THE
MANUSCRIPT

JEAN LAGACÉ

ARPress
45 Dan Road Suite 5
Canton MA 02021

Hotline: 1(800) 220-7660
Fax: 1(855) 752-6001

Ordering Information:
Quantity sales. Special discounts are available on quantity purchases by corporations, associations, and others. For details, contact the publisher at the address above.

Printed in the United States of America.

ISBN-13:   Paperback   979-8-89389-900-9
                    eBook   979-8-89389-901-6

Library of Congress Control Number: 2024923892

PROLOGUE

Lyn was not herself that morning. She had forgotten to bring Mike jam with his toast, and never came back to refill his cup with fresh coffee after he had finished his breakfast. The hair cutter had visited Al's Diner every day of the week for time immemorial, and Lyn had been waiting on him for a full five years after old Miss Lucille had decided to retire in South Carolina where her daughter lived. Her substitute had had ample time to learn his routine. First, the coffee, which he would sip while waiting for the order of white toast with jam; strawberry most of the time, but raspberry was fine, too. The choice was hers. Then after he had eaten would come the second cup of coffee that he drank slowly while doing some serious reading of the sports section of whatever newspaper was left there.

Mike always sat in the same booth at the front of the diner. He was a regular. Every one of the others knew that it was his place and would not sit there between seven forty-five and eight. Lyn was a middle-aged woman with a surprisingly low-pitched voice, what with her small frame and her fragile appearance, not one inch over five feet one and weighing ninety pounds max, if all wet. Not that he ever conversed with her, him not being very good at small talk, or any kind of talk for that matter. It was not for nothing that his mother had called him the sphinx. So, five days a week for the last five years, at seven forty-five, Lyn would say to him in that low bass of a voice she had, "How are you this morning?"

And he would answer, "I am feeling fine, thank you very much." Not a word more either from her or from him. Ever. Why? No need to!

So Lyn was not herself that morning. Furthermore, she looked like she had had no sleep the night before. Al's Diner was in the middle of a mall, one of those that had seen better days. There had once been an Albertson's Supermarket in that mall, and that store used to bring in a lot of traffic. But it had closed in the mid-nineties, and where the Albertson's used to be, there was now a thrift shop, a storage facility, and a Blockbuster video store, with here and there some space left to spare. His place of business was at one end of the mall. His father had operated Enzo's, a barbershop, at that site for thirty years, and since his old man had retired, the place was his. But his clientele, old and new, persisted in calling him Enzo.

One big fellow who worked as a butcher at the Publix on Third Street dropped his coffee cup on the counter with a bang, and that got Lyn's attention. There was nothing wrong with the meat man, though, just his usual brutish way, him earning his living by moving and cutting big pieces of dead animals. Lyn's eyes caught those of the exiting barber. He had his hands on the knob and was already in the act of opening the door. What he then witnessed in her gaze brought him to a halt. What was there? Was it pain, anguish, or agony? Or was he imagining things? She turned away from him, busy with one patron or another. Dreadful torrid air and annoying noises coming in from outside made him leave, finally. Still, he felt that some odd communication had occurred.

In the parking lot, one motorist in a metallic blue Miata convertible was honking at a truck driver stuck in a mass of cars that were either going in or out of the mall, and doing it in a very disorderly fashion. Mike saw at once that the old lady in the big Lincoln should back up five feet to let the young man in the Cadillac go through, and then the black man in the Corolla could follow, which would give space enough for the truck to get out of the way of the Miata. He walked through the confusion, though. These people were nothing to him. What did he care if they ran over each other?

At five after eight, he pushed open the door of his shop and found his first patron already installed on one of his two chairs. Those went back to his father's time when he was still a kid and liked to think that he would become an astronaut. Marvin was a "habitué," having had his hair done once a month at Enzo's since the opening of the place, many decades back.

As an old friend of Mike's father, he would entertain the son with endless stories of all that Enzo and he had done together when they were both fit and young. Mike had no such story to tell. He would have been quite annoyed to find in his life one event worth mentioning, and even more to make up a story about. His existence was made out of little things, mostly cutting hair, and what he was doing when not cutting hair, which was not much. Moreover, he found most of Marvin's narration without merit, proving just how silly the old geezer really was. If he would just stay quiet, he wouldn't reflect so badly on his father.

He finished cutting a few hairs here and there off of Marvin's skull and made a show of reflecting the end result on a hand mirror, left and right, and so, getting the usual nod of approval.

Ten minutes passed.

Marvin babbled non-stop. Then, he started a sentence with the words, "Me and your father."

That was it. Mike had had enough. He interrupted,

"Marvin!"

"What?"

"I am working here."

"Yes. On me, as a matter of fact."

"You're done."

"So?"

"You should pay me and attend to your business, whatever it is."

That kind of "exchange" between the two must have occurred previously because Marvin took it in stride. He didn't look shocked by the rudeness, and didn't even seem to mind being kicked out. He took a twenty-dollar bill out of his shirt pocket and put it into Mike's hand.

"Enzo, at least, knew how to be nice with the clientele."

"I know."

It didn't matter. Marvin would come back, and they both knew it.

By two in the afternoon, there had been four other customers in the barbershop. A slow day. Wednesdays usually were. Larry had just left the little white room full of mirrors. While sitting and having his mustache trimmed, he'd said:

"I don't know why I still come into this neighborhood."

Larry had been a lawyer at the legal office that operated in the mall and had closed shop shortly after Albertson's left. He was now attached to a big firm in downtown Tampa, quite far away, and he lived farther away still. Still, he persisted, over the years, to drive the distance so he could have his hair done by someone he was familiar with. Men were creatures of habits. If Mike knew one thing, that was it.

"Because you feel comfortable here," Mike said.

"True. But you go and take a look. It isn't safe anymore, all those suspicious characters overtaking this area. What about these properties that the banks give away or rent for next to nothing? What kind of people does it bring around? Not the right sort, I am telling you. Why! Half a mile up that street I used to come here, I stopped for gas. Nowhere did I find one friendly face to look at, and what about the lingo they used for talking? Not one of those darkies using proper English, and worse, resenting me for employing the language. I ended up giving the guy at the cash register forty dollars, expecting some change, and getting instead dirty looks from his beer drinking buddies.

"I know the place you are talking about. I wouldn't go for fuel there, either."

"Four dollars and some should have been my change. Since when are we expected to tip gas station cashiers? Not in this country, that's for sure! I don't know about in theirs."

"Here it's okay, anyway."

"Believe me, they will find this place. One out of four homes in these streets is in some kind of foreclosure or other. Most are inhabited. The grass left uncut. Even the legitimate owners don't care to try selling their homes because there is no market, what with all those banks giving away properties like they were junk."

He interrupted himself, looked at his watch, then said, "Tell me, Mike. Is my car still in the parking lot?"

Larry had a blue Mercedes, and it was still there.

—∞—

Mike first saw her from far away in the mall's parking lot, coming toward his establishment. She was wearing a scarf. He remembered having asked himself if she could have been of the Muslim faith. Nah! With a t-shirt and jeans, she didn't look the type. She had no chest to speak of. So, he assumed the girl was young. With that piece of cloth around her face, he couldn't tell if she was plain or pretty.

He was alone, busy with mopping the floor, able to recognize all who had sat that day on his chair just by glancing at the hair that covered the black and white tiles on the ground. Where could she be going? He had asked himself. To the laundromat? With no plastic bags full of clothes? If she had been there before and now was just returning, he would have noticed. He made it his business to scan every male that moved outside his store's front glass wall, since they were all potential customers in need of a clipping.

He stopped musing when he realized that the teenager was pushing open his door and had gotten herself in, quite an intrusion of his little domain. Once inside, he saw that she was carrying a purse made of cheap vinyl with a cartoon of Mickey Mouse on it. Out of one corner of that sack, he saw a tuft of thick brown hair protruding. But then the girl uncovered herself and he realized at that instant that the hair in the purse must have been hers. She said to him, "Can you fix it?"

"Who did that to you?" Mike asked her.

"I did."

"You did this?"

"She made me do it."

"Who?"

"Pralina."

She was twelve. Maybe thirteen. She showed him two plaits of interlaced, braided hair, ten or twelve inches long with the ends attached by a red ribbon. Just looking at her head around the ears, he could tell where it came from.

Astounded, he just told the name again.

"Patricia? Who's Patricia?"

"Pralina," repeated the girl, giving him an exasperated look. "What, you don't know her?"

"I am afraid I don't."

"I knew it, I knew you weren't real... Another of her silly stories. She's my mom."

"And where is she now?"

"How should I know? She must have left the diner at four this afternoon. You breakfast there, don't you?"

"Al's place, you mean?"

"Sure! She waits tables there."

Suddenly, Mike reviewed the scene from that very morning when Al was on the phone and Lyn was nowhere to be seen. Al was saying in a subdued voice, "Thank you, Officer. Yes. Irma Sanchez. She was last seen yesterday night. Yes, okay, I will tell her. Thanks again."

But Mike had paid no attention, more preoccupied with the score of the game last night between the Lightning and the New York Rangers. Martin St. Louis had had two goals and two assists, and this had gotten Mike's full attention, putting everything else in the far back of his mind. Now, he said to her, "You are Irma, yes?"

"Who else?"

"Then, Lyn is your mother."

"Pralina."

He ignored the girl's angry tone. "No need to bring around the cavalry," he responded with a bit of an attitude of his own. "Your mom was quite disturbed by your little disappearing act."

"It's all show," Irma snapped back.

"But you must tell her where you are."

"I did. I called Al's at the end of her shift."

"She knows you're here?"

"She told me, 'Go see Enzo. He will put your hair straight.'"

So, Mike invited Irma to get into one of his chairs. She was small and he had to use the mechanism to elevate her to a height at which he could work her out properly. Her cranium had the aspect of a cauliflower. He mumbled between his teeth, "This is a mess."

"Yes, I know."

"Why did you do it?"

"I hate braids."

"And she wanted you to have them?"

"It serves her right. No more of that now."

"Still, there was no need to take to the streets."

"She made me angry. I hate her."

"No, you don't. This, I know. You will see."

"You live with her, then! After, you can give advice!"

He thought of his own mother, who always argued with him over one or the other of his numerous shortcomings. The shabby way he dressed, him not being a great conversationalist, a black hole for all her gossips. His mother, who kept inventories of all that he should change in his ways, blaming him for Chrissy's leaving him, because he was childless, his passivity, him plowing through life with nothing to show for it after so many years. "What! The last movie you saw was *E.T.*," she argued against him. "And it took a scene with Chrissy to make you go." Yes, his mother could be a real pain in the ass. And quite unfair, too. After all, he was keeping his father's place going still, and what was it in it for him, apart from a meagre living? Did the old lady appreciate the fact that Enzo was still around and breathing through him? Instead, she complained that Mike did not know opera and that his father had Bergonzi singing arias of *Aida* all day long before his passing away. She was saying that under his tutelage, the place had no class. Damn! People were calling him Enzo. What was he if not the shadow of his father? Family, he knew about.

"She must love you very much. That's why she cares."

"I wish she wouldn't."

"Grown-ups do that all the time. You will, too."

Now he was using his scissors, cutting here and there on her scalp, attempting to achieve some kind of balance between pilosity and features. At last, he said, "You know of Twiggy?"

"What's that?"

"Whatever. In a few minutes, you may look like her."

"Who was she?"

"An actress, a model or something..."

"Anything will be better than tresses and silly lulus attached at their end."

After it was finished, he decided that he would take her home. So he said to Irma, "Call your mother and tell her we will be there soon."

His car was an old Chrysler Cirus that did not reveal its age easily, due to him making sure that it stayed in showroom condition. He invited Irma in, this girl who now reminded him of a boy. With her cropped hairdo, she had not seemed to mind seeing what must have looked to her like the face of a total stranger in the mirror. He had seen those astonished looks on men who would come unannounced into his barbershop with hair at their shoulders and Barbarossa kinds of beards, and those old hippie types would ask him to get it all out.

"Like Yul Brynner," he would say, just to stay on the safe side of the transaction.

Most knew Yul Brynner. After all, those guys were old, and seeing their long-forgotten faces was a shock for most of them. As for Irma, she didn't care. As a matter of fact, she said to him, "You did fine."

She was smiling at him--a Mona Lisa kind of smile, luminous and mysterious. And at that precise time, Mike decided that he liked the girl.

Inside the Chrysler, Mike asked her for directions. It was the end of the day and already the sun was setting. Night was an hour away. She told him and he remembered Larry telling him about that gas station where he had stopped to refuel. Irma's house was in that area. He wasn't afraid. Besides, the lawyer was an old fool, as dull as a five days opened soda bottle. In a discussion, you could bet your life on the good solicitor giving the Rush Limbaugh line of obvious and expected answers. It was as if Larry had that crazy notion that wherever he spoke, there were hidden microphones, and he wanted to impress the CIA or whoever was listening through those devices that he was a good American.

As soon as Irma got into her seat and put on her seat belt, she started working the car radio. She pushed the channel buttons on the FM and the AM frequencies and got nothing except static.

"You aren't much of a listener, are you?" She asked him.

He looked sideways and saw what she was doing.

"You mean the radio? No. I have no use for it."

Suddenly loud music filled the Cirus, a Latin tune with a lot of brass and ardent rhythm. A male singer was enthusiastically repeating the refrain. Some words, Mike could make out: Madrid, Eterno, Amor de mi vida. Irma pushed one button to fix that station into the audio system memory, and then dialed herself to another position. Mike said:

"Whatever you're doing, it's all for nothing."

"So, you don't mind my doing it, do you?"

"Suit yourself."

And she did."

Soon enough, Irma had found a station for all five preset knobs on the Chrysler sound system panel. As far as Mike was concerned, it was just some noises coming out of loudspeakers he hadn't known existed up to that moment. The racket left him unconcerned, though. The girl was doing her thing under his benevolent eyes, a thing that girls do, and who was he to know what they were?

There was the garage where Larry had said he had stopped this same morning. Mike tried to look inside through the windows of the store, but couldn't discern much of anything with all the beer ads that covered the glass. He saw that the place was selling twelve packs of Bush Light for six dollars. WOW! That was a deal worth stopping for.

He heard the girl saying to him, "That street over there. Next light. You turn left."

It was red and he had to wait at the corner. Traffic was heavy this late in the afternoon. It was the end of another day's work. Behind him, he saw a monster SUV approaching, perched on ridiculous-looking wheels that lifted the vehicle two feet up in the air. Mike could see nothing of the driver towering over him, like he was in a lunar vessel and most probably pondering whether he should pulverize the obstacle the Chrysler represented or just drive over it. At last, the light turned green and Mike moved ahead while the pilot behind revved his engine like he was readying his spatial module to separate from the ground.

"All kinds of crazy-looking folks around here," Irma said in a matter-of-fact tone, as the strange-looking machine hurriedly passed them in a backfiring cacophony.

They were now in a residential area made of small ground-level sinking bungalows in need of paint and more forsaken, sorry-looking, yellow, meagre grass overrun by broken-down pieces of car junk and home appliances. There were just the trees, mostly Spanish oaks, to give the place a semblance of habitability. Mike cruised through the desolation without issuing a word. From the car speakers a male voice spoke. He thought he heard the words, 'Pensa me.' That was when the music started. Next to him, Irma cried, "This is Mommy's song!"

Did he hear it the first time he listened to the beautiful rendition of the song by Luz Casal? Probably not. Later, he would ask himself if his mother was right when she urged him to use his eyes and ears to connect with the world around him. "Get involved," she would tell him. "Look around and get an interest." Could it be that he was missing things just because he didn't care they existed?

But tonight, alone in the car with Irma, what he took notice of was the girl's face during the short time it took the singer to finish the piece. She said to him, "How I would love to sing that way."

"Why don't you? I'm sure you can."

He would have expected her to argue the point. Instead, she asked him, "Why aren't you married?"

Taken aback, he objected. "How do you know I'm not? Does it show that much?"

"You don't wear a ring."

"No ring, no bracelet, no metal. No metal of any kind on me." He smiled back with what must have looked to his passenger like a bit of unmerited proudness.

"And you only shave twice a week. Tuesday and Friday."

He didn't have time to respond to that because she directed him to turn right where there was an entrance with a gate left opened, which looked upon a parking lot at the rear of a three or four stories, sixteen-unit condo building. There was no place left for the Chrysler in the reserved guest spots. Irma told him, "Move around and exit where we came in. You'll find places on the street."

To that, he answered, "There's no need for me to get out. Maybe I'll just drop you off."

"No! Mom will want to see you. She told me so."

He parked the Cirus a block or so down the street and they walked together back up to building number 2, where Irma and Pralina both lived on the second floor. Pralina opened the door of her unit when they were both walking the outside corridor, which was accessed through exterior stairs that serviced all three stories of the building. Mike found it difficult to recognize Lyn, the morning waitress at Al's diner, in the stylish woman that, now, was smiling at him. She was wearing designer jeans that showed her legs and a top that put her breasts where they could be noticed. Her black hair fell on her shoulders in a wavelike fashion. It looked nothing like it had that morning at work when it was hidden under a hideous-looking little cap with the letters AL on the front, with that same hair all flattened up and pulled out at the back. She had also put on a little makeup: lipstick, powder, and stuff. As if all that wasn't sufficient to make her a knockout, the woman who was now in front of him was well worth looking at because you could admire her beautiful eyes and that happy smile, which illuminated her face.

She must have made up with Irma at some other time because there wasn't a trace of tension in her greetings to the girl. "Little Irma, my baby and her new look. Come now, dear."

"I'm not a baby. I'm no longer Little Irma. I'm a grown-up from now on," hissed her daughter.

"You must give me time to get used to it. You look so old, suddenly."

"That was the point, wasn't it?"

"I guess you're right," answered Pralina. "Silly me not to have prepared myself for the atrocity," she added in a contrite voice.

They were all still outside the flat. Pralina invited Mike inside and he reluctantly went in.

"It's so nice of you to take care of this sorry matter. Don't take what I just said seriously. Frankly, I look at Irma and I find the cut you gave her absolutely charming. And it suits her perfectly. Gives some character to her face."

They walked through an open space with a small kitchen in spick and span condition to the left. To the right, Mike discerned a corridor with two closed doors, and then they found themselves in the dining and living area: a vast room with a glass table and four chairs at one end near the open wall kitchen, plus the usual sofa and arm chairs facing a sound system and TV cabinet. In the middle, there was a coffee table on a blue and white carpet. The floor was tiled and there was a patio door that opened on a Florida room overlooking a ten thousand square foot garden, with the street and all three buildings facing each of its sides.

Pralina had Mike sit on the sofa and settled herself beside him. Near enough, he noted. He felt uncomfortable, not used to the attention and not knowing much about what to do or what to say. The woman smelled good, though. He decided to do nothing, to say nothing, and wait it out. Irma chose a CD from a rack that contained a few dozen and put it in the CD player. He was surprised when Pralina addressed her daughter in Spanish. Then he remembered Irma's last name--the one that Al had told the police officer while on the phone. Sanchez. Why! He was in a Mexican home--first time in his life. He looked at the walls, expecting the usual paraphernalia of crucifix, rosaries, and portraits of the Pope, the Virgin Mary, and saints, but saw nothing of the sort. His father had been born a Catholic and had married his mother, who was of the Episcopalian faith, in the fifties. There hadn't been much religion in their home, and any there was, was of the Protestant variety. Now, the CD player was turning and Pralina asked him over a merry Spanish melody, "Do you want a drink? I can offer you white wine or beer."

Irma said, "She went to the store just for you and got you Coors Light."

"Irma," protested the mother, "you are embarrassing me." As she turned to him, she added, "It was not much to do."

He was red in the face and hoped she would not notice. He mumbled, "The Coors would be fine, thank you."

"And you must tell me how much I owe you for Irma's haircut."

He made a dismissive gesture with his hand. "Don't talk about it."

"I must insist."

"No. It's on the house. Irma is a nice gal. It was my privilege."

That got him a smile from the girl.

The woman got to her feet, but not before stopping in midair to put a quick and soft kiss on his left cheek.

"Thank you so much, Mike."

Then she went into the kitchen to get him his beer. She had called him Mike. Not Enzo. How did she know his name?

In the end, he stayed until nine o'clock. They dined on some Mexican-Spanish cuisine that was miraculously all done and ready. And the stuff had looked and smelled so good while the beer and the one that came after made him hungry. And with time, he started to thaw a little and they talked, her for the most part, but him also participating, in small bursts of words that he regretted saying as soon as they left his mouth. But later, he became less and less bothered over his more than welcome contributions to the conversation.

They had had white wine with the meal, and that had helped, too. And there was also, at one moment, that song that had played on the CD player. They were having dessert: upside down pineapple cake with vanilla ice cream, and then it was that song again. He recognized it instantly and it stopped him dead in his tracks as he was telling them a story about his father opening the barbershop 40 or so years before.

They all enjoyed the song, quietly. He listened to the lyrics even if their meaning escaped him totally. There was no need to understand the language to know what the song was about. It was all about love and having someone thinking of you. Piensa en mi. That, he could make out. He was now attracted to each and every mournful note and chord of the guitar accompaniment. It was then that he got his first experience of what certain people called a magic moment, and from then on, he would know what it was they were talking about when referring to similar occurrences.

"That's Mommy's favorite song," Irma announced after the melody was finished.

"It's so nice, don't you think?" Pralina asked him.

Mike came out of a trance-like episode, willing himself to say the right thing and having absolutely no notion of what it was or should be. At last, he sheepishly agreed.

"Yes, it is."

"He knows nothing about music," Irma said.

"Irma!" interjected her mother. "You are rude!"

He laughed, dejectedly.

"She's right. I'm not much of a listener."

"But you did fine just now," his hostess objected.

"My mother would say that's a first."

"And I'm happy that it was here, and with that song."

She gazed into his eyes, and there was a lot there that he wouldn't dare to decipher. She added in a voice so low that he had to read her lips, "I'm glad you love that song."

When it was time for Irma to go to bed, he chose that moment to justify his leaving. Pralina didn't object even though it was Friday night and she wasn't working on the weekends. Mike stood at the door, searching for the right thing to do or say before leaving, and Irma helped him find his way through that awkward moment.

"I liked sitting in those big chairs of yours," she said. "Perhaps you'll have me back on one of those." She smirked.

"Why would you? You're all fixed now."

Though there was not a lot to hold, she grasped a lock of her hair and added, looking at her mother, "As if I would let those grow again. Not a chance!"

After that, she disappeared, going through the door in the wall between the living room area and what must have been the space behind for two bedrooms plus a bathroom. Pralina followed Mike outside the condo. Stars sparkled in the sky. There was also a full moon that he made a show of staring at since there was not much else for him to do, or so he thought at the time. Nevertheless, he could see her out of the corner of his eye. She was not so thin now that he had a good look at her. And not so small either. She must have been forty-two, but still could have passed for a woman five or ten years younger. And she had a good figure. No doubt about that, the jeans and the T-shirt all filled up at the right places. Why had he not realized that before? As his mother had often said, it pays to have a real and serious look at things.

Pralina cut through the embarrassing silence. "I think Irma took a shine to you."

"She's a good girl." And those words were his cue to walk out of her place, too confused to say anything more except, "See you at Al's, then."

As soon as he said the words, he regretted them. Those words took away all that could have been intimate between them and brought back the business side of their connection; that of a waitress and the patron she served.

"As you say! Good night.

He didn't hear her close the door behind him, but he knew she had. From there, he would have been of the opinion that the scene was finished, never to be replayed again. Normal life would take over. Complicated outcomes from mingling with people would be avoided. He had no need to have his life jumpstarted like it was a car.

⸺∘∘◦❦◦∘∘⸺

He was walking on the street away from Pralina's condo, in the direction of the side avenue where he had parked the Chrysler. There wasn't much light around, and he noticed that some lampposts had no working bulbs, or else they had been broken out by kids throwing rocks at them. He turned the corner of the avenue. Now he could see his car a hundred yards away.

That was when he saw them, three boys or young men. Athletic looking. One was black while the other two were Cuban brown. The dark one was bouncing a basketball on the sidewalk. Seeing Mike, he threw the ball in his direction and it would have hit him hard in the face had he not caught it in time with both his hands. All three jokers were laughing at him and speaking between themselves in Spanish.

The smaller and mean-looking guy, with tattoos all over his impressive biceps, addressed his friend, who had a White Sox baseball cap on his head, "Now, look at what we have here. A gringo that plays ball."

Baseball Cap added, "It takes four to play. What do you say, Gringo? You want to make it a foursome?"

Mike wasn't afraid. Not yet. He gave the lot his best smile while returning the basketball to Black, and then he tried to pass by them. But Tattoo put himself in his way.

"Not so fast, Gringo. What's wrong with you? Suppose you don't appreciate us having a talk with you? What is it, Gringo? You don't like our kind? Is that it?"

Tattoo's nose could have touched Mike's, and he could smell the punk's sour breath. He pleaded, "Come on, men. I just need to go home. We live in a free world. You do your thing. Let me do mine."

They all laughed at that, even Mike, though he thought himself pretty stupid for doing so.

"So, what will it be, Gringo?" Tattoo insisted. "Where is it that we will be enjoying this freedom you talk about so well? Our place or yours?"

Mike said nothing and the joker continued teasing him. "But I am telling you, Gringo. You really do not want to see Paco here's place. Because believe me, Gringo, Paco's place is a pigsty. Isn't that true, Paco?"

Paco agreed that yes, his place was a pigsty. There was a lot of talking in Spanish that intercalated itself into those exchanges, and there must have been some jokes between the three because there was a lot of giggling and chuckling that made absolutely no sense to Mike.

"So, you see, Gringo," Tattoo said to him, like it was the reasonable solution and that Mike, too, should find it obvious, "it will have to be your place. You will invite us, yes?"

"Hey, guys," Mike answered, his tone now uncertain, "you have to stop this. It's not funny."

"Oh, you want funny. We'll give you funny, all right. You have a car, don't you? So, perhaps we won't go to your place, after all. Why? We'll just use your car to get ourselves a ride. What do you say?"

"My car is over there. It's the white Chrysler. Take it if you want, but leave me alone."

"No, no, Gringo. This is not to be. You must come with us. As Nimo already said, it takes two to tango."

They were all walking toward the Cirus. The avenue was as deserted as it could be for punks wishing to act foolishly. Mike stopped moving forward and got his car keys out of his pocket. "You take the car. Really, I don't mind. But I'm not going with you."

"Like you have a choice, Gringo."

And then Tattoo got out a knife that made a neat little click when it opened. There was no need to do more and Mike, defeated, started to walk again.

Baseball Cap -or was it Nimo? - took the key out of Mike's extended hand and opened the door of the Chrysler on the driver's side. He got in and Black -or was it Paco? -opened the other door and sat in front beside him. In the back were Tattoo and Mike. Baseball Cap put the key into the ignition and started the engine. This activated the car radio that had been left playing when Irma had left the vehicle. At once, there was Latin music blasting all over, loud enough that it startled them all. Black turned his head to throw a puzzled look at Mike, showing him, in so doing, the small diamond that embellished his left earlobe.

Meanwhile, Baseball Cap hit all five buttons that gave access to the pre-selected radio channels and found them all of the Spanish variety. Nobody said a word in the car and the punks acted a little weird, like the discovery of some anomaly in an otherwise quite preordained world had gotten them all confused.

And then, it happened. Out of the sound system came a song that Mike recognized on the spot, and he cried without thinking, "Let it be. This is a good song."

The song was just starting. Already, the melody, now that Mike knew it, got to him in a way that he would not have believed possible the day before.

Piensa en Mi.

When the lady singing the song got to those words, it was so nice and so sad that Mike could have cried there and then. The singer went through the piece like she was an angel visiting them. After the song was finished, Black said something in Spanish to the others. "Este gringo es bien chévere."

Nobody argued. All three bad guys looked kind of subdued, as if there was nothing left of their previous bluster; the cat that suddenly tired of playing with the mouse. Then, Black let out something that sound like an order. "Vamonos!"

Baseball Cap took the key out of the ignition and threw it at Mike. Tattoo opened the door on his side of the Chrysler and left. Black also got outside of the car and again said something, but addressing Mike this time. He looked him right in the eye and said, "Me gusta tu musica, Gringo."

Then he turned around and left. Baseball Cap was still in the car. Mike asked him, "What are you all doing? What did he say?"

Baseball Cap looked at him. He smiled at him--a friendly kind of smile that was no longer threatening. He explained, "My friend Paco, he just told you that he liked your taste in music."

And then he, too, left Mike's car. As he was leaving to rejoin Black and Tattoo, who were walking away in the direction they had all come from, he turned and said to Mike, "You are a cool gringo, man! That's what he just said to you. Now, get lost and have a good night's sleep."

Mike made it home.

Sunday, he did nothing except think. Monday, he got to work, but did not visit Al's place in the morning. He saw Pralina finish her shift at four o'clock and he waited until five to call her home. Finding the number was easy.

She answered the phone on the second ring.
He asked her for a date.
She said yes.
They had a lot in common, after all.
Breakfast at Al's Diner, Irma, and a Spanish song.

BOOK ONE

SPIROS

Spring 2008

His office was on Central Avenue in downtown St. Petersburg. The place was not far from the Haslam bookstore, and he still remembered when he was in the habit of roaming through the shop at all times. Those were the years when he could read what he liked and he was free to do so. He was now forty-eight. He was married. He had two children, Martin and Tammy. The first was just out of his teenage years, and the second was fifteen. Both had more and more a life of their own.

He was number three in the publishing firm he worked for, Diland, Ross, & Morrow. His name wasn't Morrow, though. Peter Artritis was the inscription that decorated the door of his office. A not-so-grand one at that, but still a large enough corner space on the tenth floor of the Verizon building. He was a publisher and an editor. What he did for a living was finding new talents and help those selected few with their embryonic art. His life hero was Max Perkins who, as a young man, had discovered Ernest Hemingway and Thomas Wolfe while working at Scribner.

At Diland, as the place was known, he enjoyed some kind of seniority. All three founders had died a long time ago. Therefore, Ross and Morrow didn't mind much the Diland short cut. On his walls were pictures he had painted when still in his early twenties. That was twenty-five years ago or so. Mostly oils, some watercolors. They weren't bad as they showed some talent or facility. But he had not pursued the matter to its end. Satisfied with producing what he had. Amateur stuff, he knew now. And having lost no sleep over it.

He looked at his watch. His wife had asked him to pick up Tammy at her friend's place and bring her home. It was not yet the time. He let go a sigh. Two full hours he had been at his desk and accomplished nothing useful. This was a bad day. There were too many of those since… He couldn't remember how long he'd felt that way. Felt that his life wasn't what he had expected it would be. Felt that he had not achieved much, considering all he had realized before he had reached the age of majority.

He had gotten a law degree at The University of Tampa while still in his teens. And he had not yet been twenty-one after having completed his one-year apprenticeship and passing the Florida bar examination easily. But he couldn't be certified a lawyer by reason of not being of the legal age of twenty-one, the minimum age required for practicing law in the state. The Tampa Tribune had written some article about the feat.

So it happened that Peter Artritis went to work for the Tampa Tribune at the end of the sixties. He never bothered to become a member of the local bar. As a matter of fact, he had never really intended to practice law. He'd gotten through the studies because it was expected of him, and being sixteen at the time, he was in the habit of bending to other people's wishes. Still was, for that matter, his natural disposition being quiet and docile.

What he liked was Latin and Greek. Being a Catholic, he had been enrolled in a Jesuit college that dispensed a classical education, and it was there that he had gotten interested in both languages. He was soon able to read Platon, Aristote, Caesar, and Ciceron in the original languages. One would have asked himself what he was to do with those dubious skills, but not Peter Artritis, who seemed to be at his greatest in all useless and unprofitable activities or occupations.

Since his early twenties, he had been freelancing for newspapers, mostly Europeans, with articles written in old Greek or Latin, four that were weeklies, the other, a four time a year magazine, and all shared a list of mostly the same eccentric subscribers from all over the world who fancied to take their news about the Beatle's last prank in one quite dead idiom or another.

He had an older brother who was an accountant. He wasn't considered as bright as Peter by a long shot. Still, he was the one to give advice, everybody consulting him for everything and nothing. Charles knew his way around as Peter never did. Charles, who always knew what to do in all circumstances, or would bluff his way into making you believe so. Peter didn't. Charles was moneywise. Peter wasn't. What Peter was and Charles wasn't good at: Philosophy, belles-lettres, art, and creativity.

When he was still a student, Peter had worked at the Tampa Tribune, doing errands, mostly. That daily had an arrangement with an Australian syndicate that let them publish in feuilleton older abridged versions of unknown author's novels who had not sold on their continent. They were paying nothing for the privilege, and it was good for filling spaces. It was the staff's work, in turn, to shorten these stories to fit into the allotted space reserved in the weekend literary section as in a serial, eight weeks for each. Twenty thousand words in all. Nobody was taking the work seriously, as nobody out there read that literature. Yet, it had to be done.

When the time had come for Mikes Steven to fulfill the task, he had stopped Peter in the corridor outside the room he was working in and told him, "Hey, kid, what is it you are doing right now?"

Peter had pushed a shopping basket full of material from the basement store that he had to distribute around, as well as get in all the outside stuff that had to be processed through the shipping department. He knew Stevens from having played chess with him and beaten him a few times. The man was in his thirties. He dressed like a detective in B movies. He wore a hat, even if it was no longer in fashion. His beat was crime, and he dedicated all his working hours wandering by the courts, producing stories on villains, the prosecutors who put them in jail, and the lawyers who tried to interpose in the process. He knew Peter liked to write, and he had taken an interest in the youngster. Now, he had a book in his hand that he gave to Peter.

"Where do you want me to deliver this?" Peter had asked.

Mike had the distressed look of somebody harassed with problems he couldn't be expected to cope with in a lifetime. His hair was disheveled in a stylist kind of way. A cigarette hung at the corner of his lips, Bogard like, while his eyes, Paul Newman blue, watered owing to the smoke it produced.

"It's my turn to Reader-Digest this sorry piece of shit," he snapped disgustedly.

Peter turned a few pages of the volume he had just been handed. It was three hundred pages, twenty-six lines a page, ten words a line. The title was "Amelia's Turkish Delight." The author, one Frieka Lollipoplatt. He then stated with a straight face, "Never heard of her!"

That got him the laugh he might have anticipated. He offered the book back but the journalist wouldn't take it. What he did instead was staring hard at Peter. As his elder wasn't making any effort to pick up the Lollipoplatt masterpiece, he threw it in his pannier and asked, "You care for a game of chess?"

"So I can beat you up again?"

The boast was so obvious as to be a joke by itself, and both knew it. Ashes from his friend's cigarette fell on the ground, but not before hitting Mike's tie and white shirt and leaving a trace of their passage, which he put right with a gesture of serene carelessness.

"As if you could." The boy in front of him smiled back at him.

"Pretty sure of yourself, aren't you?"

It was Peter's ambition to get into the writer's brotherhood at the newspaper. Getting friendly with those who were already members of the fraternity he craved to join seemed the right thing to do. Also, he valued Mike's humor. Therefore, he was ready for what was to come.

"This potboiler," Mike added in a disgusted manner.

Peter knew all about it but said nothing.

"If you could give me a hand with it, I sure would appreciate your effort."

And that was it. It was an easy task. He would read the Lollipoplatt romance, all sixty thousand words of it, and he would produce an abridged version of the piece over the next eight weeks. One chapter a week. He was happy to have been asked. He liked the newsman. Mike was the real thing. Being distinguished by the likes of him was what made life worth living.

As soon as he was back home that day, he applied to the task in hand. Home was his parents' house. They were in 1979. He was nineteen. That same year, ayatollah Khomeini would seize power in Iran and Margaret Thatcher become prime minister in England. The position he had at the newspaper was a summer job. He was finishing his third year in law school. He had a girlfriend that would leave him since he wasn't ready to marry so young. But that was all yet to come. What he had to do right now was getting through trashy Amelia's adventures in the Balkans. So, he started turning the pages.

He hadn't gotten far before growing bored to death. He got distracted from his task when hearing his brother arguing with their mother about the Democrats being responsible for all what was wrong in the world, which brought on a debate that continued until all were called to the kitchen table, where dinner was about to be served. He didn't think about the book again until a week had gone by, when he was stopped by Mike in the Tribune's outside parking lot.

"Where is it?"

"Why?" He answered, realizing at the same instant that he had forgotten to shorten part one of the Lollipoplatt material and not wishing Mike to become aware of his oversight. "There's still time left," he added in a bold manner that was not like him.

"No, no," the other corrected him, not yet afraid, so sure that this smart kid wouldn't let him down. "I must deliver the silly material on Bob's desk at four this afternoon at the latest. Today is Thursday, and they start printing the weekend supplement tomorrow, right?"

"Yeah, right."

"So, when can you give me the damn thing?"

"Don't worry, you will get it in time," Peter mumbled.

"You sure about that? Because if you don't, I am screwed…big time."

"Four o clock, it will be on your desk," he had promised.

And that was it. It was eight in the morning. As for the book, it was somewhere in his room. And he had to get to work.

He looked rather gloomily at Mike's back as he walked toward his car. Municipal courts were his destination. That's where you could find him before eleven a.m. As there were a lot of those, one for each town around. You could say that he was a tough act to follow, something he might have used to his advantage when the front desk couldn't reach him and he needed some excuse for his disappearing into nowhere land. He had gained quite a reputation for the stories he harvested out of his fellow citizens' misery when dealing with the local constabulary over infractions, one more exotic than the other, and their inevitable outcome in the hands of benevolent justices of the peace who settled all disputes in their town's favor.

What was he supposed to do? Was there a way out of the embarrassing situation? At the moment, he couldn't see any. He remembered the first time they had talked. He had wanted to impress the man who had looked so much to him as the quintessence of what a writer should be. Mike had intercepted him in one of the basement long passages, asking to put some mail in the box on his way home. Walking on the nice linoleum floor beside his would-be mentor had made him challenge the journalist into a game of tossing coins out, twenty-five feet or so away from a wall and throwing quarters in its direction. The nearest pitch won both pieces. That was one of the few games he had gotten quite good at in college, inspiring that crazy notion that his skills might in some improbable way get Mike to take an interest in him. That was before their playing chess together. He knew that the guy had a reputation for being good at everything, be it pool, snooker, golf, tennis, cards, back gammon, you name it.

So Peter had thought to himself, there is one thing I can beat this guy at. I am good at pitching quarters against a wall. Get them one inch or two from the partition. So, his mind had told him, Mike, he can't ever stoop so low as to do this, let alone try to make money out of it. Okay, then. That had been the plan.

What then?

When the older scribbler had accepted the dare with a big smile on his face, Peter hadn't had the good sense to turn back and run. Instead, he had shown Mike two quarters.

"I will play mine, if you don't mind."

And then, he had made a big show at choosing the right instrument out of a bundle of change he had, like it was a cue stick in a rack full of them. When he had found the coin he liked best, he had said, "How do you want to do this?"

Peter should have known better. How ingenious he must have looked to his opponent as he had stared at him with bewildered eyes.

"You don't mean you want to do it just for the fun of it, do you?" Mike had asked, incredulous.

"Well..." He couldn't back out now, could he? Some instinct made him stutter, "Whatever you feel comfortable with." Hopefully, the other wouldn't want to scare him off with stakes too high. Besides, he couldn't be good at that game. Not as good as he was, at least. How could he be? It was child's play.

"Five bucks the throw. How does that sound?"

That was a lot of money. He was making ninety dollars a week, working at the newspaper. What had he been thinking? His only experience at gambling was using nickels. And now he had gotten himself into a situation where he was risking a hundred times that much for one throw of the dice. This was absurd. Yet, he wouldn't survive Mike laughing at him. In a tone of voice he felt was more assured, he said, "Who's to go first?"

"You."

He wanted to annihilate his adversary right from the start, wanted to make him realize with his very first quarter comfortably installed three centimeters out from the wall what kind of serious trouble he had put himself in. Therefore, Peter landed his government-issued piece of silver just there and then, he had glanced at Mike, searching in his newfound friend's otherwise debonair posture some kind of disquiet, but saw nothing of the sort. What he was doing, though, was preparing to throw. Which he did in an airy way, as though he were tossing seeds to some pigeons in a park nearby. That unsettled Peter a bit. Next, he saw the coin fly through the distance and stop incredibly near its mark. An impossible shot. Mike's quarter touching the goddamn partition. Could this really be happening to him? The calamitous deed had been achieved right under his astonished eyes. Beginner's luck, he told himself. He had to, didn't he?

He had put an end to the silly massacre after losing forty bucks in just ten minutes or so, signing Mike a check. He wasn't in the habit of carrying that kind of cash in his pocket. Before leaving, quite dejected, he had barked at the other, "What the fuck! What was that?"

Mike had grinned at him, then said, brandishing the piece of paper he had just signed, "Make sure this doesn't bounce, will you?"

And that was what had started their friendship if that word could ever apply to their rapport after this odd episode.

One big bang, coming out from the street five floors below, pulled him out of his reverie. His office at Diland had a balcony, with patio doors giving access to it. They were now open since it was winter and he enjoyed being free from the edifice's air conditioning system's dictatorial imposition. There was nothing like a soft breeze coming from the outside.

A big six-wheeler had crashed into a blue Mercedes that had tried to cut its way through traffic, and he could now hear one very pissed-off lady badgering its imperturbable driver. Peter looked at his watch. Time to pick Tammy up. Last month, while she'd attended her ballet class, he'd had her wait five minutes on one street corner. She had been wearing leotards and a tutu. As soon as she had gotten into his Volvo, she had made him pay dearly. He still recalled the harsh words she had shouted at him as she'd lamented angrily all the hooting and hullabaloo her circus-like appearance had provoked in the area.

Better go now.

He was still driving the same car five years later. His mind went back to the time when Mike Stevens had beaten him at throwing coins against a wall, and had later asked him to work on the Lollipoplatt necessary distillation. Oh, he had given him the piece in its new condensed format, except it had nothing to do with what its author with the silly name had imagined. What he had done was write the damn thing himself. One first chapter of a completely new and original story. All seventeen hundred sixty-seven words of it.

He had taken refuge in the journal's library and had gotten to work. A quote from Eleanor Roosevelt had started him up. "A woman is like a tea bag. You never know how strong she is until she's in hot water." That had given him the first words he'd needed. On page one of his six-page handwritten document, he had begun his narrative this way:

"Royal King had a tea bag-like quality: one never knew how good he was until he found himself in hot water."

He had given Mike the story in time. The past remembrance of that stunt had put a semblance of a smile on his face. Where was that manuscript of his? Ten years ago, he had tried without success to find both the sixty pages of his script, each of those handwritten, and its type version, one a girl in accounting had produced free of charge, since she was Mike's girlfriend at the time.

He had done it over two months, one chapter after another, always within the prescribed time and was still surprised today at how easy and fun it had been. What pleasure to see his words put in print. His story in one newspaper, for all to read. At first, he had looked forward for something to happen, like somebody devouring his tale and loving it. At night, he mused about how strange people were, passing through everything the world offered and seeing mostly nothing. He was saying to himself, if he was to read a piece like his in a magazine, why, he would send an enthusiastic comment to the editor or write something. He would take it upon himself to make sure others read the work in order to share the pleasure with his friends. The fact that he had not done anything of the sort for all of his previous readings was a notion that didn't come to his mind at the time.

A subsequent meeting with Mike had put a term to his ingenuousness. It was after the fourth or fifth publication.

"Have you liked it?" He had asked.

The crack reporter, who was walking fast with one worry line set on his forehead and his customary cigarette hanging from his mouth, had stopped dead in his tracks. He had stared at Peter in a curious kind of way.

"What in hell are you talking about?"

"The Lollipoplatt potboiler. What else?"

"What? You expect me to read that garbage?"

Peter had received the comment like a punch in his stomach. How stupid one could be. His older self winced as he sat in his car, immobilized on a bridge and waiting for a little boat with a ridiculously high mast to pass in between its two raised parts.

"Why? He had responded the older man. "It's supposed to be your work, after all."

"And thanks to you. Yet, I can dispense with the dubious pleasure."

"Her story is quite good, though."

Mike had stared at his watch, an exasperated expression showing on his face. "That would be a first, finding anything of value out of that sorry pen pusher's shit list."

"How can you know," he had stuttered, "if you never look at the stuff?"

"What is it with you? Are you okay?" Mike had asked him with as much solicitude he might have shown his bookie when inquiring about yesterday's baseball scores.

"All I'm saying is it isn't fair to form an opinion based on prejudice."

"As if those jokers could write. They couldn't even if you were to dictate to them."

"Still," Peter had objected, "we got them published, didn't we?"

Mike had shrugged his shoulders as disposed of the protest. "Filling! Nothing but filling! One could put the Singapore phone book in there and nobody would notice the difference."

Peter, quite defeated, had then confessed, "You don't understand. I wrote the whole thing."

"As if I didn't know already. I'm the one who asked you to do this. Remember? What is wrong with you? You're not happy with the situation? You want me to pay you an indemnity?" Then he had laughed. There had been a pause. And he had laughed again. "He says he wrote the whole thing", Mike ended up repeating, as if it was the funniest thing he had heard in weeks.

"No," he had insisted, quite in a panic, "what I mean is… I created it all from scratch. What you find there is mine…"

"The silly Lollipop bitch… You… No, you didn't," countered the older man.

"Yes," Peter affirmed, thinking he would get some well-deserved recognition from now on.

Instead he'd gotten a laugh so big, so incredulous, so filled with surprised amusement that people from far away turned around to look.

"You are such a loser!" Mike had erupted between two bursts of laughter.

He still recalled the icy feeling that had filled him when hearing that. He had been hurt in a way he wouldn't have believed possible before. Even now, just recollecting the scene was like scratching a board with his nails.

Unbearable.

—∙∘○❖○∘∙—

The outside temperature was fair. In this late afternoon, traffic was heavy. St. Pete-like, though. It had nothing to do with what Northerners had to suffer in their megacities. His wife had asked him to pick up Tammy, and what else? While waiting for a red light to turn green, he tried to recall the tasks required of him and failed to do so. He harbored a sensation of failure for his ineptness at performing the simplest chores. Maybe Tammy would know.

Coming from behind, a sorry specimen of a car honked crazily, its speedy driver making grand gestures directed at him. The meaning of his insisting provocation was clear enough. He wanted Peter to move the Volvo out of his way, which was part of the street and half the sidewalk.

Because he could, he complied. One very beaten Ford Taurus sneaked ahead, the car at an odd angle since half its wheels occupied the sidewalk, ten inches above street level. Its pilot was a youngster with a Yankee baseball cap that fell over a face disfigured by metal protruding out of every pore of his skin. The punk's initiative seemed to have irritated a Lexus owner real bad. One black man opened his car door just in time to block the NY sports fan's way to more abuse. Mercifully, the light changed and the traffic ahead started to move. The Taurus could have waited to access the street if it had found one drop in the sidewalk's elevation, but its driver decided otherwise. The instant the Taurus's left front wheel hit the road, there was a scratching sound as the car's frame got stuck in a precarious unbalance, with its back wheel not touching the ground anymore. Peter drove around the struck vehicle and had not stared.

At his daughter's friend's house, he parked the Volvo on the street beneath one Spanish oak from whose branches hung odd protuberances. He could hear the sound of that outgrown flora as it brushed against the car's roof. He was ten minutes early. There was some music coming out of his sound system. He changed the station in the hope of catching the news. He was in just in time to hear the newsreader talking once more about the Mississippi idiotic extravagance.

That was the case of the sorceress, a woman who lived on the Gulf Coast and was known as the witch of St. Pierre. She now had been found guilty of murder and the Gulfport D.A. was going all the way, asking the jury for the death penalty. Her case wasn't your ordinary run-of-the-mill open and shut kind of murder. She had admitted to bewitching her victim, a physician who had practiced quite a late abortion on her daughter while drunk out of his wits, killing both the mother and the child.

There had not existed much sympathy for the good doctor in the community as he faced trouble of his own with the justice department. But whatever it was he had to respond to, it wasn't ever to be enough for the witch of St. Pierre, and she had applied justice her own way, using her very real power of sorcery to dispatch her beloved daughter's killer into a better world. She had publicly thrown a curse at the man. She had even said when he would die. Moreover, she had boasted that whatever the medical establishment would say, whatever ailment they said had bested the man, it wouldn't be right. What he would die of was just one thing and nothing but.

Her curse.

The doctor passed away in June 2005 exactly when she'd said he would. And true to her prediction, the coroner established cause of death had been an embolism. At the time, Peter remembered, it had been a tough call for the bureau of the district attorney. The one in charge had been forced out of office because he was reluctant to prosecute. His substitute, a former preacher in some fundamentalist church that had, a bit late in his life, obtained his lawyer's degree, had seen in this case a sure road to becoming the governor of his state.

Now, the case was in appeal. Not the verdict, mind you, but the trial itself. The witch's lawyer argued that there could be no crime without a direct connection between the aggressor and its victim. And then, such connection couldn't be of the spiritual nature. Still, the jury in Gulfport had taken a rather more pragmatic view that was mostly the D.A.'s perspective on the question. The local judge had let them get away with it.

The reasoning went like this.

God exists, and so does the devil. And if God can be seen accomplishing His wonders in His people's day-to-day lives, so is the devil. Then, if one can prove a conspiracy between a malevolent sorcerer and an evil spirit, and if there is an admission of cause and effect, so be it. It must be prosecuted in the Christian dominion of Mississipi, and justice shall be done.

A knock on the glass of the Volvo's passenger door startled him. Tammy was there, already making a face to show scorn at the careless way he was waiting for her. She would blame him for not having once glanced in her direction, and furthermore, for having parked his car on the other side of the street. But that injunction was for the epoch when she was a toddler. It shouldn't count anymore.

He unlocked the door and the lock, giving way, emitted a most cheerful mechanical noise that strengthened, as it always did, his view that he was driving the most technology advanced automobile in the whole universe. Tammy sat beside him and he told her, "Don't bang the door, please."

She did. He refrained from quibbling over the ill-treatment, even if the deliberate assault against the faultless mechanism cut deep into his inner self serenity.

"How was your day, honey?"

She was fourteen and rather small for her age. Because of that, sport wasn't much of an option for her. Hence the ballet, where being petite wasn't a handicap. More like a plus. And the girl was good at it. She'd been enrolled into Miss Sokolka's class for the last seven years, and showed real ability. He had the car moving before she greeted him with an answer. He turned left on Tyrone Boulevard toward the Alternate 19 and Highway 275. That would get them to Tierra Verde, where they lived. Their house had five bedrooms and a direct view on Tampa Bay.

He asked again, "Is there anything wrong, honey?"

She sobbed. He liked her better when she was shouting at him.

"What is it?" he insisted.

"Anna will get my part," his daughter whispered. "I know she will."

"Come now, Tam," he tried to calm her, "why would you say something like that?"

"We were rehearsing and I fell. Anna laughed at me and said she could get it if she wanted."

She was probably referring to some incident that had happened before today. He'd just picked her up from Anna's place.

"But," he asked with a bit of anxiety because the wrong query could prove he wasn't up to her recent history, and being caught at that was sure to get him a beating, "isn't Anna supposed to do the old lady?"

"Yes," Tammy sniffled through her tears, "but now she says that Emily's part is more to her taste."

He pondered over that. Silly Anna Wainswright was the spoiled daughter of immensely successful lawyer Leonard Wainswright and Hollywood movie star Candice Belle. The mansion they had at Madeira Beach was just one of three or four they possessed around the world. Anna was a girl who was used to getting her way, whatever the cost to her mostly absent parents. He knew he couldn't fight those people. Well. Maybe he could. But if he could, there was no way he would. Not in him to get into a brawl over such a matter. He said with as much assurance as he could muster, "This doesn't work that way. The show is in two weeks. You are Emily and nobody, not even Anna, can take that away from you."

"As if you knew."

"Believe me, I know," he lied.

She looked at him, half reassured. He took pity on her, the poor girl, stressed over an end of the year representation. One lost evening for him and yet, for his daughter, a day of reckoning with either glory or humiliation.

"Oh Dad," she added in a rather pitiful way, "I wish I were dead. I am so afraid. After all, I did fall. What if it happens in front of an audience?"

What a way they talk, nowadays, he thought. This sounded a bit over the top coming from a fourten-year-old girl. It must be from the Wainswright girl mimicking her actress of a mother's idiotic transports and ending up coloring Tammy's language.

"Don't be silly now," he said. "And, dear, abstain from talking that way. You are my girl. You know that, don't you? And I also know and you know that you will perform perfectly. You always do. What do you say?"

"Yes Daddy."

Now that he thought of it, had he told her to abstain from using future hyperbolic overstatements, or just asked that she ignored all scenarios involving her falling in front of them all?

He felt he had the upper hand now. On the 275, he moved ahead of an eight-wheeler truck that honked angrily at him, as if he had shown its driver a lack of respect. Then he turned in Tammy's direction and said, "Don't let Anna Wainswright play with your nerves. She wants to do the Emily part as long as you show an interest. Let her do it and see the sorry lass fall on her butt, as I think she will. Now, don't you worry no more about idiotic Anna. She is just jealous of you because she knows that you dance better than she will ever be able to, even if she were to go at it for the next fifty years."

Their house was a split-level with two hundred feet of land facing Tampa Bay. Tammy set in motion the massive door that serviced the three-car garage. Peter took note that his wife's Chevy Malibu was in its usual place, encroaching halfway into his own spot. Why should she care, Angela used to argue, there is space for three, and there are only two cars in this family. Still, it hurted symmetry. Balance was important for him.

Stability, uniformity and equilibrium were his thing. Shapelessness, chaos, and disorder were the real enemy.

Like in the garage.

His was a lost case. Another battle he wouldn't win. How many of those he had fought for no big result? This was the story of his life, wasn't it? Ever finding himself at the low end of all the fights he would care to enlist in. Then, if it was to be that way, better not to get involved in the first place. Much better, even, to let go and take everything in stride. He would find it easier in the long run. Disengagement was the word. Stay away from trouble. He would live happier and longer.

That was what he would say to himself in any situation in need of his arbitration. Don't meddle. Leave it to others. What is it to you, after all? Who cares if things go this side or that, left or right, up or down? For whatever posture one might adopt, there existed another, which was its exact opposite, and how many more in between? Everyone fought like mad to secure their neighbors' adhesion to their way of thinking, be it the kind of grass to put in their front yard or the best time to spray the lawn out of the city's meagre water resources. As if all these palavers would make a difference to the greenery.

He had learned from experience that it didn't. Things had a way of working out on their own. People were just plain silly, believing themselves the force behind any permutation in the order of things one way or the other and calling it progress. All self-serving idiots, the whole lot!

He maneuvered the Volvo the best he could, missing by a few inches his son's racer that had fallen on the ground from the wall it had been leaning against. Tammy got out first and he stretched out his arm toward the open space in order to prevent the door from banging shut. But his daughter, as soon as her feet touched the green painted cement floor surface, ran straight to the door that gave access to their kitchen.

"Mamma, mamma," she was shouting, "You'll never believe what happened…"

The rest, he couldn't hear. The car's right panel had been left ajar. He got out of the Volvo and followed Tammy's steps, but not before putting things in the right order, straightening Martin's bicycle properly, and closing both doors of his automobile.

When he saw Angela, she was glancing absentmindedly at their daughter performing dance steps, while moving a big spoon into a cookware from Le Creuset. It was more like a stew pot, but cast iron, French, worldly wise and very expensive. When their eyes connected, she smiled and asked, "How was your day?"

He approached her and kissed her neck. She had auburn hair that didn't show any gray yet. It was cut short but not too short. Shoulder level was more like it. She was athletic and a beautiful woman, something she would be for the rest of her life as her features were strong and capable of staying well in place for her whole trip through existence. She was five feet five to Peter's five ten. She was unassertive, but confident and direct in claiming one's rights or putting forward one's views. She wasn't dogmatic or aggressive, though. In their family, she was the one who made all the decisions. And she was good at it. Under her watch, they hadn't made a lot of mistakes. She was at her best with people. Angela knew her way around, and managed to get the better of everyone in all kinds of situations. It was a gift, and Peter didn't dispute her ability to pilot their household better than he ever could.

Tammy was still pirouetting in the dining area, and she complained, "Mummy, you aren't looking."

"Yes, I am, dearest." Addressing Peter, she asked, "Did you get the birth certificate?"

That was it, the nagging thing along his trip to Anna's residence. He had forgotten about the damn document. He told her so.

"Martin will need it if he wants to get on the Tampa University football team."

"I'm sorry. I'll bring it to him tomorrow, I swear."

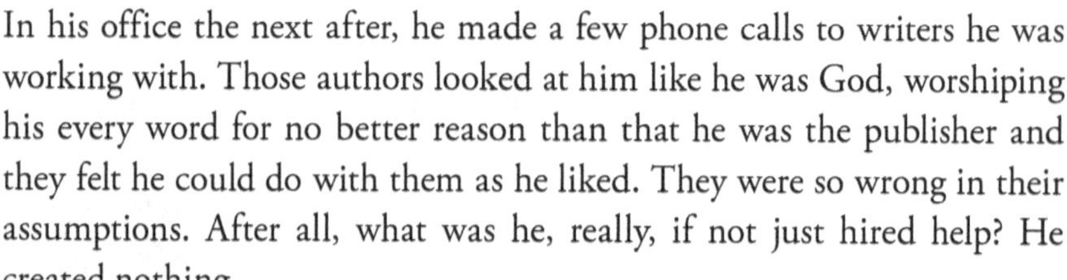

In his office the next after, he made a few phone calls to writers he was working with. Those authors looked at him like he was God, worshiping his every word for no better reason than that he was the publisher and they felt he could do with them as he liked. They were so wrong in their assumptions. After all, what was he, really, if not just hired help? He created nothing.

They did.

His role was like being a road for cars. Who would want to be a road when you could be the machine that flew its way through the wind? How much he envied all those who had shown enough talent to get published. He had tried. Oh, how he had attempted to make it himself into that business of writing novels and having them read by the multitude out there. And having movies made out of his stories.

He had written a lot of those. He had shown them to the staff at Diland and was told all the time it wouldn't fly in today's market. Now, he still wrote but kept it to himself. He couldn't take any more rejection. His only success at publishing anything was so long ago, when he had improvised a tale of his own instead of abridging the Lollipoplatt cheap output.

"You are such a loser," Mike had snapped at him.

That had summed it up pretty well, don't it?

He was so afraid.

Whoever read his work judged it to be too cerebral, and told him so. They might have had a point. He was cerebral, all right, speaking Latin like a priest and reading Aristotle in the original, like if it was the last of the Grisham thrillers. What was that if it wasn't being cerebral? Yeah! Like if it was a sickness or a disease.

He liked ideas, put didn't care much for the people who emitted them, and that showed in his narratives, which were mostly texts with no dialogue. His pieces were seen as erudite and brainy, elaborate ranting with no easily discernible point, plot, or significance. The kind of production, a not-so-kind gentleman from Brisbane had once said to him, that would put his Australian readers to sleep at once.

He looked around. He worked in very nice surroundings, with a view. Not to say that there was much scenery to look at, the nearest water being on the other side of their building. Facing the south wall made out of plate glass, he had installed a telescope. The quite powerful instrument was perched on its three-leg support and pointed to Highway 275, Treasure Island, and the Gulf of Mexico.

It was eleven in the morning. He hadn't done much work yet. Not as if it would make a difference. He was a small part owner (about five percent) of Diland. The firm was in the process of changing its name from Diland Publishing, as it had been known for decades, to Oracle Publishing. He was kind of working for free, his salary next to nothing. What he got was participation in the house profits, and this paid the bills.

He called Linda, his assistant who was also a deputy editor and loyally drudged through his own work load. She came on the phone after two buzzes and he asked her, "What about Martin's birth certificate?"

"It's on your desk, somewhere."

"Well…"

"Will be there in a sec."

She was short, slightly overweight, wore spectacles, had blonde hair, and was highly intelligent. She glanced at his desk, which had nothing on its immaculate surface, and then she looked around. She could have reminded Peter that she had, the day before, handed him the envelope with the certificate inside. But she didn't. That was one characteristic he liked in the woman. She didn't make much of his nonsense.

"So you do use that thing, after all."

That brought him out of his daydream.

"What was that?" He inquired, as the woman walked decisively toward the telescope.

"What is it you were ogling at?" She asked, making fun of him. "You can't see the beaches from that distance, can you?"

It came back to him now, what he had done with the envelope and where it might be. It had very much to do with the way he had gone through his afternoon the day before. He had read in the newspaper some article that had deplored the decline of the American car industry, and he had used the equipment to count cars as they moved, coming out of Tampa on the Skyway Bridge. He had written down his newly acquired statistics on the back of Linda's envelope. And he had most probably left it in the area as some other matter must have interfered with that activity. At that instant, his phone rang. The deputy editor found what she was searching for and put it on his desk.

"You pick up that line," she whispered. "I'm out of here."

So he did.

"Peter Artritis here," he affirmed smoothly into the receiver. "Can I help you?"

It was Arthur Morin, his lawyer of twenty years, who also was a friend. He had a nice house in Pass-a-Grille, where he lived alone. He had bought the summer residence when the price had been low. Still, it was an expensive piece of property, and the cottage was a real beauty. Maine style. A two story-building with a porch all around. Both he and Angela had helped him choose the place. And since then, they had enjoyed a few BBQs there. Arthur had never married. He could see the ocean from his living room, den, and bedroom.

"Are you doing anything?"

He recognized his friend instantly. "As a matter of fact, I was preparing to leave. I have a document I must deliver to my son at home."

"Then, maybe I could treat you to lunch. What do you say?"

"Sounds good."

"Great. You know the Pasadena steakhouse, don't you? We could meet there in half an hour, and it will give you all the time you need to play the mailman."

The restaurant was far away at the end of one immense parking lot that served a few very big name chain stores, and there weren't many parking places left. He recognized Arthur's vintage Mercedes. Luckily, up the same aisle, one black lady pushing a cart full of junk stopped beside a washed-out, yellow, beat up, discolored truck. He waited for her to pack her purchase in the back of the pickup and disappear, which she did, but not without leaving the cart where she had done her unpacking. He swore silently. There was no way to get in there without addressing that obstacle first. He would have to move the nuisance out of the way.

He opened his door carefully, but not carefully enough. A massive Ford SUV let out a hoot so loud and bellicose that he banged his head hard against the Volvo's door frame. That nearly killed him right there. He barely had time to discern from the corner of one eye the gargantuan monstrosity that passed by him like it was an express train. Wasn't any driving standard in an area like this one, he reflected, trembling? It took him another ten minutes to recover and reach the restaurant. As he was shaking hands with his solicitor, for no discernable reason, he felt like the meeting would be bad news and that nothing good would come out of it.

It was frigid inside. He should have known better, and he regretted not bringing a jacket. Arthur was nursing a Coors Light, his glass almost empty as he had been left waiting for the last quarter of an hour. Peter felt he needed to justify himself for being late. But before he could open his mouth, Arthur made a gesture, holding up his hand in such an easy and detached manner that Peter was at once filled with mute wonder. The motion was filled with such power and silent authority, like whoever was behind those signals knew they would be seen and instantly understood.

A girl with too short a skirt, which was part of some garb only female waitresses were made to wear, appeared out of nowhere and quite likely by magic. His lawyer asked him, "You care for one of those?" Without waiting for an answer, he told the attractive damsel, who had a tray in her hand and a very bored look on her face, "Get him one." Then he finished his glass in one gulp, put it back in the tray with his beer bottle and added, "Make it two, will you, precious?"

Peter would have had to search in eternity to find the right code that would permit him, like Arthur, to give pet names to perfect strangers. It didn't mean anything, he knew. Still, offhand manners like those, as much as he would have liked to reproduce them, weren't in him to do.

They were alone in their box. They had had their steak and toss salad. He had refused dessert. Arthur, for his part, was gulping down some house specialty pie, and looked very busy doing so. Up to now, they had both said nothing of importance. But it wasn't like Arthur to suggest a meeting with nothing on his mind. It was more like Peter. With some foreboding, he forced himself to ask, "So, what's up?"

Arthur interrupted his mastication of the last piece of the pie. He resumed his chewing for a moment, then said, firing little bits of crust from his mouth, "Something happened," in a kind of ominous manner.

"Well," Peter responded, "why do I not like the sound of this?"

"It has nothing to do with you." Arthur hurriedly adjusted his discourse. "The fact of the matter is… I might need your help with some business that came up my way and entered into your field of expertise. After all, you are a publisher, aren't you?"

"You can say I am, as you must know by now. Why would you need my help, though? Have you written your memoirs? Everybody these days seems to feel they have had a life worth telling about in some sort of narrative or other. What will it be, then? Some case of yours that you have won big? Or this bit of a lucky break you once told me about with your bar exam and its magic question? Is that it, Arthur?" he asked in a derisive yet amicable manner.

Now, suddenly, he felt in charge. He felt like he had some power of his own. Perhaps he couldn't charm his ways to all the "precious" ladies of this world, but what might and ascendancy he possessed was his ability to decide who, of all those having put their guts out in the form of written words, would get published and who would not. For him, this was without a doubt the greatest accomplishment of all.

"Now you're being silly," Arthur answered, a paper napkin covering his mouth. "Why would I write my memoir? I'm not dead yet. No. The thing I wanted to see you about is this."

And then, he showed his left hand on the table. In it, there was a big brown package; it was thick enough that Peter, who had stared at a lot of similar parcels, guessed what it might be.

"What's in there?" He asked nevertheless.

"What do you think?"

"It sure looks like a written piece or something."

"It sure does. Because that's what it is. What is it you people calling these things? A manuscript?"

"What is it about?" He inquired.

"As if I knew. Mind you, I am a little behind in my reading. You know, stuff like the Supreme Court rulings for the last two decades or so."

He threw a dismissive glance at the big envelope and its contents that, as far as Peter was concerned, might have carried all the hope of one poor soul of ever making it as a writer and being recognized as a creator of some talent.

"Therefore," Arthur continued, "no, I didn't read the masterpiece. Haven't even looked at it. I kind of figured that you would be the perfect guy to do just that."

"Where is this coming from, if you didn't write it?"

"It's a long story. I will explain later. What do you think?"

"Come now," Peter said, enjoying his predominant stature, "why would we be interested at Diland in shit like this? We read the hundreds of stories that we do receive unsolicited every month of every year, and you would have us doing nothing else twenty-four seven. All these would-be writers that are using the Internet nowadays. They send us the sorry results of their collective efforts, expecting us to read the material, and in this way, discover the next Hemingway or Grisham that they think they are. No. As you should know, we don't do business that way. What we do is this: we delete the embarrassing nonsense before it clogs our computer system to death."

Arthur, who had listened to the long tirade and kept a smile on his face, put the envelope between the two of them. Unperturbed, he got a pack of Marlborough out his shirt pocket and asked, "Do you mind?"

Peter shook his head no and concluded, "The chance of that piece of yours being worth something is one in a million."

"Why are you telling me all this?" Arthur asked, lighting his cigarette. "Who knows, this could be the next Pulitzer."

"Very funny."

"To say it is not, one has to take a peek. Won't you have a look?"

"So you do it, then. Or you show this work to an agent and you get him to submit it to Diland. This is the only way for us to look at it."

"You want an agent? I'm an agent. So, as an agent, I am asking you to take an interest at some work of my protégé."

"Agents read what they intend to submit," Peter objected.

"Who says I didn't?"

"You did."

Arthur, at that point, let out a sigh of repressed annoyance.

"Why are you doing this?" He snapped. "You act like you are a goddamn nun and I'm asking you to suck my dick."

Peter became red in the face and looked away. Their waitress was back. Arthur gave the girl his credit card and she left, showing them her nice little behind as it balanced this way and that in the most perfect, harmonious equilibrium.

Peter had been staring at the big brown envelope on his desk for fifteen minutes. The packet was still sealed. On its visible side was some writing he read for the fifth time--or was it the sixth? Someone had scrawled in such a challenging calligraphy, as if he didn't care if it could be deciphered or not, the words, "I dedicate this story to both the Rays of Tampa and the Phillies of Philadelphia organizations and players. I hope that my characters will be found worthy of the likes of Georges Steinbrenner, Sparky Anderson, Billy Martin, James Catfish Hunter, Dave Conception, Tony Peres, Pete Rose, and many others. Long Beach, February 2000."

At the steakhouse, Arthur told him how he had come by the manuscript. Its author was a fellow MD going under the name of Otto Zielgard out of Gulfport, Mississipi. It seemed he had gotten one local practitioner of Black Magic very pissed off for having been involved in a late miscarriage on her forty-two-year-old daughter, and for having been quite drunk while doing the procedure. In the end, it was said that the poor woman had been left on her kitchen table, bleeding to death, while her doctor had slept on the floor.

"Isn't this the story they are talking about on the news?" Peter asked, making a connection between what he was hearing and the convicted witch of St. Pierre.

"So you know!"

"Not much."

"She killed him in some way, I was told."

"It doesn't make sense. You, an attorney, should know better. Witches do not exist."

"Go tell that to that prosecutor in Gulfport."

"But," he objected, "it takes some real and direct contribution from the part of an accused to be found guilty of a crime. If wishing somebody dead is a crime, let alone a capital one, there would be nobody left to walk the streets of this country."

"This D.A. out in Mississippi seems to have convinced the jury otherwise."

Peter shrugged.

"That jury," he spat, "they acquitted O. J. Simpson, didn't they?"

"They sure did," said the lawyer. "They believed there was a conspiracy between one senile elderly voodooist and some demonic entity who, at her request, agreed to perform the deed. This, under the laws of their commonwealth, was judged enough for the silly notion to be put in front of the jury, leaving to its collective sagacity the ultimate resolution over the woman's guilt."

"She will appeal."

"That she will. It might go on for years, perhaps a decade or more. Mark my words. This is the perfect circus case for all who so desire to join in the discussion, put in their two cents if you know what I mean. As they shall, you will see."

"You make it sound like it's a game."

"It's the way we govern ourselves as a society. And it works…most of the time."

"Will it work for that poor wretched hag?"

"Who knows?"

"Come on," Peter replied, "what about the federal jurisdiction? The woman's lawyer will petition the court and argue that it can't be a crime to conjure with the devil."

"Well," Arthur said in a dispirited tone, "the woman has been tried and convicted. The defense team must have already been working along those lines right from the start, attempting to quash the bill of indictment over such grounds. But the court in Gulfport has gulped down all the Christian fundamentalist rhetoric of that little Bible-quoting preacher prosecutor they have out there, and his views about the sovereign power of the state and its indisputable right to legislate itself into legalistic lunacy."

"What is it to you?" Peter inquired.

"Zielgard was our client," Arthur confided. "Our office in Jackson had represented him once, a malpractice case for which he had been badly insured. We got him out of that mess, and he has been a regular with us since then. Mostly tax cases, litigation with his professional order over his right to practice medicine, misdemeanors, small stuff for the most part. The guy was a drunk, you know."

"Then," Peter asked, "why are you taking sides?"

"Did I? And whose side would that be? As if there was a side," Arthur added. "I don't believe in witchcraft. What I say is for the sake of intelligent discourse."

"But," Peter insisted, "if you're not involved in the lady's defense, why do you care for the writing of some wasted doctor?"

He looked at the envelope that separated them on their now clean table, thanks to Precious's ministrations.

"The point is," Arthur explained, "well…this envelope was delivered to our office manager in Jackson, that is, to Jack Bernard's home in Jackson's High. Three days ago. It came to him by Purolator, from the agent that sold Zielgard the piece of land and the shitty doghouse he lived in at the time of his untimely death."

"Did he have family?" Peter interrupted.

"Just a cousin, and from what I heard, a dreadful one out of fricking East Germany. One serious asshole, that Kraut. Doesn't speak a word of English, and he hates our Americans' guts. Thinks our lot are nothing but hopeless, capitalistic warmongers and desecrators, taking advantage of people, vegetation, world temperature, anything atmospheric, water, animals, natural resources, and whatever else can be put to work to senseless profitability in one inexorable, useless, long-run, assets-exhausting, crazy process--"

"Aren't we doing this?" Peter broke in.

"I'm sorry," Arthur condescended, "I'd forgotten that you had a soft spot for those issues."

"All I say is there is a logic that applies to them issues, and one should show respect to those few who remind us of such. They might have a point."

"Whatever," Arthur said, "what I mean is…this idiot is pestering the firm with that sort of diatribe in his marxistic lingo, and then we have to translate his inane ramblings into proper English to realize that he's actually accusing us of robbing him blind and using the CIA to spy on him."

"Then, this German will end up receiving some cash, I gather?"

"As if I care. From the selling of the house a few bucks maybe. He could, though, if you were to find some merit in his kid brother's last words."

"The chances of that--"

Arthur cut him off.

"Yeah, one in a million. You already told me this."

"Statistics don't lie."

"You might have exaggerated that one."

"No more than my point deserved."

"But," Arthur argued, "the guy is a celebrity. That should be worth something. Give him some pull. Don't you think?"

"A dubious one, if I may say so."

"Still, a celebrity of some sort. He isn't any Joe Blow who ends up being killed by his wife, girlfriend, or partner. Our guy got on the wrong side of one very bad bugaboo. You are the editor. You should know. You look this thing over and work it out. Will you?"

"Don't expect too much, though."

"Seriously, you do that for me, I'll owe you one. And whatever you decide in the end, I will respect your judgment. All I need is a professional opinion to put in the file so I can show that I did ask. Don't get me wrong, I would like this to be good, but I don't expect it any more than I'd expect to find a pile of gold if I were to dig into my backyard all the way to China."

"It's okay, I'll do it," he agreed.

"The office in Jackson knew we had a publisher as a client, and they sent me this because I am the lawyer who handles you. As simple as that. Again, all I need is your take on this Zielgard's story, and if it isn't good, as it most probably will not be, so be it.

So Peter had capitulated, as he'd known from the start he would. There was no way he could have refused this little favor to Arthur. It had been fun, though, playing hard to get.

The buzz of a fly in his ear interrupted his dreaming. He recalled being in his office, and he wondered how the annoying creature could have gotten into such a secure environment as the Verizon building. He couldn't quite figure that out. What a racket the beast was making, though, for so tiny and trivial an animal. Now, he would have to stop whatever he'd been doing, get up, and dispose of the silly disturbance.

Damn! He wasn't happy with himself. He had let himself go at the restaurant. Hadn't been able to resist the twelve-ounce New Yorker they'd had on special at that restaurant, with the girl whose skirt was so short that one would have thought she wanted to prove she was a female. At that instant, with the insect around, he was paying the price for the transgression with his eating habits, which were normally frugal at lunch time. He was suddenly feeling so heavy that just the idea of going after the fly seemed like an impossible task. And the worst of it was he wouldn't be able to eat anything substantial tonight. He should call Angela and tell her.

He searched for something he could use to kill the vexing insect. That's when the fly decided to land on the envelope, moving along, undisturbed, as if it hadn't a care in the world. It stopped moving in the middle of the homage from the author to both the Rays and the Phillies. His right hand found last week's issue of Time magazine, a special on the coming summer Olympics in Beijing. He hadn't read it yet, and would have preferred not to use it as a weapon but, there was nothing else nearby, and the creature was in a spot where it might be disposed of with no great exertion on his part. Folding the periodical in two, he took position, and then, with more force than needed, brought it down hard onto his unfortunate prey.

Having performed his task, Peter stared at the mixture of blood and pus. What a sorry mess, he thought. Now there was nothing left to do but throw the magazine away. No big deal. Olympics, he didn't care that much. The stain was covering Steinbrenner's name, and part of those of Catfish Hunter and Dave Conception. He wondered if Arthur had read the handwritten note scrawled on the back of the envelope and decided he hadn't.

It had taken him a full ten minutes to make sense of the short inscription, working at it like it was a puzzle, and then getting its meaning mostly by deduction. Arthur wouldn't have bothered. How could it matter one way or another? It didn't. Strange, the digressions the mind did all the time like it was losing control. What a miracle that anyone could still function properly with such a random apparatus.

With a bunch of Kleenex, he wiped up the vile pudding that defaced Arthur's parcel, with the Zielgard manuscript inside. He got a letter opener out of his desk and broke open the sealed envelope, then pulled the manuscript out and looked at the last sheet of paper, searching for a number. He found it. It wouldn't be that bad, after all. Two hundred and fifty-three pages, twenty-two lines each, double-spaced, ten words a line. About fifty thousand words, all written out from a typewriter Zielgard must have acquired second hand when he was a student in the fifties. Not enough of those to make a book out of. Not of the kind he cared to read, anyway.

He looked at his watch. Not much of a watch, for that matter. Bought at Costco ten years before. He had managed to keep it, though he'd lost his two expensive ones, one of which was a gift from his wife.

It was not yet four in the afternoon. Better read this thing now. The story was titled FAITH, those five letters in capital in the center of page one. On page two, Zielgard had typed, "A tale about baseball. The Devil Rays of Tampa, the Phillies of Philadelphia, and the World Series. Where richissime Rays club owner, Franck Richantall, fights with his very stubborn manager, Joe Black, over having Manuel Garcia to appear in a game."

He started to read. At five thirty, he called Angela.

"How was your day?" he asked.

"Fine. How about you?"

"Lousy. Arthur called. He wanted to talk to me about some business. I had to have lunch with him."

"Oh, poor you," his wife mocked. "How I pity all those suffering men at work. Where did you boys go, looking like men of consequence?"

He ignored her sarcasm.

"You know that steakhouse on Pasadena?" he answered.

"We went there with Bob and Lucy."

"I couldn't resist the steak, and I had too much wine. I don't feel like eating right now."

"Great!" she exclaimed. "I'm just entering the house and had nothing fancy in mind for dinner. I bought some cold meat, cheeses, and salad."

"Like a picnic. That sounds great."

"When will you be home?"

"Something came up. I might stay a little longer at the office. I should arrive around eight, nine at the latest."

"I'll wait for you to eat, dear."

"Sure," he said.

He heard her breathing through the phone. She said, "I love you, honey."

Even though it was the way she ended all their phone conversations, it sent a little jolt of happiness through him, much like one gets when hearing a few notes of music he likes.

"See you later, then."

He made kissing sounds, as was expected of him. This was their usual routine.

He finished fast reading FAITH at a quarter past eight. How strange it was for Zielgard to have imagine a duel in the World Series between the same teams that everybody in the business was sure would oppose each other this next October. Zielgard had neglected to inform in what year the action took place. If this piece was to find a publisher, the year 2008 would be fine. Before leaving, he put the manuscript inside his safe. As for the soiled envelope, he chose a new one and destroyed the other. Passed it through his shredder without thinking.

The trip back home went quickly, as it always did. St. Pete was a town with streets that made sense, the kind that are straight and get you somewhere, without the older cities' capricious impositions. Outside, it had been raining. The glimmering neon lights of stores and shops he passed on both sides of Central Avenue reflected on the wet bitumen. With his windows partly open, he could smell the cool air, hear the roar of the Volvo's tires racing through the thin layer of water on the asphalt. He turned north on Thirty-Fourth Street and then right on Fifty-Fourth Avenue, passing by Eckerd College toward Pinellas Bayway and its bridge. He got on it without stopping, an electronic device on his windshield giving him the right of way through a special lane.

Before the second bridge that would have gotten him to St. Pete Beach and The Don CeSar, he found the road leading to Tierra Verde, and a bit farther to the south, Fort DeSoto Park.

Angela was home, waiting for him. She wore a soft fabric rose dressing gown, and while he pressed her to his chest, he could see she hadn't much else on under it. He felt her, her lower back his place of predilection, and she purred in his arm. How he loved that woman. And he knew he was loved in return. That, at least, he had gotten right.

They had their picnic. The sight of the food displayed on the kitchen table had stirred up his appetite. They drank white Zinfandel, the inexpensive kind that he used to buy at the local Publix. Later they watched an episode or two of NYPD Blue . . . . He couldn't remember when he'd taped those as he did that a lot, shows to be put away and listen to in times like these.

Seeing Sipowicz worrying about the huge Greek orthodox wedding ritual and reception Sylvia, the woman he intended to wed, was planning, had been fun. He and Angela had married in a simple ceremony. No big fuss. He didn't like being the center of attention or worrying about what was expected of him. He'd envied his peers at college for their easy demeanors, compared to what he perceived as his own clumsiness. He felt out of place in all circumstances and situations.

His wife, from the day he'd first met her, had given him an anchor to hook his life to. For that and plenty more, he would be forever grateful to her.

They went to bed at eleven. That night they made love, an unforeseen affair as it was the middle of the week. Sometimes one had to do the unexpected, hadn't they? Life was that way. He woke at five and couldn't find sleep after that. Instead, he thought. Searching, probing, scrutinizing, dissecting, testing, questioning, and then, reviewing all the previous reasoning and starting the process all over again. So it happened that when he heard the sound of his alarm clock radio and the voice of the BBC anchorman at the local PBS station reading the seven o'clock morning news bulletin, he already had a plan.

FAITH

PART ONE

He wasn't much of anything, this Manuel Garcia. As a fourteen-year-old, he was still quite small, but that could change. One never knew for sure with boys that has the power to transform themselves from one year to the next. Girls, he didn't care for yet. Or so his mother thought. Which was a mistake, since Manuel liked a girl from his school, but was too shy to say so, and too proud to admit it. The girl lived in their neighborhood, and her name was Irma. Both she and Manuel had played together since the Sanchez's had moved to St. Pete ten years before. And then Irma had grown breasts and her silhouette had become that of an adult. In a matter of months, she had aged in such a way that made Manuel felt lost and forsaken.

Manuel had dreams. Not that he was good at interpreting them. As a matter of fact, he neither knew nor cared anything for that science. No! He was into having dreams. A lot of them, he told people later, like they were fairy tales. In this way, he became a kind of celebrity whenever he procured an audience, and was addressed by all as Dreaming Manu, which didn't bother him at all. As long as Irma remained his number one fan. And that she did, up to the day she became a woman and he got stuck in his boy's countenance.

2 o o o 2

There was that dream that contributed to make him famous with the crowd of youngsters that visited the Gulfport Library. He was eleven or twelve at the time. He had told the dream to Irma. They were in the park that split the town in two, from the public library to Twenty-Second Street. They were alone. In that dream, there had been one big black bird that croaked like mad near his bedroom window. He'd awakened and saw the crow perched in the highest branch of a Spanish oak on their neighbor's lot.

Suddenly, the crow had looked at Manuel and dared him. To do what? He couldn't say, and there was no time to figure it out because in the second it takes to blink an eye, the bird had taken flight. There was not much else to do then but to follow the animal, which he did. He relished the run outside, at night, in pursuit of the flying crow. Couldn't think of anything he had ever done before that was more exciting than that ride. His guide had touched the ground and picked something up, enclosing it in both of his claws. He took flight again, Manuel chasing after the creature.

They flew back over the Tampa Bay, and then he recognized the inverted pyramid of the Pier, the 275 highway, Boca Ciega Bay, and Gulfport. The crow began its descent, landing at the rear or Irma's mother's small gray stucco apartment condo building, a few streets away from where Manuel's family lived. The crow cawed, a repetitive uproar of noisy, agitated nonsense that got him a response from another crow to the east, and then it was gone. Its catch, however, it had left in the grass near the doghouse. Manuel had approached the object. It was a woman's wallet, kept firmly shut by one blue elastic band. At that instant, something weird happened. Manuel knew that inside that wallet there was a one-year-old ticket from the Florida lottery, and that the ticket was a winner. Four good numbers out of six, a one-thousand-dollar value.

That was the dream as he had told it to Irma. The girl had braids, and the end of the left one was in her mouth. She munched it in a distracted kind of way. She said, "You're making this up!"

"Why would I do that? It's just a dream."

"It's weird."

"Why? Dreams are supposed to be that way. If they weren't, we wouldn't need shrinks to interpret them, would we?"

"What do you suppose this one means?"

"I don't know. You tell me."

"As if I knew."

"What about you? Don't you have dreams?"

She looked at him as if he was talking about some sickness or other. She remained silent.

He walked her home. It was four in the afternoon, and Irma's apartment was on his way. At her building, a woman was in the parking area getting some bags full of groceries out of the trunk of a white Nissan Sentra.

"Hi, Aunt Paola," Irma welcomed her.

"Oh, hello, Irma. Back from school now? I'm just coming from the Publix. Got some stuff for Pralina. Why don't you ask your friend if he'd like a glass of lemonade?"

Once inside the two-bedroom condo, Paola had said to her niece, "You will never imagine the fright I had this morning.

Paola was visiting them out of Tallahassee. She had slept in Irma's bedroom while Irma had joined her mother in her double bed. She served them lemonade.

"What?" Irma had asked, who was the most curious of them all.

"I lost my wallet this morning. You had already left for school, and Pralina was getting ready to go to work. It was terrible. Your mother did try to help me find it, but you know she has her regulars and she had to leave. So I drove her there without my driver's license or papers. Imagine if I'd had an accident! And then I came back here. Why, I was in a state! What if I didn't find my wallet and all my documents and cards everything?"

She got it out of her purse and brandished the small object.

"So, you found it in the garden, near the doghouse," Irma said.

"What?"

There was real bewilderment in Paola's eyes. She looked at her niece as if she were a squirrel reciting verses. As for Manuel, he recognized the . . . . . wallet from his dream with the elastic band around it and said, "You should call the Florida Lottery and check the number for the Mini Loto you have in there."

Paola had made the sign of the cross and wouldn't go near Manuel after that. She had even refused to use the lottery special line to verify the ticket number's validity. Instead, she'd emitted a little cry, more like a bark, and shredded the ticket. Both kids had watched the fragments fly around like butterflies, and when the pieces touched the ground, Irma picked them up. Paola left an hour later, a two full hours before she'd planned to leave.

Manuel had learned a lesson from that experience. People didn't like tricks much, and when they looked at you as if you were the reincarnation of their great-great-grandfather, the feeling of their astounded stares on you wasn't so great. From that moment on, he remained discreet about his dreams.

Before her aunt returned to Tallahassee, Irma had shown her the shredded ticket, which she had taped back together. She had asked, "Do you want me to collect the money for you, aunt Paola?"

"I don't care what you do," Paola had mumbled while trying to get a golf cart in her car's luggage compartment.

"Take it," Irma insisted. "It's yours."

"I don't want it."

"Why?"

Paola closed the boot with a bang.

"Show me that ticket," she hissed.

She took it out of Irma's open hand, then returned to the condo and flushed it down the toilet without saying a word more.

Irma said in a matter-of-fact tone, "Now we'll never know, will we?"

"I know enough already. It would be a good idea if you didn't . . . mingle too much with that fellow, Manuel."

"We go to school together."

"Is he a good Catholic?"

Paola was, but not her sister. Nothing in the house showed she was one. There wasn't even a Bible to remind them they were Christians.

Her aunt added, "Never mind that. Manuel is bad news. Better for you to keep away from him. I will say so to your mother."

Pralina had laughed at the concept. Her silly sister and her religious nonsense.

"I fear the Holy Spirit is not welcome in your home," Paola had said to her over the phone.

"Nor any other kind," Pralina had responded.

And that was that. Her sister would get over it. She always did.

3 o o 3

Years passed. Manuel was good at school. He had many friends, but he kept his dreams to himself. There were others, and most were unremarkable. Sometimes they seemed to allude to something real, but he was unable to link them to any actual events, so he forgot about them and was happy for it. He didn't like that dreaming business much. In fact, he was a little afraid of the dreams. Once, he was skateboarding and passed a parked car. Somehow, he'd known that there were firearms in the trunk. That very same night, he'd heard on the news that the bank the car had been parked in front of had been held up. Nobody injured, though. There had been three masked gunmen using the very same weapons he had perceived in his hallucination. Was he a psychic? He didn't like psychics. He liked down-to-earth people. He liked reality, and he disliked the notion of losing his grip on it. He didn't appreciate lunatics of any variety. And psychics were lunatics. There was to be no discussion about that. Too many people had looked at him as though he were a talking dog. Dogs, he tolerated. But one that spoke? There were enough humans with that ability on Earth. He didn't want the life of a performing dog.

Manuel liked sports, and as he grew, he became better at them. He practiced several, basketball, football, baseball. He would never be big enough for football, but he was fast. At five feet ten, there wasn't enough of him to make it in basketball, but still, he was very good at moving the ball, and was one of the best for long-distance scores. But what he liked the most was baseball. He was a passable hitter, and a very good short stop.

4 o o o 4

Joe Black was fifty-four years old. He was a big man, and his hair was thinning, but he kept his weight under two twenty, and that gave him a fair silhouette. He was a man who knew what he wanted, and what he wanted, he usually got. He liked to think of himself as a no-nonsense kind of guy. He didn't talk much, but when he did, people listened, because he was not one to repeat himself. His motto was: "If I said it, it must be true." He knew his way around, and how to make things happen. That was why he was the Devil Rays' team manager.

He was on his way to pick up both his kids. They were living with their mother in her new husband's mansion. The guy was a solicitor, and was super rich. He was one of those guys with the idiotic addition of 'the third' or 'the fourth' at the end of his name.

The residence looked over the bay of Tampa, near where its water converged into the Gulf of Mexico. He got off of the 275 at Fifty-Fourth Avenue South, and turned right on the Pinellas Bayways. He drove his black Lexus 450 over the first toll bridge that overhung the water separating Boca Ciega Bay from Tampa Bay, turned left and then left again where there was, at the end of a small road, a very exclusive gatehouse community protected from undesirable characters by a guard in full uniform, who accomplished his Cerberus-like task from a sentry box that looked more like a small cabin. A control over a gate could open it with the right code, or through the sentinel's gracious help. Joe didn't recognize the watchman of the day, who was looking at him with suspicious eyes, even though he was driving a Lexus 450 and was the Devil Rays' manager, for Christ's sake. Not to mention that he went there on a regular basis.

The guy looked foreign. He was probably into soccer. Silly game. With his left arm stretched to the max, he punched in the number he had been given under the critical stare of the Mediterranean alien. 4571. He waited for the gate to open.

It didn't.

The guard was glaring at him now. He glared back, his eyes laser-like, passing through the insignificant individual and making him disappear, or deleting him computer-like. What a nasty business that was. Barbara had insisted from the start that he comes to pick up the kids himself. That was years ago. Now they were almost adults, but there wasn't much public transportation in that part of town, and his children had gotten used to the royal treatment. If he wanted to see them, that's what he had to do, isn't it?

He had called on an impulse. Wanted Thalia and Martin to be with him at the stadium that night. The Boston Red Sox were the visitors. The Rays were playing .666. And it was Thalia's Birthday. They would have hot dogs and such. They would put on the Rays' uniform so they could be with him and the players during the game. His kids were living with their mother and her witless lawyer millionaire, the fourth of the fucking line, or was it the fifth? She'd married the pedantic, useless, raving moron a few years back, a ridiculous prig who appeared either pompous when he was right, or plain silly when he wasn't. Barbara had nothing planned for that night. The family tradition was that birthday parties were always the first Sunday after the actual date.

So he'd asked to get the children for that night, even if they weren't children anymore, what with Thalia being twelve this very day, and Martin seventeen already. They would get to see the game with him, in the dugout. And it had taken five minutes of palavers and Barbara throwing out all her capricious objections, not one of them making any semblance of sense, and still, he had listened and said nothing. Let Barbara tire herself out, as she usually did. At their age, one would have thought the kids could do as they pleased. But he refrained from saying the obvious. She was a lawyer. She was intelligent. She knew all that. It was all just a show. Better let her do her thing. He would get what he wanted in the end. So she wanted him to drive them out and back? He could live with that. That was why she'd given him the password. That damned password that didn't work. And this S.O.B. of a guard who did nothing, offered nothing, just looked at him like he was a carpet peddler. He punched in the number again, but now his shoulder hurt. He was too far from the machine. Because of that, his index finger lacked assurance and the contact with the device's button seemed approximate to his sense of touch. He locked his eyes onto the guard's very dull and annoying face, those eyes that were used to instant submission, which luckily wasn't his foe's attitude at that precise moment.

"Is there a problem, sir?"

He spoke with a heavy accent. Greeks talked that way. The Zorba like character had the trait of an opponent manager when he had just seen the pitcher for the Rays strike out three of his own players in a row. Very, very pissed off. Joe had an impulse to sit him on the bench. But instead, he said, "What are you looking at?"

There was a TV running in the little room, out of which silly Zorba planned with uncommon brilliance the best strategy to make a real fool of himself. Now, the sentinel affected to show interest at the image coming from the television. Joe imagined some bimbo rolling a big wheel full of numbers because he heard the voice of a woman shouting, "B-24." So Zorba was learning to play Bingo. Joe sighed and put in the number again. His left hand extended as far as he could make it and still, the gate refused to budge. Would he be forced to maneuver the Lexus in a way in order to gain easy access to the push button apparatus? He could sense the smirk on the bonehead watchman.

He mumbled, "Can you open the damned gate, please?"

"Don't you have the number, sir?"

"My ex-wife gave it to me. It won't work."

"What was the number she gave you, sir?"

He told him the number.

"But that was last week's number, sir."

Joe looked at the guard, saying nothing. Behind him, there was now a Chrysler 300 with a guy half his age driving it, red hair, and very red in the face.

Unperturbed, Zorba said, "Last week's number won't work, sir. Can't you punch the right number, sir?"

Incredulous, Joe erupted, "What?"

"What I mean, sir, is this week's number."

Where were these people coming from? He asked himself. Could this guy be descended from Plato or Aristotle? He cursed Barbara, who most probably had planned all this. He surveyed the simpleton as he would a recruit who didn't have a run in him for the Major Leagues.

He barked, "I came here to pick up my kids. Will you stop that nonsense and let me in?"

5 o o o 5

At last, he made it to the Tropicana Field on time. On the way to the stadium, Tammy had him stop at one of her friends' places to pick her up. Irma was her name. Not much money in the family, based on where she lived. He knew that kind of neighborhood. He had grown up in one of them. Not that he would care to return to such a life. But he wasn't a snob. Irma looked like a nice girl. Furthermore, she was a real knockout.

Both girls were babbling happily in the back of the Lexus. He said to Martin, who sat next to him, "Sorry business, me getting stuck at the gate."

"Yup. Mummy isn't good with numbers."

"That's the understatement of the year."

That got him a laugh. Martin looked too serious for his own good, and needed loosening up. To their right the massive stadium appeared and he signaled his intention to get out of the auto route at the next exit.

From the rear, he heard Thalia say, "That can't be true. You're making this up."

Martin, who didn't care about girls' gossip, asked him, "Will the Rays make three in a row?"

"We sure will try, Son."

What were the girls talking about? They were whispering, and he heard the name 'Manuel.' What was this about? Maybe one of them was with child and that fellow Manuel was the father. Just that same year, two players for the Devil Rays had ended up in similar situations. He interrupted the girls.

"What are you two scheming?"

"Oh, papa, you will not believe the story Irma told me."

But Irma didn't want to share it with him.

"You don't want to know, sir. It's a silly tale, and it's not for me to tell."

"Then," he responded, "I assume it's an indiscretion."

"Yes, sir, it is. My friend wouldn't appreciate it if he were to learn that I betrayed his confidence."

"Oh, shoot, Irma," Thalia objected, "this is the greatest story ever! If he told you, it must be because he wanted it to get out. Don't fret like you're a virgin nun."

Joe said, "Thalia may have a point."

Then Martin said, "Is this about the magic bat?"

6 o o o 6

That was the night Joe learned about Manuel and his magic bat. The Red Sox had had the best of the Devil Rays. Joe wasn't happy about the loss. They had played 40 – 20 before that game, and now they were 40 – 21. He felt like he'd gotten on the bathroom scale and discovered he'd gained five pounds. Or found a scratch on his car door. He hated the feeling.

They were all having a shake at the Dairy Queen on Gulf Boulevard near Pasadena. Martin was commenting the match while his quite dejected audience sipped thick chocolate beverages out of straws the color of the American flag. Joe looked around and noticed here and there placards for the Republican candidate in the coming presidential election.

"A home run in the seventh would have done them right," Martin concluded his monologue.

The Rays had left three men on bases at the end of that one. Harry Zed, called the Marvel, with an average of .331 and twenty-one big ones up to now, had hit a pop fly that had been caught easily by the Boston short stop.

"Yup, that would have finished them up," mimicked Thalia whom, Joe was sure, wouldn't know the score of the game, maybe not even who had come ahead.

"Home runs usually do that," he said.

Martin was burping his way to the last of his milk shake and his sister shouted at him, "Will you stop that racket, you horrible slob?"

Martin looked at her, then smiled and said, "I'm not finished."

He made a noise inelegant enough for three or four patrons to turn around and look at them.

"Gross", Thalia hissed, with a frown that did nothing to lessen her natural good looks. Martin picked a note out of his breast pocket and passed it to Joe.

"Dad," he said, "this is from Mom."

His father unfolded the message and looked briefly at it.

"Nobody told me Clem was sick.

Clem had been his dog, which Barbara had insisted he part with when they had separated six years before. The animal had been eight years old at the time, and he'd known she didn't care for it. She had pretended that the children were used to the canine, which had probably been true. He had missed the old beast, though, and now Clem was older and sickly.

"She's okay," Thalia reassured him.

"Four hundred dollars okay." He smiled with a straw in his mouth.

"Anyway," she countered, "Manuel would have gotten you a home run."

"Yeah, right!"

Thalia turned to Irma and begged her, "Please, please tell papa your story."

"This is childish," Irma objected. "Your father will laugh at me. With reason."

"No, he won't," Martin said. "What he'll do is sign him up."

"Can't you be serious once in a while?" Irma retorted.

Joe looked at the three youngsters. It wasn't so late that he couldn't listen to the silly tale. He was with his kids, and he was happy in spite of the loss of his team, his newfound average of .655, and the two wins he would need to get back to two over one. Let them entertain him with this fellow Manuel and what…his magic bat! Clearly Irma didn't put much stock into the yarn. Thalia was another story. She had a proclivity toward credulity, and had always been an easy target for all things that didn't make much sense, but looked good, nevertheless. Reincarnation, levitation, moving objects from a distance, exorcism, and all other kinds of exotic beliefs. She was a natural for those. As for him, he kept an open mind for all hypotheses that could be proven true. Martin, for his part, affected believing in nothing except republicanism, and constantly hit him with comments like they were little jabs in his ribcage, criticizing his liberalism, his soft heart, his belief in God's great design, and his complacency toward Barack Obama. Martin shared his mother's new husband's opinion that the black candidate was no better than an American Fidel Castro. His son could get on his nerves sometimes, but he was seventeen, quite honest and balanced though maybe a bit overextended on the right side of politics. At least he didn't attach himself to lampposts when he didn't get his way.

He looked at Irma and said, "I'm all ears."

"I don't—"

"Who is this boy, Manuel?" he insisted.

"A friend from childhood," Irma reluctantly admitted.

"He was in school with us," his daughter interrupted. "Now he's in college."

"And he plays baseball for the Raiders," Martin announced.

Joe knew about the Raiders. He expected Martin to make the team himself in 2009. Except sports didn't seem to be on his son's agenda these days. Organizing a campaign in school to promote republicanism was more to his liking, and that didn't leave a lot of time for athletic accomplishments.

Joe said, "So, what's the big deal about Manuel?"

Irma looked him in the eyes. "As a matter of fact, it's an incredible story. I wouldn't blame you if you thought I made it up. But I didn't. I swear. I couldn't even create, let alone imagine, a tale like this."

"Spare us the suspense. Go ahead," Joe said.

7 o o o 7

March 2008

It was a Saturday afternoon. The Raiders were playing against the Invaders, a good enough team for a college in the second district out in Pensacola. The Invaders were winning six to five at the end of nine, which Manuel could do nothing about. He'd struck out with a runner on second. Mr. Reynold, the Raiders' coach, had still given him a slap on the back, and that was what hurt the most. Receiving that little encouragement, the kind a coach in college baseball gave to a loser player who needed solace, was humiliating. On the bench, nobody had looked at him. It was a bad day. The game was lost. The next and last at bat wouldn't make any difference.

That was when he had his vision. Nobody around him noticed anything. It just came and went. No trance, no dazed stupor, no ecstasy, no hypnosis, no somnambulism, no psychic-like absurdity. Just some quietness that took hold of him for not quite five minutes, and him seeing a scene like it was a movie on a screen.

He saw himself. He was wearing a shirt with shorts. His shoes were loafers and he was barefoot in them. He walked down a street. It could've been any street in any big town in North America. Some old town, not the kind you'd find in Florida. More like a town up north. Like New York or Boston. A town with tradition and history. A town with streets that seemed to say, "Don't expect us to go straight, or anywhere." A town with old edifices and multitudes crowding its sidewalks, getting in and out of stores in one inextinguishable torrent of insatiable bargain chasers. A town with buildings so high. A town standing upright. He walked in that town on a street that seemed to him like a canyon. Everyone bumped into him left and right. He couldn't progress in any direction without facing a barrage of serious-looking pedestrians charging into him. Then he saw an alley between two close structures. Where did it go? He didn't care. After all, he was going nowhere, and the trip was hard enough. Why not hide in that dark spot and wait it out?

The sun had no business there, and at first he didn't see much of what surrounded him. Gradually his vision cleared and he could make out the width of the passageway. Not enough for a car to get through. Seven or eight feet at the most. He proceeded further into the lane, twenty, thirty feet maybe, and then he saw dustbins and a pile of green bags that rose higher than him, protruding three or four feet from the wall that supported this sorry assemblage. One of the many bins had been left open, and he could see all the rubbish that had accumulated in it. Before he could take inventory, he heard a stifling sound, like the noise made by someone sleeping. Lying in the mass of detritus was a man napping, all muffled up in one decrepit sleeping bag. The mendicant had all that he possessed in three brown bags near him, and looking at those, it was difficult to tell a difference between his stuff and the waste he dozed in. The man had a five-day-old beard. In his left ear was a black and yellow earring. His bare left arm showed a Mickey Mouse tattoo, and his t-shirt announced CAPITALISM IS. He couldn't make out the rest of the quotation.

Behind him he heard the honking of the occasional car, and for the sound of it was like the useless protestations of beaten-up machines. He asked himself what he was doing there. The place was filthy, and vermin were most probably crawling in all holes, gaps, cavities, and recesses.

A sudden gust of wind moved his hair in his eyes, and he put it back in place, seeing a piece of newspaper that had been displaced on a bin without a cover.

And then he saw it. The baseball bat, that is.

It was an ordinary bat, quite like the one he used with the Raiders. The kind that was Major League approved. He could discern one small red strip up where the bat's circumference was the biggest, and when he took it out of the bin, he noted that there was another red strip in the area of the grip where the wood piece was at its leanest. This bat was splendid, and Manuel couldn't help but ask himself who in his right mind would have thrown it away. Why? He would keep it that was for sure. And find a way to give the Raiders a few hits out of it. That was when he heard a voice, and he looked around for the speaker.

"So, you have come."

He realized it was the old beggar talking to him. He had the bat in his hand, and the shock of hearing the voice had made him hold it in a way that looked aggressive. Seeing no danger ahead, he readjusted his posture, let the bat touch the ground, and used it as if it were a cane, at the risk of looking a bit silly.

Nevertheless he said, "Are you talking to me, sir?"

But the man just repeated, "So, you have come."

"What do you mean, sir?"

"You are the one this bat has been designed for. Listen to me now, young man, and you listen good, because I'll only say it once. This piece of wood that you are now holding is special. Very special indeed. It will give home runs at will to you and to you only if used in Major League Baseball. Do you understand what I have just told you?"

"Yes, sir, I do, sir. I really do, even if it doesn't make much sense, sir. I am sorry, sir. I mean no disrespect.

"This is not for you to decide. What I am telling you is the truth. Now, act upon it."

8 o o o 8

His friend, Peter, had gotten him out of the dream by crashing beside him on the bench. It took Manuel a few seconds to adjust to the reality of losing the game, more irksome for the fact that they had been ahead five to two up until the seventh inning. The coach would have them pay dearly for that slip up.

Peter said, "I got my old man's Mustang. You care for a ride?"

They had a few beers in a joint in Clearwater, and that was it.

Two months later in June, the college organized a trip to Chicago. Participants were to sleep in the gymnasium and take their meals in the cafeteria of whatever institution they would sojourn at. In that way, the four days to sites and museums could be offered at minimum cost. It was still two hundred dollars, and he had put sixty of his own toward financing for the journey. His parents, who were far from being rich, had paid the difference. An excursion like that was too good an opportunity to be missed. So, he went.

On the last day of their little adventure, they were all preparing to leave for the airport. It was three in the afternoon. Their TOD for the plane from US Air was 18h00. Mr. Camlot, the art professor and trip organizer, had looked at his luggage. There wasn't much, and that was probably why he had noticed the baseball bat that Manuel carried. He most certainly would have ignored the matter if it had been an easel, a set of paint brushes, or canvas. But a baseball bat? Really, those athletes were a silly lot. He could have asked, "When did you get that?" or something. He didn't. Just stared at it in a dismissive kind of way, stared and stared a moment more, as if he were trying to think of something witty and didn't find anything. So he just looked at Manuel as he would have a pupil who couldn't spell properly. Why, those poor illiterates, you didn't want to be rude with them.

From nine to one on the last day of the trip, the students had been free to move around town as they wished. The school they were bedding in was at the corner of Halsted and Chicago in the downtown area. Manuel had decided to walk the two miles to the beach. The temperature was mild. He had dressed in his usual outfit, shorts and a t-shirt. Chicago was a gigantic city. Beautiful, too. The buildings around him were so huge and massive, with the busy crowd driving through or walking its streets and sidewalks. Chaotic-looking, and yet all of them moving in an orderly and determinate fashion.

And then, something happened.

Hundreds of clerks flowed out of a building and in a matter of seconds they were all around Manuel, knocking him left and right and pushing him against a wall, looking fierce and resolute in their decision to bulldoze their way to the entrance of a mall on the other side of the street. Manuel had a sense of déjà vu.

Then he saw the opening in the wall and remembered the passage between the skyscrapers from his dream eight weeks back.

He entered into the canyon-like alley and walked resolutely toward the dustbins and the piles of green bags that protruded three or four feet from the wall. As he expected, the snoring old man was there, too, all muffled up in his sorry-looking sleeping bag. It was the same man. He recognized not only the face, but also the black and yellow earring in his left ear, and the Mickey Mouse tattoo on his arm. He could make out the full citation on the soiled t-shirt. CAPITALISM IS DOOMED. All he had to do was move the newspaper that had been wedged between other stuff and here it was, a baseball bat with its little red strip bands on the top and bottom. He didn't hesitate to take hold of the bat. He waited for the beggar to wake up, even though he didn't need to be told a second time what the bat was good for. And then the poor man snored. Beside him were a few bottles of cheap vodka, two empties and one almost full. From where he stood, Manuel could smell the sour breath of the decrepit old man. He didn't feel like getting the poor wastrel out of his slumber. So, he took his prize and walked toward the light and the street.

——∘∘∘⟩●⟨∘∘∘——

Irma was finished and a little out of breath. They had passed over the bridge on the Pinellas Bayway and Joe turned left on a road leading toward Isla del sol. Another gated community of singular residences, mostly mansions, sat on an almost island that looked upon the Gulf on its northern side, and on a canal that separated it from its opposite bank. At the gate, the guard recognized the children and let them in, no questions asked. It was eleven thirty at night. Irma was quiet, now.

Joe sighed and said, "That was quite a yarn."

"You asked for it, remember?"

From the back seat, Martin said, "I sure could use that bat myself."

Thalia cut him off. "To do what? I bet you couldn't hit a basketball with it. What about a baseball?"

"Who cares about striking silly balls or balloons? I would build a cathedral and put this piece of wood in it, and have everybody pay a buck for the privilege to look at it. Ten to touch it and a hundred to swing it. What about that?"

That got him a laugh from his father. Joe asked, "What about you, Irma?"

But Thalia was now rebuking her brother, "You obtuse, slow-witted dummy. You respect nothing but moneymaking schemes."

"I don't care much for baseball, sir," Irma answered.

"I didn't mean that. I'll get you home, now, all right?"

"Look who's talking now," countered Martin, "my big sister the democrat, who would build a cathedral with public money if given half the chance, and worship her own new divinity in it, the one with the name that starts with 'Barak.'"

"Idiot!"

"Thanks," said Irma.

"It's on my way home," Joe answered. "No problem."

He had dropped his kids at Mr. Nobody the fourth or fifth's house. The place had all the cachet of a public building, big, comfortable, and undistinguished. One unsuspecting pedestrian could have confused the premises with a small museum or the St. Pete main library.

Then, Irma.

Joe lived in Pass-a-Grille, on the Gulf and the sand of the St. Pete beach. His cottage, Maine style, was a nice two-story wood structure, shingle covered, with a large veranda facing the ocean. Cozy, large, and beautiful. He loved that house. He loved his children. He loved the tale he had just heard. That night, he was ready to love everything. He was feeling good. Contented. He didn't know why. After all, the Devil Rays had lost their match tonight. Forty to twenty-one! He had to get back to a .666 average. Two wins. That was all what was needed.

9 o o o 9

The first article appeared in the Tampa Tribune August the third.

That day, and before the game against the Toronto Blue Jays, Joe Black's Devil Rays ruled their division with a record of sixty-three to forty. They were trailing the Chicago White Sox by two games for the league Championship. His team still had fifty-nine games left to play. Joe was confident he would get there in time. This was to be the Devil Rays' big season of all time. He felt it. He knew it. The same, as he knew, that Obama would win in November. He was good at prediction. He had never missed a presidential one before. And if a black candidate could make it in the US of A, the Devil Rays could certainly make it to the World Series.

It was ten in the morning. Outside temperature was the usual South Florida summertime hot, humid, oppressive, and untenable. If you weren't a native, that is. As he wasn't.

From his living room, the ocean drove weak surf over the sand that reminded him of the Great Lakes, and Ontario in particular. He had been born a Canadian. He was from the north. And some day, he would return there. If he had to choose where he wanted to live, the American east coast would get his vote. Not too large a town, more like Portland or Atlantic City. Near the great metropolis, but not too near. He no longer had a wife. There was nobody important in his new life. Just his children, and they were part of the old. He would stay near them if he could, but soon, they would go their ways, and who knew where work or romance would move them around the continent? So, when the time came, he would go up north where a tree was a tree, and where the word 'season' meant something.

He originated from Toronto. That was the place of his youth, where he had met the woman of his dreams, the girl he had dated when he was nineteen and whom he married at twenty-three, after he completed a master's degree and she became a lawyer. She was his first love, and the only he would ever get, since he didn't believe that kind of experience would happen again if you had it right the first time. He had lived with Barbara twenty-five years. They had had two kids. He still loved her. Love, once given, couldn't disappear totally. It would always survive somewhere, whatever you did, or whatever rationalization you put in its way.

What had gone wrong between them? He couldn't say. Just that, in some kind of imperceptible way, she had stopped loving him, and that was it. His job didn't help. He couldn't blame her for not having wanted to follow him to California ten years back. Then, she had met the guy she was with these days. He had been a big shot lawyer in a well-established firm out there in downtown Tampa Bay. And a multimillionaire in addition. He had offered her a job. She had accepted.

That had started it all.

Some asshole of the fourth or fifth fucking generation had made her a partner, and then she had moved over to his place. He knew that life wasn't easy. Those days had been a difficult time.

Fate had it that he got an offer to manage the Devil Rays in 2004. So, there he was, living two miles from Barbara, who had married her new, very rich boyfriend. But that changed nothing for him, did it? You could move out of your parents' house and they would always remain your parents, right? As far as he was concerned, it was that way with couples like him and Barbara, in eternity, if not on this earth.

In his eyes, it was so obvious that it needed no demonstration. But if one was needed, one need only look at images of both of them when they were young. That was the most difficult thing to do, glancing at those mementos of the past, pictures taken out of booths in pharmacies, showing them as kids so juvenile, guileless, and naïve, believers in things absolute. The kisses she had given him… He would never forget the first time he had touched her. Those moments were for him and him alone. Nobody could take them away from him. That was what life was worth living for. Those moments, he would cherish for the rest of his life, as well as the woman who had made them possible.

They said that nowadays, a man had one wife when he was young and another when he grew old. He didn't believe that doctrine applied to him, even if it certainly looked true enough for other people. No. For him, there would be no other woman. Not because he had decided that. Rather because he knew it. He didn't believe that he could do it again, have anybody the way he'd had Barbara. Repeating that process was impossible, and if he couldn't do it the right way, there was no point in trying to do it.

It would be mimicking. A mockery. Faust was a damned fool for having tried it, and so was Goethe to have penned down the silly dramatic. All he would achieve by engaging in another relationship was sullying what grace and magic he remembered from the initial experience.

END of Faith part One

That same morning, the first thing Peter did when back at the Verizon Building, was to call his lawyer. He was lucky that Arthur answered before the third ring, it being eight thirty a.m. and the staff getting in at nine.

"Morin, Fansworth, & Hochik. How can I help you?"

"It's me, Arthur," he stated.

"Ah, Peter. So, what do you think? Will the Zielgard piece be worth anything?"

On Peter's end of the line he faltered a bit, and then charged his way into his prepared dialogue, his voice as decisive and authoritative as he could make it.

"How would I know? You don't expect me to have read it yet, do you?"

"As a matter of fact, I did. I thought that was what you guys did for a living. Sorry if I got the wrong impression."

Arthur was annoyed, and it showed enough to make Peter uncomfortable.

"And I'm sorry if I have failed your expectations. It isn't like I had nothing else to do, you know."

"Look who's talking now. Is it the same fellow who has teatime every damn afternoon at four, and who watches Dallas on his TV set at the office?"

In a kind of confidential mood, he had shared his liking of the show once, and the price Arthur had extracted since then was pure sadism.

"This is so untrue," he protested. "What a vile thing to say! You sure sound like a lawyer, now. Talking nonsense and expecting to be trusted. No wonder you tricked your way to some success in your profession."

"Oh, that hurts a lot," Arthur moaned.

"It better," Peter laughed. He added in a more conciliatory disposition, "I might take a look at it this weekend. All will depend of this trip we're making to Orlando. It's not yet decided since they're doing some work in Angela's sister's house. Either it will be finished this Friday and we go now, or it won't and we'll make the trip the next weekend."

"You do that," Arthur said bluntly.

"You know I will," Peter said.

"What I would like is a little more enthusiasm on your part."

"You want excitement, Arthur? You buy yourself a lottery ticket. It has a twenty million jackpot this month. What about that for stimulation?"

"At least you humor me. Not an easy thing to do so early in the day, and me not having sipped yet from my second cup of Starbucks."

"You have a busy schedule today?"

"No. As a matter of fact, I might pass part of my day looking at this sorcerer's case on the court TV network. You know that the jury is expected to announce its decision on sentencing at eleven. Will it be death or prison?"

"But," Peter objected, "the woman is kind of old, isn't she?"

"She'll be sixty-seven next month. So, not so old, but old enough."

"I can't believe this was an issue that needed to be put before them."

"Oh, but it is. Not that the state will have much of a chance to act on their decision if it were to go that way, though. With the appeals and us lawyers' artifices, stratagems, and tricks, not a chance for that to happen within fifteen years, and by that time, she'll have gone in the usual fashion."

"This is all very comforting. I still can't see how they could make a case out of this. The facts don't add up."

"Point of appeal number one," Arthur interjected. "Who would have ever thought that in such a country like ours, its highest court would end up having to decide if an angel, good or bad, is a 'person' in the sense of the law?"

"And when that happens, let's see what the politicians will do with the question," Peter pondered.

"Just go take a look at what's befallen Mississippi right now," Arthur said. "The governor has felt the need, in his last address to the people a week ago, to affirm that he is a true believer in God. He said it three times, when the subject of his discourse was the urgency of putting more money into their roads."

Silence fell for a few seconds. Peter asked, as if it were an afterthought, "Do you know if Zielgard ever showed his manuscript to anybody?"

"So what if he did? Why would I care about that?"

"I don't know."

Peter could well see that this was not the right kind of inquisition. He changed track before Arthur could become suspicious.

"You told me the story came to you through the agent selling the house."

"Yup."

"What if this agent wrote this thing and now wants to have a free shot at being published?"

Arthur laughed.

"Now, that is preposterous. You must be an author yourself. You do have quite an imagination, Peter! Besides, that makes no sense. What would be the point?"

"So," he asked, "what's his name?"

"Phil Leclerc. He's out there in Gulfport, Mississippi. You care to find him? He's in the phone book. You go and ask him about his artistic disposition. Well, Peter, with this last one, you made my day… Ha, ha, ha! I have to go. You have some reading to do, haven't you?"

He searched for the agent's name in Gulfport and found it easily, since Phil Leclerc Real Estate Agency was at the top of a page. An advertisement showing his picture promoted the quality of his services. With such a name, French Canadian by the look of it, he was protected from confusion with the competition, being the only one with a Gallic surname. Although, there was a Leclair woman who advertised her talent at reading the future in the palms of your hands, tea leaves, or the feathers of your favorite bird pet. And then there were the Leclerk brothers who were in the XXX motion picture business. Peter called the number for the agency and got the broker on his first try.

"Phil Leclerc Real Estate, "a deep and resonant voice said on the western side of the Gulf of Mexico.

"Bonjour, Monsieur Leclerc," Peter articulated in perfect French. "Are you the one who handles the Zielgard property?"

"Tout à fait," the other said, also using his mother tongue. "How can I help you, sir?"

"My name is Peter Artritis from the St. Petersburg/Tampa area. How is life treating you, Phil?"

"I'm okay. From where I am, I can see you guys on the other side of the pond. What's up, then? You want to move into the beautiful state of Mississippi? By valor and arms, that's our motto around here. So, when are you coming? You will like the weather around here."

It was spring, and the temperature in downtown St. Pete wasn't so bad yet, not like it would be come summer, when the thermometer would reach ninety-eight in the middle of the day and the humidity would rise so high that one felt he was walking through a Turkish bath. Still, to the agent he said, "What about the hurricane? Camille in 1969 and Katrina in 2005 destroyed half the town."

"We are good up to 2041, then." Leclerc answered with a chuckle.

"Still, you are too far north. Snow, I don't like much."

It was a lame joke that the agent had the good sense to laugh at anyway. "Ha, ha, ha, that was a good one," he lied. Then he added, "I have the Zielgard residence to sell, though. You would like the site. That is, if you care to live in such a place."

"Tell me, this residence of yours," Peter said, "is it coming furnished?"

"Peter Aristis, I can see right from the start that you have a great sense of humor."

"Artritis," he corrected.

"Sorry, Atristis. But no, it isn't coming furnished, as you suggested. Whatever waste was in that pigsty, you wouldn't have appreciated much. I can tell by the way you talk, believe me."

"So, what did you do with the furniture?"

"Throw it all on the street. Nobody would touch it. That tells it all, doesn't it?"

"And what about the stuff that didn't go in the gutter?" Peter insisted.

"There wasn't much of that, mind you. The few pieces that we could salvage out of the mess, the metal, I gave to a junk dealer who took it free of charge. Electronics and such, I gave to the Salvation Army. And then I heard that there is some German buffoon across the ocean who doesn't like my philanthropy."

"Cultural differences," Peter commented.

"Ah, this I know about, me being of French extraction. Still, I get by."

"I am sure you do. But tell me, Phil, was there a typewriter in the junk you threw out or gave away?"

"As a matter of fact, now that you mention it, there was."

"And what did you do with it, if I may ask?"

"You want it? It might still be at the Salvation Army on Anniston Avenue."

"You have the phone number?"

"Let me look on my cell. I talked to them last week. It should still be there. Yes. Here it is."

He gave it to Peter.

"Ask for Jason."

Peter wrote the number down, then said, "You've been a real pal, Phil. I appreciate your help very much."

"So there will be no moving into this area, I take it?"

"You know, St. Pete isn't that bad."

His next communication was to Jason, who was not yet there. He left his name and phone number. Linda opened his door, the Diland owner's massive frame behind her now filling the space so that it dwarfed everything around him.

Spiros Artritis was eighty-two, but looked easily a full ten years younger. The man had the bearing of a king, and he knew it. He could have been Anthony Queen on a movie set, just about to dance a few steps to a bouzouki tune. His Zorba-like father was everything Peter wasn't. Wherever his patriarch found himself, with the rich crowd at some charity ball at The Don CeSar, or the Waldorf in New York, where he lived most of the time, he attracted attention, dwarfing all near him, man or woman, to the status of faire valoir compared to his prestige, his subdued roughness, and his quiet deportment of reliable and undisputed authority.

He was on his way to Montreal, and the house he still maintained on Lake Memphremagog, a place that had been in his wife's family since 1921 when her grandfather Ernest d'Allemagne had bought it. Québec being the land that had started it all, he had and would keep the cottage, and persist to visit there till the end of his life. Peter remembered well that mansion on the lake from the days when he was a kid, before the family moved to New York City in 1968. His father, in his mind, was the best example of an industry mogul like one read about in novels. The man was able to play a great number of roles all at the same time: a performer with the ability, in the blink of an eye, to put his audience in a state of wonderment, capable of astonishing and provoking at will, annoying or irritating, and then with a clap of his hands, he would have them revelling, as delight as if he had given a new meaning to the word 'happiness.'

He could be impossible, absurd, vexing, unpredictable, fascinating, affectionate, tender, enchanting, and sometimes bewitching. He could also be cold-blooded, harsh, brutal, rude, and tasteless, as well as attractive, lovable, and seductive, if he needed. All those traits he collected and cared about no more than if they were clothes on his body.

Depending of circumstances, one uses what will fit, and some of the most fortunate people end up always looking their best without really trying. This would sum up Spiros Artritis pretty well. In 1959, he had married Peter's mother in Québec City. She was Madeleine d'Allemagne. It had been a good marriage. Spiros's wife had died of cancer ten years before.

Peter got up from his seat. He looked at his father, who occupied the space in his office in such a way that it didn't look so grand anymore. Suddenly, he felt small and insignificant. His father had not always been easy to live with. He could crush you, overwhelm you, or shame you into insubstantiality. He could do all that without even realizing he was doing it. Peter had been the first victim of his father's brilliance. He still remembered with pain in his heart how he had tried as a child to make his father look at him, with his small deeds and accomplishments, but he'd missed the target most of the time. Never were his efforts considered adequate or worthy of his father's attention, which he craved. Yet, he loved his father as his mother had. And he knew that Spiros had reciprocated the sentiment in his own way. Still, all his life, he'd been under the impression that he had fallen short of what was expected of him, had failed his father in one way or another. He recalled as a child always missing his old man, who traveled a lot, and then, when he was around, being afraid of him.

Otherwise, life for Peter had been pleasant enough, and quite comfortable. With his mother's family, the d'Allemagnes from Québec City, he had had an existence that could have come out of a story of the Comtesse de Ségur, with all the cousins he'd had and the summers they had enjoyed together in the big house on Lake Memphremagog. "Les Vacances" had been his favorite book in those early years of his childhood, his father looking much like as the men in the story, aristocratic and distant.

Spiros had joined and then succeeded his father-in-law, Marcel who had started Quincaillerie Marcel D'Allemagne & Fils with the help of his father Ernest. This business, created in 1931, had prospered and become, with the passing of years, quite a successful wholesale concern, an enterprise of a good reputation in the Québec City area, an unavoidable player that you were sure to find if you were of a mind to build anything. From the little store Marcel D' had started at twenty-one, he had added on by occupying the adjacent building, and then, he had bought the whole edifice from the owner. The fellow had gotten tired of the worry of dealing with tenants who didn't always pay their rent on time, which didn't stop them from complaining nonstop about this or that. Marcel, on the other hand, had never given him any trouble. On the contrary, he was the reason why he had kept the building so long. And then, when he had wanted to retire, he had offered his tenant the building at conditions that were difficult to refuse.

It didn't take long after the transaction until all the flats on the second and third floors were put to good use--that was, the enlargement of the hardware business, which had become wholesale by that time. That was 1957. The same year, Spiros Artritis disembarked from the Athena in Montreal and found his way to Québec, and then Marcel d'Allemagne Quincaillerie en gros. Spiros had had a big personality even so early in his life. Nevertheless, he was a perfect nobody, with no money to his name, and he didn't know the language, except for what he had learned in school. What assets he had were immense ambition, a good intellect, capacity for hard work, and the most important, his word, which you could depend on with your life.

So it happened that Spiros met Madeleine d'Allemagne and by that time, he had improved his French in order to be able to charm his way to the girl's heart in the belle's own language. Pictures of him in those years showed an individual with elegance, a superb and virile beauty that could only be found in movie stars of the time. He was quick-witted, had a laugh that was contagious, and made you want to share in his cheerfulness. If he had a mind to do it, he could use his bouzouki and sing you a ballad with a melody so sad that it was sure to bring tears to his audience's eyes, men or women. That was the way he was. He had facility, aptitude, and ability. He was overpowering.

He and Madeleine were married in 1959. Early that same year, Fidel Castro worried the world by seizing power in Cuba. Spiros who kind of looked like the dictator shaved his beard and went to work for his father-in-law. From there, the business took off in a way that took Marcel d'Allemagne by surprise. It amazed him out of his wits and beyond all his previous expectations. He had thought himself good at was he was doing. But what Spiros brought to his operation was life-changing, like the coming of the fax machine would prove to be a few decades later.

After all, there was a limit at what one could do with a hardware business. Spiros had certainly proved this to be untrue. How had he done that? In his own unobtrusive way, as he could be discreet if need be. He showed that he could also be a master at diplomacy. Marcel d'Allemagne was approaching sixty, and didn't look the picture of health as much as he would have liked. Hence, Spiros's road to predominance had been quite easy, while his wife's father enjoyed the slowing down of his work routine, and even more so since there was always more money coming in. He had to give credit to his son-in-law. Whatever he had achieved up to that point had been, in his mind, well enough to qualify as undisputed success. But he was forced to admit that he had seen nothing. It looked like success didn't have the same definition in French that it did in Greek. Under Spiros's gentle and vigorous orientation, things started to happen.

They became a company. That newly created commercial society bought all the land next to theirs, and connected together all existing buildings, or erected others. This expansion had been done between the years 1962 and 1970. Marcel was no longer active, and left most of the day-to-day business to his daughter's spouse. This man, by the late sixties, he considered his own son, and the best gift God had sent his way after his own wife and daughter.

There was no great man without good fortune playing a part in his ascendancy, victory, and triumph. After all, most illustrious characters enjoyed good health of body and mind and likely died of old age. This was the prerequisite to gain prominence in one's field. Luck was involved. Chance, opportunities, and the ability to seize the last when it came your way. In this manner, war had been good for Quincaillerie Marcel d'Allemagne en gros Ltee. Québec had a harbor, shipbuilding yards, and a lot of other trump cards, like manpower, as well as proximity with the sea that put it right into the Canadian Army supplies authority's radar. In those days after the war, the military had an enormous appetite and unlimited means. It happened early in 1960 that one cargo of PT-235 truck-like vehicles, designed for the conflict in Vietnam, it was said, had been railway delivered to a colonel in Val Cartier. It had been later discovered that these trucks were useless by reason of one faulty piece. There was then nothing else for the officer to do than to change the defective wingnut if he wanted to have the machines on a boat and shipped to Asia.

They had met at some lunch organized by the Québec chamber of commerce. Laflamme had been suggested to contact Marcel D'Allemagne and ended up talking with Spiros. The latter proposed they rendezvous the next day at the QCC gathering since they were both member and the colonel could then explain in detail what his sorry situation was.

"One wingnut like this one," the colonel had ...... complained to Spiros, taking out of his spotless uniform's side pocket one small scrap of metal half a centimeter thick and as big as a silver dollar, "what do you think?" Colonel Marc Laflamme had added in a dejected tone of voice, "Damn, as far as I know, those silly gadgets could have been designed on the moon. I may only get my hands on some when the big wheels in Ottawa find a way to bargain with the fricking Martians."

"Martians on the moon?" Spiros had observed.

"Don't get smart on me Artritis," the Colonel had countered with a benign smile on his lips.

"Let me see that piece of junk," Spiros said, taking it from the colonel's open hand and examining the object the same way he would if it had been a rare specimen.

The Hellenic entrepreneur wasn't yet three years in North America at the time of that conversation. At 33, he might have been intimidated in the presence of an officer of the Canadian Army. After all, as far as his father-in-law was concerned, the young man was still learning the business, and Marcel d'Allemagne kind of enjoyed the notion that there was a lot to learn. Yet, with that Colonel that he had never met before, he could talk as if he were ten years older and much wiser.

Like they were equals.

Which they weren't.

Spiros was so sure he wasn't in the same league as this petty officer, with his stupid intendancy problems, who couldn't imagine a solution to his problem that didn't come from higher up in the military hierarchy. The problem with most people, he thought, was that they did things the way they were used to doing them, and resisted all changes without thinking.

They were in the gardens of the hotel Clarendon in Québec City. Spiros had been relishing the cognac he had been served after a meal he hadn't touched much, a routine affair organized by the town's chamber of commerce. He had arrived at the dining room alone, and then been made to join a table with a vacant place beside a gentleman of the military. While waiting for the invited guest of honour to reach the lectern and make a speech, Spiros had introduced himself to the other people at their table, and then, with Laflamme at his side, they had talked.

Spiros scrutinized the wingnut.

"What's wrong with them?" he asked.

"They come loose," sighed the Colonel. "It causes the transmission to fall apart, somehow. How should I know? I'm no mechanic. My job is just to move tonnage. For now, I'm being told that these screws, when you bolt them fair and square, will break down anyway. So the shipment, it stays with me until the trucks are declared fit and ready to go. I might as well prepare to have them in my face till the end of this war."

He moved to take the wingnut from Spiros.

"Like this piece of scrap out here. Would you believe it," he added, "the silly nuisance opens up like it was a fricking nutshell."

Spiros had felt the weight of the morsel of metal, handling the piece as if it were a baseball and he was getting ready to throw it at the advancing barman in his waiter's garb.

Compared to him, the khaki uniform the Colonel was wearing appeared a tight fit as the man looked a bit unsteady, but then, he was gulping scotch and was now asking for a second. Besides, Spiros had seen him drink a full bottle of a millésime Château Latour, which had been suggested and presented to him by a very affected head waiter, an older French native who proclaimed himself a great admirer of "the Marechal," and who had had the nerve to blame the British for the sinking of the French Fleet at Mers-el-Kébir. His view had been expressed with gusto, as it was shared by a prelate who later had bored their whole table to death with the full life of Ste Thérèse de Lisieux.

"It's American made, isn't it?" he had asked.

"Chrysler is using the stuff. Get it from a manufacturer in Arizona or some other shithole in the desert. How would I know?"

"I could make them for you. They're just wingnuts, after all. Those Pt-235 vehicles must have been equipped with the wrong batch of hardware. It happens, and they wouldn't be that difficult to reproduce if I were to get the right specifications. You need how many?"

Marc Laflamme had stared open-mouthed at the man sitting beside him.

"Are you talking seriously?" he asked. "Sapristi! Do you suggest making it right here?"

The supply officer threw a very skeptical gaze around him, beyond the Clarendon garden's wall. Here, in Laflamme's mind, meant obviously out there, in this little nothing of a place where there wasn't even the semblance of a car industry, except for the manufacturing of mini statuettes of the virgin Mary that people hung from their Ford and Chevy's rear-view mirrors. They were all that way, Spiros concluded with some exasperation. It was all over again the sorry repetition of Groucho, who wouldn't join a club that would have him as a member. The natives themselves ignored their ability to build things, and would never conceive of one turbine originating from such a place with a name like St. Pie truc machin.

"If I say so, it is because I know that we can make them for you," repeated Spiros. "So, how many will you need, then?"

"Sapristi!" the man repeated. "I have one hundred of those stupid vehicles piling up in my backyard. Ten dozen would do just fine."

"Three days. Give me three days, and I will deliver them to you. Let's say it shall be our society's contribution to the war effort. This way, if my wingnuts don't fit perfectly, nobody will be the worse off for it."

Back at his office, he had found Rocco, the chief of Atelier. The man knew his business, and he proved he did by recognizing the wingnut just from looking at it.

"The same as our model 133," he said. "Maybe one or two millimeters thicker. Picton Tools manufactured those for Chrysler, who used them to place the panel that supports the eight-cylinder engine of their S-300 truck. They don't sell those in Canada. That's why we don't keep that kind in stock here."

"Can you duplicate this, smart ass?" he asked.

"Yes. I keep here Picton's book of specifications for all that they produce. We have one for all the big players in the car industry in North America. I'll get you a full company of such soldiers up and ready to go to the front in no time."

While saying this, he took down a very dirty catalogue off a shelf in the dusty cubbyhole that served him as an office. The catalogue looked the same as many others all lined up in some semblance of order. Once opened, the chief's fingers moved through the pages. There were business cards everywhere, and a single sheet menu from the restaurant La Belle Place fell on the floor. It was the diner Spiros visited every morning for his breakfast of toast and coffee.

"Here it is." Rocco pointed to a picture of a look-alike wingnut on a page that displayed several. They all looked the same to Spiros's unpracticed eyes. "What's wrong with that specimen of yours?" He asked, giving it back.

"No, Spiros objected. "You keep it. I'm told they break under pressure."

Rocco, who was an Italian, had sneered, "Yup, like those Franchouillards on the other side of the ocean. We know these things can happen, can't they? As for this…" He pointed to the wingnut on his desk. "…a wrong batch?"

Spiros ignored the cheap aside and the politic beyond. Instead, he asked, "What is it made of?"

"Steel. Just take a look here. You read this. SW 243-560. Dofasco does that. It's delivered to us in one-hundred-pound plates. I can get them in all thicknesses as need requires. All I have to do is settle the tool-making apparatus to the proper measurements and then the wingnuts you need will multiply like puff cakes in a Jesus story."

"How do I know that they won't be useless like this one?"

Rocco had laughed the objection away. "I will guarantee them with my life," he had said. "How many do you need?" As if this would have settled for good the matter of his product's excellence.

"One hundred and fifty."

"A piece of cake. It will be finished before the end of the week. I will see to it myself," he promised.

"Rocco," Spiros said with a very serious look on his face, "you fabricate the silly little buggers as if your life depends on it, you understand me? Take all the time you need, but I want perfection, you get that? If I pull this off, we'll attract the attention of the big shots at National Defence in Ottawa, and God only knows what it might bring us. I mean contracts and future business."

It had worked out just like that.

The wingnuts had been delivered to the colonel. The man had disappeared for the next few weeks, so after thirty days had passed with no news from him, Spiros had shrugged his shoulders and said, "Really, those soldiers type have their ways…"

Much later, though, when he had given up on the matter, someone out in Ottawa had called his office to ask if he had space where he could store some things.

Marcel d'Allemagne owned at the time four of five pieces of land around his place of business, in case he wanted to build on them, and he used them, in the meantime, as open warehouses.

"Well," Spiros had answered without thinking straight, "what we do here is selling hardware wholesale. So—"

"You are that Greek fellow, aren't you?" the stranger on the other end of the line interrupted.

"Spiros Artritis, that's my name."

"I've been told," insisted his interlocutor, who had introduced himself as Pierre Francoeur, "that you also went under the name of Mr. Fix It."

"Well…"

"You know who I am thinking about?"

"I believe I do, yes."

"He made you a hell of a reputation up here, you hear me?"

"I am most flattered."

"What does that mean?"

"The colonel remembered me. I'm glad."

"He told me you were the man who could deal with my problem."

"It all depends on the puzzle," he responded rather pitifully.

Pierre emitted a sound that could have passed for a laugh.

"Believe me, Artritis, you don't want to know the answer to that question. So I'll ask as if it never came up, you follow me?"

Spiros didn't. Pierre Francoeur didn't mind. He continued as if he were confiding in a longtime friend, "It doesn't matter. Here in bloke country, they have a name for this. They waffle around. In French, we called it the 'langue de bois.' This is an art form that has sprouted up over time at Defense, and you civilians wouldn't even conceive of such elaborate and refined nonsense. Seriously, now, let's say it's a supply problem. Transport, also. And then what to do with the stuff while waiting to get it out of our way. That's not even half of my predicament, mind you, and to make it worse, it's the easiest part…"

"I could help you with the supply bit. I can deliver directly to the Quebec Harbour. Transport, we don't do in a way that would mean anything to you guys. As for storage, well, that remains to be seen. I got plenty of space here. So if it pleases you to use those…"

"Splendid. I'll tell you what. Major William Carey will contact you, let's say tomorrow, and then he will arrange a meeting at a moment convenient for both of you. You can discuss the details of what his needs are and how you can help."

It just so happened that Major Carey was the perfect embodiment of Spiros's idea of a Greek Santa Claus. That is, if you didn't mind Santa being short, neat, crisp, and silly. He never asked the cost of anything. The man had appeared at the shop at eight in the morning the next day. He hadn't cared to call before, and never knew his luck that Spiros' scheduled visit at a project site had been canceled at the very last minute. As for Marcel d'Allemagne, he no longer worked so early, rarely gratifying them with his august presence at the office before ten a.m., and then, not every day.

There was at La Belle Place a waitress known as Mado. She always kept a sweet caporal in the left corner of her mouth. Carey hadn't touched the cup of coffee the woman had served him. He must have thought that some of the dust particles floating in his beverage were embers from Mado's cigarette. They sure could've been. None of the diner's regular patrons minded the occasional seasoning, though.

Spiros would remember for a long time after the words the major had said right at the beginning of their talk, "When you get out of bed, which foot hits the floor first?"

Spiros had no idea. He said so. He couldn't discern if there was disappointment showing in his new acquaintance's inquisitive physiognomy. But the major wasn't finished. He asked, "What is it you do from the start? Shave? Brush your teeth? Shower?"

Once this strange introduction had passed, which Spiros had attributed to some martial thinking gone awry, it had seemed to him that magic had taken over and things went on by themselves after that. They had strolled back to the d'Allemagne office. They had walked the ground. The buildings looked like the factories that had been built the century before. They were all red brick, four and five stories high, huge with outliers here and there that made them look operative, efficient, and capitalist ugly. The unlikely and disjointed structure had its front entrance on Dufour Street. The land facing that road measured a hundred and sixty feet, while in depth it carried on along Barclay Avenue for over eight hundred feet, up to the Five Rose milling plant. As both men were walking on the sidewalk, trucks with the d'Allemagne logo on their cargo box passed them by.

"They are starting their delivery run," Spiros explained.

At that moment, Major William Carey had come to a halt, looking pensive, staring about in a distracted sort of way, and Spiros wondered if he was still wondering what task it was better to accomplish first, be it shaving, showering, or whatever. Take a leak, he had answered on an impulse to the idiotic interrogation. Why hadn't the major suggested that as a possible answer?

Without looking at the big man towering over him, Carey said, with his right arm pointing toward the Five Rose's deserted expanse in front of him, "It's a bit tiny, but it might do for now."

Spiros could see in his mind the manager of the flour plant next door. That man had mentioned two years before at one of their Kiwanis monthly dinner meeting that they could sell them those adjoining acres. Since they had built themselves a new shop three times bigger in Trois Rivières, business had slowed down in Montreal and those two acres didn't fit anymore into the company's future expansion. At the time, he had said that he would think about it. Nothing had come of it. He would need to speak with this guy if he could. Major Carey was still talking. He didn't seem to care much if he was listened to or not. Spiros wondered if he'd missed something important.

"…yonder, where there is, what? Could it be a garage?" And without waiting for an answer, he continued. "We will build a two-story warehouse, two hundred thousand square feet on each floor. It shall be enough. A pity you do not make use of more land in this area, though…"

"It might be arranged," suggested Spiros. "Listen, Major Carrey, you announced that you intend to do some construction work. Why don't you find yourself some existing edifice?"

"No time, Spiros. By the way, call me Bill, will you? Furthermore, either those places you talk about are not available, or they don't meet the specifications. Getting them to the right specifications might end up costing more money than the prefab, we'll raise here. You know, us in the army, what we do is very basic. Nothing fancy, if you catch my drift. We ain't building no pyramids. You heard that joke about the kid boasting about his army father's construction skills?"

He hadn't.

"Let me tell it to you, then," the major said. "This kid, whose old man was in the army, said to his friend, 'You know about the Alps? Well, my father built them.' The other boy, he answered back, 'You know about the Dead Sea? My big brother in the Navy, he killed it.'"

Spiros was too preoccupied at that moment to laugh at the joke. In his report of their meeting to his superior, Carey would write that their "fixer" didn't have much of a sense of humor. While in his presence, he had been content to change the subject.

"After all, this friggin war in Viet Nam, it won't last that long, will it?"

"And what is it you guys are going to do when you have those commies on their knees?"

"We give you the keys. In the meantime, we pay you some rent for the use of the land."

It had taken just two short months. Before the reddening leaves had had time to fall to the ground, he had managed to get an option to buy all the land that Five Rose Mill didn't care for, at a price so cheap that he would no longer be able to look their chief officer in the eyes for the rest of his life. And then, some form had risen out of the nothingness, one construction with no aesthetic attribute, misshapen and squalid. Yet, it appeared very functional, the spitting image of the organization who had conceived the hideous contraption.

Because of their acquiring of the adjacent lots, the project was a lot bigger than had been anticipated at first. In the blink of an eye had appeared at the back of their place of business an armada of tractors, mechanical shovels, bulldozers, and tipper trucks, who then proceeded in no time to dig a hole into the ground, take out the earth, and get it out of the area. In this huge hole, as long as two football fields and six feet deep, engineers had laid a slab of concrete, out of which they had elevated cement and steel structure. It would support the walls, floors, and roof of the giant future warehouse.

As for finishing, there would be no dressing up. They had put in an asbestos covering of a gray-green institutional color, sad and undistinguished. There were to be no windows. Plumbing was nonexistent. Electricity was reduced to a minimum, as there was no heating except in a six-hundred-square-foot section laid out as offices near the enormous access door. Inside, there was a ramp that small trucks and lifts could use to move from one floor to the other.

When all was finished and done, William Carey came to visit Spiros, carrying proudly on his uniform the rank of a full colonel. He looked radiant and very pleased with himself, as if it had been in him to put an end to the war, and today was the right time. The newly promoted officer certainly cut a fine figure as Spiros congratulated him for his elevation, which he had been attentive enough to notice. It was hard to miss the added gold crown to the already present maple leaves that garnished both sides of the Colonel's regimental starched collar.

"Bill, the Colonel had reminded Spiros. "I owe you that crown, since it is you who made me look good in certain circles. You must call me Bill since we're old chums, aren't we?"

Carey had a bunch of paper in his hand and he passed the lot to his friend.

"Now," he had said, "this here is the lease. I hope that you can see yourself through all this big wheel gibberish. I didn't look at the damn thing myself. Not my cup of tea. Still, I have been told that you might find its terms satisfactory. Everybody always does, anyway."

"I don't doubt for an instant that we will," Spiros approved. He knew quite well all there was to know in the book like document, thanks to his late dealings with Francoeur. As a matter of fact, the terms were very much to his liking, indeed. There was even a provision that exempted those lots from property tax as long Defense would use the site as their tenant.

"One other thing," William Carey said, "this literature contains somewhere a list of the material that shall find its way into these storage spaces. There is a section that concerns you. My boss wants to know what items you can take care of: your rate of delivery, in what quantities, and your prices. So, you work that out and don't let that guy wait too long, if you know what I mean."

Peter looked at his father, who filled his office door frame. What was his old man doing there? The last he had heard of him, he was in his New York apartment, a five-bedroom affair that looked directly on Central Park. Nowadays, he liked that place best, more than his country of birth, which he hadn't visited for the last decade, or the California beach house near Los Angeles where his older son lived alone. Charlie! He was a financial genius. Taking after his father, or so he said, managing the family's quite substantial portfolio. He didn't have his patriarch's merit, though. Spiros had made it alone with no great effort. Everything he had accomplished was made to appear the easiest thing in the world. How was this possible when he, Peter, couldn't decide anything without agonizing over everything? It could be the time of departure on a fifty-mile journey, where to eat, restaurant or picnic, and if the latter, what kinds of sandwiches, the itinerary, what to do once they arrived and so on.

Spiros had taken a little hardware operation in Québec City and made it into PLUS, the giant chain store it had become. It had helped that Charlie had graduated from the Harvard School of Business. What he had learned there was how to be careful. What Spiros hadn't needed to learn was how to make things happen.

Still, Charles had done quite well at growing the businesses in his father's footsteps, having acquired a knack at expanding all he touched into bigger and better. In doing so, he had become quite rich by himself—unlike Peter, who could read Latin as well as a priest and do crosswords in ancient Greek, small achievements that hadn't impressed his elder brother and father. Then, he'd gotten his law degree before he was old enough to practice as a lawyer. He'd had to wait five months to apply for the Florida

Bar exam, and then he'd never applied. This had earned him one derisive observation from his sire.

"You missed Plato by twenty-four hundred years, Cesar by two thousand, and missed the Bar by five months only. I guess it shows progress of some sort, don't you think?"

Indeed, Peter didn't resemble Charles. Neither had he succeeded in doing what he wanted most, which was to author a novel of his own and have it published under his name. Until now, all the words he had written—and they were numerous, be it short stories or longer works—had been rejected either by the few publishing houses he had cared to show them to, or by his own. The results of his efforts at writing, he had been told, were too cerebral and intellectual. Words shouldn't be like a puzzle, to be put into their right and meaningful place by the reader. They had to make some sense from the beginning. Otherwise, people might lose interest. *But*, he protested vehemently to his critics, *who cares about regular, usual, everyday life bullshit? I can't write about me eating ham and eggs in the morning and discussing later with my wife what we will do in the afternoon, walking through the mall or returning some book to the local library.* One editor at Diland—his own house, soon to become Oracle—after such a protest, had said,

"It sure beats finding yourself in a house with no doors, or drinking tea in a cup with no bottom."

Peter now looked at his father, his solid presence overpowering him, as it always did. He didn't have much of the Artritis blood flowing through his veins. He was molded more like a d'Allemagne, with their fine, well carved, and slender features.

Peter was sitting at his desk. Embarrassed at being caught once more at doing nothing, he said, "Papa!"

"Hello, Son! C'est une surprise, n'est-ce pas?" his father answered, using French, as Peter had.

"Why didn't you tell that you were visiting?"

"I'm doing no such thing. I have a house here, remember?"

Spiros was referring to the place he maintained at Pt. Brittany, a mansion-like palace that overlooked Tampa Bay, not far from where its water merged with the Gulf of New Mexico. He had bought the residence in 1967, when the family had moved to Florida after Precision Corp., the investment trust his father had created in 1966, had gained control over one small chain of stores that cared for small contractors and hobbyists in need of building materials. Over the next forty years, they'd expanded into almost all fifty states in the USA. Canada had been left alone though, since there were stores under the PLUS banner in all its ten provinces. The PLUS name had been the driving force behind what had become, thanks to his sibling's wizardry, the Artritis Empire.

Without waiting for an answer, the older Artritis threw a book on Peter's desk. It was a Bantam pocket edition of the Ken Follet bestseller, "The Eye of the Needle."

"I read that on the plane coming in. When will you guys get me an author like this one instead of silly recipe circulars, psychoanalytical self-help books, and how to mess about with anything else?"

"This is hardly what we are doing in here, dad," he said.

"Whatever!"

His old man shrugged, as if he didn't expect much from him. He turned away from Peter.

"Is there any place to sit around here?" he added, as he did doing every time he visited.

There were three chairs, but he always pretended not to notice them. In 1983, Precision Corp. had started acquiring newspapers in towns like Atlanta, Augusta, Jacksonville, Tallahassee, Tampa Bay, St. Petersburg, and Miami. Spiros had had the good sense to buy those from consortiums who didn't know how to make money out of printed words, and they'd surrendered them to him on the cheap in order to pursue what they really liked doing, which was getting oil and gas out of the ground. It hadn't taken long for Charlie to figure how to make some real money out of the new venture: sports, sex, and the small ad section. With the St. Petersburg newspaper had come Diland, a local and trivial publishing house that had operated out of the Verizon building in downtown St. Pete. In 1994, the papers were doing great, and Precision sold them all at a very substantial profit to Rupert Murdoch. Since the British magnate didn't show an interest in the Diland business, Spiros got to keep the company, which had to be severed from the St. Petersburg Herald they also sold. It was a hard job for the accountants, since nobody cared to separate one company properly from the other. That was when they had changed the name from

Diland to Oracle. It was still an adaptation that Peter had some difficulty with.

He'd been working at Diland since the mid-eighties. At the time, it had been a way to recover from his failure of having the novel—which had taken him three years to produce—put into print. He wouldn't ask his father to do it as a favor to him. Neither would he do it as an act of authority because of his part at Diland. The fact that he could was the point. As for self-publishing, it was out of the question. If his stories couldn't make it by themselves, so be it.

So he had been put in charge of Oracle in the early 2000. It wasn't making much money, but neither was it losing any. Which was success, wasn't it? Who knew when it might serve some purpose in Charles's global capitalistic ambition and grand design? Meanwhile, it gave Precision a foot in the artistic crowd and kept Peter occupied. Still, Spiros couldn't understand how his younger child could be happy in revising and editing the silly ramblings of other while being incapable of producing a literature of his own that would sell. Wasn't that the perfect illustration of Peter's problem? Using his gifts and intelligence in the pursuit of everything useless, futile, and utterly unrealistic? From early childhood, if he were to be good at anything, you could be sure that it wouldn't be something that suited his father's tastes, but something from the most unfathomable topics. If, by miracle, he were to take a fancy in anything as trivial as sports, you could bet your life that he would end up meddling his way to its most insipid issue or non-issue, like what was a baseball made of, or creating a story where pitchers threw cubes at batters who swung at them with frying pans.

Spiros had resigned himself to the fact that his baby boy lived in his own world, a universe he had never been able to get into, nor felt comfortable in. He had judged from early in Peter's life that it was better to let him be. He was making a living. At least, Oracle was seeing to that. He had a family. He had a wife who loved him. Who was to say which of the brothers had a better life? To each his own, Madeleine used to tell him. From the door, he forced a smile on his face and asked his son:

"How are Angela and the kids?"

Peter stood and pushed a chair in the direction of the older man.

"They're fine," he answered. "Why don't you sit down?"

Spiros moved around the seat, ignoring the offer.

"We could go out and have something to eat," he said.

"Sure, Dad. How about you? There's nothing wrong, is there?"

"I must have felt lonely. Getting old does that to you," his father added, laughing. "You know, it makes you think of stuff that would be better off left untouched. I wish your mother were still around. And then, there's more family to see here than in California.

"So, that is all? You came for a visit just to see us?"

"What's wrong with you? You think of me as careless and unconcerned? I have grandchildren, haven't I? I might want to see them."

"Bien sûr, Papa. I'm glad you feel that way."

"I don't know how I feel anymore from one hour to the next. I have mood swings, I've been told. I'm telling you, Son, never confide anything to doctors. They will invent all kinds of silly speculations to your most innocent communications. Believe me, growing old is a full-time occupation."

"You look well enough, though," Peter answered with a real trace of envy in his voice.

"The Artritis curse!" his father shouted. "Dying, and taking a long time doing so. Not looking the part. Besides, it keeps me busy."

At that moment, the phone on Peter's desk rang.

His father said, "Damn these chairs. Don't you ever meet anybody important in this office of yours? You would have them sit on these government-issued, ugly plastic appliances? Where am I? In some slum doctor's waiting room?"

Peter ignored his father's nonsense and took the call. It was a boy from the Salvation Army in Gulfport.

"Was it you, sir, who asked about a Royal typewriter?"

"I'm interested in such a machine that belonged to a doctor who died not so long ago."

There was some noise in front of him and he saw that his guest had sat finally.

"Right. That would be the guy who was cursed. Why sir, are you a collector buff?"

"As a matter of fact, I like those old machines," he corrected. I'm used to writing with one that refuses to deliver the letters E and P anymore. So, if this one still works properly, I might take it off your hands. How much are you asking for it?"

From where he sat, he heard Spiros's mumbling mixing into his conversation.

"The chairs. And now a vintage piece of shit."

"It works as fine as could be expected of such an antiquity," the kid on the other end of the line assured him. "To know more, you might need to talk to Bill Nesbitt. He handles the Zielgard stuff."

"But," he protested, "I've already been told this. If you are not Bill Nesbitt, why are you calling me?"

"Bill isn't here at this moment."

"Is there anything else I should know about?"

"I'll have Bill call you, sir, as soon I see him."

"I appreciate it," he responded, a bit mollified.

"Sorry for not having been of much help." He concluded their talk by offering Peter his thoughts on the doctor's circumstances. "I do hope the lady who killed him fry, though. It sure will give some extra value to that piece of scrap, am I right, sir?"

The criminal division of the Superior Court in Gulfport was in session on this particular day in June of 2008. The jury that had found Rosa Maman Tour de l'Isle guilty of first-degree murder for having caused the death, with malice and forethought, of another human being, namely one doctor Zielgard, was now deliberating over her sentencing. Would the guilty verdict they had rendered the day before result in capital punishment? Or would her passing the rest of her life in prison be considered sufficient punishment? The six men and four women, plus the two alternates, were at that moment in a back room on the second floor of the Law Court. The time was twelve fifteen. The previous afternoon and all morning, they had heard the assistant District Attorney ask them to apply the law in its utmost severity, and to send the vile murderess to her death, while the lawyer for the defense had begged them to save her client's life. After all, she had told them, the Negro woman was herself the victim of stereotype, prejudice, and implacable beliefs!

Why had the lady advocate lost the case in the first place? That was the question that liberal America was pondering nonstop over thousands of blogs, forums, websites, and chat rooms all over the country. How was it possible in modern times? Obviously, the issue of the connection between the victim and the accused and its ultimate conclusion would be for the higher court to decide. Yet, to have such a debate in the United States of America, for all the world to examine their denizens' incongruous division over religion, belief, and faith, was a step that most would have preferred not to be taken.

Still, that particular attorney would soon find it very difficult to survive the ordeal of being the first in modern world history to have one of her clients accused and found guilty of murder by way of a conspiracy with a supernatural entity. She had been labeled a non-practicing Catholic. That explained it all in a state that, from then on, professed through its jurisprudence some evil spirit's supremacy in its dominion. Furthermore, evil spirits were now an official doctrine, and such a tenet, although highly improbable, had become the law of the land.

One would have believed that the few people burdened with that huge a responsibility would feel overwhelmed by the impossible task asked of them. But in this jury's deliberation room in Gulfport, Mississippi, it wasn't so. Far from it! They were now discussing whether to have pizza or Kentucky Fried Chicken for lunch.

Finding the lady guilty had been easy enough. The woman had admitted everything. Ollie Devott, the assistant District Attorney, said she had confessed, hadn't she? First, she'd wished her victim dead. Then she'd pricked a Zielgard puppet full of pins, and the doctor had died on the day and at the place she had predicted. She should have stayed quiet, as her lawyer had said she should. But she wouldn't. She'd asserted from the start her right to be heard. And the judge had let her. Worse, he had tricked her into the worst incriminating evidence. She'd claimed full responsibility for the doctor's killing. She'd fought her advocate, who wanted her to be declared insane. She'd done her best to convince the court-appointed shrink that she was sound of mind, an opinion the specialist hadn't felt like disputing since he was getting paid by the county, and played poker every Friday night with assistant D.A. Ollie Devott and his fun crowd. So, his report to the Court concluded that the witch was legally sane. In higher circles, the joke was that the average dog on the street would have passed the test.

It was a very simple case, as the prosecutor had emphasized over and over, even if his female opponent had tried to confuse the issue by putting in front of their judicious Christian wisdom her own undisguised heathen and atheistic, self-serving discourse. When all was said and done, Ollie Devott had argued, in cloture of his mostly pious conjectures, all his case rested on faith.

The good people of Marriott County, who were all firm believers in Jesus and staunch supporters of The Good Book, had graciously accommodated the silly woman. She had wanted to be found guilty. The jury had indulged her. So be it. Now, all that was left to be decided what was to be done with Rosa Maman. However, this could wait till they had their lunch. At that moment, the floor belonged to a very dignified gentleman who was telling his audience of fellow jurors the story of his arrival at the court house that very morning. The poor man had gotten mingled into a gathering of suspicious, unshaved characters all dressed up with the same black pants and shirts, and who had stuck together all around him as they invaded the building. While he had been lost in the middle of the gypsy-looking assemblage, one bailiff had approached their cluster and addressed them all.

"Found?" He had snapped.

Next, one of the clique virile representatives, who stood beside him with a red bandana in his jet black hair, and a five-day beard that looked so rough and spiky that it would defeat all razors, answered something in a strange dialect that the court officer must have taken for a 'Yes,' since he terminated the exchange by yapping at the group,

"Found in a house of game and debauchery, court number one, to your left."

"You imagine, the distressed narrator man said, me being confused with that lot of Mediterranean lowlifes!"

A member of the jury, who had been born in the Balkan, said:

"You sure look like you could use a little fun yourself, though."

That had got him a few laughs here and there. He ignored the furious gaze of his humiliated colleague. One overweight woman asked again,

"What will it be, then? Pizza or fried chicken?"

"What time is it?" Asked another.

The woman sighed, exasperated. Getting that bunch to make a decision was a hopeless assignment.

"Twenty-five after twelve." Someone answered back.

"Can't we settle the matter before lunch?" Asked a black lady in a green dress, clearly concerned about dragging it out too long.

"They don't expect us to decide that quickly." Objected the dignified gentleman.

"We've been discussing it for a full hour, insisted the exasperated jury member. I suggest we take a vote right now and be done with it."

"She is right, concurred a younger white man with a ring in his right ear. If there are two of us who feel for the bitch, better we learn of it now. And then, we might best appreciate the job left to be done."

"I'm not ready to take such a stand at the moment, countered the overweight woman. If their silly assembly couldn't decide over pizza or chicken, she sure as hell wouldn't let them get out of this room that easily."

Most of the others glared at her, but stayed quiet nevertheless as they sensed that the rebuke had more to do with appetite than wavering over the life and death issue.

"So, let's decide what we'll eat, one alternate resolved."

"Pizza would be fine," said the other alternate, his first words since they all had been put together the day before.

"We had chicken yesterday."

"Why can't we have Chinese?"

VIII

On the ride back home to Tierra Verde, with his father sitting beside him in the Volvo, Peter remembered that his old man had wished for Peter's mother to be there. Whatever the faults he could lay at his father's feet, there was one thing he had witnessed from him, and that was true love between man and wife. His father had loved his mother, and had been loved in return. He knew it. Every day of his life with them, it had shown, in small things and gestures. In this way, he had learned and been able to duplicate his parent's behavior as his own. In life, people always reproduced whatever they had been exposed to. He was driving on Route 19 toward the Pinellas Bayway. It was four in the afternoon. The second movement of the unfinished symphony was just starting on his car's stereo system.

"You always listen to that sort of music while driving?" His father had asked.

"Angela likes it. I don't mind. I find it relaxing. Don't you?"

"As you like."

"I must have some CD with bouzouki music somewhere. You want me to find it?"

"Anything that will match with the sun and might make me want to shake my bones a bit would do fine."

Peter took out the Schubert disc from the CD player and introduced another in the starving automaton's aperture. It gobbled the new offering as a lizard would have a passing fly. Instantly, joyous sonority inundated the car's cockpit, the instrument's crisp intonations putting them both in a trancelike agitation, their bodies suddenly reacting to the rhythm like they were liquid in a bowl at the moment it reached near-boiling temperature.

"This is good, his father approved. Where did you get it?"

"YouTube! This is one of those parties they have back there where everybody finds themselves in a restaurant to eat, dance, and sing."

They were at that intersection where the 19 merges with the 275, and the bridge that will get the motorists to the other side of Tampa Bay. Peter turned right toward St. Pete Beach. He passed in front of the entry for Pt. Brittany, where he would have to drive his father back later at night. At the junction of Pinellas Bayway and road 679, he went left. They were five minutes away from his house. Out of the car's speakers came the voice of a Greek woman. He recognized instantly the song's beautiful melody. Somehow, it filled him with melancholy and tenderness. Tears filled his eyes. He was happy to have his sunglasses on. What was wrong with him? He'd had these episodes on a regular basis, ever since he had passed the age of forty-five. They seemed to come from nowhere. What he was thinking of was his life with Angela, like if it was something to be talked about in the past tense. Which made no sense. Yet, it felt like being at the hospital and doubting the doctor's words when told he wasn't sick. Or like dreaming of driving on a road and being certain of having lost his way. They were both quiet as they listened to the song. Could the awkwardness be the result of his father's presence in the car? Damn! How intimidating that man could be. Could anyone be sure of anything while near him? He loved that man, though. Was he loved in return? Spiros was mouthing the lyrics of the ballad. Peter looked at his father, who appeared to him like someone lost on the sand of some Aegean beach, with a smile on his face. Would he ever know the answer to that question? His father, who had loved Peter's mother and not anyone else. Or so he had felt.

Whatever Peter had wanted to accomplish in life and hadn't, paled in comparison with his existence's real success: his family, and the love he felt for Angela, which was neither more nor less than when he was in his twenties. He couldn't imagine himself going through life without her. In that way, he had followed in his father's footsteps. Who cared if one couldn't put a dollar figure on that feeling? It was nevertheless the best of all for the fact that it was invaluable. What was the worth of the sensation of utter safeness and invulnerability he felt when at night he touched his wife in that soft spot he so liked, and she caught his hand in her sleep? Nothing bad could happen to him, then. Sometimes, it pleased him to envision that they would die together, she holding his hand, and this being so, his passing away would be made easy. Why was he such a sentimentalist in life, and yet useless in his writing when came the time for his characters to show human feelings? Why were his narratives, he chided himself, read like algebra equations, or Freudian gibberish?

Once at home, he left his father to Angela's care and excused himself to his study, since he had some unfinished business to attend to. His wife didn't like her father-in-law that much. The man was so full of himself. He was sure of his ways and dismissive of everything that didn't interest him, as if such an outcome was some failing in the subjects or fields thus put aside. It seemed that everything worthy and deserving on this earth must win a passing grade through him.

To be fair to the man's prejudice, Spiros wasn't impermeable to new things, and he was still grading some as late in his life as he was. But he was used to his biases, and worse, he kind of liked those he had. Once a topic had been looked over and discarded, he could be quite acerbic in his dislike, intolerant in his judgment, and insensitive of the effects his questionable pronouncements might have on others.

"What is he doing these days?" Spiros had asked Angela when they were left alone.

"Just the usual routine, she answered while adding a cover on the table where dinner would be served later. "His work downtown and a bit of writing I guess."

"Yeah, he said with a smile, those stories of his that make no sense."

"How would you know?"

"He asked me to read them. He gave me two new ones today. I have them in the car. They sure will put me to sleep tonight. What will it be this time? A war between letters and numbers? Or some hero of his who will find himself imprisoned by freedom?"

"Some people might like that if you don't."

"Do you?"

Angela threw a cold look at her father-in-law.

"How dare you…?"

"Show me one! Anyway, Spiros sadly carried on, seemingly unaware of the effect his talk might have on his daughter-in-law, this son of mine was brilliant as a child. Quite a lot more intelligent than me. And he had a lot of schooling put into him, you know? Too bad it never showed in anything he did."

"Leave him alone, she snapped at the old man. By my standards, he did well enough."

Spiros must have sensed that he had overstepped his welcome because he adjusted his discourse to his host's sensibility. He was wearing a light suit with his shirt open. Angela couldn't miss the man's natural elegance. It was as if all his gestures had been staged crafted and made for an audience.

"You're right. I'm sorry. You must excuse my words and attribute my ramblings to a father's nostalgic longing."

Spiros looked around him, and then, into Angela's eyes. He had abundant white hair that he pushed to the back of his head. Why did he look so healthy, mighty, and not a bit contrite, she thought angrily?

"He has a family, thanks to you." He said to her.

"He is a good husband."

"You love him, don't you?"

"You know I do."

"Then, he's got already the best of what life is about, didn't he? Who cares if he writes silly tales?"

There was a silence. And then, Angela added, as if an afterthought,

"He loves you very much."

"In his own kind of mythological way, yes."

"Do you love him?"

"Why are you asking?"

Nothing in Spiros's stance showed that he was unsettled by the turn of the conversation.

"You never did, did you?"

"That's what you think?"

"No. That's what he thinks."

"He is my son, his father replied, as if this was the correct answer to Angela's question. I just feel sorry for him."

"Please don't."

Angela was dressed in jeans and a t-shirt, her usual attire for a weekday. As a watercolor artist, she was very good at painting gardens. She had done all those of her friends, then of people in her neighborhood, and now, her fame had extended outside Tierra Verde to St. Pete Beach, while a few galleries in the area exhibited her work and sometimes sold a piece or two. Her red-brown hair was cut short. Reading glasses dangled on her chest from a string that hung around her neck. She wasn't tall. If she looked delicate, her strength showed through the burning in her eyes, which were grey and could become cold and furious when provoked, or cut to the quick. She loved her husband and had his mother, but despised his family on the Artritis side right from the very start. At least there wasn't that many of them. She had married Peter in spite of his father. The man was conceited and rude, carrying with him at all times the absurd notion that whatever he prized and liked was all what was worth knowing in the world. What curriculum he ignored was to be put away for their not having made it yet in attracting his benevolent attention. Still he had the nerve to argue that his mind was a field always open for philosophy, social science, and modern art to compete at receiving his blessing. Not so big an imposition as long as scholars studying these matters got their acts together and impressed him with a concept that made sense. He couldn't stand the arrogance of those who couldn't, if their life depended on it, come up with an original idea, and still gave themselves the right to be the arbiter of taste and aesthetics in society.

Angela directed her gaze right through Spiros. It was all scorn and disdain. Why should she engage the man? She didn't care for his advice. But Peter did, and her motto was "better known thy enemy."

"Why are you sorry for him? She asked at last, her voice frigid. "Are you suggesting that he is a failure?"

Spiros didn't like the woman that much, either. Sure, his boy's wife had been the right choice for him, and he, at the least, should be happy for that. But the fact of the matter was that the woman had no ambition. She was the last person who would put good sense into his son's mind, or some strength into his bones. She originated from New York City. Her parents had been teachers. She had been raised an east coast liberal, and Angela wouldn't believe anything that didn't come through the correct channel, which was one with a left inclination. He forced himself to smile in her direction and admitted:

"That depends of how you define success. My point is, what he wants is not there for the having. As for an author, the audience he cares to please might as well come from another world. I never saw anybody in all my existence who runs into walls as much as Peter does."

"So, he has courage."

"Losers are like that. They can never learn from experience."

"He is no such thing, she said. And if he is, it is because you made him so."

"Now you sound like my wife."

She discerned and amused pout on his lips, as if Spiros was making fun of her. And then, he added, "Why, if I may ask?"

Angela said with as much fury in her voice as she could get, "Not being like you doesn't make him a failure."

"I just don't understand him, is all."

"So, perhaps you are the failure."

He had to give her that. It was a good line. From the corner of his eye, he saw Peter walking out of his office toward them. He decided to let Angela have the last word.

"I guess you're right. Perhaps I am, he said."

They'd had their supper in the garden. Peter had made his best to cheer them up, sensing mistrust and belligerence in his wife's attitude toward his father. He knew he had displeased his dad in some way, and he had come to accept over the years that he was the one to blame since he had failed to reach any of the man's standards of excellence. It had been this way all his existence. He had always known what his father expected of him. He might have wanted to deliver. He hadn't. His father was right to be disappointed in him. Who wouldn't be? Peter himself was! So, he had come to accept the situation and would have liked Angela to let it go. His father was his father. He wouldn't change. Neither would his younger son. If his old man wanted to make jokes at his expense, he didn't mind. So what? He knew his role, and had come to enjoy playing his part.

He had cooked steaks using the BBQ on their deck overlooking the water. Spiros had complimented Angela on her garden, flower beds that sprouted out of all the nooks and corners. The same could also be seen in the house on colorful paintings that hung from walls all over the place. 'Greeneries' was the term Peter's father used in real life when talking about grass and such. He must have had a lot to be forgiven for if he were complimenting his wife's own way of fooling around.

After a while, Angela apologized and left them alone. The temperature was usual for a Florida summer: unbearable, hot, and humid. But they were used to the inconvenience. Peter sat by his father, enjoying the last of the day, both of them sipping at a shot of Ouzo. From the water flew an ineffective breeze. The sun was low on the horizon. Spiros had Madeleine on his mind, as he had most of the time he'd been there. He looked at his son and said:

"I was lucky to have your mother."

"And then, you had me."

Spiros rolled his eyes.

"Why are you saying that?"

"It evens things out, Peter said dejectedly."

"This is you talking silly again, his father complained."

"You deserved better."

"Charles is doing okay. And you manage Oracle."

"I do nothing of the sort, and you know it."

"How would I know what you are doing with your days?" His dad replied, showing a bit of exasperation. What he hated the most in his son's disposition was this inclination of his for contrition, remorse, and self-flagellation. What was wrong with the lad? How could he have sired such a poor specimen of a human being?

"Nothing much useful to your affairs, I'm afraid."

Spiros had been there and knew now what was coming. He closed his eyes and brought his glass to his mouth. It was a blessing that his son couldn't see the tense line that barred his forehead. It wouldn't have changed anything if he had, though. Peter was just doing his thing, being Peter. That was the effect he had on the boy. Dissolving his brain into mush.

"I contribute puzzles for the Latini, he said, and I write film critiques and stuff in that antique language. Nobody cares anyway."

He could have marveled that his son knew Latin enough to be able to create crosswords using that dead tongue, or to read Julius Caesar's "De Bello Gallico" in the original. But this was beyond him.

"So, his father offered as advice, work out your subject."

"You mean, like, make them sexy?"

"What's wrong with that? If you're a writer, you write something that readers might care to read."

"Yeah…you're right. Silly me not to have thought of that before."

"So, you did? Then you know what you have to do, don't you? If you were to put your heart into this, you would shame your competition out of the business."

"My stories, Peter carried on, are not in line with current taste."

"Why don't you make them?"

"They wouldn't be my stories anymore, would they?"

"They would if it were you who wrote them."

"They would be stories written by me imitating somebody else, he corrected."

Spiros sighed, showing his displeasure with his son's airhead reasoning.

"You are doing it again, getting me all confused, he complained."

"Sorry if I disappointed you."

"Well, you have your ways."

"Your way or the highway. You remember that soccer game you wanted me to play in?"

"You must have picked that one in some sitcom you listen to with your wife, he answered. Anyway, how could I? It was years ago."

"Me not wanting to play soccer, or get into any sport, for that matter, made you angry, didn't it?"

"I sure would have preferred you to be more of a man like I was, he admitted. Still, it doesn't mean anything."

"I am the nerd son of the Brassens song "Les Philistins." Un enfant non voulu, chevelu, who writes poems and flighty stories and would die to get them publish."

"You run Oracle. I wouldn't worry about the publishing bit if I were you."

"It can't be that way."

"Why is that?" His father objected.

"I will not buy myself a book. I will only get published if my work is judged worthy of being put into print."

"As you already tried, I would presume."

"Without success, I regret to say."

"Your time will come."

"As if you cared."

"Now, Spiros countered, you are doing it again."

He looked worriedly at Peter. He knew what was coming, those same sentences exchanged between them before, old conversations, conflicts, and regrets revisited.

"Crying like a baby will get you nowhere, he mumbled. Neither will make faces if us ordinary folks do not appreciate or understand your erudite, wordy production."

"You are not ordinary people, he protested."

"Oh, yes, I am. And you are, too. All you need to do is act the part for once."

"What? Are you suggesting I am a phony?"

"Tell me the last book you read, Spiros said."

"Tacitus, Annals, Book XII."

"You see. Good old Tacitus. How did I miss that bestseller?"

"It was written two thousand years ago, and it's still around. We shall see in four thousand years if this Follet book you read on the plane is still in print, let alone Thomas Mann, Jane Austen, Dostoevsky or Tolstoy."

His father shrugged.

"As you wish."

He got up and concluded rather abruptly, "Time to go!"

In the car that would bring him home, he started the conversation where he had left it.

"You have enough money?"

"Thanks to you, my family and I enjoy a comfortable living."

"Are you happy?"

"Sort of."

"You should be."

"I would like to be a success in my field, and I am not."

"Who is?"

"You are."

"Because I specialize in the feasible. Take it down a few notches. Try something easy for once. Change lanes. Get in the one that plays into people's taste. You want eminence? You adapt your style, and success will come to you like fleas on a dog's back."

"Sorry. It is not in me to do that."

Spiros looked at his son, astonished. Did he really believe such nonsense?

"Are you to telling me, he erupted, that you can't find in yourself to write a story about A and B making a trip and meeting C in some hotel and having those doing something sensible? It is more like you don't want to, isn't it?"

"I already did. It was called *Titus visits his father.*"

"Is it the one, Spiros laughed, where the hero is the only one on this earth who can understand the language of the trees, and he metamorphoses into one when he discovers an old oak which he recognizes as his long lost father, or so he thinks? You call that gobbledygook a story? How many pages that one? Why? You must hate your reader really bad, torturing the poor fellow the way you do."

Peter decided to change the topic of their conversation. He asked his father,

"Et toi, Papa, are you happy?"

"I have been. I wasn't like you, though. When I found myself in a tight spot, I would get the hell out, while you seem to cherish those. You're a moth for everything abstract and incomprehensible."

"I wish I weren't, Peter admitted sadly. I am sorry."

"Stop saying you are sorry all the time. What you like or don't is your business. At the least, you could fight me over the validity of your preferences like a man. My point is, you have more brain power than your brother and I put together. Use some of it before I die to write me a story I might like. One I will understand from start to finish. Can't you do that for me, Son?"

"I will, Papa. I promise you I will."

And then, Peter couldn't stop himself from shedding tears. They came with no warning and ran down both his cheeks. The distressing display took Spiros by surprise. Before he could emit one word, his disturbed son repeated that long-forgotten gesture of wiping his face clean with his forearm, like when he was a kid and such a scene happened at regular intervals.

"I am not myself lately, he sniveled in between two hiccups."

"You're not sick, are you?"

Spiros was relieved when the Volvo stopped at his house. Its driver, with his composure regained, looked at the older passenger as he prepared to get out.

"Don't worry about me. I'm fine."

His father put his hand on his son's knee and squeezed hard. He had never been demonstrative in his affections, but at that moment, instinct dictated to him what to do, and he did it.

"I love you Son, he articulated with some difficulty. Now, you write me that story, you hear me?"

On those words, he left, like the god he was, walking slowly toward the mansion's massive front door framed between pillars that gave the place the allure of a Greek temple.

A few hours before, Peter had talked to Bill at the Salvation Army in Gulfport. He had been made to wait a full five minutes. Perhaps it was a way for the salesman to distinguish between a patron's capricious impulse and serious interest. He sure had let it show that he wanted the Royal machine real bad. Then, Bill had come on the line. The voice was high-pitched and the tone authoritative and judgmental. Peter felt intimidated at once.

"Bill Nesbitt here. In what way can I help? From his side, Peter heard his interlocutor whispering to someone else. "Not now, I'm busy." And then, directed at him, "Please, tell your business promptly."

"I already called about the typewriter."

"We got a few of those. And some computers, too, since more and more people prefer to use those devices nowadays."

What was wrong with those guys? He marveled. Why was he played like in a game of cat and mouse? His interlocutor must have known of Peter's interest since he had explained himself in great details and been told that this fellow Nesbitt was in charge of the dead doctor's personal property.

"Didn't they tell you about me being interested in a Royal typewriter that got into your establishment through some real estate agent named Phil Leclerc?"

"As a matter of fact, I was informed of that, sir. I couldn't tell if it was you, though."

"Well…"

"I know of such an instrument, sir. That, and other stuff, too. Would you come into the store so I could show you?"

"That won't be possible, I'm afraid."

"We sell as is, as you must know. There can be no guarantee that it will work."

"Is it whole? He asked. I mean, it should come with some cover or in a case, am I right?"

"Yes, sir. As it is, the machine looks like a box, and you can carry it by a handle on the top."

"And there was just one such typewriter in the doctor's estate, wasn't there? He inquired."

"I can't attest to that, sir. The fact is, from that real estate person you mentioned, we have received just one typewriter, which is the one we are discussing right this moment, sir."

"I will take it off your hands, then, Peter said. I mean, if I can afford the expense and we can find a way, you and me, to deliver it to St. Petersburg."

Bill Nesbitt must have caught at his attempt to be humorous as he then said to him,

"Your command of the English language is very good, sir. I couldn't detect any Russian accent in it."

"Try Tampa."

"Then, I suppose it could be arranged, sir."

"How much?"

"Twenty dollars."

"Let me think it over, Bill. If I were to give you one hundred dollars, would you care to go to the nearest Greyhound station in Gulfport and put the machine on the next bus that departs either for Tampa or St. Pete? That way I could get it at the terminal and retrieve it."

"I don't know of any Greyhound station in Gulfport, sir. And I don't know what time those buses operate. You would have to give me directives, sir. But, if you were to do that, sir, one hundred dollars would do fine. I could perform as you have asked me to, provided there is a bus station in Gulfport as you have suggested there is, sir."

While talking, Peter had looked up the schedule of the Greyhound bus company and accessed their website. When he finally got in, he saw a page where there was a map of the United States. He hit Mississippi with his mouse and there was a choice for places of departure. One was Gulfport. He clicked it. On the screen appeared all the information he needed for his newly acquired middleman.

"There is a bus leaving town at 6:40 p.m. out of their terminal on Pass Road, near the Convention Center. Or you could go there tomorrow morning at 9:50."

"It would be better, sir, if I were to do that outside my working hours. Tonight would be fine, if it is okay with you, sir."

"The package will arrive in Tampa tomorrow at 06:00 a.m. So there is no problem on my end."

"How are you to pay for it all, sir?"

"I can use my credit card, he answered."

"I could charge twenty on it, sir. What about my fee? I can hardly put it through the system now, can I, sir?"

"I have my check book right in front of me. Give me your full name and address and within the next half hour I shall mail you a check for eighty dollars, I promise."

"I will have to take your word for it, then, sir, won't I?"

"You already have my phone number, and my credit card number, as well. If you insist, I could have Phil Leclerc vouch for me, he offered."

"That shall not be necessary, sir. I can tell that you will do exactly as you say you will."

So, it was in this way that he came into possession of the typewriter that Zielgard had used to write *Faith*. It was not yet clear in his mind what he intended to do with it, though. However, if something were to happen, he knew he would need the machine. When he later got to work with the apparatus, he was happy to realize that the device was in good working order and equipped with a ribbon that still had some ink left on it. He had no definite strategy in mind when, using the Royal machine, he started rewriting a few pages from one of his pieces of comparable length with the Zielgard work. He could still pretend that there was nothing inauspicious in his activity, but he would be deluding himself, and he knew it. He just avoided thinking about the matter and preferred to consider he wasn't doing anything wrong. After all, if he wanted to reproduce a few sentences of one of his stories, he could do it without submitting himself to a third-degree investigation over his intentions, whatever they really were. He chose paper similar to the one of the manuscript he had received from Arthur. He conscientiously applied himself at formatting his words in exactly the same way the author of Faith had done. One hour later, he had three pages done, and if one didn't care for substance, it was impossible to detect any difference between those and the first one thousand words of the document he had attempted to imitate.

One month later, he had a conversation with Arthur. His lawyer had called, leaving him a message. He was almost done with the new transcript. It was more work than he had thought as he had to insert spelling errors all over his own words, since the good doctor was short on orthography and grammar, as well. Just like he had been found lacking in his physician skills, or so pretended the voodoo witch who'd put a spell on him. The good news was that he doubted Zielgard to have shown his story around in its present state. It needed editing. Obviously, it hadn't been done. Peter imagined that the doctor had given into an irresistible impulse which had moved him to write his story, and had then forgotten about its existence later, possibly in a drunken slumber. The man couldn't have known that what he had created was this good. He couldn't have known that he was that talented. He was a scientist, after all. Why would a wasted practitioner have cared about literature? Zielgard must have known enough to realize how unlikely it was for him to produce something of that quality. And there had been no books in his home. Could someone who didn't read books produce something as perfect as *Faith* was? This was no less than a miracle, and miracles of that sort were his and Oracle's business to expose and exhibit everywhere that would have them.

So things happened, and the Zielgard manuscript had come into being in this strange and unusual way. A few years later, its creator had perished at the hands of a vengeful sorceress, while Peter was entering the picture under the guise of a thieving Nibelung grabbing the ring out of the Rhinemaiden's grasp.

The copying of his novel then. What about it? He had considered asking some typist to do the work, but it would have meant the need to invent a tale to satisfy someone else's curiosity over the task's purpose. He didn't care to do so. Moreover, he would have been hard-pressed to explain why a well-written text should be puffed up with spilling mistakes and bad grammar. Those changes were not so easy to make, if they were to look the way Zielgard wrote. He had needed to isolate in the doctor's style what made his prose unique, and focus on reproducing the same on the pages he hoped he would soon send back to his lawyer. Not that he anticipated Arthur would scrutinize his work of fraudulent manipulations. As for delivery, it wasn't yet the time for that. He would have to deal with that part soon enough though. His friend did expect him to read the Faith novel and give him an honest opinion on its worth. Would he act as he was expected to? Even with all the work done that should have made it easier for Peter to answer that question, he was still deluding himself and believe that he would chose the righteous way in the end. What he was planning to achieve wasn't right, he blamed himself for the hundredth time. And still, he couldn't undo what he was actually doing, or fight against the craving that engulfed him at the thought of seeing his name on a novel. He was carried away by the notion of harvesting all the praise that was sure to come his way as the soon-to-be applauded author of such a faultless tale. Peter had good sense enough to fully realize that what he prepared to bring about was no real accomplishment from his part. He never would enjoy the success he so much craved for. He knew full well there could be no fruit worth ingesting coming out a tree whose branches were named deceit, trickery, falsehood and fraudulence. All the same, he had made his bed, and in it he must lie. Would he? He would know soon enough.

Angela was in Orlando for the day, preparing a show of her art in an exhibition that brought together two dozen or so southern painters who excelled in watercolors depicting all sorts of budding flowers in their sun-inundated Floridian bungalow's backyards. It was Monday morning. Peter called his assistant and told her that he would work from home. He learned this way about Arthur having left him a message on his office answering machine, like he had done Friday afternoon at his home. He instructed her to call him back and tell the solicitor that he wouldn't be at Oracle today, and to promise that Peter would get back to him the day after. This would give him time to complete the task that he had started early in the weekend, laboring non-stop day and night. In this manner, he might be able to deliver back to Arthur the revised Zielgard manuscript no later than Thursday. When his wife returned from her short trip to Orlando at five in the afternoon, he was still typing furiously, and she could hear the click-clacking of the Royal keys as they hit the white page imprisoned in the machine's roller. She came by his room and kissed him on the cheek.

"What are you working on, dear? She asked him. Is it a new piece?"

"As a matter of fact, it is, he answered." She had asked the same thing two weeks before.

"I'm so happy. It's been a long time since I saw you working like this. What is it about?" Then, she looked at the pile of words covering the sheets to his left and added, "Oh, this is quite a long one, isn't it?"

He was suddenly afraid that she would start reading and discovers his deception at once by spotting an earlier theme in what he now pretended was new material. On top of that, as the author of *Faith*, he would have to prepare her for his radical change in style and inspiration.

"Well, he said, it's just a project. It's not ready yet. All I know is it will be different from what I usually produce. But if you don't mind, I prefer not to talk about it right now as it is bad luck to give away one's story before it is finished." He didn't add that he had promised the story to his father. It wouldn't have helped anything.

The next day he phoned Arthur's office at a time he knew the man wouldn't be there, his friend being in court almost every morning. They had talked at the end of that same day. Although he had prepared for the ordeal, he was convinced, out of all good sense, that the lawyer would see through his scheme and would promptly pull the rug out from under his feet, leaving him helpless in defending his lies as soon as his duplicity encountered some resistance.

But luckily enough, Arthur didn't care much about creative writing, neither had he any inclination in believing that any white trash doctor in deep south USA could come up with anything of value if he were to try his hands at literature. It just so happened that Arthur was very much ready to accept the sad news Peter imparted to him, since he'd already expected this conclusion from his editor client, his argument being that if you dig a hole in the ground, you don't feel sorry for yourself for not finding a treasure. As he had no reason to doubt Peter's word, the matter of the manuscript's worthiness had been readily disposed of, its return being the only thing left to be discussed.

"I'm sorry to hear that, Arthur had said. You took a damn long time to tell me, though."

"I've been busy on my end. I just found the time to read the material this last weekend. I agree, I could have performed a bit sooner. So, here is what I will do. I will send you no bill. What do you say?"

"I say you seem to be in great form, don't you? Now, tell me more about the piece."

"It is not particularly well written, Peter had argued. And there are a lot of misspellings."

Arthur, who knew a lot of his kind were afflicted with poor writing skills, refrained from commenting.

"Well, he asked, what does the story look?"

"It's a bit muddled. I couldn't summarize it to you even though I just finished reading the thing. That's one of the pieces' other problems."

It sounds like what you do, Arthur almost let slip from his mouth, but didn't. He had once looked at one or two of Peter's stories and couldn't make head nor tail while reading them. Instead, he concluded:

"So there's no money in this. That's what you're saying, are you?"

"You read Eternity yourself, Peter countered, a bit on the defensive. This is the name of the piece. And then, you tell me."

He then listened hard to see what the reaction of the lawyer would be. If he would have said: "What about Eternity? Wasn't the title of the piece I gave you, 'Faith?'" This would have sufficed to make him renounce to his scheme. But Arthur hadn't cared to know about the title of the piece he has shown Peter to review. The coast was clear, wasn't it?

What he heard instead reinforced whatever notion he entertained to explore the pro and con of that venture.

"Like I told you already, the other retorted with a dismissive laugh, I am quite behind in my reading schedule. I have a million depositions to peruse through, and all those court decisions that seem to make it their business to contradict one another. You're so funny, suggesting I read the stuff. What good would that do? Now, let's get serious. I want you to put those findings of yours on paper, let's say five hundred words. It will go to the file with the rest of this sorry business. So, tell me, can you send it back by taxi or something? I will pay."

"I'll deliver it myself. By the way, it won't be in the same envelope that you delivered to me. I destroy it while opening it. Sorry for that. I hope you won't mind."

"Who gave a shit about wrapping? It's content that matters."

"Maybe I might see you. We could have a bite somewhere if you would invite me. You owe me that much, don't you?" Peter laughed, somewhat reassured.

"Sorry, old chap. This meeting of the minds will have to wait. Tomorrow is appeal day, and I will be out in Tallahassee. I'm catching the plane in two hours out of Tampa Airport. Leave the package with the receptionists and they will know what to do with it. Just address it to my name."

"And what will you do with it? Peter asked."

"Put it in the vault as a case closed. It will most probably stay bury in there till the end of time. What else?" Arthur answered.

This was most reassuring, wasn't it?

FAITH

PART TWO

10 o o o 10

Joe had the Tampa newspaper open in his lap. What in hell had made him wander like a lost and sick puppy? On page one of the sports section there was the picture of a smiling teenager in full Devil Rays uniform with a bat in hand, and in the right position to dispatch a baseball up to Orlando. Below the picture was the heading, "Could This Be the Next Barry Bond?" followed by an article by one Bill Latuque.

"He declares this bat he is now holding will give him home runs at will. If he can make use of it in Major League Baseball, that is."

Then followed Irma's tale, but with all the flourishes of professional penmanship as seen in luminous publications of the National Enquire variety. There was even reference to the episode of Aunt Paola's purse, with an added journalistic surprise. The author, it was claimed, had surpassed himself and proceeded with some investigation of his own. He had checked the Florida Lottery and the draw for the now-destroyed ticket Manuel had declared was a winner. As a matter of fact, it had been learned by the Woodward-impersonating scribbler that there had been two unclaimed one-thousand-dollar prizes out of a hundred, and of those, one ticket had been acquired in a 7-Eleven two streets from Paola's residence. Bill Latuque himself had talked to the employee in that store and learned that, yes, he knew Paola well, and had even volunteered that he remembered having sold her that ticket, the first and last time she had ever procured that kind of product of vile speculation in his place. (Latuque's words). And, oh, yes, sir, she was a regular, coming in one or twice a week. Mostly a bread, milk, and butter lady, if you know what I mean.

But there was more.

The Tampa Tribune had put into its crazy editorial head the notion to pay Manuel to assist in all the Devil Rays' games from now on up to the end of the season, and the kid was to receive a thousand dollars a week for the privilege, him in full player gear and ready to respond to the call of duty if ever the Rays felt the need for the boy and his magic bat's services. There was also a Facebook page where the readership was invited to post its sanction of the newspaper's initiative to get Manuel in a game, in a poll-like fashion. At that moment, not even one day into the asking, more than twenty-eight hundred avid participants had already responded positively.

He had had a mind to call the editor and give him hell.

What, Joe would have barked at the guy, are you out of your fucking mind? What kind of plot is this? Have you people gone mad? This circus of yours is complete lunacy..." and so on, and so on… The more the words of great affront and outrage formed in his mind, the stronger the impulse to get on the phone and shout his way back to serenity by abusing whoever was either responsible for the sorry business or found himself on the other end of the line. That was when he heard his phone ringing. Who could that be, so early in the morning? Better not be that troublesome bulb peddler from the Institute for the Blind. The guy pestered him every three months, asking him to buy his silly commodity, and Joe now had a closet full of the useless junk, enough to last him two lifetimes. He shouted angrily into the device's mouthpiece.

"What now?"

There was a bang where the caller was, like the person had dropped the phone on the floor. Joe then heard the sound of a chair grating on tiles, followed by a sigh.

"Is it a bad time?"

The voice was the club owner, his boss Franck Richantall. Joe then said in a more subdued tone,

"Is that you, Franck?"

"Who else? You good, Joe?"

"As good as it gets, he lied."

"I don't know. You sure sounded a little piqued when you took that call."

"I'm okay. So what's up, Franck?" Joe forced himself to ask.

"Must get you to answer Bud. That way, maybe he'll leave me in peace."

Bud was Bud Selig, from the Office of the Commissioner. Everybody in baseball knew that there was a feud between the two men, and for the last three months, they hadn't been talking to each other.

"Bud will come over, Joe lied again."

"Yep, I do hope so. The son of a bitch is a hardhead, but not as hard as you, though."

Joe let that one pass. From his Versaille-like castle in East Hampton, one the fifty richest individuals in the country cleared his throat and asked,

"You saw that sports section in the Tampa Tribune?"

"You mean that crazy business about that Manuel kid?"

"Not so crazy if you think about it."

"What?" Joe couldn't believe he was hearing this.

"Well…"

"I mean… You're not… Why… This shit knocked me over, literally. Why, I…"

"There are possibilities here, Franck interrupted."

"Yeah…like this organization mixing with devilry and wizardry. And what about me? Am I to transform myself into Santa Claus or Merlin?"

"No need to do that, Joe."

"What the fuck are you getting at here, Franck? Don't tell me you believe the silly nonsense?"

"Watch the language Joe and NO, there is no need to do that, either.

"So…"

"This is an opportunity, don't you see? I did some thinking over that situation down there in Tampa. And some research, too. I know for a fact that people will react to a miracle. They will like it. And they will ask for more. Game after game after game, they will come as if we'd invited them to Christ's Second Coming. People are natural suckers for tricks and delusion. Here, they tell me that they will eat the stuff like mad."

In Joe's head, a thought infiltrated, like a pop out taking over his PC screen.

"You are behind this crazy shit in The Tampa Tribune, aren't you, Franck?"

"I beg to differ with your way of putting it, though, his boss admitted."

"So, you think this will work?"

"There is nothing bad about getting a full house. After all, the Rays have a great season, and there are still ten thousand seats unsold every night in the Tropicana Field."

"And you figure that little scheme of yours will gut the place?"

"I know so. You will see. All it takes is a little magic."

11 o o 11

It was September first, and the Rays had eighty-three wins and fifty-two losses, and they were still trailing the Sox by half a game. As for the Tropicana, it was now packed to full capacity and more, as Franck and his minions in research had announced. Packed not only in their town, but wherever the team played. It was sold out everywhere. Money from On Demand TV was going through the roof, and the last ten games of their regular calendar would be broadcast, plus the play-offs, in Cineplex movie halls all over the country, like the Metropolitan friggin' Opera.

Franck Richantall was kid-happy. He didn't remember having had as much fun in all his life, and the man had a boat as big as an aircraft carrier and a plane that could rival Air Force One, *and* more money than he could care to count. The only thing he had ever done that was as much fun as this was when he had played the lead role in some high school play at the age of fourteen.

Newspapers all over the country had picked up the story and, these days, that kid Manuel was a celebrity, his notoriety and eminence equaling both the democratic and republican candidates in the coming November election. Manuel had made the front page of *Time* magazine, *The New York Times*, and all other publications worth reading in America. He'd also made it abroad, appearing in *The Times* in London, *Paris Match*, *Der Spiegel*, *La Gazzetta dello Sport*, and so many others around the world that making a list would have been a challenge. While Hollywood studios were bidding millions for the movie rights.

Even churches were looking into the phenomenon. The Catholics weren't so keen over the marvel, thinking they had some kind of exclusivity on episodes of the supernatural variety and all things miraculous. Clergymen of all denominations were baptizing people like crazy. Reality shows with religious content were the fancy of that summer, and why not?

Franck wasn't opposed to starting a new one if he could find a way to make some more money out of the process. Of all the artefacts that had made it into one faith or another, a baseball bat was as good as any. Who but God himself could have made that piece of wood the ultimate baseball bat? It had to be blessed in some kind of way.

As for Joe Black, if he had ever entertained the notion that he, himself, had some prestige as a member of society, that was before this season started, and because he didn't know then the real meaning of the word. These days, he felt as if he had been caught in a whirlwind that had dropped him into Wonderland. He had enjoyed a kind of normal life up to now, able to get milk at the Publix in relative anonymity. Since that Manuel frenzy, there was no place on earth where he could expect to be left alone. Paparazzi were all over him, from morning till bedtime. A crowd of curious gapers had taken over his house on the beach, a gathering of zombie-type creatures that stared cowlike through the scenery, scaring him, appearing alien in their asinine passive behavior. His neighbors were keeping their thoughts to themselves, but he knew they blamed him for the unsolicited attention.

Security guards and officers from the St. Petersburg police force were all over the place with their cars and sirens. Pass-a-Grille wasn't downtown St. Pete. Residents in Pass-a-Grille didn't care much for transients, bums, or vagrants with rings in their noses and ears and bodies besmeared with tattoos. Local restaurants were fed up with the nuisance, the sorry assemblage using their facilities and consuming next to nothing of what they offered. Worst of all, they were giving the area a bad name, since the clientele that counted stayed home or went elsewhere.

Joe resented Franck Richantall for having originated this insane circus, and for the role his boss made him play in it, since he was the one who would decide it, in this scenario of his—that was, the scenario imagined by whoever was pulling the strings in this wily conspiracy against reason and intelligence. They had promised that he would retain the last and final word. What good was that supposed to do him? As if he could ever decide in favor of the kid going to the plate. The chance of that to happen? None. Zero. Zilch. Over his dead body. No way. Who were they thinking he was? Franck had said to him:

"No reason to get excited, Joe."

"I'm not excited. I'm just telling you, Franck. This boy and his funny bat, I will never manage."

"That's for you to decide, Joe. What I suggest is you keep that decision to yourself. You don't let anybody know about that, you hear me, Joe?"

"How am I supposed to do that? I have a thousand assholes every day pestering me with the same goddamned question. Will I put the kid in the game tonight, and if not tonight, when will I put him in the game?"

"Sure, Joe. That's what we like, them worrying about that.

"I'm going to put an end to their misery, tell the sorry lot that this will never happen. Not on my watch, anyway."

"No, Joe. This won't do. This isn't the plan."

Then, Joe had erupted.

"I don't give a shit about any plan that doesn't initiate from the Tropicana Field. You hear me, Franck? I am the fucking manager of this team. I have a fucking contract. And you fucking know, and I know, and your lawyer as well as mine - remember Horace Lott? - know, as we all know, that I alone make the decisions as far as playing baseball in one field or the other is concerned. So, this is the fucking end of it, Franck."

Then came the soothing voice of his billionaire club owner, who was now probably sipping a Martini and looking at some Tropical Island from his transatlantic pleasure boat.

"Please, Joe. Listen to me now, and listen good, because this is not open to discussion. Ask Horace. He will confirm. I do agree with all you just said. You are the manager till the end of the season, and you will get us the division Championship, and you will bring the team to the World Series. We all know you can do it, and all this, you will accomplish your way. Nobody differs on that. What you do not have authority on, on the other hand, is the politic of the company that owns the club. And this is me. And what I want you to do, Joe, is to keep an open mind on the kid. And if it means that you don't go babbling about your heretic dispositions in a world where souls are craving for the spiritual, so be it. So, all I want you to do, Joe, is to indulge other people's beliefs. Can't you do that, Joe?"

"And for the sake of the moronic multitude, I must let them think that this Manuel getting at bat, maybe tomorrow or later, is a possibility, a decision that I must debate at all times during a game?"

"Don't make it too hard on yourself. After all, it is the same on my end."

"You mean, when you utter to reporters in front of the crowd, 'this is for the manager to decide'?"

"Well, I could always respond that I will not permit you to use that Manuel fellow. You know I would never do that to you, Joe. Letting you decide the players in a game is your prerogative and yours only."

"Nicely put. I'm the one who is to be made to look like a halfwit."

"Whatever. The way I look at it, there's nobody left to make the difference."

12 o o o 12

There was a cult-like quality in the hysterical media display of excitement over so insipid an issue as his belief in Manuel's ability to score home runs. He couldn't say no because of Frank's specific command, while a positive view over the dilemma was not an option either, because he would be asked over and over why he was waiting to put the youth in the line-up. Therefore, he was playing with words and he, not being a lawyer like Horace, was not so good at it. He looked like a damned fool most of the time, and hated the wretched feeling that it brought him.

He was on local TV every day, snaps of him, mostly, in late night news bulletins. He was also plagued with uninterrupted solicitations to be part of shows, requests that he invariably declined, which made the bloodthirsty producers double their asking by reason of the rarity his posture provoked. This was without counting the crowd of journalists and freelancers invading his privacy in and outside the Tropicana Field with their idiotic agendas and cliché questionnaires.

It was now September eighth. They were playing the Yankees, and silly Margaret from some west coast tabloid was asking him what Manuel's astrological sign was. The dame had the nerve to question his ability as a manager because he didn't know or care. But, had said the ridiculous reporter, if you were to know his sign, you would learn when Jupiter goes into orbit or aligns itself with one planet or another, shit like that. And in this way, he would know the right time to put the boy in a game. She had even given him the card of one Stella Galacta that had declared she was ready to help if he would just call her. So, that was what he had to endure. That was his life nowadays. That was no life at all. It was torture. And still, in spite of everything, his team won games in the good old ordinary fashion, by scoring more runs than the other team. At least, he had that part well. It helped to get over the rest.

13 o o o 13

A few weeks before, Barbara had landed at his place, the first time since he had moved there. After separating, they had kept contact to a minimum. Communication was through notes or the children. There had been the knock on his door, and instantly, he had known who it was.

Knock, knock… KNOCK, KNOCK…knock.

Strange, the ways some people do things all their lives, replicating little gestures. His wife was like that, knocking on his door in a way that he would remember till he died, her own special way that dated from time immemorial. He doubted she would knock this way for Mr. Big Shot Lawyer the fourth or the fifth. He got to the door and she was there.

Barbara.

His wife, whom he had not seen up close more than three times in the last six years. What age could she be now? Who was he fooling? He knew perfectly well. She was fifty-two, and in his eyes, still the Barbara he had dated when he was nineteen and married when he was twenty-three. The same woman he still loved, and who was now living with another man. What was she doing here? Why had she come? It was not like her to act impulsively. Between the two, he had been the sentimental one. But she had loved him, of that, he was sure. He knew it. And what they'd had done together, he believed she would never do with another the same way. Or so he hoped. Then, she had said:

"I knew you had a nice place, but didn't expect it to be this good."

"Thanks. Will you come in?"

And he had gotten out of her way to let her pass. From the street, flashes of light exploded out of cameras that would produce pictures of the encounter for tomorrow's gruel-like dispatches that an ever-expanding mass absorbed, as if they needed the stuff to maintain themselves in a state of delirious rapture.

"I came to say hello."

"I'm glad you did."

In his living room, there were pictures of him and the kids in all kinds of activities and situations. And then, his wife's eyes caught one of herself at twenty-four, in its original frame of twenty-eight years. She'd worn the dress he had so liked at the time. She'd been smiling. She'd been smiling at him. She remembered that day the picture had been taken. They'd been in Maine, in Kenny Shore, in a little cottage on a side street with the ocean and the splendid beach of Old Orchard less than three hundred feet away. He had had his first job in professional baseball, and those two weeks had been paradise.

"I see you still have that one, she had pronounced."

He had stayed silent. Then asked her if she would care to drink anything. He knew she would say no. She usually did. He drank tap water. She bought bottled water. As expected, she declined his offer.

At last, she said, I heard you had a rough time.

"Nothing to it. Just the routine craziness that we get at the end of all seasons. I will get by."

"I know. You usually do."

He asked himself: did she know how he still felt for her? She couldn't. Seeing her was difficult. It was like looking at a loved one through the plate glass of a prison cubicle where you communicated by phone and you knew that you were there for life. He said to her,

"Don't you worry for me. We'll finish on top."

She smiled at him. Her smile was beautiful; it illuminated her face. She had perfect skin, no wrinkle, and her color and scent, so good, exactly the way he remembered, like in the picture of her with that light blue dress.

"At the office, I am no longer the lawyer so and so. All people cared about was that I was once married to you."

The mention of once being married made him wince. He hastened to hide the feeling by contorting his face into a dejected sneer.

"They say I would have beaten Reagan for president."

At that, she laughed, the sound crystalline and light. They had been happy, as happy as one can get. He knew they had been. What, then, had come between them? She had said:

"You would have been great at anything you tried."

He looked at her. What was that? Maybe she was sick. Maybe she had learned she had cancer and… He sensed something squeeze in his chest. With a little quiver in his voice, he asked her,

"Everything is good for you…?"

"Thank you for asking. Can't be better."

If she had been sick, she would have told him.

"I am happy, he lied."

Still, to be sure, he asked,

"What about your health?"

"I feel wonderful."

"Thanks for that, his true self emitted with a sigh of relief, imperceptible to her." She looked around.

"This house reminded me of the Weaver."

It was a cottage they had rented for many years in Biddeford Pool. It had had three bedrooms upstairs, and a covered gallery all around, and a perfect front view of the Atlantic. There were pictures of them and the kids in that house all over his place.

"I thought so, too. That was the reason I bought it, as a matter of fact."

"So, she then concluded, it was not that difficult, us talking to each other, don't you think?"

"I am glad you stopped by. Feel free to do it again."

"I am glad I did."

She got up and he followed her to the door. She turned toward him and offered her face to be kissed. He skimmed her cheeks with his dry lips and then she was gone. She hadn't talked about Manuel and he was grateful to her for that small mercy.

14 o o o 14

The Baltimore Orioles were not at their best during that summer of 2008, even if they counted Trevor Vaudon on their team. The organization was losing money, and the inconvenience, which had never been a concern in the past, now was. It was common knowledge that the owner, Charlie Luserfelt, who was seen, up to that time, as having very deep pockets, had lost a bundle in the Lehman Brother's fiasco, and for reasons he couldn't even fathom, all the get rich fast schemes they had put him on or his trust fund or his companies, all those were imploding in his face all over the planet. All those nice countries he had patronized for the last six or seven years and had liked so much, those Irish and Portuguese and Greeks, they were all turning on him. Those ungrateful bastards. Why were they doing that to him? He should have known better. Stay home. Don't push your luck. Play safe.

So, times were difficult for "Old" Charlie Luserfelt, and he was not in the mood to lose more of what was left of his hard-earned money at some sport he couldn't stand looking at for more than ten minutes in a row without being put to sleep. He knew what the problem was with his team. They were losing more games than they won. That was it. No need to be a genius or a great financier to figure that out. That was what he was telling Billy Thorpe, his manager of six years. And that was what Billy didn't seem to comprehend, the losing of so many games. Billy always had reasons of his own to expound on the sorry situation, reasons that he could talk about for days, and always ended with him putting more money into that rat hole. Better getting screwed by the Europeans, who at least did it with some elegance and breeding, them always showing some count or baron on all their board of directors.

A sinking ship! That was it. He was in a sinking ship, and he had to get out. These people who would be left on the boat, he didn't care for them. They didn't deserve him. They didn't understand the essentials of baseball. His version of it. Baseball essentials. It went like this:

IF YOU WANT TO WIN, YOU MUST NOT LOSE.

15 o o o 15

Friday, September 9, 2008.

The Devil Rays had a double against the Baltimore Orioles. All the talk shows in town were speaking about one thing only, and that wasn't Manuel. What everyone was babbling about at the start of this wonderful weekend that promised to be sunny, windy, and fair, was the trade, the eventual exchange of the century, and that included the last one. This exchange that would dwarf one involving Gretsky for Lemieux into meaningless unworthiness. Not even an exchange for that matter. More of a sellout.

Unbelievable but true. The three years and seven year option contract of Ace reliever Trevor Vaudon had been disposed for one hundred million dollars to the Philadelphia Phillies.

The weekend before, one Indian millionaire offered through the Telegraph, in Calcutta, fifty million rupees ($65,000.00) to Manuel if he would consent to visit his country and play for the Bengals, which was the town team for the game they played there that they called baseball. That was enough for the kid to get himself an agent. From the day he had one, it was no longer possible for him to appear on TV shows for free. And the Tampa Tribune had to pay him five hundred thousand dollars if they wanted him to continue playing the mascot in their little publicity stunt, a five hundred thousand bucks that they made sure would be reimbursed to them out of the contract Manuel was expected to sign in the Major Leagues, if ever. It was a good deal that Manuel couldn't lose. Happen what may, he would still keep the money. As for the journal, it was making cash like crazy out of this, and the board knew a good thing when they saw one. It would have been better getting it gratis, but one could be honest sometime.

That Friday, the Devil Rays lost their two games against the Baltimore Orioles, thanks to the Wonder, as he was called in the press, the ultra-famous Baltimore relief pitcher Trevor Vaudon alias the Voodoo. Some said… no! Most said he was the best of all time for that category. He was to end that ominous weekend by playing his last two games in the Oriole uniform against the Rays. His coming exile to Philadelphia for a bag of money made it into the world's newspaper. Thanks to him, the Orioles evened the score, returning home with a 3 to 1 predominance which wasn't much for letting them forget the Voodoo and his flying away out of Tampa on a plane not the same as theirs.

Manuel might have been forgotten a bit in those early September days thanks to ace reliever Vaudon shine and sparkle. Still, the poll Richantall had started early in august showed there were now more than seven million fans in the USA that had posted a YES vote to the Tribune's question:

"Do you think the Rays should give Manuel a chance?"

16 o o o 16

To whoever cared for baseball and professional sports in general, Trevor Vaudon was, at twenty-seven, already a living legend. For most who had an opinion and an audience to deliver it to, he was the greatest of all professional sports heroes, all disciplines included, reducing all who had preceded him into popular psyche to the role of "faire valoir." Not even Tiger Woods could compete with the brilliance of Trevor Vaudon.

He was known in the league under the surname of Voodo Warhead. He was the most phenomenal relief pitcher of all time, one who threw old statistics of idols from the past in the dustbin. He could put out a candle on a birthday cake with a fast ball at fifty feet. Birds on wires weren't safe if he had a mind to it and they were singing the wrong tune. It was said that his curve ball was so convoluted that it had forced the French to redesign their tire-bouchon. Nobody could hit him. He had statistics that made no sense. Just that year alone, he had struck out thirty-six players in a row. He was from outer space, inhuman in his perfection. He was a God out of the Greek mythology.

He was Voodo Warhead.

And this Monday morning, September 12, Voodo was no longer working his miracles for the Orioles, thanks to good old Charlie Luserfelt, who had sold him - sold in the literal sense of the word - to the Phillies, in exchange of one hundred million dollars. The Phillies could use him, while he was a waste in Baltimore baseball. The Phillies had signed him for ten years, which included the three left in his Oriole contract. He would receive fifteen million each year for the last seven, plus one bonus signature of twenty-five million. Within one week of this infamous deed, the team owner, who couldn't show his repulsive face anywhere in town without risking a public lynching, peddled the company that owned the club, network, and organization for fifty million cash, and no questions asked about the one hundred million that had never made it into the Orioles' bank account. The new direction, one trust fund out there in the Midwest had made very clear, was that they wanted to start from scratch with real players who enjoyed good old fashion baseball, and didn't need nor want tricks or godlike prodigies to add up wins.

So Charlie had been asked to get rid of Voodo Warhead before the deal was to go through, and to take the blame for it. What if he had to move out of town? Poor Charlie would have to live with the hundred and fifty million he had left. Was there a place on earth where that would be enough? He might regret the crowd at the Hampshire Golf Club, though.

17 o o o 17

September 13 2008, Lehman filed for bankruptcy protection, and the end of a certain way of life drew near without anybody realizing it. It had been a bad week for Joe's team, them losing five games in seven and they had sixteen games left to play. They were still ahead in their division, but were leading by one game only. That was when he decided to make Manuel a visit. The pressure to put the boy into a game was becoming unbearable. As long as he was winning, he could survive the ordeal created by crazy fans who were all over the Internet criticizing him left and right in a kind of lunatic discourse that made you question humanity's intelligence.

His reasoning was, if the time were to come that he would be forced to do it, better to know whom he had to deal with. So, he needed to have a meeting with that fellow Manuel. But it was imperative that he proceeded in organizing the encounter in such a manner that the media wouldn't know about it. Otherwise, there would be no end to idiotic speculations. He thought about the matter. Then remembered that Thalia knew Irma, who knew Manuel. He asked his daughter over one Monday night when his team wasn't playing, and had her bring Irma. At the same restaurant where her mother worked, under the cover of absolute secrecy, he asked her if she could contact Manuel.

Irma said she could.

Then, he asked her if she could organize a meeting somewhere private that he could visit incognito. She had measured him with eyes green and piercing. Next, she had said to him,

"You look like you need a haircut."

"What if I do?"

"Mike. I could ask him to fix it. He did mine, once."

"I don't care much about my hair right now, young lady."

"You asked me about a place to meet, didn't you, sir?"

"Actually, I did."

"What if, at Mike's place, you find out that Manuel is in the barber's chair?"

"Oh! Now I see what you mean. Well…who's Mike?"

"My mother's beau. You know what I mean…?"

Joe looked at the waitress that had served him coffee. Irma had took his order and delivered it to him before taking place on the seat facing his. The woman smiled at him and he saluted her briefly with a movement of his head and eyes. He said:

"Your mother?"

"She is a real fan."

The lass was good. Really. He was quite impressed with her. Neither girlish nor childish. To the point. Fast and direct. He murmured as if to himself:

"This could do. Everyone needs a barber once in a while. Why, you think you could make this work?"

"I know I can. Manuel will be happy to meet with you, sir. He has great respect for you and the plight you are in right now."

"If he really is, that makes him a very wise young man, Joe concluded."

18 o o o 18

September 22, 2008

Ninety-two to sixty-two.

Just one more and they would play six hundred. A comfortable number, that one. And nice to look at beside your team's name in the statistics section of your local newspaper.

Enzo's Barbershop was in a mall that had once hosted an Albertson supermarket. Now, all that was left in the desolate surroundings were deadbeat business, small shops of all kinds, mostly food, costume jewelry, and a tattoo parlor. Occupying the deserted Albertson's space was a gigantic indoor flea market. In all these free enterprise ventures was the same hope and desire to make a living out of peddling trinkets for profit. What a pitiful existence! Was there a more rueful way for a Jack to earn his pittance?

What the place had in abundance, though, was parking space, which was quite impressive and very handy if you were to look at the privilege from the point of view of a New Yorker. While in St. Pete, every store had those. That was what Joe was thinking about in the Toyota Echo he was using after having left his Lexus at the garage for a two days inspection. This would serve his trip allright as he wanted to stay incognito. He turned left to cross the south section of Route 19, which earned him an impotent toot of aggravated outrage from one absurd lunar-like vehicle pop backing his way three feet off the ground on wheels massive and impractical. No doubt that improbable contraption of a car and all its crazy-looking and useless permutations must have cost its owner a whole lot of cash, maybe even the price of the Echo he was driving. How was that possible? So much silliness, when the country that had produced such a sorry specimen of an inhabitant had put others on the moon.

Enzo was in the same mall he had visited to meet Irma at Al's Place. He oriented himself with the given instructions. Enzo's was at the mall's other extremity. He parked his car where there were others that formed a little cluster and would ensure his Echo had some anonymity. And from there, he walked. He passed the flea market entrance and got stopped by a beggar who asked him for spare change. He didn't have any. He never carried money. He started to explain, but the man had already figured it out, from his body language, perhaps. While he was looking into the man's eyes, he saw nothing of the bitterness he would have expected to see in there. That vagrant gaze was as empty as the celestial void. He could discern no expectation of any kind in those eyes, which looked through him as if he was no longer there.

Mike was his age. He had one patron already sitting in one of his two chairs, and didn't see Joe since he had been made to face the part of the wall that had no mirror. When Mike saw the Rays' manager, he apologized to the quite hairless man he was working on and took Joe by the arm, telling him,

"I have all the accounting you need to look at in my office. And your apprentice is there, too. Take all the time you need, and please, save me some money from the tax man, if you can, that is. I need to have some left if you care to be remunerated for your services."

The so-called office was more like a closet in a submarine, with just enough space for one person to move around a desk and two chairs. He recognized the young man who sat, thanks to Franck Richantall far away on the player's bench. He had never addressed the boy up to that day and made it clear for the kid to stay away from him. Now that he was near him and Manuel was still standing, he took a look. He was a medium built, nice-looking fellow. He could see the kid as a good runner on bases; maybe he could steal a few. Joe sat behind the desk while Manuel installed himself as comfortably as he could on the folding chair. After a few awkward seconds of silence, Joe invited Manuel to sit and said:

"They tell me that you play baseball."

"Always did."

"Are you good at it?"

"I could get you home runs, if that is what you mean."

"Come now, son, not with me. There's no TV crew around, is there?"

Manuel looked at Joe with intense eyes.

"So, you don't believe."

"Why should I?"

"I can understand that. If I didn't know, I wouldn't believe it myself."

"What is it that you know? Joe asked."

"I know that I can hit a baseball at will and put the damned thing over the fence. That's what I know, sir."

"And how can you be so sure of such a performance, pray tell?"

"You let me do it and you will see for yourself."

"So, young man, what you are telling me is I must gamble my name, my reputation, and my sanity on your word alone, is that it?"

Manuel's posture contracted as if he was suddenly in pain and his features showed concern. Then, he said in a low voice that made it hard for Joe to hear,

"You see, I have these spells. Can't say I appreciate those. Never did. Makes me look like a freak. But still, I get the damned things. Always did since I was old enough to remember having them. I kind of see things. It's not as if I have any control over the silly process. Don't ask me who will win the World Series or who will be the next president. I don't predict on demand. And I am useless for your average people's problems. Neither can I help the law to catch serial killers. I don't do tricks or magic. I do not communicate with spirits, neither am I into paranormal bullshit or parapsychology, fiction science, or anything else."

"So, Joe then asked with a semblance of a smile on his lips, what is the branch of the lunacy tree that you fancy for yourself?"

At that, Manuel set free a laugh of his own, and for this, the fact that he showed he had a sense of humor and a realistic take on his situation, Joe gave him some points.

"I am very good at interpreting dreams. Mostly my own."

"I have always found that dreamers were useless."

"Dreams usually are, conceded Manuel. Most of mine are, but you see, sometimes, they mean something."

"Yup, like Aunt Paola's purse and the lottery ticket that was in it?"

"I had plenty of similar dreams that all proved themselves true later on."

"And that bat of yours, Joe added, that you first dreamed about and found two months after in similar circumstances?"

"That's proof enough for me, Manuel declared in a dismissive and obstinate tone."

"Tell me more, Son."

"What do you want to know?"

"Tell me one of those dream stories. You must have thought of some. Indulge me with your best shot."

19 o o o 19

Arthuro Blazon from the Santa Monica Police Department was patrolling the little road that hugged the coast. He liked that beat, getting near the beach houses and imagining himself having one of those and awakening in the morning to the sound of the surf crashing on the sand just a few hundred feet from his back patio door. What he would do to have a dream of a place like that. He would run every morning before going to work, and in that way, keep in shape, which he wasn't doing much out of Culver City where he lived. Alone. In a one bed, one bath condo duplex that looked over one highway or the other, take your pick. How much had the places he was passing cost their owners? They weren't mansions. Far from it. Mostly cottages, not very big, but big enough. Summer houses? Kind of. Meaning that whoever had their name on the title for those places must have some other residence in town. How could they afford it? Arthuro was still young and had a lot to learn in world affairs and the art of money making.

He was now cruising a stretch of road that was five miles long and quite level with the ocean, with nothing between him and the white sand at his right. That was when his attention was alerted by something that wasn't what it should have been. In front of him, Pacific side, he could make a picnic area and one dark compact car that was stopped near one table. On the table, there was the usual stuff one eats on similar outings, plus one inert body, a woman's, her head resting on the table while her short hair moved with the wind. His first thought was, too much wine, and he searched for the Gallo container he was used to buying at the grocery. There wasn't any jar or bottle that he could see.

He parked his big Chevy Impala near a blue Toyota Echo with one bumper sticker that preached LOVE THY NEIGHBOR. He came near the napping lady. He could see now that she was an older woman. Though she appeared to be sleeping, something was wrong. The sandwich in front of her had been left half-consumed, as was the bottle of soda that her right hand still touched but didn't hold. And then, he noticed her eyes and knew that instant that she was dead. He called for help and stayed there to secure the scene, getting out of the way and making sure not to touch anything.

The deceased was sent to the nearest hospital, where the cause of death would be determined. At first sight, the general opinion had been some medical condition. Within twenty-four hours, though, there was a report on the desk of the state District Attorney that stipulated that one Claire Raditch, a teacher from Hollywood, had died from a shot in the neck that had injured her spinal cord. The weapon was a .22-caliber rifle, long range, and it was believed that it had been sawed off for the purpose of easy transportation and more convenient usage.

Miss Raditch was divorced at the time of her demise, and rumor had it that there had been some bad blood between her and her ex. Also, the couple had had two sons and one daughter, the latter disturbed and under psychiatric therapy with medication that she was supposed to consume on a regular basis and didn't. She also had a friend that she was seeing, and one older one that she no longer did, and was believed to be quite pissed off by the lady dumping him. But, worst of all, she was at the time of her death a member of a jury who had presided over the trial of a mobster boss. Deliberations over culpability or innocence had been going on for over four days. And last of all, one couldn't ignore the possibility of a crazy ocean drive serial killer rampaging the area. Bill Murray, the detective in charge, had a lot on his plate. The murderer could be anybody. There were so many leads, and he didn't know where to begin.

So, it was a relief when, three weeks into the investigation, his office received a tip that proved itself highly useful. It was suggested that the bullet had originated from a boat two kilometers off the coast. Nobody in the department had thought of that possibility. It was impossible to think of somebody seriously wanting to dispose of another human being by using such an improbable method. Firing at a target from a moving object? But what if it had been an accident? Which was this here communication's point, wasn't it?

It didn't take the police very long to locate four Marinas and twenty-eight possible vessels carousing in the area that day when poor Miss Raditch had been dispatched into another world, accidentally or otherwise. Out of the twenty-eight boats, from the description given in the note, they could eliminate twenty-five. They visited the other three and, in one of them, easily located one .22 caliber rifle that matched the bullet extracted from the teacher's neck. They got from the boat's owner his declaration, which was put in the file. And the file was closed. Accidental death, it was concluded. One guy trying his skills at some fly fishing or birds, and one mad projectile with eyes that must have ricocheted on one wave or another and finished its course into one very unfortunate woman's spinal column.

END of Faith part Two

2010

Spiros was back in his home in Pt. Brittany. He had been lucky, everybody around insisted rather clumsily, he believed. He didn't appreciate much being reminded how frail and breakable he had become. He had had a stroke. Nothing heavy. A very small one, as he had been told by consoling doctors. One that would leave him with no limitation of any kind. Yet, it had been a stroke. There was no way to skip that. While it had passed through him, time had hung suspended, the world as he knew it had immobilized, and for what had looked like the half-life of eternity, he remembered having thought, "les jeux sont faits," and heard in his mind the crazy clicking of the small white ball as it was jolting its way across the moving roulette that his life had suddenly become. Nobody liked to think that the next big event in one's existence would be lying in a coffin. Spiros could well imagine his own funeral in the d'Allemagne clan's favorite Québec church or cathedral, a place they would visit en masse when marriages, baptisms, and deaths made them pious.

The Artritis mansion on Point Brittany had a full view of Tampa Bay. He had come upon the place in the late eighties. In those years, they were long established south of the forty-fifth parallel. In 1982, he had purchased, through Precision Corp., one small Floridian chain of stores that specialized in hardware and construction material, an activity that matched its already ongoing business. David Nielson was the principal shareholder of the society whose shares he acquired. He was also selling the house he had built for himself as a way to dispose of all the surplus he had accumulated over the years, which he couldn't get out of his inventories except by giving the stuff away. This was bad business, since he wouldn't sell the good merchandise to those lucky customers who had benefited from his generosity. His wife had broken a leg on the grand stair that separated both wings of the small palace. Now, she hated the place and wouldn't live there anymore. Her very words. The infirmity had also turned the lady against the house, which she had ferociously described lately as a pile of crappy, out of fashion, surplus scrap. Disparate marble tiles were everywhere. There was a granite exterior wall on the front façade, bricks at the back. The walls inside were painted with washout colors that nobody sane would have wanted for a seven-hundred-square-foot condo, supposing there were people willing to live in such a place. Really, this was a surprise, the poor husband explained to Spiros as his spouse moved on crutches, out of hearing and musing over her misfortune, the dampness of everything, and most probably, of that damn floor, slippery when wet. That, he explained, had caused her to collapse on one step. As for not living there anymore, how uncaring with words one could be. They hadn't yet lived there two years and then, calamity had struck. No more! Can you believe this? His seller bemoaned. Marital differences could certainly do with a little consistency. True, it had been his project. But she had wanted out of their previous home, and approved of the site. Who could have resisted all that water around? In this way and from the start, she had been his ally. Reluctance had come over time. Although she had accepted the concept of creative building and architectural expediency as a way to save money, it hadn't helped that she had had no say in the finishing and decorating of their residence-to-be. All her frivolous suggestions were vetoed on the grounds that he had to use his own supplies, or employ all that he could get from others at rock-bottom prices, he being quite good at finding incredibly good deals, if one didn't care too much about having what he really liked, and could make do with the "occasion du jour." And, his host proudly admitted, he was that way. "Who cares what a table looks like?" he rationalized to Spiros, who was listening politely to the other man's ramblings while making all kinds of calculations in his head. "A table is a table, isn't it? Function is what matters." The marble was of a very good quality, but the color was wrong. So it was for a lot of other details in that improbable chateau. It had a sort of heteroclite quality, ill-assorted components and disparate assemblage mixing without direction toward a set-upon outcome. Furthermore, it wasn't just the house his wife had turned against. She wanted out. Out of the south, out of the sweltering purgatory that Florida was in summer. She wanted to go back home to the West Coast, to sunny San Francisco, where she had been born and all her family was. If she were to be a cripple, she now shouted at him at night, better be one where there were people to take care of her.

Spiros ended up getting the other guy's company, though not as low of an asking price as he would have liked. On the other hand, he had plucked the Point-Brittany mansion for a song, thanks to his whiz kid of a son, whom he had introduced to the seller. Charles, although only nineteen, had arranged matters in such a way that the stricken husband winded up making more money out of the loss on the edifice than he would have by selling it at triple the price to the first Joe Blow showing an interest.

They went to the Don CeSar in St. Pete Beach a few weeks later in celebration of their deal. Madeleine and Spiros had dined with David and his wife that no longer needed artificial help to get around. She walked as fine as a New York Rockette readying to kick her legs over her head in unison with a line of others. Also, the happy woman prepared to embark with her gloomy spouse on a boat that would sail four days later and cross the Atlantic toward Le Havre, and then, the gay Paris of Leslie Caron and Maurice Chevalier. In the celebrated rose pastel palace's dining room facing the Gulf of Mexico, they had had champagne served by a very French attendant. The man looked very impressive in his full attire as he had expertly filled their glasses out of the bottle of Veuve Cliquot that Spiros had judged the occasion deserved. When it was finished and the Napoleon-looking servant had put back the celebrate flacon in its silvery ice casket with a show of ceremonial gestures, Spiros thanked him, using the Frenchman's language.

- Merci beaucoup. Vous pouvez laisser la bouteille. I will do the pouring from now on.

Their server had looked down on Spiros as if he had doubted his ability to do what he had just said he would, and then, he clicked his heels and moved his head slightly forward, like if he was a military man giving them some kind of old-fashioned salute.

- Bonne fin de soirée, messieurs dames, he said, and then moved away.
- You speak French, Irene wondered as she looked at Dave with a bit of chagrin. She considered the poor man boorish, uncouth, and oafish to her polished urbanity and chic. How short he was of everything that counted in her fantasy world, like right now, as he gulped the succulent Gallic nectar filling his flute the same way he would have the Coors Light he had first asked to be served with to their impeccably well-dressed waiter. Her unrefined husband wouldn't know the difference between "merci beaucoup" and "bonne nuit." Otherwise, Irene was a nice enough woman whose idea of music was the Mantovani Orchestra playing Johann Strauss waltzes. Furthermore, she had asked for ketchup to go with her prime rib roast beef, which she had accompanied, against the advice of the maître d', with a glass of her favorite sugary white wine.

"It is no big deal, Spiros had answered. I also speak Greek." He proceeded to fill more champagne into Dave's glass. By that time, the chain store ex-owner had caught his wife's watchful eyes and managed to stay away from his second serving, which he sipped, like he could see her doing. As far as getting into the conversation, he knew better than to try as long as it strayed into that nebulous subject of foreign languages. What he couldn't figure out, though, was all those unfortunate people having to get into the trouble of learning them in the first place.

"How nice, Irene condescended."

"My wife was born French, Spiros explained."

"Canadian French, Madeleine d'Allemagne corrected. My family has lived and prospered in North America for the last three centuries."

"Then, Irene surmised, you must have originated from Québec."

"As in the city, yes."

"You hear this, Dave? Québec City. We should go there some time, don't you think?"

David, sipping some more of the Veuve Cliquot wine promptly concurred, "Yes, we should". He didn't add what was on his mind, which was if he had known he could have gotten the new infatuation with anything French out of his wife's system with a trip somewhere on his own continent, he would have pushed that option very hard before embarking on a ship and hoping for the best after that.

—◦◦◦—◖◗—◦◦◦—

It had now been almost thirty years that Spiros Artritis had lived in that very same house. Not on a yearly basis, mind you, since he had that apartment in Manhattan and another one in Athens. There was also the d'Allemagne summer place in Notre Dame du Portage, near Riviere du Loup in the province of Québec. It was a spacious cottage overlooking the St. Lawrence River. They used to go there from June 24 up to the last week of August every year with the kids, who played and interacted with their numerous cousins on their mother's side. The three-story Victorian had plenty of rooms for them all, four full bathrooms, two kitchens and eating areas, as well as one guest house that could have easily accommodated a family of six.

Peter was now driving the Volvo toward his father's house in Pt. Brittany. He was bringing him the full 252 pages of the *Faith* manuscript that, over the last two years, he had copied into his word processor. All this work done in utmost secrecy. During all this time, he didn't know if he would persist with this project, contenting himself to go through the motion, accomplishing what was necessary in order to be ready if ever he was to decide to do what upon the last minute he still persisted to denounce as an unthinkable transgression.

He had printed it, and all he wanted now was to show the work to his dad, as he had promised he would. Being a procrastinator of the first order, he would have preferred to wait. His father had just survived a stroke. This time, he had been lucky. Would he have another? Difficult to say. It depended. There wasn't much the doctors could say to reassure him. He was left with the impression that from now on, anything could happen. Chances were he would have a relapse, most probably within a few years, if he were to give credence to what he had learned on the Internet. And this time, it might be better if he didn't survive, because otherwise, his father might be left helpless, his mind forever a prisoner of a no longer functioning body. That thought had been enough to push him over the edge. He needed to act upon his impulsive and dubious project. Either he did it now or he forget about the outrageous deception.

He decided to proceed. Soon, he would announce his achievement to Angela. But first, his father. Angela was out, dining with friends and colleagues in the local art milieu. He called his father against his better instinct and invited himself to supper, saying he would bring steaks, and then, Spiros had cut him off:

"What! You want to put me in the grave? The doctors have put me on a diet."

"So what is it you can eat these days?" Peter inquired.

"Don't ask me. You don't want to know. Dreadful stuff, take my word for it. Just thinking about eating depresses me."

"I could bring Chinese."

"You could do that, Spiros hesitated."

"There is nothing wrong with egg rolls, is there?"

"I guess not."

"So I will be there with the food within the next hour."

"Oh, and by the way, his father added at this juncture, you better go through the back door. I will wait for you. In this way, we might avoid the nurse's suspicious scrutiny."

They had not met that night. When he showed up an hour late at his father's place, the front door had been left unlocked. He found Spiros in his bed sleeping. Peter ate some of the food he had brought, alone. He put the rest of the Chinese delicacies in the fridge and the manuscript on the dinner table with a note that he wrote on the spot.

"You were sleeping when I arrived. I am leaving you this little story of mine for you to read. I think you will like it. At least, I hope so. I will call you black later."

Peter was now ready to go public with *Faith*. His father would read the work he had left in his home the night before. Now was the time to show the story to his wife. He did it that very morning. She had known there was something coming, though. She had seen him make copies out of his Canon home office printer and asked him, thinking he was creating something new:

"Finally, using that old machine helped, didn't it?"

The year before, she had seen him labor out of the Royal typewriter and was curious enough to pry into his reason for such. He had given some thought at the possibility of inquiry into what was for him an important change of demeanor. So, he was ready for her:

"I used the machine as a diversion, he had explained his wife. See if it would give me some inspiration. Well, I must admit that it did. I resurrected lately the first chapter of a piece written a decade ago. I have decided to use those few pages to create something new. I'm quite surprised to have authored a tale that started with a kickoff as good as this. So much so that I find it difficult to believe I authored it."

Peter stopped talking and touched the Royal machine with his left hand. "The surprise, you see, was to realize I had used this old here contraption to write those first few thousand words of my FAITH story. Yes, it already has a title and even if it isn't finished yet, it's all in my head and I know for sure it will make a great book."

Angela had given him a little smile of her own and he had been well aware this instant she didn't believe what he was saying, patting him on the shoulder like one does with a child that showed around his very average drawings. It was better that way, Peter concluded. After all, he wasn't sure what he really wanted to do. As long as it stayed that way, he didn't feel like the swindler he knew he really was.

One year had passed. His wife had forgotten about the Faith story. Never asked how the work was progressing. He didn't tell her either. Up to that morning he showed her the manuscript, that is. He knew she would read it. She always did. Without protest. Even if she anticipated the usual deception. She must have thought it was part of the job of being his wife. At least, Faith wasn't long. After reading it, his wife had come to him and brushed his lips with a kiss.

"It's a wonderful story, Peter, she had said."

He'd known it was. Whatever he had produced in the past, she had never told him anything like this, and somehow, it hurt him more than all the rebuffs he had endured while he was hacking his way, over the years, through the literary underworld. He was grateful to her that she had not started her complimentary observation with some offensive preliminary like, "I can't believe that you wrote this." The tale might have been good, but it wasn't quite so good that the woman he cherished the most on that earth might not believe he had written it. He had disengaged from her embrace. Without even realizing it, he had started to cry, at first silently, then, sobbing like a baby as his wife gazed at him, dumbfounded. The crisis must have lasted for a full five minutes. Angela had never seen her husband like that before. The word 'depression' came into her mind. In the end, she asked,

"What is it, darling?"

"It's the story. You like it."

"As I like all what you have written."

"But you like that one better, he sobbed."

"It's different, and you didn't have to explain its meaning to me, she defended herself."

"It's not me."

"What do you mean, it's not you?"

"It's a pleasing piece."

"What's wrong with that? One writes to please an audience, I would assume."

"Not this way, he whimpered."

"The fact that you have created this marvelous story, that you can do it if you choose to do so…"

"I don't know, he interrupted, I don't know…"

At that moment, he had almost been ready to tell her everything, but somehow, he hadn't.

He turned left into his father's driveway, which could easily have accommodated half a dozen cars with enough space left for a Hummer to move around. He was bringing Won Ton soup with shrimps and broccoli. The food smelled awfully good. He got out of his vehicle and walked along the side of the posh residence toward its large garden, the waterfront, and the Four Winns 435 Vista boat attached to a wooden dock that advanced one hundred feet into the ocean. He could hear the water hitting the sea wall that protected the ground from getting swallowed by the bay, ten miles long at that point. He had left the FAITH manuscript for Spiros the week before, and now he would collect it back.

They had finished eating their meal, devouring it all with the help of a few Heinekens. Then his father looked at Peter from the bench seat built into the wall of his mansion's kitchen. His son was cleaning his plate on the other side of the table.

"How do you know what baseball is all about? He asked Peter."

"You don't have to know that much to write a story, he responded, his mouth full."

"You wrote that? Spiros had challenged while producing the *Faith* manuscript out from under the table's wooden surface, where it had remained hidden beside him."

Peter ran his hand through his thick head of hair, which was a brown color that projected a bit of a red when hit with light. His were the eyes of a hunted animal that got snared in the glare of a car's headlight. His face was still unmarked, his skin free of a beard, soft, unlike Spiros, whose cheeks carried the harshness of sandpaper six hours after shaving. Peter was fifty but didn't look his age. From pictures of him that appeared in the Tampa Tribune, a few people had thought they represented the actor William Macy. Both men were built the same, and if one were to try hard, it could be said that there was a bit of a resemblance between the two.

"I wrote the words THE END on this piece last page just two weeks ago, he answered, avoiding looking into Spiros face."

"This is damn good, his father declared."

"So, you like it?" Peter said, his voice morose and miserable. What had he been thinking? Fortunately, Spiros didn't catch on to his son's mood as he continued enthusiastically:

"Do I like it?" Peter could well detect something like awe in his father's voice. He'd never looked at him that way before. "Son," he added, "this is the best fricking story I ever read."

"From me, you mean."

"My boy, I know how to recognize a winning piece. This is the best baseball story ever, you hear me?"

"So, Peter emitted joylessly, perhaps I will get published, after all."

"If you can't get that tale of yours published, you are not worth much as an editor. Show this to the Oracle's board. They will like this potboiler."

"Well…"

"This comes as a real surprise, Spiros interrupted. I sure didn't anticipate you had in you the stuff needed to create a splendid story like this one."

"It's a silly little tale, Papa."

"Now, you are doing it again. Being your old self and babbling nonsense. You wrote this, Peter. I am so happy that you did, Son. As for sentences and paragraphs, this is what writing is about. I am sorry, but all my life, I felt that you were searching the world for all the places where you could be sure not to find me. I thought you were doing it to spite me."

"I wouldn't know how to do that, Papa. "He protested lamely. Still, a sad kind of smile had appeared on his lips.

"Getting on my wrong side that is."

"I wouldn't want to go there, either."

"Anyway, his old man said, I am sorry…"

"No need to."

"…for not having been the father…"

"Don't say that, Papa. I'm sorry if I have disappointed you."

"If I didn't know better, Spiros continued, unaware of his son's interruption. I come from the old country. You, on the other hand, were born after the war. In America! We might be father and son, and yet, we are part of two different worlds. In mine, you grab at things. In yours, you discuss them to death."

"Why did you leave Greece?"

"There were too many grabbers and not much to grab at."

"And how do you feel now?"

"Much better. I am so impressed. This new work of yours will bring you far, there can be no doubt. Who knows? Maybe one day I will be remembered because I gave you life."

"Don't overplay your hand, Father."

"Let me show this to Charles."

"I am not yet ready. I would prefer you didn't. You are the first after Angela to have read this thing."

"Thanks for the privilege, his dad acknowledged."

"I am happy to have shown it to you, Peter lied."

"And I am certainly glad that you did." He took the manuscript in his hand and, looking at Peter, he added, "This, I couldn't do, and you did it perfectly. I am so proud of you, Son!"

"It's just a story, Papa."

Spiros let the bundle of clipped pages drop on the table between them. He took a fork and played with the utensil in silence. Then it fell on the floor. Peter bent and picked up the small instrument as his father concluded:

"How I would like good old Charlie to read this. That pompous bully. He thinks he is the only one in this family with brains."

2015

Tammy had married at nineteen that Italian boy she had liked so much after graduating from her art class. She had also tried her luck on the Tampa theater scene. If one didn't care about earning money, she wasn't doing so badly. But it paled in comparison to her husband's success. Marcello Bellato had Jimmy Stewart's good look and Mediterranean charm. To Tammy's eyes, he was more than attractive. He could move. And sing. As for his acting, let's say that he had presence of the sort that made the screen appear more luminous when he was in it. He would have been a star without really trying. Wherever he was, he shined.

They had known each other five years and had been married for the last three. In 2014, things had started to unravel the wrong way. First, it had been learned that he was heavily in debt. He was playing the horses like mad. He had managed to stay even up to the year before. Then, his luck had turned. That was when he started putting more money into his gambling than he was able to earn from his acting. His take on the industry, while being far from what his idol Al Pacino made, was still quite a lot of cash for a Jimmy Stewart lookalike. That same year, he had been served with a claim from some federal agency that made it its job to collect unpaid income taxes to the US Department of Revenue. They were demanding immediate payment of the sum of seventy-six thousand dollars that he didn't possess. He didn't even have the funds necessary to honor his actual current taxes and ignored the need to make quarterly compulsory provisional payments for the year to come. If that wasn't enough, he owned his bookie fifty thousand dollars, and he was receiving a lot of disturbing phone calls from that corner as well. He should have known better by paying attention to the scripts where he played dubious characters, who always wound up in places he didn't care to visit for making the same mistakes he persisted to repeat in his real life. There were loans one would be better off not doing because they were bad for your health. Literally. You borrow from the wrong person, things start to happen.

The good news was that he had signed a contract with a major film conglomerate for three movies. Hopefully, as he had been told by his agent, the signature bonus would take care of his bookie if he could receive it very soon, and the damn government didn't seize the cash before he could put his hands on it. In addition, if the matters were not bad enough as they were, the actress he was to perform with in the first motion picture had taken a shine to him. Being distracted with all his financial worries, he was not as cautious in his indiscretions as he had been in the past. He had been caught red-handed with the girl, quite a regretful kind of situation since the silly actress was nothing to him. Moreover, there was a big part of him that really loved Tammy. Most of the time.

Yet, he was an actor. Was it his fault if all those women had a crush on him? Life wasn't supposed to be this way. Men were expected to do the chasing. He didn't chase. How could he be guilty, then? Not as guilty as Tammy, who was crying as he had never seen her before, had said he was. Jesus! How it hurt just remembering that dreadful scene. Seeing his wife tormented by such horrible pain, and sensing that he was the cause of it all. He really had felt sorry for her. Words didn't come easily to him. He was used to repeating those learned from a script. Now, he was on his own and he had no nice little line from a script to cut his way out of the tearful situation. One part of him would have liked to swear he loved her, had loved her from first meeting her, and always would. He couldn't find it in him to do that. Such a discourse sounded so crass even to his ears. How could he have created such a mess? In his miserable and inappropriate way, he saw now from a distance, he had tried to tell her all the right things, but she was in too much agony to be receptive or to understand his rather unconvincing and self-serving exonerations. He realized that he had upset his wife really bad. True, this wasn't the first time. Yet, in their past disputes, he had always managed to hold some footing, some intimate conviction that all might be well in the end, as it usually was.

However, this time, since he had been caught with another woman, he couldn't be sure of anything anymore. This looked like the real thing. After so many episodes of his wrongdoings, he comprehended at last that too much was too much, and he couldn't blame her for wishing to dump the useless fool he certainly had proved he was. She had vacated the condo they owned in Queens. The note in his hand said the place would be put up for sale soon. It also asked him to move out. He couldn't object. Hopefully, the expected transaction would cover the mortgage. And if there was money left, he knew he would get his share. She wasn't the type to keep it from him.

It was the end of a rainy afternoon. He had come back home to change at a time he knew she wouldn't be there, his best chances of recovering from his present difficulty being in letting her cool down. Meanwhile, he would stay clear of Tammy and kill time by playing poker with a bunch of guys from the technical staff of the movie he was filming at the moment. And now this! The note didn't say how much time he had to pick up his belongings. His circumstances had changed for the worst, hadn't they? He couldn't pretend that this development came as a complete surprise. What else could he have expected? Collapse, debacle, and destruction were the norm for all he seemed to be doing. What, then, could explain all that had gone awry with his life? He hadn't wished it to be so.

Not so many years ago, his future had looked bright enough. It had promised plenty of the best the world had to offer to its elite cast of the young, talented, and beautiful. He had more than his fair share of those attributes. He, the Italian Romeo with the Jimmy Stewart resemblance. How had he let matters deteriorate to this point where he was in debt with mafia-like characters, had the US Treasury threatening to seize his assets - a silly concept in the first place since he had none - and he no longer had a wife and would soon need a place to crash in.

The bimbo he had been sleeping with wasn't an option. Who would help him in this dire situation? He couldn't think of anyone except Tammy. So, he decided he would call her and appeal to her better sentiments. He took a shower. One of the gang had told him that Bill would be at the game tonight. He didn't know Bill. He had just heard of him. He wanted to meet the man, to see if he deserved the reputation he had, and to see for himself why his fellow players had taken a fancy to the guy. His wife could wait.

The note had said she was at her Greek grandfather's place. Tomorrow, he would know what to say to her. He might win her back. He always did.

Spiros had been happy to see his granddaughter. She had appeared at his door on the twenty-sixth floor of the cooperative apartment building he still kept in Manhattan. The Plaza on the Park, it was called. The place was huge, and he lived alone in it, if one doesn't count the couple that shared the five-bedroom extravaganza with him. Besides, they had their own quarters with access on the other side of the kitchen and their separate exit to the outside corridor, so nobody would know they were there if not told so. Wherever he lived in the United States, this couple went with him. The woman was a cook and maid. The husband acted as his chauffeur and his wife's aid. The first of May, he had flown out of the St. Petersburg airport while Robert and his wife had driven in the Lincoln up to the Big Apple with all their luggage. He had been in town for four months when Tammy had dropped by, looking kind of strange. She acted like she had a severe illness and didn't want anybody to know. In her hand was one small suitcase, and the sight of it sent a chill through his old bones.

"Hello, Grandpa, she had said." He could see at once that her smile was not to be trusted.

"Well, he replied, what a nice surprise." He had opened the door since it was Friday and Marie and her husband had used the weekend to visit their son, who lived in Hoboken, New Jersey on the other side of the Hudson River. He had let them have the Lincoln.

Approaching ninety, he felt vigorous enough to persist in acting manly. He grabbed the valise out of Tammy's hand and got her inside. He couldn't restrain himself from covering the awkward silence with small talk, throwing away ten, twenty years, how old was she now? And conducting himself as if his visitor was still a little girl of five who was coming to stay at her granddaddy's, and he was babbling joyously of all the things they would do together.

"Oh, he said, aren't we going to have a great time? First, we'll go eat at the Cantina, and then we'll visit the Blockbuster on the corner of Seventy-Eighth Street and you'll choose us a real good movie and we'll watch it together. That is, if you can work out the silly equipment."

It had always been his line with her, and she had always managed it. As for him, he liked to delude himself with the idea he still could, despite the fact that he wouldn't know when he had last touched his very elaborate appliances. That responsibility was normally left to Robert's wise manipulations. "Marie will make us some popcorn," he added. And then, he remembered that the help wasn't around. He told her so.

"Whatever, he finished, we can manage the popcorn ourselves, can't we? What do you say?"

"I am most sorry to barge in on you like this, she said as she followed him in the living room and then in the room she always occupied when visiting."

It was more like a suite, with its own bathroom and a small balcony overlooking Central Park. Spiros went to the sliding door and pushed it wide open. It had stopped raining. Temperature was mild. The drapes in front of the overture started to move, pushed by a light breeze.

The bedroom was exactly the same as it had been all those years ago when she was young and hadn't a care in the world. Outside, the same two beach chairs faced a table that she remembered using for drawing her dad souvenirs of her trip to the city. Sparkles of water now shined briefly on its white surface, ignited by an isolated ray of sunlight that had just made it through the clouds' cover.

"Don't be, honey, he insisted. I am so happy you are here. It is like a gift from heaven."

He had been afraid to ask her what was wrong. Because something, he knew, must have been wrong. Young women were not in the habit of crashing unannounced at other people's places, let alone their grandfather's, unless they had good reasons to act that way, as she must have. And it wouldn't be pleasant news. He blamed himself for not having listened more when Tammy was the object of other people's conversations. They'd mostly spoken of her accomplishments and such. Or he had been told and had forgotten, as it was happening more and more often.

- No need to worry, Dr. Collard had tried to reassure him at his last visit. You will soon be an octogenarian. At your age, it's normal to lose memory. The more recent the information, the less is one's hold on to it. It is like a selection process that the mind is doing as you must have done it all your life. Today you attribute your amnesia to forgetfulness and old age. When you were young, it was indifference.

Spiros made an effort and remembered she was involved in the fringe theater scene of the city. Had even gotten herself a job in some administrative body that distributed public funds, where she was a consultant with responsibilities of choosing who, among the seekers, would get subsidies and grants. The salary was miserable, as it should be. Still, he knew from Peter that he paid her a monthly allocation without her husband knowing. Furthermore, Spiros had paid her half of the down payment for the condo she owned in Queens. It had been his gift to her when she had married that dandified Italian soap opera bit player. And what else? What was he to do? Should he call his son and ask him about Tammy? No. Certainly not before he talked to the girl. Why make a fuss before he learned what the situation really was? She would tell him soon enough, and then he would decide what to do.

"Now, he said to his granddaughter, I will leave you alone. Refresh yourself. Take a shower. Enjoy the place and be comfortable. Put your things in those drawers." And he made a show of opening one out of a commode in the style of one French king or another.

He departed, thinking of nothing but getting out before being hit with what she was there to tell him. He didn't want to hear it yet. He walked the distance separating Tammy's suite from the living and dining area just in time to pick up the phone on the second ring. Hopefully, it would be Peter or Angela with some news of what was happening. But no. The communication was from downstairs, where the doorman informed him of a package that had just been delivered, and of somebody who wanted to speak with Tammy. The gentleman was waiting in the lobby, he was told. Should he send him up?

Spiros snapped, "Who is it?" as if he was thinking perhaps it was the Italian fellow Tammy was living with. Everyone around pretended they were married, which he doubted.

"Marcello Bellato is the gentleman's name, sir." He heard the doorman tell him, as he had figured out already.

Why had the idiot not told him the tiresome intruder's name in the first place? He didn't want the man near his place if he could help it. What might be the man's business to come barging here? He had been there before. Spiros had realized from the start what kind of character that weasel charmer really was. While drinking too much white wine, he had persisted in dropping lame jokes all night long, ignoring his host's annoyance with all the inappropriate interruptions in his party's conversations. Worse, the actor had collided with a pedestal with a bronze reproduction of Épictète on it while leaving the apartment. It had chipped the marble floor when it landed. He could still see the damage when he cared to look under the Persian carpet.

"No, he shouted in the mouthpiece. Keep him where you are. I will join you soon."

When he finally made it downstairs, he had had to dress properly. He wouldn't be seen in shorts by this celebrated humbug. But when he arrived, there was nobody waiting in the lobby. He approached Roger's desk and was shown an enormous bouquet of red roses, three dozen at least from the look of it. There was a note with Tammy's name on it.

"Who are those for?" The doorman asked him.

The man was a dunce, Spiros decided. Why? He must have let his granddaughter in, and the girl's name was right there under his nose. Why hadn't he called to let him know she was coming upstairs, though? This could wait though. Instead, he asked:

"Where is the man that brought this in?"

"I informed him that you were coming." The doorman answered. "He left me those. He asked me to give it to you with the note. He said that he couldn't stay and that he could be found at this number." Roger passed Spiros a piece of paper with the Plaza on the Park's logo on it. Someone had crossed its surface with a ten-digit number. Spiros picked up the small communication of precarious script, as if its author had staked his life on its outcome.

"Do you want me to send them up? Roger asked again, showing the parcel that rested on the granite counter separating them. Those will need water soon, he added."

"No, thanks. I can manage." Spiros responded. And then, he had turned abruptly with his burden and started walking toward the lift. So, he decided, here is the story that was soon to be disclosed to him. Lover's stuff.

—∞◦◦}◦◦{◦◦∞—

Meanwhile, in her grandfather's sumptuous apartment, Tammy had left her suitcase unpacked. She had moved to the patio door and unlocked it. Once opened, she had walked outside and rested her body against the railing as she looked distractedly in the direction of Central Park, the Hudson River, and Secaucus. How long she had been lost in thought, she couldn't say, even if her watch told her it was past six p.m. Why had she decided to come here in the first place, she asked herself. She had not even been sure that Spiros would be there. She had acted impulsively, without thinking, his address the first that had come to her mind when answering the driver of the taxi she had hailed on the street. If he'd been out, would they have let her stay? She obviously wasn't thinking straight. The way she had barged in was ample proof of that, entering the lobby through the locked door in another resident's wake. She could still hear the man complaining at Roger's absence as he had needed to find his keys, and he'd had plenty in his hands to make the operation perilous. It wouldn't be long before Marcello showed up. What would she do then?

She entered the bedroom. There were two beds, one single and one king. It still was large enough to accommodate a desk, two armchairs and a big TV with enough space to look at it from far away. She sat on the single bed. She recalled the list of things to do she'd made that morning and extracted it out of her shirt pocket. She and glanced at the words she had written in capital letters.

PAPA, I AM SORRY. That was a reminder to call her parents and apologize for her neglect of their relationship for the last few years.

GRANDPA, as in, can I stay with you for a while?

AGENT. She had to find one if she wanted to put their condo up for sale.

WORK. She must call the agency and tell them if she didn't feel like going to work on Monday.

Her boss would also need to know her new "coordonnées," that is, where she could be reached from now on. How long would it take for Marcello to vacate the premise? Would he even do it? She couldn't tell. She had heard a few dreadful stories involving other people's breakups and them warring over children and who would keep the house. But they had no children. That was a blessing. She didn't care that much about the domicile. Happen what may.

She looked again at her list of tasks. Perhaps she could dispose of number one right this instant. Was there a phone in here? She put the folded note on the bed and left the suite, leaving the patio door open.

While walking through the apartment in search of one, she heard a knock on the unit's front door. She let a few seconds pass. Something rapped again, but louder and more frenetic this time. Where was Spiros? She looked through the peephole and saw an old lady on the other side. When she opened the door, the woman was surprised not to find Marie or Spiros, as she must have expected, but a young woman. She took a little while to recover. Then, she said:

"You must be Tammy, yes? Don't you recognize me? I am…"

"Miss Ray…burn, the younger woman said hesitantly." She was finally able to identify the visitor, remembering the lady that had joined her grandparents for late afternoon cocktails, and had been present at birthdays when those happened to be celebrated in New York when Tammy was a kid. Once, this same neighbor had offered Spiros complimentary tickets for a Met matinee of *Madama Butterfly*. Tammy had inherited those, since her grandfather had seen the Puccini masterpiece numerous times. As she hadn't, it was judged to be a nice introduction for her to the operatic world. She had gone with a friend. The pair had loved the Italian tearjerker. It must have been nine or ten years she hadn't seen the old lady, which explained her previous confusion. Her visitor had the careful eyes of those who needed help with their comprehension by reading other people's lips.

"So, you remember me, beamed Miss Rayburn."

She lived on the same floor five doors away.

"How could I have ever forgotten you? Countered Tammy. You were so nice in introducing me to the Met. You've made me an opera buff, you know."

"I used to go a long time ago. I don't hear so well anymore."

Miss Rayburn looked frail and distracted. Tammy asked her:

"Are you allright? Can I help you with anything?"

"Silly me, the other mumbled. I am no good at anything nowadays. I locked myself out of my apartment and I can't open the door."

The woman was on the verge of tears. She held in her shaking hands a ring of keys that all looked the same, and no wonder, in the state she was in, that she couldn't discern the proper one, let alone insert the tiny instrument into the lock. Tears formed on both sides of her eyes.

"You must not tell, she sobbed. I can't call the desk downstairs since my son will be told. He wants to have me in one of those homes, you know…"

"Tut…tut…tut, nobody will do anything of the sort, Tammy reassured the very distressed Miss Rayburn the best she could. "Now," she continued, "let me have those keys of yours and see if I can get in. Please show me to your door. I would very much like a cup of tea right now. Will you fix me one?"

"God bless you, dear."

In this way, Tammy followed her into the carpeted passage that led to unit 2607. To avoid putting herself in similar circumstances, she made sure that the door of unit 2614 stayed unlocked. The set of keys in her left hand emitted a clattering sound. There were too many of them, without a doubt, most no longer of any use for any existing latch. The assemblage was the sorry résumé of a life winding up in oblivion with neither direction nor purpose. Once in front of apartment 2607, she started working one key after another until she rattled her way up to the true one. Then the lock clicked its surrender, the obstacle she was fighting against stopped resisting her efforts, and the complacent aperture swiveled submissively on its hinges. As both women entered, the lift reached the twenty-sixth floor.

The lift regurgitated Spiros with his package of roses, which he resented carrying since it made him look like a fool. At least, that was the way he felt. Mercifully, there had been nobody to see him parading with such a ridiculous load of nonsense. At his age, and his dear wife dead since 1998, who was he to offer flowers to? And if he did, what is it the trivial gesture made him look like? An older Mr. Bean, perhaps? He had his hands full with the enormous bouquet. Before he could find his keys in his trousers, he realized the door had been left slightly ajar. He pushed it open with his foot and called:

"Tammy?"

There was no answer. He had a strange feeling at that precise moment. Why, he couldn't tell, but he became very much afraid. He felt a knot in his chest and a chill in his spine. He walked into Tammy's bedroom, calling her name again. Maybe she was in the shower. She wasn't. Next, he felt a draft and saw the patio door fully open. He recalled his sister, Despina. She had been a teacher, and at twenty-three, she had met a colleague who'd professed great love for her. They had dated for two years, and then they had announced their engagement at a party where they had danced and sang in the Greek tradition to the accompaniment of Zorba-like bouzouki music. Christos! That had been the fellow's name. He had given his beautiful and wonderfully happy sister a ring, but not much more, and certainly not his name. He hadn't married Despina after all. Never explained why, either. He had just disappeared at the end of the semester when he was supposed to meet her one Friday night. He hadn't shown up. His poor sibling had never been the same after that terrible shock. She was devastated, destroyed, wasted. Some said that she had started dying then and there. She had been thirty. She was his big sister. He remembered her having been there for him, and he had loved her like a second mother. The family hadn't known what to do to help her, so a trip had been suggested. It had been a cruise on the Mediterranean Sea. Yes, they had thought, this could help. He had been designated to go with her. It had been the summer of 1938. He'd been twelve. They had had a suite with two rooms, one beside the other. Both had a balcony. On day three, while at sea, once out of the shower, he hadn't found Despina where he'd left her, reading. He recalled she had been in good spirits, though. In her room, all was neat and sparkling. There was a note left on the bed where she slept alone, and he could see through the balcony door that had been left gaping a knocked-over coffee table beside the railing, the only protection against plunging into the tumultuous water twenty meters or so below. She had jumped. He hadn't needed to read the note that said, "I am sorry." He knew it already. It had killed their mother. His father had never been the same after that. As for him, he couldn't stand Greece anymore and knew right then and there he would leave the place somehow.

It looked like the same thing was repeating itself all over again. He saw the note on the bed. He had time to make out the words, "Papa, I am sorry." His heart was beating too fast. Still, when he realized that, there was no time left to be afraid.

When Tammy returned a few moments later into apartment 2614, she faced a locked door. So, her grandfather, who had left for one reason or another, must have come back. She envisioned how frantic he might have been over her vanishing act. She rang the bell. She couldn't hear if it was working. She decided to use the silver-colored hammer in the shape of a lion's head to bang herself in. And still, nothing happened. What a bizarre coincidence, this re-enacting of the Miss Rayburn's predicament, but now with Tammy in the role of the damsel in distress. What was she to do? She must ask for help.

One day later, they announced the formation of cyclone Patricia. It was October 2015. That same day, Peter was told about his father. For the rest of his life, he would associate his death with the calamity and colossal destruction nature brought down on Central America in what would soon be described the world over as the strongest hurricane ever to hit the earth. This was illogical. His usual nonsense, Spiros would have said. Yet, in his immense grief and sense of irremediable dispossession, he was past all that was rational, sound, and sensible. The fact was that he had heard of both calamities at the same time. For reasons he didn't care to revisit, he entertained for a brief instant the notion of his old man transmuted into a ghost and showing anger for having been tricked out of this world under a false pretext, hence his blowing a bit of wind over the Gulf of Mexico.

It had been a difficult time. He was immensely grateful to Angela, who had been there to support him. Tammy had come back to St. Petersburg to live with them. From her, they had heard the full story and the horribly wrong set of circumstances that had swept his father away. He had known the full story of his aunt Despina, who had jumped out of a boat when she was in her twenties. So that was what had killed his father. Reliving that grisly scene and assuming erroneously that his granddaughter was repeating the past. Looking on the matter from a distance, he couldn't say if he would have liked it better if Spiros had died at the hands of the silly disturbance that Patricia had been. It was better than thinking that if Tammy hadn't shown up at the Plaza when she did, his father would still be with them. Of course, he didn't tell the girl as much. He let her assume the obvious, which was that her grandfather had been eighty-nine and his time had come. Better that Tammy ignored the fact that she had somewhat caused the old man's death. He couldn't get the thought out of his mind and was angry at himself for entertaining the notion. But still it stood there, whatever his efforts to get over his resentment, a feeling that was diffuse and unfocussed as it was directed at a lot of everything that didn't square up in his life. His father had been the rock he'd always felt he'd needed to protect himself against all that could go wrong in existence.

For Peter, it resulted in him not being able to distinguish whether the lifeless feeling in his innards was due to his father's disappearance, or to some other dysfunction in his body.

Life didn't stop, though. Hurricane Patricia didn't hit Florida, which was a blessing. His existence continued to flow lazily, with nothing much happening except the occasional highs and lows. One could always build some protective wall against those. Days passed. Then, months. 2015 became 2016. Peter went through that period without writing a line, the drive to do so no longer there. He felt like he had nothing to say anymore. As if he ever had. Whatever he was fond of, nobody else he knew felt the same. He still received publications penned in Latin or ancient Greek. He didn't look at them. He didn't find it funny anymore to read about Donald Trump campaigning to become the next president in those dead languages. Neither did he contribute, as he used to, articles of his own. It must have been the effect of some accumulated lassitude that made him adopt Charles's view of the activity. Angela knew better than to bring up the subject of writing. After all, it looked like her husband had survived the ordeal of Spiros passing away. Routine and normality had taken over, as it usually did.

Life still offered a lot of what they both enjoyed, though. Peter was working at Oracle, and the small publishing house was doing surprisingly well. It fulfilled all the needs Peter had of doing something useful. Furthermore, he and Charles had become mega millionaires in their own rights. Charlie had taken their father's place as president and CEO of Precision Corp. Peter's whiz kid brother had managed to stay well out of the financials in his investments. So, he had avoided the worst of the crisis when Leehman Brothers went broke and you could buy shares of Citigroup for forty-nine cents apiece. The chain of stores that had been created in 1978 after Precision Corp. took over a Floridian hardware wholesaler was now a giant in the industry, in direct competition with the likes of Lowe's and Home Depot. Thanks to Charles's wise steering and guidance, Precision Corp. had opened the first two PRECISION stores in Tampa in 1982. At around sixty thousand square feet each, they were more like cavernous warehouses imagined into existence to dwarf the competition in its stock-keeping unit capacity. From the start, associates, as employees were called now, offered the best customer service in the industry, guiding the clientele through projects such as laying tile, changing a fill valve, or handling a power tool. Not only did store associates undergo rigorous product knowledge training, but they also began offering clinics so customers could learn how to do it themselves. PRECISION revolutionized the home improvement industry by bringing the "know how" and the tools to the consumers, saving them money. Over the years, PRECISION had bought out competitors and multiplied stores all over the country. It was now a public company in which Precision Corp. owned a participation of thirty-seven percent. Which was still enough to exert a very big influence on the company's management.

In 2012, the Rays had finally made it to the World Series. Peter had been very much tempted to use the jubilation and euphoria the team maintained around itself that summer and show The Faith manuscript around. It sure would put a term to the harassment coming from his father, and to a lesser extent from Angela, that couldn't understand what he was waiting for. He couldn't tell them he was afraid.

Not only afraid. Terrified.

What if Zielgard had narrated his story verbally to someone? It was almost impossible to imagine he hadn't done so. A splendid story like that. It must have been a real challenge to keep it inside oneself. And then, he countered in his mind, the man was alone, had no friends and nobody to confide in. Also, there was always this saying that it was bad luck to divulge the punch in one's tale before having it put into a book.

What about Arthur then? Arthur would suspect something fishy the instant he learned about his accomplishment. He knew his friend numerous tries at producing tales and his hoping at getting them published. He had been shown a few pieces and returned them unread. A blessing if true. Because if he had and compared with the manuscript Peter had returned to him in 2008, he would know Zielgard couldn't have produced what he was reading, so similar with his friend's production. But knowing Arthur, chances were good he hadn't cared to look at the material. Still, upon discovering Peter's actual success at producing a piece that makes sense, even that many years later, what if he started to dig and ask questions? He might want to look at the piece Peter had returned him. What then? If he were to show it to Angela, she would recognize his style instantly. How long lawyers kept file once closed? Five years? Anyway, Peter didn't doubt he would fail miserably at any confrontation with his solicitor if Arthur was of a mind to cross-examine him.

So he waited. 2012 came and disappeared and he waited.

2013.

2014.

Nothing changed. Those years found him always frightened, faint-hearted and perturbed.

And then, his father died and something shifted. After a period of mourning, one morning, in late May 2016, after Tampa Bay had had three straight wins, Peter got out of bed with a kind of new swing in his gait. He had looked at his wife sleeping on her side of the bed and he had felt a jolt of intense and passionate affection toward her. He had made love to her then and there. What had passed through him, he couldn't say. But something had lifted from his shoulders. A weight that had been there no longer was. What it had been, he had no clue. What it changed in his perspective, or in what way it affected his attitude, he didn't know. It just gave him back an appetite. That morning, he had felt twenty years younger. He'd craved for a breakfast of eggs and bacon. Suddenly, the game's happy result clinched things in his head.

Somehow, he knew that the time for *Faith* had arrived. The Zielgard story had finally come to life like a movie playing in his mind. He would arrange the work a bit; adapt the piece a bit. And then, he would publish the story. He knew what to do. It was a marvelous feeling. He was happy, and he had confided as much to his wife. She had looked at him, thrilled and beaming. All he had to do, he told her enthusiastically, was making some adjustments to the story she had already read a long time ago so as to reflect the actual 2008 baseball season and its final sorry denouement. This got Peter in a frenzy of intense activity. While it happened, it revived in him the sense of being creative. His input in the narrative gave him the illusion that a few added words and color here and there would suffice to dissolve the other man's novel into his own. Such delusion was enough to keep him going. To remember the last time her husband had been that cheerful, Angela had to go back a long way. That summer, Peter had a great time working out the manuscript, adapting the drama so it fitted with the Rays and their quite magical 2008 performance. He was so much into it that it didn't bother him that he had stolen all of Zielgard's forty thousand words. It had been so long ago. Time enough to clog arteries, diminish memories, and make peace with the devil.

BOOK TWO

PETER

Winston Farmer didn't care much for the east coast. He had been born in Los Angeles. When he was twenty, he'd moved to Montreal. Career-wise, it looked at the time like the sensible thing to do. He had an uncle who worked at the Montreal Star. There had been an opportunity for the young upstart he thought he was. He took a job there. Crazy moves like that, you had to do them at a tender age, when you could still learn something. Like a second language. All things considered, he had done well. By the time of the strike that precipitated its demise, the Montreal Daily had made him an assistant editor. In 1979, Farmer caught the attention of one of the Southam Papers' directors. Southam owned the Montreal Gazette. They made him an offer and he took it unenthusiastically. The Star had folded. Furthermore, he had come to detest the city's winters and silly politics. He would have preferred to go back home to California, but there was no job waiting for him there. The only offer credible enough coming from that side of the continent would have forced him to live like a monk in San Diego. At least the cost of living in the Québec metropolis was cheap.

He had to wait fifteen more years to move out. In 1993, he received an offer from Oracle Publishing. They wanted Winston to come south and replace the chief editor, who was to retire in 1994. The man had held the job since Precision Corp.'s acquisition of the firm in the late sixties. Moving out of Montreal had been a blessing, though. That city was of a schizophrenic temperament, the town divided in two between its French and Anglo citizenry, the formers resenting the latter for speaking the wrong language, and Québec's political class behaving as though ignoring the lot would make the "blokes" disappear. He had learned to live there like a native, though. He had made friends of Gallic origins. Even the separatists, after a few drinks, were not as bad as they looked. And the place had ended up producing a very special kind of North American, so different from those born south of the forty-fifth parallel. He had become one of that new breed, bilingual in French and English. He found it a very chic combination. Somehow, he would miss the place and its restaurants, which gave you a "dining" experience for half what it cost elsewhere to enjoy meals half as good. And he would miss films like Elvis Gratton, which he had seen four times. It was now a favorite of all time. Those folks could be quite funny in their own way.

Montreal also reminded him of his former life with Marion. No. Better not to think of Marion, the woman who was like a sore on his skin that he persisted to scratch. Yet, he was constantly doing it. His mind was like that. Refusing in all times and circumstances to listen to his better self. In his professional life, it had been mostly that way, too. He constantly messed with issues that would have been better off left alone, while he'd neglected those he should have cared about. Maybe he liked to act rebellious. To provoke. Say things that set people on edge. Perhaps he was appreciated in his present job because he had that quality. That was, the ability to detect the fault line in everything that attracted his interest. He could be a real pain in the neck sometimes, reading other like they were the dashboard of a 747, and finding in a matter of seconds all the buttons that were better left untouched.

While a resident in the province of Québec, he had lived with Marion in a Beaconsfield bungalow. That was on the so-called west island. They had bought the three beds, two baths in 1977 after the ultranationalist Parti Québécois came to power and the market for houses had plummeted. Their place had been two streets away from Marion's parents' cottage. That close proximity hadn't prevented their daughter from betraying him with a piano-selling fellow in Sherbrooke, a town that had no other distinction than to find itself at the end of an auto route. Eugene was the name of the guy who had sold them the piano. He'd been pretty good that Eugene. Quite formidable when playing one of his instruments, as he had a way to tickle a keyboard. You gave him a chance, and he would sell you the device in the time it took him to strum out your favorite tune. For Marion, it had been "Unchained Melody," their mascot song. That peddler, who played his clavier like he was an Arthur Rubinstein impersonator, must have entertained his wife with the silly exhibition a hundred times. And he, the idiot extraordinaire, had bought the thing to make his companion happy. He recalled the sorry episode like it was yesterday.

They had put the piano in their living room, and nobody had touched it except their son, Eric, over a season of fast evaporating ambitions. From then on, it had become no more than a piece of useless furniture in an already congested space. After having put the blame on her one time too many, Marion reacted in spite by confessing to her affair with Eugene. She'd then abandoned him. Not for her virtuoso concert player in Sherbrooke, though. She'd just left him, leaving their kid's pictures where they were, on top of the piano. And the kids as well. He could keep them, the house, the furniture, and the mortgage, whatever! Éditions Robert Laffont, where she was working, had offered her a job in Paris. She had taken it. While in the French capital, she had met a Corsican and married him. She was now living somewhere in the Ajaccio region, on the Mediterranean coast, in a superb villa with a quay and a thirty-four-foot yacht to go with it. At least, so Eric said, since both he and his sister had visited the little emperor's birthplace. He doubted it was as good as his son pretended. Still. Damn his wife. Damn Corsica. Damn Ajaccio. Damn the fricking boat.

His father had been responsible for the name 'Winston.' Not long before he had come into the world, his dad had written to Churchill, and the great man had answered back in a letter with his own script. He must have loved his American fan's letter very much. But going solely by his response, it was impossible to guess what his dad's original transmission had been about. The then British Prime Minister might as well have used a secret code and an enigma-like machine, the only method to decipher the message's meaning. When asked, Lawrence Farmer would roll his eyes and insist they talk about something else. Being young, he hadn't made much out of the situation, or his father's whimsical attitude. The letter was treasured, from the time it was received, as a relic. It had been preserved in a glass framed picture that had hung on their house's best walls for everybody to see, only to be rebuffed gently if one asked too many questions. This had been the apex of the Farmer family's otherwise very plain existence. Once, Winston had said to his old man when he had come for a visit to the second-largest French-speaking town in the world,

- "Why didn't you correspond with Général De Gaule? Charles would have been a nice name."

It was two or three years after the general had come to Montreal and shouted his highly controversial "Vive le Québec libre." Why was he recalling all that? His poor father had been dead fourteen years, since 2002. Perhaps it was because he had inherited the Churchill souvenir that was on his office wall, which he was gazing at right at that moment. Better to muse over Churchill's pen craft than to recall his ex-wife. Marion, who spoke French with a Parisian accent, and enjoyed herself out on the Ligurian coast. Was she swimming in the nude on those beaches they had there? Go figure, with that clique of European exhibitionists she hung out with. How old could she be now? Fifty-four, fifty-five? She had been blessed with good bone structure and a nice silhouette. So endowed, as he remembered her, she had always been well positioned to fight life's inclination toward ruin and decay. She would do it by exercising at the gym, running, bicycling, and subsisting mostly on fish, salad, tofu, and lait de soya. He sure didn't miss having to look at the dubious concoctions she mixed herself in lieu of breakfast in the morning. Why couldn't she eat corn flakes and toast like everybody else? That, too, he must have told her one time too many. It was no wonder, then, that she might be running around half-naked on a silly pile of sand, lost in the middle of one stupid sea or another. Damn! There was not much fun in recalling his ex-wife. It was his life's big mistake, never to be repeated as he would never marry again and certainly not his present companion. With time, he succeeded in getting Marion out of his system. For a while, anyway, as she had a way of tickling her way back into his thoughts. Her and that damn Corsican, the villa, the boat, and the CIAO at the end of postcards, with snapshots of her beaming in an all sand, water, sun, and tits scenery. What a sore it was that jarred on his nerves again and again. The hell with her. He could stand the comparison between that rocky island and his own life here in

Florida. After all, his two-bedroom condo in Gulfport, St. Pete, had an oblique view on Boca Ciega Bay.

He was in his office in the Oracle headquarters out in the Verizon building on Central Avenue. Outside, the sun was excruciatingly hot, the humidity stifling, and not a breath of air - no breeze at all, if not for the birds' contributions, except there was none in sight. Employees couldn't complain, though, since there was air conditioning and the temperature maintained inside was a shivering seventy. There was a knock on his door, and he prepared for his meeting with Peter Atritis. The day before he had been shown a new piece of the man's writing, an achievement from his part since words that circulated were to the effect he had put a term to his ambition of producing a novel. He was now coming back to receive his verdict for one he had just finished. The poor schmuck could have done as he pleased and have the phone book published under his name, selling it as urban poetry if he liked or cared. It would be nothing for his colleague to make the bestseller list if he would just arrange to buy himself one hundred thousand copies of his own book. But Artritis would have none of that. He had to give credit to the man for not purchasing his way to instant celebrity. The rich and ineffectual scribbler couldn't put two words besides each other that would make any kind of sense. That there were individuals like Peter around who survived in the world was beyond his comprehension. Winston Farmer was of a spiritual disposition that didn't leave much room for poetical license or idiotic prose. He shouted:

"Please, come on in."

The party that entered his office had the sad look of a dog that you could beat up, and the animal would stick around. Peter was moving in his direction. Winston stood up, indicating the sofa they both were to occupy to have their chat. Why, he thought, his guest might as well have been a two-bit manager from the building's administration team, running in for no better reason than that Winston had snapped his fingers.

Could it be that such a wimp was the author of the book he'd read and reread just to make sure he hadn't hallucinated? This wasn't the work of a loser. And if Winston had ever met one, Peter was a champion. His story, though, a prize-winning one. How come such a character with so many flaws had found what was needed to transform himself, in quite a miraculous way, into every editor's ultimate wet dream? The individual that stood in front of him sure didn't look the part. Yet, he could discern a bounce in Peter's steps, and a never-before-seen sort of confidence in that otherwise illegible smile of his.

"Hello, there, Winston said with as much benevolence as he could master. Please, take a seat."

"Did you read it?" Peter asked anxiously.

"Yes, I did, he answered back. Pretty impressive!"

"You think so?" His visitor mumbled. So much for the self-assurance, Winston accredited.

"Coming from you that is."

Peter laughed sheepishly. "A break in my old ways, you mean. Yes…"

"It's sure not in your usual style."

"I have decided to investigate real life."

"As if you could, snapped the other."

Peter raised his face, but Winston couldn't catch the man's eyes, which looked beaten up. The Oracle's chief editor let pass a few awkward seconds, then added,

"What game are you playing here?"

Peter, who sat in front of him, winced, suddenly appearing frail and vulnerable.

"Well, I wrote the piece, no matter what you might think."

Winston shrugged.

"If you say so."

"Do you like it, Peter asked again."

"As a matter of fact, I do love it very much, yes. What intrigued me, though, is the origin."

"I am bringing the work to you, as I did all the others, don't I? So why are you making such a fuss now?"

"Because, Farmer said, this can't be yours. You can't have written it. Therefore, you tell me. Whose story is it?"

"What? Peter resisted. Are you telling me to my face that you doubt my word?"

"I am sorry."

"You have always disliked my stories, his visitor complained, changing the subject."

"Dislike is not the word, Winston countered. What I did is this: I told you that what you persisted to write and show me wouldn't fly."

"And this will?"

"If it doesn't, nothing ever will. You sure you authored this?"

"Why are you asking? Who would if not me?"

"You could have had it ghostwritten in India."

"Preposterous."

"Or somebody sent it to you and somehow, you have convinced the sender to let you publish his work under your name. Better yet, you paid him a small fortune for the story rights. But it won't work; these schemes never do. When this thing makes a hit, your secret collaborator will come out, and Oracle can't have that."

"And I am the one who has a reputation for making no sense, Peter uttered morosely."

"What do you expect?" Winston protested.

Peter was taking it all as if he were an eight-year-old boy accused of plagiarism, while Winston certainly wasn't enjoying the role he was playing. Why, he pondered incredulously, wasn't Peter acting like a man and stop the silly struggle? He felt like the other's passivity left him no choice but to persist in torturing him. He wasn't getting any pleasure out of the exercise.

"This is so much out of character, he explained. It is like you told me that you could fly from one trapeze to another, fifty feet off the ground in some circus. I wouldn't believe you. And this is like the same thing, isn't it? You, at fifty-six, and with your background, finding yourself capable of assembling words in the right order, producing such a story? This is beyond me."

"You know, Peter elucidated in his unbearably submissive manner, writing *Faith* wasn't that difficult. Once I decided to make it this way, I mean."

Why wasn't the man angry? "What gave you the idea? Winston muttered."

"The World Series of 2008."

"A World Series from a few years back." Winston repeated, making sure to show in his tone of voice the astonished perplexity that he felt. "From somebody who never, since I work here, uttered a word to me about professional sports, let alone baseball. I wouldn't risk asking you who Tiger Woods is. And yet, your first try, and you get it all right like you were John Grisham or John Connelly."

"It's not Einstein's theory of relativity we're discussing here, you know, Peter interjected."

Winston looked at the man. Artritis was intelligent. More than he was, no doubt about that. After all, the guy could do crosswords in fricking Latin. Was it possible, then, that he was so prejudiced against him that he could now be mistaken? Could this imploring buffoon be trusted? Was it possible that he had misjudged the fellow? He answered:

"True! We are now talking with our noses very near the ground, and I was under the impression that it wasn't in you to do that."

"The fact is that I can do anything that I put my heart into."

Somehow, this bluster caught the chief editor's attention. Why not, after all? Would Einstein be able to produce the Faith novel? He could if he had lived in the right time and put his mind to it. Sure, Peter was no Einstein but he was bright and he was to decide to use his brain gainfully, who was he, he Winston Farmer, to turn down whatever came out of such a process?

"That, you very well might, he admitted. At least, from where I sit, it certainly looks that way."

He decided he had tortured Peter enough. If he insisted he had done it, it might be true. Better make peace with the poor fellow. He picked up the manuscript and brandished it in the air. "As I already said," he repeated, "this impressed me very much. I mean, the fact that you could do it."

"I am glad…"

"Maybe, Winston compromised, I sold you short one time too many."

"Indeed, perhaps you did, Peter approved with a timid smile."

Why was the man incapable of looking him straight in the eye, though? He prepared to capitulate to his slightly younger co-worker's logic. "I have to say this," Winston carried on. "Whoever owned that story would have published it already. Hence, you must have written it after all. So, let's say that you have convinced me for now. As much as I still think it is quite an impossible tour de force that you have created, I am ready to believe that you might have performed the deed after all. Therefore, I must confess to you right now, I am overawed to my wit's end."

"So, Peter implored one more time, you think it's good?"

"You should know, Peter. Let us put down this insecurity of yours to the fact that your personal experience with literary success is near zero. We both know this is soon to change, don't we?"

Winston Farmer, looking very mercurial, raised himself from his chair. He took his visitor by the arm, leading him toward the exit.

"Let me check this out with some others in the field. Perhaps I was so caught up by the wonder of liking something that you wrote that the surprise alone got the better of me and altered my judgment."

"I do respect your judgment very much, Peter offered as he was exiting through the door the other had opened."

"Let me get back to you in a few days, will you? And then, I promise you the experience of a lifetime. Because, if I am right, and I don't doubt I am, this book will get you to places you never anticipated in your wildest dreams."

This was a prophecy that would come back to haunt both of them.

All who cared to read *Faith* submitted positive feedback. Most said they had enjoyed the story, some reading late at night to finish it. Winston had a friend at Eckerd College who worked in the creative writing section of their literature department. Eckert College looked upon Boca Ciega Bay, whose waters merged into Tampa Bay and blended into the Gulf of Mexico a few miles away on the other side of the strip of land that was St. Pete Beach and Pass-a-grille. Eve Lamont not only had liked the story, she had made her students read it and grade it according to her own set of standards and criteria. In exchange, Oracle would pay sixty dollars for each of those critiques, a sum that had helped a lot in ensuring the undergraduates very welcome collaboration. As they were adult would-be writers of both sexes, all ages, and multiple backgrounds, Winston had concluded that whatever judgment they would collectively produce in the end was well worth the money invested. Oracle could have published Peter's story, but as it was a rather small house, they didn't do much fiction, and what they did in that genre was not in the habit of reaching the New York Time's bestseller list. Winston believed that *Faith* had a good chance to interest a major house like Random, Bantam, Harper Collins, and such. Oracle would act as an agent, and in doing so, would ensure a fee. It could even coproduce the book by taking an interest in the venture. Furthermore, it might look better if *Faith* was to be picked up by an outsider since it would take out of the equation all the cheap comments about self-publishing and the vanity presses that otherwise would be sure to come their way from one corner or another. So, Winston prepared a letter of introduction with the best lines taken out of adjudications collected from his Eckerd College readership, as well as one titillating résumé of the tale. He followed with phone calls here and there, built a list, and fired his first salvo to those few he had thus selected. He didn't have to wait for very long because four days later, Marc Lafleur, his best friend in the business, called him out of the Penguin Group USA's headquarters in Manhattan.

"I like it, he said. But I will sell it to the boss only if you guarantee me complete exclusivity right this minute."

"Marc, he objected with a laugh. What is it with you this morning? You know I can't do that. What if I were to receive an offer and you come back to me in two weeks with the 'I am sorry' bit?"

"What I say, Lafleur countered, is I know what I'm doing. I know I can sell this package upstairs. But I will not convince the ninth floor to show much of an interest if the possibility of us being turned down exists. I must be able to tell them that they must act fast, and if they do, they will get the deal as long as it is fair. You know what I mean. We did this before…"

"It's a great story, Marc. You don't see the likes of it that often."

"Come now, Winston. After all, Peter Artritis is a perfect nobody."

"As you would be if you were to…"

"Anyway, the other interrupted. Give me until tomorrow at noon. I will have you a confirmation by then whether Penguin has an interest. And if I'm wrong, I'll owe you dinner next time you visit the Big Apple at the place of your choice. Do we have a deal?"

"Well, Marc, you better make sure the outcome is right, because you make me feel like a passenger in a Cessna, and I have to believe you when you say you can land the goddamn plane."

"Don't expect too much, though, you hear me?"

"My author doesn't care much about money. But you know I do. So, you beware. Seriously, Artritis wants to get published. Therefore, the usual conditions for a first timer will do just fine."

"So, Marc said eagerly, we have an accord?"

"Get that plane on the ground, will you?"

"I will but you must give us a chance…"

"Yup, he answered. You better come up with the right email tomorrow, though."

"You will get it, don't you worry."

"Or you will remember the dinner I will get out of you for the rest of your life, you hear me?"

And that was it. Winston had looked as his watch. Ten past eleven. He understood that Marc had most probably played him, as he would have already had the okay from his board to make him a proposition if he had pushed it. Whatever, Penguin was good, and to him, the knowing was better than the waiting. And now, he was sure *Faith* would get published, as he had known from the start. And it would most likely be with Penguin. He knew Marc. He would get a good deal out of him.

FAITH

PART THREE

20 o o o 20

"So, that was you?"

There was actual amazement in Joe's voice and composure.

"Who else?"

"How did you know?"

Manuel made a move with his hands that showed extreme annoyance at what he was about to say.

"Well, I saw the damned thing happen. That's all. Therefore, when the story got in the newspaper, or perhaps it was on television, anyway, one way or another, I knew that it was not the crazy daughter nor the mobsters nor the ex-husband, nor the flushed boyfriend. Why? It was an accident, and I was kind of surprised that they didn't think of that possibility themselves."

"Tough call to make, I would say. Highly unlikely."

"Whatever."

Joe was thinking really hard. This was too much. He felt uncomfortable. And it had nothing to do with the exiguity of the space he was in. He said:

"Then, you saw this happen before it actually made it public?"

"Exactly."

"Why didn't you warn anyone?"

"Didn't know the location. This vision of mine could have been anywhere. On the east coast, the Gulf, The Great Lakes, the Adriatic, or the Black Sea for all I knew."

"And still, from the TV or the newspapers, you were fully satisfied that you had the right event?"

"I had a good look at the woman and the way she was dressed. No place left for any mistake. And what about the silly cliché on her bumper? Love

Thy Neighbor! Beware thy neighbor would have been more appropriate to her circumstances, don't you think?"

Joe extracted himself from the chair. All throughout their meeting, Manuel had stayed put, stuck against Mike's desk. Now, there was no place left for both of them to move at the same time. So, Manuel didn't move while the older man opened the door, which he couldn't do properly because of the boy's presence behind it. Before leaving, Joe looked at the youngster and said:

"You take care, Son."

And then, he was gone.

Manuel waited fifteen minutes before leaving, but not before getting on a chair and having Mike give him a clipping.

21 o o o 21

One week left in September, and they were two games ahead of the Yankees. In the National League, the Phillies dominated, the more so now that they could count on Voodo Warhead in their ranks. They used him almost every day. What they were doing was taking the lead early in the game, which they managed easily with all the heavy hitters they had, and then, come the fifth inning, they would send the Voodo to the mound. The Warhead would finish it all up in his usual fashion, which was by striking out the opposition. Voodo was a chimera. A demon out of one's worst nightmare. He raised up dread, horror, and panic in all the NL players, managers, and owners, but didn't have such an effect yet on anyone in the American League.

Now ten million people around the world demanded to see Manuel at bats for the Rays. The pressure on Joe's shoulders had become intolerable. A day or two earlier, a Mexican clergyman had become a media celebrity for making a case that Manuel Garcia's not playing in the AL was race related. Why, Joe fumed, it was complete nonsense just to think this, let alone say it out loud, shouting such silliness any place that would have that priest, and there were plenty who did. The silly cleric who was never made to explain how come more than two thirds of the players that made up the Rays alignment were of Black American, South American, Mexican, or Cuban Spanish origin.

179

The Tampa Tribune had decided to honor the ten millionth respondent to the question "would you like to see Manuel play in a game" with a ten-thousand-dollar prize and a trip to Tampa for two, all expenses paid, to attend all the games of the end-of-season series, including the World Series, if Tampa should qualify. It came out that the happy winner was a European Greek used-car salesman who didn't know much about baseball, who couldn't remember having participated to the survey and who asked when he visited the Tropicana Field for the first time where the goals were. Luckily, he had asked in Greek and the interpreter hadn't cared to translate.

About that time, Joe decided to ask Horace, his lawyer, to check Manuel's story by calling The Santa Maria Police Department and learning what he could, and most of all, anything that would corroborate Manuel's tale. But when he called his lawyer's office, he learned that Horace was away on the east coast, involved in a case before some New York State jurisdiction with local members of the Bar who were working under his supervision, since his office had the plaintiff as a client. He wasn't expected back before the middle of October.

So much for substantiation.

He saw this setback as a sign. No way he would put the kid on the plate. What had he been thinking, anyway?

22 o o o 22

The Rays played the last game of their regular schedule against the Yankees, and at stake was the East Division Championship and automatic qualification into the end-of-season 2008 series. It was the most important game since the Texas Rangers were second in the West Division, and would beat the Rays for second best by one win if they lost tonight's match. Joe's team had slowed the tempo a bit, lately, while both Yankees and Rangers had multiplied victories in the last week or so, proving that they were right on the money, outdoing themselves when that counted, earning their manager and organization the ultimate praise, glory, and honor.

Everybody in town who had a bit of baseball in mind, and there were a lot of those, had a field day about why and how Joe had let slip his prevalence over the competition - not that it had ever been so big domination, but why? Some fans, who were not so articulate in their arguments, referred to Tampa Bay's statistics of July 2007 and their twelve-game lead over Chicago, to strengthen their gloomy reasoning, which was that the Devil Rays were declining into trifle and coming fast obliteration.

Around Joe, things looked frantic enough. Everybody was maintaining an air of artificial joviality and relaying instructions with such cheerful affectation that he would have thought he was living his last hours on earth while waiting for a giant comet to crash into the earth planet. It was so weird that when Joe was asked by some Japanese tourists where the lavatory was in the gigantic Tropicana building, he said: "Sure, no way, the Yanks don't stand a chance." So, that was the general atmosphere. But he knew he would win. He had been there. He would survive this.

Then Franck had called him and said to him that same afternoon,

"I got you that fellow under contract."

The silly business again. Ignoring it wouldn't do. Still, he asked:

"What are you talking about?"

"Come on, Joe, you know."

"Whatever, he grumbled, don't count on me to use the lad."

"You sure could welcome some help, wherever it came from, Joe."

"You want him to play, Franck, you come yourself into the dugout and you manage the team."

"You got it all wrong, Joe. I'm the owner. I pay you to do what you do. Dearly, if I may say so."

"Go to hell, Franck."

"Listen, Joe! What is there to lose? We drop that game tonight, we're history."

At that, the Rays manager repeated, like a mantra,

"No way. The Yankees don't stand a chance."

"I know, I know, but listen to me, Joe, if we trailed them in the ninth and needed to score one or two runs, you better see what the kid is worth. We understand each other, don't we, Joe?"

"Do I take this as a vote of non-confidence, Franck?" He asked.

"No, it's not, the other whispered like he was in a church. I have faith in you, Joe."

"Faith, he repeated. So that's what it's all about, isn't it, Franck?"

"They say faith moves mountains, preached the other."

Joe couldn't believe what he was hearing.

"Are you going pious on me, Franck?" He asked.

"Have a little respect for the beliefs of others, Joe."

The Rays manager could visualize the enormous beam of light that opened the owner's face from one end to the other. He said:

"Anyway, it is not your call to make."

"The Rays better not losing tonight's game without having given the boy a chance, you hear me Joe?"

"I hear you loud and clear, Franck."

"So, you do it."

And then the phone went dead.

23 o o o 23

Fate had it that they won that game against the Yankees. Quite easily, at that! Their ace pitcher took the lead early on and their heavy hitters did the rest. All the winning was done before the end of the fourth inning. Five to zero then, and the Yanks never recovered. After that triumph, it all went like in fairy tales where nothing could go wrong. They beat the Soxes, white and red, back to back, without hesitation or remorse. They were winning left and right, crushing their opponents in all kinds of ways, all players excelling and making the other teams look downcast, wasted, and clumsy.

They felt indomitable. They felt like nothing on earth could get at them. They felt great. They felt brave. They felt unique. They felt like winners. All those feelings were good. They were all ecstatic, and they were no longer afraid of the Phillies. They were no longer afraid of the Voodo, as they had started to call him in Tampa. Who was Voodo Warhead, anyway? And what a silly name he had. Warhead! Of that pétard, they would take care in time. They would defuse him, you wait and see.

So, that was the state of mind at the onset of the World Series. It was Tuesday, October 20, 2008. They were starting that night against Philadephia at the Tropicana Field. Since the signing of his contract, Manuel had been part of every game, in the dugout, sitting on the bench with the members of the team, in full uniform like the others, on a par with the greatest of players, being called and allowed to call legends of the sport by their first names.

Everybody was very nice to him, even if, sometimes, he noticed from their part some circumspection, some holding up, some artificiality into their otherwise apparent cordiality, as if they feared, against all reason, that too much of him could charm or bewitch or change them into a frog or something.

His agent had proved very dexterous in obtaining for him, a few weeks back, a Major League contract of one year for two million dollars—that was, what was left of the 2008 season. It meant that, in two weeks at most, his obligations and responsibilities toward the team would end and he could keep the money. One million and a half, of it since he had had to reimburse five hundred thousand dollars to The Tampa Tribune.

And he was in no doubt that when asked to perform his magic, he would score the required home run, and then, the world would be his to seize. He was ready to do his part, and anxious to do so. So far, the team had accumulated wins without his services. However, he knew, his time would come. It had to.

24 o o 24

Horace was back from New England. The case he had been working on there was postponed to the winter session of the Federal Court of Appeal. And when he had started to explain to Joe the intricacies of the jurisdiction and the fine points of the law as they applied to his Corporate Client, five minutes into that meaningless jargon had put Joe into a state. At last, he had interrupted,

"What is it you are doing, Horace?"

"Why, the point is, they misinterpreted Article 178 as they didn't know about Scott C. Willowdale and…"

"Por favor, Horace, tell me who the fuck you slept with in fucking Boston, for Christ's sake. That I can understand and disapprove of, by the way, since you are married with three kids. But please, do keep your judicial niceties to your black robe audience, will you?"

Horace caught the gist of Joe's meaning. After all, he was a lawyer. He was fast on his feet.

"You are right, Joe. I am sorry. I see all is going great for you, you doing the World Series and all that…"

"You got that one right. But…"

"I got your message. You phoned the office while I was away. You have my cell number and didn't call. So, it must not be so big a deal."

"I called you for a reason, though."

"What is it?" Horace then asked him.

And Joe told him about the case in Santa Monica. His lawyer said he would look into the matter.

<h1 style="text-align:center">25 o o o 25</h1>

The first game, the Rays had won easily. Four to zero. And their ace pitcher, Royal Davies, had proven his worth once more, limiting the very frustrated Phillies to four hits. No chance for the Voodo to show his six feet three inches black American frame at the mound.

The second engagement on November 22 was another story. They had still gotten the better of the National League champions, but it had been a bit more difficult. They had taken the lead again, but were never in position to ensure themselves real dominance and the early surrender of their opponents. It had gone like this:

One to zero.

One to one.

Three to one.

Three to two.

Three to three.

Four to three.

And it had stayed that way with horrible suspense into the ninth inning, when the Phillies put two men on bases. But then, Joe had used his own ace reliever, and if Willie Corrall wasn't as good or spectacular as Voodo Warhead, that night, he had gotten the job done.

October 24, they were in Philadelphia, Rocky Balboa's country. It was raining, cold, and windy. So that was it. The temperature had beaten them up really well! Like the team had been hit by a tornado. Nine to zero. Suddenly, matters were not looking so great anymore. Perhaps their little trip to prominence, fame, and everlastingness was not to be the walk in the park their past invincibility had made them to believe. But Joe knew better. Sure, he was disappointed. But not surprised, and certainly not losing spirit over the fiasco. This was bound to happen, and the sooner the better. They couldn't win them all. Not against a team the caliber of the Phillies, who had a great organization, great players, and the Voodo. The Warhead hadn't been put into its search mode yet, but that would come soon enough. And they would be ready. He had figured it all out. The only way to neutralize the Warhead was to get ahead and to stay ahead. The minute the Phillies had one point over the Rays, there would come the Warhead, and then, it would be the end of it. One hitter after the other, three strikes at a time, and who would be next? And that as long as it took. So, the Voodo, he shouldn't be allowed to pitch.

If he managed to do just that, they would win this thing.

October 27

The fourth game into the World Series had started well enough for the Rays. However, in the end of the fifth, all hell had broken loose, and in no time, the Phillies had gotten four hits, two stolen bases, and three points, leading three to two.

Joe changed his pitcher and so did the Phillies.

Voodo Warhead had been true to his reputation. Twelve strike outs in a row on forty-nine pitches. Joe's hitters were either batting at wind or looking at a baseball coming so fast it became invisible to their incredulous eyes. They finished that fourth game trailing the Phillies five to two since the Rays' relief brigade was not as good.

The team had made it back to Tampa quite dejected. While anybody, media or public, that cared to emit an opinion, had adapted their discourse to present circumstances, seeing the flaws in their previous reasoning, saying now in quite unanimous fashion the exact opposite of all their previous learned conjectures and claims.

The experts, whom one could look at on TV or listen to on the radio, were no exception. Nobody seemed to worry too much about defining what an expert was, anyway, the common wisdom being that an expert was someone who emitted an opinion that duplicated one's own, and a very great expert was someone who shared the multitude's beliefs. As a matter of personal policy, Joe stayed well away from the so-called experts, those commentators who prattled their way into dubious celebrity at the price of professional sports' efforts, sweat, and anguishes.

Franck had called him in the afternoon before the game.

"Still feel up to it, Joe?"

"What do you think, Franck?"

He was looking at his line up and found it missing. He had used all his best start-up pitchers and would have to make do with a young one that had been judged very promising by their scouts the year before, and had given them nine wins this year against eight losses. The recruit had a good fast ball and a pretty impressive curve, too, when he had a good day.

"We lost the last two, didn't we?"

Franck could be a real pain in the ass, sometimes.

"You know, he protested, they are the Phillies. Not a bunch of start-ups, or bumpkins, those…"

"What, Joe? You're not afraid of that lot, are you?"

"I kind of resent this, Franck."

"Sorry if I invade into your zone of sensibility, Joe. The point is, this World Series, you have to wrap it up for me."

"I'll do what I can. I don't carry a bat out there, Franck. You do know that, don't you? I'm just the manager."

"Speaking of a bat, Joe, there is one I sure would like to see in action."

"The little prodigy would have made no difference, he grumbled."

"Whatever. I gave this esoteric fucker 2,000,000, and the little son of a bitch owes me one grand slam for my money."

"I will see what I can do, Franck."

"You better do that, Joe."

Franck's voice grated like an old barn's door. And that was the last he heard of it as the communication went dead. Joe hated that kind of pressure, even if, in this job, he had had to learn to live with it. All those pushy owners that thought money could buy anything, a company, a boat, or a championship. Sometimes, he felt he had more than his share of other people's silliness and idiotic criticism.

Joe wasn't ready to let Manuel play. He would either win this thing without him, and then, no one would care to bother about the lad and his magic apparatus, or he'd lose. If that was to happen, he would be history in Tampa, anyway. Still, he would get out the same as when he'd gotten in. Whole, unbroken, self-preserved. He would not convert into mania and craziness. The world wanted to believe that the kid could do it. Let them. Believing was easy. Performing a miracle wasn't.

He knew well enough what all the believers would do after Manuel failed to give them that home run he seemed so sure he was able to procure. They would all look in Joe's direction and he would be the one to go into the Guinness Book of Records as the most credulous of them all. He would be called in eternity Joe Black, the sucker extraordinaire. No way was he going to permit that to happen. And screw Franck Richantall.

26 o o o 26

October 29

They say there is an advantage for the home team to play before their supporters. There is a never-ending debate between those who affirm this to be true, and the others who oppose the tenet as an unprovable doctrine. Still, it could make a difference, and in that night's game, the fifth in the confrontation, it most definitely did. The crowd was so loud, vociferous, and belligerent, that it couldn't have but stamped the fear of God into their opponents.

The Phillies had played badly; they had made three errors. The first was in the second inning. The left fielder let the ball drop after securing it safely in his glove. That had given the Rays two points. Later in the sixth, the shortstop had let pass through his legs one slow strolling baseball that the center fielder was so sure he would catch that he didn't move in time and he had to run after it, which cost him three or four additional seconds, enough for the Rays to score three more points. The Phillies had made it back to a semblance of competition in the eighth, but it was cut short at five to three. And, it finished that way.

The Rays were resolved to put the matter at rest the next Saturday in Philadelphia. They were determined to finish them, those recalcitrant Phillies, right there in their own turf. That would serve them right. That night, they would crush the bastards. They had been repeating the injunction so much that they often woke up reciting the words, and ended up believing them due to an human inclination that went like this: "If I said it, it must be true."

Unfortunately - mankind will never learn - nature doesn't work that way, and the sixth encounter was lost. Voodo again, coming after the Phillies, had made it three to two in the sixth. The Warhead grinned his way to total devastation of his adversaries' will to fight with his lightning-like pitching arm. What a pity, Joe had thought, this crazy circus moving back home again, and the ordeal to be duplicated one more time. He was tired. He was sick of the ceaseless strain.

And he was afraid. He had never won a World Series. Some managers did and others didn't. He had a good chance to make it into that exclusive fraternity, and still, this Tuesday, November 3, a few hours before the ultimate and final duel, he felt like the prize was so far away as to be almost out of his grasp.

27 o o o 27

Sunday November 3, 2008

They were in the middle of the seventh. The Rays were at bat. In the Tropicana Field, the fans were restive and jumpy. In the beginning of the fourth, one of the umpire's decisions had caused a roar of dissatisfaction, which had deafened the close space they were in, making it brutal and oppressive. In no time, a rain of junk had inundated the field. Fifteen full minutes had been needed to clean the ground and for the assistance, the players in the field, and the field itself to get back to normal.

Meanwhile, once the chaotic display of unrestrained emotion had passed and they'd been back in the game for a few minutes, there had been a ring from the in-phone communication line that connected both benches with the administration offices and the VIP boxes hanging up high under the gigantic building's ceiling. Sam Kouts, the Chief Umpire, took the call and then shouted in Joe's direction.

"For you, Joe."

Don Ferguson was at bat. He hit, and when Joe put the receiver to his ear, the small and very fast player was already at first.

"What are you waiting for, Joe?"

"Get out of my way, Franck, will you? You're starting to get on my nerves really bad. I am the manager of this team, I make the rules, and I will take no order from fucking nobody. You hear me Franck? So piss off."

"So, Joe, this is the way you want it, don't you?"

"Listen, Franck… Joe stammered, a little mollified."

He was interrupted by the thunder of fifty thousand yelling fanatics as Don Ferguson stole to second base. Willie Mack was pitching for the Phillies. There was one man out. Tom Gruber was at bat and had just missed a second time. The count was two balls and two strikes.

"I am all ears, Joe, said Franck when the pandemonium had subsided a bit."

"What I mean, Franck, is the Phillies are ahead seven to four. Ferguson is at second…"

The baseball arrived fast and Gruber saw it pass right on the plate at knee height.

Strike 3.

Joe sigh dispiritedly and carried on.

"We already have two out. Alvares is next. Why on earth are you pestering me right this minute? Getting a home run this instant will make it seven to six. Seven to six, Franck! We'll still lose the damned game."

"Well, seven to six is better than seven to four."

"That, Franck, is the most asinine observation of all time. What is it, your wife left you?"

"Find a way, Joe."

And he was no longer there. Joe put the receiver back on its cradle just in time to see Alvares hit a fly that got caught in center field.

28 o o o 28

They contained the Phillies in the eighth. Willie Mack dispatched them fast and decisively. One, two, three. The first, three strikes and out. The second, a hit that got caught by the shortstop and relayed in time to first base. The third, a foul ball that found its way directly into the catcher's glove.

The Phillies came very near in the ninth to add to their three-point advantage, but relief pitcher Pedro Montalva saved the situation for the Rays, that is, if there was anything left to be saved. Then it was their turn at bat. Tampa Bay's last chance to make it to immortality.

And that was when it all happened.

They got one hit. Then another. Men on first and second. Ensued a long interruption while the Phillies' manager confronted with his ace starting pitcher, Willie Mack. He could bring out the Voodo now, but he owed it to Mack to give him the chance to finish the job he had handled so well up to that moment. From where he was, Joe could see that Mack wanted to stay. Who wouldn't?

Avaredo, the Phillies' manager, let him.

And it looked like it had been the right decision, because the next two at bat had been struck out neat and clean, Billy King on three pitches and Elmore Glen on five. And then, Mitch Plante had hit the ball really softly and it looked like the second base would get it, but then the ball had made a strange rebound and gotten through to center field.

Seven to four. Three men on base.

The phone in Joe's breast pocket started playing, "The Star-Spangled Banner." He furrowed his brow. Franck again? Not on his cell! The game had stopped, and out of his left eye, he saw Willie Mack leaving the mound. Now, he thought, this will get us the Warhead. He took the call.

It was Horace. In the stadium, they were all shouting in cadence, "MANUEL, MANUEL, MANUEL!" He couldn't hear a thing. The clamor was deafening.

"Horace? Is that you? I don't hear you so good."

"Joe? You there?"

"Yup, and as you must know, quite busy right this moment."

"Just one thing. I got a call from the office a few minutes back, about that business of yours in California. Santa Monica. Is that it?"

Voodo was now walking to the mound. He would need five minutes to drill himself to perfect execution. In the mouth of his cell, Joe shouted over the rhythmic wavelike outcry of the crowd,

"Where are you? It's past ten o'clock at night here. Where is this office of yours that works at such an hour?"

"Hawaï. I'm in Honolulu, countered Horace. Just finished a round of golf and one lawyer here talked this morning with somebody in our Boston office. Someone who spoke today with a guy named Bill Murray from the Santa Monica Police Department. And that fellow, Murray, he confirmed all you told me. He confirmed having received a letter from one Manuel Garcia saying that the bullet that killed his victim had originated from two kilometers off the coast out of a .22-caliber rifle, long-range…"

Joe interrupted the lawyer. He needed to hear no more. This was a sign. It had to be. Arthur calling now to tell him about Manuel, when there were now three men on base and they needed four points to bag the World Series. He knew now what he would do.

"Thank you so much, Arthur. This helps. I'll explain later. I must leave you now."

He put his cell back in his pocket and approached the bench where Manuel sat. He asked the boy:

"Do you feel like giving us that grand slam now, Son?"

The other was already on his feet.

"I kind of worried you wouldn't ask."

"I don't know. What if this doesn't work?"

"Then, why are you letting me hit?"

Joe gestured to the crowd with his right arm.

"You hear them? If I don't, I may not get out of this place alive."

At that, Manuel smiled. There was so much confidence in that grin that it got Joe into a kind of poetic disposition.

"Don't you worry, chief. I'll prove them right. I will have that ball out of this field in no time."

"I know you will, Son. I know you will, he repeated, and maybe he was at that moment believing what he was saying. As Manuel started moving out of the dugout, Joe caught him by the elbow, turned him around to face him, and then he scribbled something on a piece of paper on his block note, which he detached, folded in two, and put in the back pocket of Manuel's Devil Rays pants uniform."

"Let this stay where I put it. You may look at it after you win us that World Series. Now Son, you go out there and you hit the Warhead into shame and oblivion."

As soon as Manuel showed himself outside the dugout, the Phillies' manager ran to the chief umpire and complained. Sam made a sign to Joe, who joined them both. On seeing Manuel, the crowd had gone ballistic.

"He is not on the players' list for tonight."

"What about that?" Kouts shouted at Joe.

Who then had addressed his grumbling opponent.

"Cut the damned red tape, will you, Avaredo? The public will kill me if I don't play the wonder boy. Bob, you've got this in the bag already. Don't tell me you believe this shit about the kid's magic. What, you think the Voodo won't be able to take care of him?"

And then, Kouts, who liked a good show like anybody else, said:

"Well, the kid never played pro baseball in his life. What are you afraid of, Bob?"

Avaredo spat on the ground to mark his disapproval.

"Shit. Do as you like. Let's play ball."

And leaving the other two, the Phillies' manager had got to the mound where everybody could see that he had a very serious talk with the Voodo that left a scowl on his grim face.

29 o o o 29

The people in Tropicana Field were shouting so loud that it sounded like a hurricane was hitting the place, without the wind. It was a rumble of the variety that gave gooseflesh. It was intimidating. It was belligerent. It was invasive. It was dreadful and alarming. It was crazy. It was hypnotic. It created dizziness. It was like looking straight into the eyes of insanity.

Joe felt giddy and had to touch the wall to steady himself. He then saw Manuel as he was taking his position at the plate. The boy was now mimicking the usual preparatory moves of swinging his instrument this way and that, and looked foolish, doing that, as if it would change anything. Joe mumbled through his teeth:

"Don't overdo it, kid. Stop the silly display with that bat and show your stuff."

At the mound, the Voodo looked at the scene as a spider would look at a fly. Joe caught a signal the catcher sent him with his free hand.

So, that was the way Avaredo wanted to play this thing. Joe was not that surprised. Always expect the unexpected, was his motto.

And that was when the most preposterous performance in professional sports occurred in front of fifty thousand astonished and unbelieving eyes.

Voodo threw Manuel, one after the other, four balls, all very high and very far from the plate, as if he wouldn't want to risk any chance of Manuel trying to take a swing at them. It was all very fast, and very disappointing, like a balloon popping.

Manuel, looking a bit dejected, moved to first base, and the player at third jogged along to the plate, making the game seven to five.

The hitter Joe sent after that was no match for the Voodo. Three pitches and out.

The Phillies won. The crowd went catatonic. They were like zombies on a set of *The Walking Dead*. A very sorry spectacle.

30 o o o 30

Joe was alone in the dugout. He was taking his time, looking around and telling himself that he wouldn't be there long, now. He'd lost the World Series to Franck Richantall's immense ambition. The hell with it. He would get another job in another organization somewhere. He was rich enough. He was worth a few million and could live on that easily. He didn't need that much. He wasn't worried about his future.

He heard somebody call his name. Was it Barbara? When he saw it was her, his heart constricted. He got up and said,

"I didn't know you would be here. If I had, I would have gotten you good seats."

"I am sorry for you, Joe. I know what this meant to you."

She took something out of her blouse pocket. It was very small, a little blue earring that he recognized instantly. She offered him the object.

"Look what I found, she said. Couldn't get my hand on the other, though."

She smiled at him. He was twenty years old again.

"You remembered?"

He had given her the trinket when he was nineteen. It was one of the first gifts he had bought for her, three months into their relationship. Her birthday present. She had been eighteen at the time. That night he had touched her under her blouse for the first time. Had known then the feel of her perfect skin. He still felt, thirty-five years later, the sensation of total bliss that her letting him do that had produced in him.

From around his neck, he produced a chain and showed her, hanging from it, the other piece of the same pair of hearings, a small morsel of blue glass nicely carved in elaborate gold-looking metal. She, in his mind still his wife, moaned, or not a moan, but a sigh, and said.

"Oh, Joe."

"You know me, he acknowledged, always the romantic."

He was surprised to see tears in her eyes. They were in his, too. She murmured,

"What has become of us?"

"Well, we grew old. That's all."

"I am so sorry, she said."

He assumed she was referring to his team's loss. He gave her his best smile.

"Too bad, he said, that I'll move out of Tampa just when we started to talk to each other again."

She took his hand and held it.

He let her.

31 o o o 32

There could be some truth in the saying that faith moves mountains. The Baltimore Orioles had offered Manuel a ten-million-dollar contract for three years, and an undisclosed bonus package depending on the number of home runs he procured the team. The organization figured that it would cost them a bundle, and that it would be worth the money.

However, Manuel never got to bat even once in the Major League. Every time he faced a pitcher at the plate, that pitcher would give him the first base free. He finished his very short career in baseball by earning himself the nickname of Mister Base on Ball.

After three years of the same, he quit professional sports with enough money that he'd never have to think of the damned nuisance ever again. Then he went to college and became a lawyer.

After receiving his law degree from the University of Tampa, he had a small party at his mother's place. While he was in his old room, he saw in one closet his old Devil Rays uniform that he had discarded after the team lost that last game against the Phillies that day in November 2008. At that instant, he recalled Joe Black giving him that piece of paper. He had completely forgotten about it. Could it still be where he had put it? Those clothes had been in a wardrobe since time immemorial. His mother had cleaned them and put them there for him to pick up at his leisure, and they both had forgotten the matter afterward.

He slipped his hand in the back pants pocket, and yes, he felt something. It was there. He took the piece of paper in his hand, opened it, and read Joe Black's washed-out scrawl in capital letters.

IF THEY LET YOU.

He recalled the time, more than seven years back, now, he had said to Joe,

- I will have that baseball out of this field in no time.

If they let you, Joe had written. Not bad for a prediction.

Manuel smiled.

And that was that.

THE END

Manhattan, New York, marsh 2017

Sister Simonne, who was of French origin, dispensed religion classes for the senior students at the Convent of the Sacred Heart, on east Ninety-First Street in Manhattan. Sacred Heart was an all-girl school. It was very exclusive. Sister Simonne was short and dressed like the fifty-one-year-old spinster that she was, classic and conservative. Her pupils liked her, for she was perceived as nonthreatening, her field mystical and spiritual seen by most as insignificant. Nobody expected much from her lectures. Nevertheless, she had that quiet determination proper to those on a mission. Every day that she confronted her very bored audience, she would consider herself successful if she happened to catch the interest of just one or two of the young women facing her. As for the rest of the class, they were at best benevolent, sometimes hostile, and always patronizing. Sister Simonne was sensible enough to attribute the occasional resistance and hostility to the need of a few to mark territory. This was why she ignored the stifled laugh that her discourse provoked in certain quarters, and she kept reading in her clear and resounding voice that contrasted with her restricted frame.

She was reading comments out of St. Thomas d'Aquino, St. Augustin, and other pillars of the Catholic faith, but St. Thomas d'Aquino more than all the others combined, since there seemed to exist between the two a special connection. One could hear the resonance of her words when she shared passages of the Summa Theologiae, so luminous that it looked as if the words were irradiating out of her. Still, it wouldn't reach the kids who, in their present circumstances, didn't care much for self-induced substance-free nirvana. At that moment, for instance, one sunny Friday afternoon in late April, they could see Sister Simonne's eyes roaming without seeing, those same eyes with the myopic and contented quality that characterized people in the know. Those few that had made the trip to the other side of the mirror, where revelations would come your way depending on the right gesture or correct incantation to show readiness to be saved.

Through the open windows a slight breeze blew papers off a girl's desk and she bent to pick them up. From a church nearby, bells rang. Sister Simonne finished the sentence she had already started reading and seemed on the verge of initiating another one. She looked at the clock on the back wall, a place nobody else dared to visit since it needed a contortion of the neck and shoulders. One risked being caught at it, which drew the taunts of professors, who could be, when provoked that way, quite ferocious in their sarcasm, giving witty observations that could make a crowd of hysterical teenagers die laughing. Those unfortunate transgressors who found themselves on the wrong side of their elder's humor would painfully remember it for life. At last, Sister Simonne pushed both sides of her book against one another and the result was a bang, like if a door had been made to close hard in its frame. That got the class's full attention. All the girls stared at their professor with uneasy apprehension.

"Might as well stop now, she decreed."

"Now, we won't ever be able to find our way to that place again, one girl in the front row said sarcastically."

Here and there erupted some burst of contained laughter. From the middle of the room, one anonymous girl snapped loud and clear,

"Any page will do."

Sister Simonne moved toward the student who had talked last. "So, Marie Claude," she proclaimed, "I presume that you voice the views of all your comrades."

She placed the book in front of the good-looking, freckle-skinned, yellow-haired schoolgirl.

"Before we all leave, let us see if you can find that place."

Whatever bookmark that should have been there had disappeared. Marie Claude took the volume and let it rest on her desk, where it opened by itself. She looked as the pages settled. She then picked up the treatise and started to read aloud from a page of her choosing. Her voice proclaimed, as calm and unconcerned as it could be:

"God has created the universe out of nothing…ex nihilo. And then he also created time, so that time and the universe have coexisted since day one."

The nun took the volume away from her.

"Those are not the author's words. You are making them up."

"They were your own last words, though. Or the gist of it, at least."

As it wasn't far from the truth, Sister Simonne let that pass. Instead, she said, addressing the whole assembly of students:

"Time. What an interesting notion it is."

"Hard to conceive, someone interjected. How could such a notion could have been created? After all, why would time need to be created?"

"So, their teacher said, I see that there are some among us who are adept at formulating questions. I shall ask all of you, then, to produce a one-thousand-word essay on this very subject. I will collect your work same time next week."

If a lesson was to be learned from that exchange, it is that educators always have the last word.

The two girls faced each other from both sides of a booth-enclosed Formica table with its cracked vinyl upholstered benches. Outside, they could see passersby walking alongside boutiques and traffic fighting for every few feet of asphalt two cars could occupy at the same time. It was a long time since they had had snow on the streets. Four in the afternoon was the hour when schools and colleges in the vicinity poured out their flow of young people. Some were in the habit of stopping at Paulie's Corner to sip a Coke or a milk shake.

"Hello, you guys. What is it with you, Roxanne? You look like you are gonna to be sick."

"You got that right, Marie Claude acknowledged the newcomer. Please, Marcelle, tell us a joke. I can't think of any others that will remove this dejected façade from Roxanne's face."

"What is it? Marcelle asked Roxanne, you don't care for the menu?"

A plump woman in uniform stopped in front of their table, ready to write down their order. To tiresome Marcelle, Roxanne burst out, "Get lost. We came here to do some work."

"So, asked the waitress standing beside them, will it be the usual?"

A look from Marie Claude gave her the answer she needed, and she departed. As for Marcelle, she was hailed to another table by the people she'd come to mix with in the first place. From behind the counter, they could hear the sound of the machine that was mixing their milk shakes.

"So, we work, then." Marie Claude suggested as she extracted from her purse a flacon filled with a yellowish substance. She opened the miniature container and put a few drops on the tip of one finger, which went behind both her ears in a kind of mechanical gesture.

"You want some?"

"Why? You think I smell, the other snarled."

"Ooh là là! Aren't we in a horrible mood today? Why is that? That silly composition we got stuck with?"

"Thanks to you."

"Oh you the poor lad, Marie Claude mocked her friend. "I will do yours, what do you say?"

"Don't be idiotic."

"It is called Éternité. Maman sent it from Paris."

"How is that possible? Roxanne complained. I am the last to learn this."

"Time…the universe. Boundlessness, eternity…"

"You should have told me, complained Roxanne."

"…and God."

"You are leaving, and frankly, it doesn't seem to distress you a bit."

"As if I could change anything in the situation, Marie Claude muttered with a sigh. For sure, it hurts me, but what is there to do? All my life, it has been this way. My father is a diplomat who always move us from one place to another. Romanichels, that's what we are. Anyway, we both are finished here at Sacred Heart. And you're moving back to Tampa with your father this summer."

"Still, we would have managed. But now, you are going back to France."

Their milk shakes came and both girls took a sip.

"For a few months," Marie Claude tempered, "and then, some shit place in the Middle East. No, you are the one being fortunate to have a place you can call home."

"You could say you don't want to follow your family. Ask them to let you stay here."

"And make an American out of me? They think I have enough of that already."

"What will become of me? Roxanne exclaimed, her eyes watering."

Marie Claude took her hand in hers and smiled.

"You have a family. Your parents..."

They are divorced.

"But they might make up, won't they?"

"This movie business is not helping a bit, though."

"How romantic, Marie Claude chuckled."

"Dad doesn't care much about all that."

"What do you mean? You told me that it was all like in the book. That your mom had left your father because he was like mine, had his family moving around all the time and your mom having her own career to think of"

"You made this all up, Roxanne snapped back. Pestered me with all your conjectures, and now, you pretend I am your source?"

"Still, your dad, he is the real character in that book, isn't he?"

"He has been the Devil Rays' manager from 2006 up to 2014. Since then, he pilots the Chicago White Socks."

"And that would make you Thalia and your mother would be Barbara."

"We discussed all that before. This *Faith* you like so much is fiction, as its author has repeated over and over from day one of publication. It has nothing to do with reality. Furthermore, I don't have a silly republican brother. And my mother has a new husband whose name is Edward. We all live here now."

"What about the old one? Will Barbara return to her true love?"

"How can you ask me this at a time like this? You're leaving me. Soon, you will be in exile, 4000 miles out in some desert land or the other and all you think of is associating my family and me with characters in this book you happen to like."

"You did too."

"As if I cared."

"You should. It is your folks, after all."

"Will you stop that nonsense?" Roxanne suddenly erupted. "What's wrong with you? Is this your idea of facilitating our breaking up? You making jokes about my mom and dad's past relationship, inspired by a book that I am quite certain neither of them have read?"

She remained silent for five seconds, after which she added, "Edward did, though. He found the book in my room after he heard on his car radio a silly panel of Monday morning quarterbacks discussing him, as if he was some character in an afternoon soap opera."

"Did he?"

"It sure didn't make him happy at finding from that bunch that people were discussing his private life on the air."

"Still, they met that day when the Rays lost that last game against the Phillies, like in the book."

"They are my parents. Sure they met. They do all the time. What do you think?"

"So, Marie Claude exclaimed, that part was true."

Roxanne shrugged, her composure that of a harassed animal.

"Not quite like you imagine. They met, yes. Why wouldn't they? Eight years ago, my father was for a time one of the most popular men in this country. His team almost won the 2008 World Series. Furthermore, he got us good seats in Tropicana Field. Do you remember that game when they were ahead three to two and could have finished the Phillies then and there?"

One of those tickets was for Edward. Roxanne's stepfather had had a golf tournament and had decided he would pass on that trip. So they had brought Marie Claude instead. They had flown to St. Petersburg one long October weekend. She had been nine years old at the time. They enjoyed the game, but the Rays had lost, like in the *Faith* narrative.

"Yet, she made contact. Did she tell you about it?"

"You are being ridiculous. Of course they had contact. They had been married twenty years. They had one child together. That child being me. And then, he had to pass on the tickets, didn't he?

"I don't mean that kind of connection."

"You make all this look like it was a conspiracy. Can't you tell the difference between fiction and real life?"

"Can you?"

"I am the one about to lose her best friend, and I act the part. What about you?"

"Your father never remarried."

"He was hurt bad when it happened. It was difficult, then, not to hate my mother for what she had done."

"Did he carry a piece of her jewelry around his neck, like Joe Black did?"

"Please, stop, will you? You can be a real pain, you know when you put yourself to it. Still, my mother once told me that he was a good man, and that she had loved him.

"Does she still?"

"They both have a new life. Made new choices. At least my mom did. What would be the point?"

"Perhaps she realized in all those years that she made a mistake."

"They have been married ten years, Marie Claude…"

"Maybe Peter Artritis knows more about this than you think. What if he knew both your parents and they inspired him to write what he did? They all lived in Tampa at the time. They could have met."

"I can't argue this no more, Roxanne grunted, not yet angry but on the verge of becoming so."

"Come on, now. Don't clam up. There must be something right in my conjectures. I am sure your mother met with your father after the game and something happened and Peter Artritis found out."

"As if she would tell me if that was so. Whatever, I would know. And I owe to Edward to uphold his relationship with mother. Their union has been a success. It's not something susceptible to break down like in this story you drive me crazy with. How childish you can sometimes be, Marie Claude."

"Your father didn't make it a secret. I mean that he still loved her. You told me so yourself."

"You should know better. This was the unfortunate result of us both having read the FAITH novel and yes, there were some similarities between mine and Joe Black's family and the Artritis book. So I might have overplayed my romantic hand and imagine things for no higher motive than wanting to make an impression on you. And have some fun in the process. I didn't know that it would fuel your lunatic side as to become obsessive and compulsive."

"Now you are being unreasonable. Better work on St. Thomas d'Acquino, then."

"Perhaps we should, Roxanne agreed."

But neither did. Instead, Marie Claude said:

"Then, he didn't tell her that he still loved her."

"Perhaps he had ways to show her he did. I don't know. With all your nonsense, I find it difficult to differentiate between what the book suggests and my father's real actions, or what he might have told me over time about him and mom."

Marie Claude pulled paper and a pen from her school bag, putting them on the table between them. Her silent message was, "You prefer St. Thomas. I will give you St. Thomas." However, with her mouth, she said:

"Yet, don't you find it singular that both Joe Black and your mother match so well?"

"I am afraid it is coincidental, countered her friend." It was clear Roxanne made a visible effort to keep her voice low. "Don't try to see anything more into this. What a blabbering idiot I've proven to be, letting you go that far with this delusion of yours."

"TV show hosts started this circus to boost their ratings. We just dipped into their spinnings."

"Still, if my father were to know about his being part of our numerous conversations on that subject, he would be disappointed. He would be in his right to expect more discretion out of me."

"This may be so, Marie Claude graciously conceded. However, your father, who isn't Joe Black, has seen his contract renewed with the White Sox for three years and this was two years ago; and next year, he will be sixty or so. Time to retire. No more running around the country in search of a team to coach." She smiled mischievously at the other girl, adding, "I am telling you, they will make up."

"Don't start this up again, please."

"L'éternité alors. Better talk of that. Eternity, the universe, and time."

XIV

A few months after that meeting between the girls, it had been announced by a Hollywood major studio that it had bought the movie rights for *Faith*. The book had hit the stores just in time to find its place under Christmas trees. The baseball fairy tale was on the bestseller list of all the newspapers that counted in the country, and elsewhere. Its author, Peter Artritis, had become the darling of the media, being invited to more programs that he could possibly attend to. The public had even been told which actors were to play the leading roles. Tommy Lee Jones was to interpret Franck Richantall, while Kyle Chandler would do Joe Black, with Annette Benning as his wife.

At first, Peter liked the whirlwind of attention. After all, he had been ignored all his life. Finding himself suddenly at center stage with everybody around playing the role of a complacent sycophant, clapping their hands at anything that came from his mouth and debating later to uncover the hidden meanings of his most insipid declarations, was a first. Not to say he had no originality of his own, but being himself, whatever he said in an interview was most likely to be beside the point. Which explained that compulsion of others to discover the correct interpretation of all the great man's statements. These critics were quite good at what they did, though, and the collection of jumbled nonsense they built up out of barely anything certainly demonstrated to Peter that the end result of such analysis looked better than his initial enunciation had. He came to believe that he pronounced maxims whenever he talked. As for those who worked with him and knew him well, the question they hadn't yet formulated to his face was how such a low caliber had shot a bullet so much out of its predicted range.

At the same time, some part of him didn't enjoy the new existence. That part, he did his best to keep away from his conscious mind. The intense public scrutiny to which he was now subjected didn't help. He, who had always slept easily, lost that ability. He began using pills. Nightmares jolted him awake at dawn, with his pajamas all wet, and his heartbeat so fast that it scared the hell out of him. Angela, the first time such an incident happened, was sure her husband was having an attack or something. He reassured her. He blamed the medication. He blamed the mattress. There were too many blankets. He blamed his diet. He blamed anything but, and he knew it. He was afraid. He understood very well what his problem was. He would have liked to discharge part of his load, if only by telling the truth to his wife. However, he was not ready to disclose that much, because then, she would know. He couldn't resign himself to that. Yet! He knew if he were to tell her that she would be there for him. He could count on it. Yet, better to wait. The relief she would provide was the trump card he kept as a last measure.

The fame he now experienced came with nasty side effects. He realized that he couldn't hold his new station better than a man who makes a fool of himself after a few stiff drinks. He sensed he was losing control. He felt that getting admired for something he hadn't done wasn't fun. The louder the cheers and applauds, the worst the perturbation. What about the movie business? The success was immense, then. His mind couldn't take it anymore. He longed for the ordinary existence he had left behind. The life he'd had before. He couldn't be happy with being described in the media as an individual he wasn't, and would never be. He was now a character in a play without any director to prompt him with the right dialogue or tell him how to react at another actor's intrusions. He couldn't do it. He dreaded the moment when he would be confronted with his accumulated platitudes. The day would come when someone would do the math and realize that the figures didn't add up. That he was a fraud, an impostor who couldn't have written *Faith*, no more than he could have flown a helicopter. Surely, any time now, one of those show hosts who cared to invite him would ask him the question that would make him trip, provoke a response on his part that would expose him for the swindler he had become.

Angela could see that Peter wasn't his usual self. As she had enjoyed her new prominence of being the wife of a very successful author, she couldn't make out why her long-time companion didn't seem to relish all the attention that came his way. Not only that, but he no longer had an appetite, and he complained of not sleeping properly. He would start crying for no reason. These were signs. Her husband had been a simple man with simple tastes and needs. Peter had never suffered from mood swings, let alone depression. That same man was now imploding right in front of her when triumph had at last berthed alongside his very own dock.

Which made her think. She remembered when Peter had introduced her to Faith seven years before. So long ago that somehow, the seditious reflections she had entertained at the time had been put aside, just to come back with a vengeance. Nowadays, the disturbing speculation constantly occupied her mind, a very annoying and repetitive concept that she had to fight over and over. The notion that the Peter she knew might not be the author of Faith. But if it wasn't him, who, then? This was the only reasonable explanation for the long waiting at publishing the novel and then, that disaster zone they had penetrated early in the winter after a brief period of felicity, those first few months of waiting to get the book into their hands, oh those days had been heavenly, full of laughter and happy projections. All the old doubts born out of troubling inconsistencies had been put away in blissful euphoria. It had been like they had both awakened into a new world of magical anticipation where reality gave way to fantasy. The period he had been planning and making the book ready for publication was the best they had had, with the proofing and accepting the congratulations of friends, colleagues, and coworkers. Yet, after the book had been published in its hard cover edition and had become an immense success, the media had taken notice. From there, the pressure had started to build.

They were approaching the end of 2017. A big studio was making a movie out of Faith. That was when things had turned bad.

—∘∘•❈•∘∘—

2018

The film business had been a calamity. Angela could well see it now. What had until then been no more than a literate success with an impact limited to those who read books grew instantly to gigantic proportions when the story made it out of the newspapers' literary page and got upgraded to their cinema section. It multiplied by ten the crazy scrutiny of the unquenchable medias over her spouse's slightest actions. Peter was the living proof of that old saying's validity, "As long as you stay quiet, you do not prove yourself a fool." Which he wasn't really. He was highly gifted and intelligent. His problem was thinking ahead of others and forgetting he was doing so. People resisted those who couldn't formulate straight answers that fit their expected anticipation. That was Peter's way. Hence he had been dismissed in the past. He didn't look like the type of person he was now trying to impersonate, and it showed. His "bons mots" or witticisms were of a kind that might have made an impression on an audience made out of fans of his own writing. His attempts at jokes always fell flat on the ground. Whoever heard his humor invariably let go of a little inquisitive giggle and worked hard afterwards trying to figure out where it was coming from. It wasn't difficult for Angela to see what was inappropriate in Peter's performance. She kept wondering why he couldn't do what a ten-year-old kid would easily, which was to adapt his discourse to present circumstances. Was that too much to ask? But this was her husband. He was that way. He always had been. She liked that side of him, though. Who cared if others didn't?

He was depressed. That must be it. But why would he be, in a time of triumph? That was the question, wasn't it? That was Peter, all right. Doing the unexpected. Being unforeseeable. Not being able to perform properly in the world he lived in. When he managed to do something people liked, he conducted himself in such a way that he looked defeated and miserable.

While the movie was playing in theater all over the country, Angela drove Peter one night to the St. Pete General Hospital Emergency, where he was given sleeping pills of a stronger variety. They had kept him as he was judged in such a state as to merit a psychiatrist's evaluation. That episode had been three months ago, and since then he was under a light medication. She made sure he honored his weekly appointment with the therapist. This had helped somewhat.

They had made a movie out of his novel. He should have been happy with this development. Anybody in his place would have been. She would. He wasn't. Once he had said cheerfully, "They will put this tale on the big screen." And now that he was proven right, it was like some calamity had befallen him. She didn't know what was to be done with Peter. She might have to question him. How was she supposed to do that? She had no clue. What if she was wrong and he realized what wild suppositions she had entertained? Perhaps it was just a matter of him not being so great at handling good fortune, as was Dr. Sopratee's opinion. The learned man's advice had been: withdraw. Get him out of the country. Avoid the spotlight. Retire. Let Winston Farmer handle the mechanics of his success.

The more Angela pondered over the sorry situation, the better she liked the concept of leaving it all and disappear. This had to be the best solution to their dilemma. They had money. But that was the point, wasn't it? They had no need of money. Whatever Peter had done or didn't, it couldn't have been for the money it might have brought them. Proving himself would have been more like it. That he was somebody to be reckoned with in the world of literature. To get the approbation of his peers. Why was it, then, that when it was given to him, praise consumed him like it was acid on metal? Or was it the secret of having done something wrong that was eating him away?

In that case, the best way to cure him, like indigestion, would be for the truth to get out. The sooner the better, come what may. And if she was wrong in her deduction, he would deny it and she wouldn't dispute him. She would accept his word. All she cared to do was give him an opportunity. She knew her husband. He was distressed. She could see it in his drawn face and haggard composure. He needed help. He yearned for her to take charge, as she usually did. He wanted her counsel. She was prepared to give it to him. Whatever he had done, she wouldn't judge him. That was her plan. That was what she must do. She would act upon it then. That very day, he had been invited to the David Letterman late show on CBS.

- It will be Thursday, next week he had announced to her, his voice wild and frantic.

It was Monday. Ten days left. This was big. Better wait before hustling Peter too fast or too much. She would coach him as best she could, and later, after that final public appearance, she would put an end to that sorry media circus that was swallowing her husband alive. She might even convince him to announce on TV that they were leaving on a trip around the world.

Gulfport, Mississippi 2018

The strip mall was on Thirtieth Avenue, near Thirteenth Street. There once had been an Albertson's supermarket in that mall. The store had brought in a lot of traffic. It had closed in the mid-nineties, and where the Albertson's used to be, there was now a thrift shop, a storage facility, and a Blockbuster video store, plus a few other business operations that cared for a deadbeat kind of clientele. Here and there, an empty space could still be found. Those were advertised with big rental signs on their cheap-looking windows, all smeared with crude graffiti. Bill Mitek, the agent whose smiling grin illustrated those ads, was actually walking the premises accompanied by two nice-looking and well-dressed young men who could have been doctors, accountants, or lawyers on the make. They didn't care that much for the location's shabbiness and irrelevance. What they did like, though, was the easy access, the parking facilities, and the area's latent potential to provide the required number of patrons. Forget about the accountant. It was more like a doctor or criminal lawyer's place. In that mall, there was also a restaurant and a barber shop, both of them at opposite sides of the U-shaped building, with its open space looking on Thirtieth Avenue. The parking lot was mostly empty at that late hour, except for migrants in their beat-up RV. Mitek knew about them. They were part of his job's bad side, those irritating distractions that needed to be dealt with and that ended up stealing all the fun out of one's performance. What was he to do? He had called the authorities numerous times. The local constabulary had proved ineffective at protecting the property against the gypsy-like community's invasion, and considered the task of cleaning them out below their station. It befitted the services of a security firm that sent them weekly reports of wrongful trespassing, and could produce witnesses at will and for a fee, if they were of a mind to make it a court case. They had done it before. Fines had been distributed to offenders no longer there, replaced by a new batch of property violators. The syndicate that owned the mall would need to threaten to sue the town again if it wanted to obtain some services for the taxes they paid. Meanwhile, Mitek was better off looking the other way.

Pralina Sanchez got behind the wheel of her old Toyota Corolla parked not far from Al's Diner, where she had been working as a waitress for the last twenty-two years. There, she was known as Lyn. She had a twenty-four-year-old daughter who was six months short of becoming an accountant. Irma was still living in her mother's two-bedroom condo not far from the Gulfport/Biloxi International Airport. Their second-floor unit was one out of sixteen in a cluster of similar buildings that had once formed a gated community, which no longer existed after it had been divided into parcels of eight independent edifices. A long time ago, the early occupants had enjoyed beautiful common grounds and spaces that served them to practice sports, relax beside pools and spas, exercise in a gym, get books from a small library, and meet each other in a multitude of shared activities. Not anymore, though. Original collective structures had been integrated into more units at the millennium's beginning. They were still there, unfinished, work abandoned, a sorry display, somebody else's loss. At first, the residents that had been left with the mess created by those short-on-cash investors had tried to maintain the association they needed to apportion services, right of ways, and some degree of civility. All such efforts had fizzled out, though. Gates had been erected. New names had been invented. Pralina's stucco four-story dwelling became "The Rose Garden Drive." It was a ridiculous name, if one were to consider the absence of a garden, let alone grass or trees. Pralina's place was all concrete, asphalt, and a backyard made out of greenish gravel. Nobody complained about the lack of greenery. It would have been considered bad taste to mention it. You wanted nice, you go live near the water.

She got the key into the ignition and started the car. It resisted her at first, and then came to life in a vacillating mode, all dull and irresolute. She could smell the oil lubricating its way past all the engine's metallic objections. As she breathed carbonate monoxide into her lungs, the notion of suffocating herself made her think of that woman they were about to execute by lethal injection later that month. That same afternoon, she had had two patrons who'd been discussing the Zielgard's case while she served them late dinner. He was a physician who'd died under mysterious circumstances. But not so mysterious, at that. The state District Attorney had convicted a local witch of murder for having consorted with evil spirits to have the wretched drunkard doctor taken out of this world. The woman had certainly not denied the fact. She had even come forward, claiming full responsibility for the deed, telling first the media and later the members of her jury that she had wished Zielgard eternal rest and then had made the proper arrangements for death to happen at a time and place she had correctly predicted. As for motives, she believed the physician responsible for her daughter not surviving her child's delivery, since he had arrived late at her daughter's place and was later found sleeping on the floor with both the mother and her child dead. Right from the start, things had gone rapidly from bad to worse. It had been discovered that Zielgard was in a state of advanced inebriation when operating on the woman.

The witch, known under that epithet throughout the world, still waited ten years later to be executed in the state of Mississippi's maximum-security prison. Her case had made an impression on the judicial population, as well as the media's and the country's general population. It had initiated the setting up of more groups of special interests than any other cases, litigation, or instances ever. It ended up opposing both democrats and republicans into a deathly struggle with the 2008 election at stake.

There had been so many questions, all of them submitted, after treading a path through the lower courts to the United States Supreme Court, in one never-ending repetitive process where one side did not know the meaning of defeat and had the capacity to get reborn from one rejection to another out of new ideas, arguments, concepts, and justifications. The country had had twelve years of that from 2006 when she had been found guilty and condemned to death up to October 19, 2018, the date fixed for her execution by lethal injection. There was now only the governor left to interpose between the woman and her verdict. He had let it be known that he wouldn't interfere. Furthermore, the last try at appealing to the highest tribunal in the land had been fruitless. When all was said and done, the issues had reduced to state rights, jurisdiction, and sovereignty. Hardly the stuff to get a chap much excited about.

At Al's Diner, in the restaurant's booth with the window overlooking the parking lot, an older man could see his pickup truck piled high with bags of soil and seedlings waiting to be planted later in the afternoon. His helper munched a cheeseburger. He pushed toward his boss his plate of fries, signaling an invitation to pick some if he wanted. Tony looked at his newly hired juvenile assistant's tattooed forearms and ignored the offering. Swallowing a morsel of his tuna salad, he couldn't imagine himself eating the greasy junk food. He had hired the youngster one week before for jobs like this one, since he tended to get more of those in spring and early summer. Otherwise, the business, as advertised on the doors of his pickup, was landscaping and gardening, mostly cutting grass or gathering dead leaves off the ground of his regular clients' real estate.

"I can't believe it took so much time, he concluded his long monologue."

"There will be no more wait, the helper concurred. The governor's office has said so, anyway."

"He got what he deserved, though. The old contractor was in the habit of changing track, as conversation with him was chiefly one way."

"Right, the employee approved tactfully."

"Those damn doctors…"

"I am glad I am not a judge, the tattooed helper added wisely while eating the last of his fries alone." He was a student and would get his degree after the end of the next year.

"Why is that?" Asked the older man.

"I mean getting involved this way. I wouldn't want that witch to come after me."

"The silly woman had it coming. She claimed credit for the guy's death. Let her enjoy the benefit."

"She might not have been in her right mind."

"The bitch wasn't crazy. And she was a churchgoer."

"You mean to suggest, said the youngster, that lady sorcerer entertained some kind of faith?"

"God, angels, the good fight against Satan and his cohorts, isn't that enough theology for you?"

"The more reason to stay on her good side."

It was early spring, a Monday in late afternoon. Irma was at the condo. Most of the time, she had the place to herself since her mother slept more often than not at Mike's. He owned a two bedroom, two-bathroom unit in a better part of town that was two streets away from the ocean. From his side of the building, he had a bit of a view of the water. The apartment had belonged to his mother, and he had moved in after the old lady had died. The phone rang. Irma picked it up. It was Pralina. She was very agitated. It was important. Something had happened. As her mother was babbling her way to tell it all without revealing anything useful, Irma heard Mike shout over Pralina's voice,

"Stop it, Lyn. Just tell her to come have supper with us. You will explain it all then."

"Where are you? Irma asked her mother."

"In Al's parking lot. Driving away, toward downtown. Can you make it?"

"I will be at Mike's place at six, she answered.

"We will have shrimp, Pralina concluded, making an audible effort to calm herself."

The explanation for these uncommon turbulence in her otherwise very ordinary life was a book she had read over the weekend. It had all started the previous Friday. Pralina had visited Mike's condo. They had just finished supper and were enjoying the night breeze on his balcony, which he'd called a Florida room because it was screened all over. Pralina had held a book in her hand. It was a hard cover written by an unknown author. It was titled Faith. She had heard about the novel. What was this book doing in her lover's domicile? She had asked him. He had told her that it had been left in the barber shop by one of his customers. He would give it back next time the guy visited. Mike was no more a reader than she was. She had discovered a postal card while browsing through the pages. Out of some light coming from the lamppost illuminating the street they were facing, she read the words silently, and then she him,

"Did you read that post card, Mike? She had asked."

"What are you talking about?"

Pralina started reading aloud.

"There is a scene that takes place in a place called Enzo's, a barbershop in a mall where there is an eating place that goes under the name of Al's Diner. Since you have had your hair cut at Enzo's for the last twenty years, I thought it might interest you to read that story. It is a big success and you should give it a try…you might like it, as I did.' And it was signed: Your loving niece, Nickie."

Pralina finished the glass of wine that she had drunk at supper. She had cooked pasta the way he liked it.

"This makes no sense, she added. He must have left you the book on purpose and suggested you take a look at it."

"He knows me better than that."

"Strange he didn't tell you about the postcard."

"Can't remember if he did. Why would I care?"

"Well…aren't you curious?"

"Not a bit, if it means me reading this bestseller."

Men, she thought, they can be really dense. She had met Mike many years before and he had proved a blessing in her life. She hoped it had been the same for him. While they sat alongside each other, she was satisfied that it was. One knew these kinds of things. Even if that barber of her wasn't so good at expressing his feelings. Yet, there were small gestures that didn't lie, if you were good at interpreting them. From the inside of the flat came the voice of Anna Moffo as the diva sang, "Un bel di vedremo" from the Puccini masterpiece Madama Butterfly. Since his mother's death, he had inherited her condo with the furniture and the vinyl records of his father, mostly operatic. Mike's most basic instinct had been to sell the stuff in bulk. Lyn had objected. It was a memory of his father. This was music that they had both enjoyed, Enzo and his mother. They would get pennies for selling the collection. So, he had kept it all, plus the cabinet in which the albums stood, numerous, with their composer's names in alphabetical order. The assemblage helped give the living room and its inhabitant an aura of distinction and quiet respectability. And then, she had started listening to some.

She knew nothing about music. Still, it wasn't long before she discovered *Carmen, Traviata, Aida*, Mozart's *Marriage of Figaro, The Magic Flute*, Rossini's *Barber of Seville*, and Puccini's bests. Even Mike got used to it, no longer formulating silly objections when she moved toward the turntable. Once, he had said, defeated, "From now on, I will really sound like my father." Enzo had in his time regaled his clientele with such arias sang by tenors of the fifties and sixties, like Corelli, Bergonzi, Tucker, Bjorling, and DelMonaco. What they heard at that moment were extracts taken out of the 1956 version of the full opera with Moffo and Valetti. For her, it hadn't been love at first sight with the music. Its proximity and Mike's complacent acceptance of it had made it possible for the harmonies to take hold in the part of her brain that ruled over taste. In this way, she came over time to recognize the tunes, which translated into an inclination to hear more of them. She could tell it also worked for Mike, that if you gave anything a chance, you might end up liking it. After Butterfly was finished, there was an orchestral interlude to give Sharpless time to knock at the door of her house.

Again, she brandished the hardcover edition of Faith toward her paramour. She had been intrigued with the piece since it had been referred to on TV. A talk show she had been listening to had mentioned it, but she hadn't been giving it much attention, though. But there had been nobody at Al's in the middle of that afternoon. The show host and his guests had been debating that very same book, a discussion she wouldn't have given a second thought if it had not been for the extreme ugliness of one participant, while at the same time, the words that ran through his mouth were the most beautiful sound she had ever heard, like God talking, the voice warm and resounding, the diction impeccable, the message illuminating and vividly brilliant. And then, one day later, she held the same book on her lap because someone had forgotten his niece's gift at the barbershop. Mike's reaction was so inadequate. She asked him,

"So?"

"What?"

"I can't believe you didn't have a look at it."

"He should be the one left with the privilege to do so in the first place. It was his gift, after all."

Pralina sighed. Her suitor could be quite aggravating sometimes.

"He left it for you, didn't he?"

"Forgot is more likely."

"Well, it was his niece's birthday present to him."

"Told me she wasn't good at choosing gifts."

"But the card mentions both Enzo and Al's places. Don't you think this is worth looking over?"

"This is geography, he said with a teasing smile. Why should I be concerned?

"Because, she answered heatedly, this is the point. This is why the guy has asked you to read this."

"Well, Mike protested. He never did anything like that."

"You mean to have me believe that he left you the book with no directive of what he intended for you to do?"

"He might have told me to look it up if it's what you are getting at."

"Did he suggest why he wanted you to do so?"

"He told me his niece thought I was the barber in the story."

"He told you that, then, Pralina repeated."

"Complete nonsense, don't you think?"

"And you didn't care to check it out?"

"No reason to. That novel is number one thousand on my must-read books priority list."

"As if you had one, she erupted with a laugh."

"Precisely."

It was all a game. Mike could be that way, working very hard to dodge atypical challenges and situations in a joker-like style. She delivered the next awaited line.

"I find it amazing how aloof you are."

"Perhaps I am."

"You don't mind if I keep the book for a while?"

"Suit yourself. The volume is all yours. Just be sure to bring it back. I wouldn't want my friend having to confess to his niece he lost her gift."

Normally, Pralina didn't read fiction. She had done a few, books recommended by friends and such. But it took her so long to get over one that she couldn't remember anything of what the story was about from one reading to the other. That being said, Faith was one that she would decipher from first page to last. She would complete the task in record time.

That had been Friday. Three days before.

Gulfport, autumn 2004

Al was getting ready to slice in four equal parts the club sandwich he had just finished putting together. The knife he held in his right hand was huge, and he suddenly became afraid of what the shining blade could do to his thumb. It was such an undemanding extension of his body that found itself always at the forefront of work hazards that routine gestures and careless mistakes were sure to generate over a lifetime. All the carpenters he knew were short of a finger or some other small piece of their appendage.

He had awakened in the middle of the night. He hated when that happened. Hated the silly thoughts that visited him when he was alone, lost in complete blackness with nothing else to do other than be afraid of everything that could go wrong, wait for sleep to take away the anxiety. What was it he now remembered having pondered rather foolishly in the depths of the previous night that made his breathing quicken? What if he couldn't do it anymore? Just thinking about that had him wheezing in no time. And, now this! In plain daylight. As if the instrument had gained a life of its own and could turn viciously against him. He had turned fifty that year. Was he growing old? Mentally, he shook himself up. What is wrong with you? He asked his reflection in the mirror that faced him, a fixture that permitted him to have a look at the room and his eating patrons while he labored. Al de Marco took hold of his tool in a resolute manner and finished slicing the dish. He then threw onto the plate one helping of French fries. He was about to get a pickle, but Lyn stopped him in mid-motion as she seized Zielgard's lunch. She hissed at her boss,

- The doc hates those, as you should know. Get him some cole slaw instead.

As she waited over the meal, protecting it from unrequited, unsavory additions, Al grabbed a bit of the whitish vinegar dripping substance out of a plastic container using the metallic pincers he normally reserved for serving spaghetti. Now, thanks to Lyn, he would have to wash the damn utensil. He dropped it on the floor. The device clanged its way to the attention of the few clients' present. The physician turned his unshaved face toward the racket. He was an older man, in his early sixties by the look of him, a boozer, also, who would gulp three Budweisers while having his lunch. He was dressed in designer jeans, a starched white shirt with no tie, and a gray sports jacket. He wore on the top of his head a cap of one baseball club or other. In such an outfit, he looked casually elegant, like on a cruise ship when you are permitted to enter the dining room in informal attire.

Zielgard's eyes locked onto Al's, and being a doctor, he could see the discomfort in the man's glance. The chef was furious at himself for having been surprised thinking, "What if I am losing my mind? What is it that keeps me sane?" He had been caught. He felt like the doctor could read his mind. He saw Lyn leave Zielgard's table and approach the barber to deliver him his bill. What if he were to do something crazy? Stop this, he ordered his scary reflection in the mirror, trying to get a hold over his silly divagations.

He picked up the pincers and resisted the urge to throw them at Lyn back. She was talking with Mike. He would have bet that Lyn liked that guy. He operated Enzo's, the barbershop at the other end of the mall. Al had known the real Enzo, who had started cutting hair in the area in the fifties and moved his business here where his small boutique, beside what was today a doctor's clinic, had been in full operation before the Albertson's grand opening. The son appeared quite impermeable to the attention shown to him by the waitress. He was a good customer, the first to get in every morning, since he had taken over his father's place at Enzo's many years before. Mike removed himself out of the booth and walked toward the cash register, where he presented the invoice Lyn had left on the table. He said to Al:

"What is he up to, you think?"

While issuing those words, the hair cutter had thrown a side glance at Zielgard, the doctor who wasn't eating his club sandwich. At that instant, seeming oblivious to his surroundings, he could be seen scribbling furiously, adding words, phrases, and paragraphs to a piece of paper that was already half-full of his handwriting. Near him, there was a red folder with the name Pfizer Pharmaceutics on it. Out of that file, a pile of similar-looking darkened pages could be spotted.

"You should ask him next time you cut his hair, Al responded."

"That was last week. Can't you see?"

"Nice work!"

"Baseball is all what he talks about. I remember him getting very much excited over... Well, what's the name of that shortstop who plays for the Yankees?"

Al gave Mike his change and ignored the question. Instead, he said:

"He started bringing that stuff over two months ago. Told Lyn he was working on a short story."

"A short story, Mike repeated in a tone of voice showing incredulous amazement. But he is a doctor."

"So?"

"Doctors don't write short stories."

"Mentionned to Lyn he was almost finished."

"Well, Mike said, I don't care much for what doctors do or don't do."

Something in his host's tone wasn't quite right. Mike had a good look at Al and found him restless, his manners fidgety. His eyes had a strange lifeless glow.

"Are you okay? He asked the older man."

"I'm good!" Al said. Then, he shrugged. "It is just that I didn't sleep well last night." The man had lost his wife six months before, and it was no secret that he had trouble adjusting to his new situation.

Out of the corner of his eye, the barber could see in the mirror the subject of their conversation as he abandoned his pen and took a bite of the club he had been served a few moments before. Then, he gulped down his half-empty beer glass. Mike confided to Al:

"They say he is a drunk. Alvin told me once he had arrested the doc on a DUI charge."

Alvin was an officer of the law who had his hair cut at Enzo's and informed Mike of all the gossip at City Hall.

"The guy has taken his meals here for the last decade. I don't mind the way he drives."

Mike accepted the rebuke gracefully, as shown in the comment he uttered next.

"He took care of the arm I broke... When was what... six, seven years ago, I guess... And he moved his left limb up and down in order to demonstrate to his audience of one that it was fully operational. "Still works fine," he added.

"Then, Al concluded with a smirk, the doctor, he might become the next Pulitzer."

Al could surprise you sometimes with cryptic remarks that he would throw as if they were coming out of nowhere, curveballs that could pass undetected under a batter's nose. Mike, who wouldn't have been able to tell the difference between a Pulitzer and a howitzer, decided to ignore the quip and said,

"Have to go now."

Lyn looked at him as he made his way out and disappeared, walking toward his own shop a few hundred yards farther down. Al caught his waitress staring at the diminutive figure strolling out of view, and he became more convinced that it wouldn't take much of an effort from his neighboring entrepreneur if he were of a mind to start something romantic with Lyn. The woman was good-looking. She had class. She knew how to behave in good society. At the mayor re-election party, fifteen months before, Al had bought tickets for a full table of eight and invited some friends, Lyn, Mike, and Zielgard being part of that group. Lyn had been like a fish in a bowl with that crowd. She had sipped her wine ladylike. She had even started a conversation with the big man's first lady, who was herself a teacher. At the end of the event, it was like both women had been in school together.

Mike was simple and he was dependable. Lyn would have been a great catch for him. If only he would show an interest. Al knew that type. He had been that way. Solitary. Unattached. Individual. The bachelor type. The sort that liked to do things their way and resisted all alterations in their routine. Lyn had a ten-year-old daughter. Irma was her name. A nice girl.

The doctor had finished eating. Al saw Lyn approach his table and take away the soiled dishes. He heard her asking, "You want anything else? Another beer, perhaps?" He had had three. As he expected, the answer was no. Again, Al reproached himself for his idiotic wanderings. "What am I, now? A matchmaker?" Still, those thoughts were better than being afraid of dying or turning crazy all of a sudden. There were three patrons left in the diner. He turned away from them and started washing dirty plates.

Gulfport, Mississipi, 2018

Irma would forever remember Mike by a song that she associated with him, ever since that day when they had first met at the barbershop and he had saved her from peer derision by fixing the mess she had created by clipping—in frustration—both her child braids, when she wasn't yet in her teens. She had liked the man at first sight. She had liked that he was quiet and calm. She had liked that he could sit still in one of his barber's chair, in silence and not looking miserable, as she was when left alone in her room. She had appreciated that he'd taken care of her that day he had helped her change her appearance. She had liked the ride in his car when he had let her meddle with his radio channels' programming. Now that she enjoyed her own car, she doubted that she would have tolerated such an invasion of her private space by an unknown infant creature. She had liked most of all that he had responded the way he did to the song, "Piensa en Mi." And for having wished it from the bottom of her heart, she had been overjoyed when, after that night's mugging, Mike had called back her mother and started right there a relationship that was still working. She could now better understand her mother having taken an interest in that man all those years that he was her client at Al's, without them exchanging more than a few words. Mike was the taciturn type, reserved and saturnine. He had inherited his father's placid character. Nothing could get on his nerves. He didn't talk much, but when he did, it usually meant something and was worth listening to. The man could be a real pain in the ass, washing away all protests, objections, or disputes by saying, "I don't care," or "Why make a fuss?" or "Forget it!" or "It is no big deal," and such. This was his way for dealing with life's inconveniences and disturbances of the sort that rendered other people edgy, skittish, or fearful. Pralina saw it as a kind of protection that he needed against life's perils, and respected his inclination.

It wasn't like he couldn't accomplish anything. In fact, he was doing a lot. He was good at avoiding obstacles. Another of his sayings was, "If a road is blocked, one can always find another one." He wasn't good at expressing emotions. She had known he had them, though. It was just not in him to exhibit his feelings. He was substantial, reliable, and solid. One could rely on his word and bet his life on him delivering what he had promised he would. Irma had known her share of shallow men who talked big and were a no-show when time came to put cards on the table. Mike wasn't that way. You followed his act, and when the scores were in, he was on the winning side most of the time. Furthermore, he was nice and had a sense of humor. Hence, it had been a blessing when he and her mother had gotten together. They had been good for each other. Mike had been reluctant at first to engage in a serious relationship. Still, it had happened as love and dependence had grown on him. Both Pralina and Irma were now part of his life, for better or worse. As he would joke with Irma that Lyn was the good part, and she was…well, she could do the equation.

Monday night was the day of the week Irma had her tennis lesson. She had started practicing the sport to be with a girl she liked and who could introduce her in the right circles. Her mother knew her schedule. Yet, it had not stopped her from summoning her to Mike's apartment. She would stay there until seven thirty, have a bite, and listen to whatever Pralina had on her mind. Her mother had sounded very upset.

On her way to downtown Gulfport, this had gotten her thinking. Lyn was not that way, had never shown any inclination for histrionic displays. What was the frenzy about, then? Was someone dead? Everybody who counted in their family already was. Therefore, what could explain the commotion? Maybe Lyn had lost her job at Al's. That would qualify for drama. But after more than two decades of faithful services, it was highly unlikely. Lyn's boss was like a second father to her mother. Plus, the diner was doing okay. So it couldn't be that it was closing down. What else, then? Was somebody sick? That must be it. Why hadn't she thought about that possibility? Suddenly, she felt cold. What if it was Al? Better it be Al, she prayed. What if he wanted to sell the business because of some disease or another? Irma made an effort to remember the conversation with her mother, the words she had imparted over the phone. It had been quite impossible to guess what the woman had wished to talk about out of her eruptive redundancy. Yet, if it had been some radical life-changing incident that Pralina wanted to discuss with her daughter, she would have found a way to let her know in advance, and Mike, who was a no-nonsense individual, wouldn't have contented himself with suggesting she comes to have supper and that all would then be explained. Ergo, the matter Lyn wanted to discuss had to be trivial. As Irma was comforted by that conclusion, she prepared to exit Highway 49 and moved her car onto Twenty-Fifth Street. In front of a liquor store, she saw a parking space and decided on an impulse to stop. She would bring them a bottle of Henkel Trocken, her mother's favorite sparkling wine.

She was still on time when she rang the bell at Mike's door. From where she was, she could see a small part of the Gulf of Mexico, blue water between two multi-story apartment buildings similar to the one she was actually visiting. Mike opened the door and let her in. He took the cheap champagne out of her hand and addressed his longtime girlfriend, who was working over the stove in the kitchen. He shouted over the noise coming from the food she was cooking.

"You tell her your story. Meanwhile, I'll get this bottle open. There's nothing to celebrate, though."

It was plain from the man's attitude of aloofness that whatever the big announcement was, it didn't have much to do with him. He was making quite a show to look unconcerned, as if he wanted to stay well away from what he knew was coming. After the portentous scenarios she had contemplated on her way, this came as a relief. Mike returned with three glasses and filled them all. Pralina was still busy cooking the food. The table was already dressed up and looked inviting, with a yellow tablecloth. Where she was to sit, Irma saw that Pralina had lay her favorite chocolate delicacy. This went back a long time when she was five years old. She still liked the silly sweet. Out of hearing of her mother, she asked Mike:

"What is it?"

"Your mom got herself into something."

"Is it something I should be concerned with?"

"Not a bit, he answered with a cackle. My advice to you though... Stay away from it if you can."

"You don't listen to that dope, Lyn appealed to her daughter as she joined them."

Mike put a glass in her hand. Pralina saluted her daughter with it.

"You shouldn't have taken the trouble."

"Don't mention it."

They all brought glasses to their lips. Mike gulped the yellow liquid down in one big sip.

"I doubt Irma will want to hear your news on an empty stomach, he pronounced next.

"Let's eat now. I know Irma must soon be on her way."

"She's made your favorite dish, Mike revealed Irma. Shrimp and scallops."

"Splendid, she answered. Then addressing her mother, she added: "Let me help you."

They invaded the kitchen, Mike following them for no specific reasons except opening the refrigerator's door and looking pensively into it. The place instantly became overcrowded with the three of them piling into it. Lyn was laboring over a bowl half-full of lettuce, adding tomatoes and mixing it all with a garlic dressing. This would go perfectly with the juicy mollusks simmered down to delicious irresistibility. A ring from the microwave put an end to Mike picking bits and morsels out of the cooking utensil, because he dropped his fork in the sink.

- That would be the rice, Lyn murmured.

- This looks like a feast, Irma interjected. Are we celebrating something?

Mike extracted a bottle out of the fridge and moved toward the dining room. Irma saw from the corner of her eye that her host had suspended his car keys to a white and nicely carved key holder. It had been Irma's birthday gift to him when he had moved there after his mother had died. She had been a teenager then. He'd had the condo renovated to his and Pralina's taste. Hence the granite counter with its dark mauve reflects. She remembered having arbitrated the issue of where to put the device as both Mike and Lyn couldn't agree on a location, each other persisting to veto their way to positions that made less and less sense the more the idiotic process was left to simmer up. She had known instantly the object's correct location and was confirmed right when her mother, upon learning of her choice, claimed it was the first spot she had suggested. Mike had rolled his eyes for Irma's benefit when he had heard that boast, but had said no more. Instead, he had picked up his tools and installed the gadget where she had proposed, on the side of the cabinet that supported the heavy piece of granite, forty inches off the ground. There were four hooks and tonight, both Lyn's and Mike's sets of keys hung alongside each other. From the dining area came Mike's voice, who shouted after having filled his glass with what was left of the sparkling wine,

"I drink to our newfound celebrity."

"What does he mean? Irma asked her mother."

"This is incredible. You won't believe it."

"What are you talking about? Stop doing this. Tell me now. You are killing me."

The shrimp and the scallops were sizzling in the frying pan and appeared better for all of Pralina's ministrations. She cut the heat under her cooking utensil and promised her daughter:

"I will tell it all. But first, help me with this."

She had in her hands two plates generously filled with the savory food. She passed both to Irma, signaling with her chin Mike's portion. Irma picked up the load and asked in a voice nervous with anticipation,

"It is something good, though?"

As she left with both plates in her hands, she heard Lyn's answer.

"Nothing for you to worry about, dear, if that's what you mean. Yet, it is about us, you, me, Mike, and Dr. Zielgard. You remembers Dr. Zielgard, don't you?"

"Isn't he the one who got bewitched?"

"The same. Who would have thought that the man could write?"

Irma sat at the table beside Mike, who was busy uncorking a bottle of white Soave Bolla. She addressed her mother in front of her:

"He was a doctor. Give him some credit."

"I mean a successful writer, countered Pralina. A published writer. And selling books by the millions in multiple languages. And being talked about all over the country.

"But Zielgard is a long time dead, Mom."

"He may be dead, but he sure found a way to come back and make a triumphant reappearance in our lives, let me tell you that."

Irma gave her mother an exasperated look.

"Stop talking in riddles, will you? Tell me something I might understand."

"Supper is on the table. Enjoy the food. I'll explain later."

"She sure will, Mike commented. You wouldn't be here otherwise."

"You had me worried, though. I don't remember such a summons ever happening before in this family."

"Welcome to the club, Mike pronounced derisively. Your mom has a lot of issues I admit she keeps to herself most of the time. Meanwhile, she has in her mind to get us involved in this one. By the way, he added, Lyn, this thing is really delicious."

"But you are part of this one, like it or not, Lyn insisted, oblivious to her lover's praise."

Both women had started eating. Irma poured wine for the three of them. Mike gulped his share and proceeded to fill his glass to the brim under the young girl amused disapproval.

"I know Lyn observed with a sigh. We won't ever make a gentleman out of him, will we?"

"You do your fancy sipping, Mike fired back. You will not tell an Italian how to drink wine."

That started a conversation on the Romans and the city his family was from, Rome, and when they would be visiting the place. It was more of a dialogue between mother and daughter since Mike didn't offer much in the way of participation.

"What is it, then? Questioned Irma as she turned her attention to the matter at hand. They had finished eating. She could well see that her mother was dying to impart her news. Pralina had managed to have her dinner with a book on her lap. She took it out from under the table and showed the volume."

"You know about this book, don't you?"

"Why? Everybody does. It's a bestseller."

Lyn glanced at Mike, who was in the habit of eating slowly and still had a few shrimp left on his plate.

"That oaf didn't. And to tell you the truth, I might have missed it myself if it wasn't for that customer of his whose niece flagged me to some very peculiar passages in those pages."

"From what I have heard or read, Irma commented, it is just a baseball story. In what way can such a tale develop into anything that gets detected by your radar?"

"Useless nonsense is what it is, Mike emitted."

"Will you please stay out of this, Lyn scoffed at her companion."

Irma was not deterred by the interruption. She pursued:

"You said previously that it was all about us and Dr. Zielgard. What is it that you mean by that?"

Pralina pushed *Faith* toward her daughter. Look it up, she urged the other. At page five, it is stated that it was published in 2017.

Irma perused through the volume, found the page, and agreed.

"I read it all, Lyn continued. It is all there. I mean, us, that is, you, me, Mike, Al's Diner, Enzo's, the mall. The only variance is the location, St. Petersburg, Florida, instead of Gulfport/Biloxi Mississipi. Even the place where we live, the author got it right. My two-bedroom condo in Palm Harbour. He put it in Gulfport, St. Pete. How convenient, don't you think? Yet, it is the same place. Whoever wrote that story must have known us. And known us very well, indeed."

"Are you implying that we are characters in the story?"

"Yes. And we play ourselves."

"Don't you worry, though, Mike cut in, his voice full of sarcasm, we all look good in our little parts."

Lyn brushed away the disturbance. "Well," she followed, "right from the start he involves you, Irma, with this fellow Manuel who is the hero of the novel. Dreaming Manu, he is called, because he has visions, and you, a girl of ten, are given the role of his complacent audience. Here, look for yourself."

Pralina pulled the book out of her daughter's hands and gave it back after she had found the required extract. Then, she waited eagerly for some incredulous response to show on the young girl's physiognomy. Irma, looking absorbed, stared at one page, then the other, turned that one over. When she was finished, she looked up and said,

"I like it."

"You are missing the point, dear."

"Well, what is the point?"

"You're doing it on purpose, aren't you?"

"I'm sorry mom. You sure have put in a lot of work figuring this all out. As for me, I am not yet five minutes into it. So bear with me, will you? Who wrote this?"

"Peter Artritis. Take a look at the book's jacket. There is his picture. It says he was born in South Florida and has lived there all his life. In the St.Pete/Tampa area."

"Therefore, Irma surmised, the question, let me guess, is how this Artritis fellow from St. Petersburg could be aware enough of our existence to put us in his book.

"Precisely, Lyn approved."

"Well, the daughter conjectured, perhaps it is just a coincidence. There's a lot of written material out there with people sharing the names Lyn and Irma."

Her mother protested against the asinine hypothesis.

"Give your mother some credit, please. What are the chances of Artritis having in his novel a Lyn who is a waitress in an Al's Diner out of a mall similar to the one I have parked my numerous second-hand cars for the last twenty-five years? And if this isn't enough to assuage your skeptical disposition, tell me the odds for the Lyn name to come out of Pralina, and for the same Pralina to have a sister rightly named Paola and a daughter your age named Irma?"

"He might have known somebody who knew us. Why? For all I know, he could have been a friend of the dead doctor and learned our details from him."

"Right. What are you making, then, of that scene in Mike's place?"

Again, Pralina grabbed the book, this time her composure showing some sign of disquiet, her fingers trembling as they searched for the right passage. When she had found it, she showed the pages to Irma, who took five minutes to read it through. It was the scene where Joe Black met Manuel in Enzo's. When she was finished, Irma looked at her mother, who said,

"Whoever wrote that scene had to visit the place, don't you think?"

Irma had no choice but to fold all her previous objections right there. "I agree." She then turned to where she thought Mike was.

"There is more, her mother insisted, not fully aware of her daughter's latest capitulation."

"Where is he?" She asked Pralina.

"Oh, let him be, hissed the other. He doesn't approve of me getting into this."

"Why?"

"He wants me to forget about it. He says it is of no concern for us. He says he doesn't mind being part of some silly narrative that nobody he knows will read anyway."

"He has been proven wrong already, Irma laughed aloud. What is he making of this client of his who loaned him the book?"

"He argues that if we ignore the matter, it will go away. And if it doesn't, the worst-case scenario will be a little bit of celebrity for Al's and Enzo's, and we agree that both can live with that. What he doesn't like is the rest."

"And what would that be?"

"My proving that Peter Artritis didn't write that book."

"Who did, then?"

"Can't you see? It has to be Dr. Zielgard. I am sure he wrote Faith. I feel strongly that we owe that very unfortunate man to put the matter straight."

Mike chose that instant to reappear in the sunny living room and dining area out of the bedroom he shared with Pralina.

"We owe the man nothing of the sort. Please, he implored the younger woman, you must talk your mother out of that crazy scheme."

"What scheme? Irma asked him."

Mike didn't notice the glare his female companion gave him.

"That grand plan of hers, he explained with some relish. To redress conjectural wrongs, such as attributing doubtful merits to a dead, drunk, no-good, white trash doctor who couldn't perform his job properly. Now, she fancies the son of a bitch hit a grand slam, producing on his first try a yarn so good that it became the book of the year, as it was announced on the tube, and now, even Hollywood got interested and put out the tens of millions to produce the movie actually playing throughout the country."

"That's what the so-called author of that book did, though, and I can prove it, Lyn insisted."

"It is not your fight. That's all I am saying. Let somebody else do it."

"What you have here, Irma suggested to her mother, is quite impressive. Yet, it shows only that the author of Faith must have known about us all and the site and locations, like Al's and Mike's. It couldn't have been that difficult, let alone impossible, to achieve such a result. He would have visited Enzo's just once and it would have been enough for him to get all the details he describes in the book. As for the rest, he could have learned it easily directly from yourself as you served him toast and coffee one morning and made small talk with him."

"This is so true, Mike approved, clapping his hands. Your mother can't keep a secret, and divulges them all to complete strangers if they address her the right way."

"You might be right, Pralina graciously admitted." She looked at the author's picture at the back of the book. The man that smiled back at her wore a three-piece suit that didn't sit well with his otherwise impractical façade and odd abstruseness. "The biographical note, she added, reveals Peter Artritis is a lawyer and the head of Oracle Publishing. If he is, he certainly doesn't look the part. What he does look like is an overdressed janitor in a third-rate hotel establishment who writes amateurish poetry after work."

"I see you have developed a prejudice, Irma lectured. The man doesn't look that bad. He is just plain a bit."

"Yet Pralina insisted, I wouldn't have forgotten serving such a person."

"Mom, Irma objected, it would have been more than ten years ago, and Artritis could have been dressed differently. I doubt he would have been traveling through Mississippi and pulling up at Al's Diner in such an outfit. One other thing. There were a lot of people in 2008 who visited Gulfport in order to investigate Zielgard as he was the victim in a trial at the court house downtown, where a witch known under the name of Rosa Maman Tour de l'Isle was found guilty and condemned to death. Reason enough to look around and discover the good doctor was a client of yours. Easy from there to learn bits and pieces on your own life, Al's, Mike's and mine."

"Why 2008? For all we know, he could have come in Mississippi six months before publishing the novel."

Both women looked at Mike, astonished.

"He is right, Irma whispered."

"I have more, insisted Pralina while throwing at her lover a look that meant don't get into this."

"What is it?"

"That scene that you just read with Joe meeting Manuel at Enzo's. You might have missed something. Try rereading page 124. You start with paragraph 4."

And while Irma obliged her mother, she could hear her press her point.

"Ask Mike if he ever had him as a customer. And if so, if he ever brought him into his so-called office at the back of his store. As Zielgard did once. The answer is: he didn't. He has already admitted that much, at a time when he didn't know why I was asking such a question. My point is that you will find in that office a 1967 calendar displaying a half-dressed vixen drinking a well-known beverage, and the month shown on that piece of useless trash is May. You care to see that outmoded vintage of the sixties? You can, for it is still there."

"It is a remembrance of my father, Mike parried. He added rather piously, "He could come back and find the store like he left it."

"Isn't this enough filial partiality for you? Lyn mocked the man of her life. How thoughtful of you. This is quite a dazzling performance, what a man will do to rationalize his way out of a good clean-up job. The sorry point is, as she kept trying to make an impression on her daughter, what are the chances of Artritis ever finding out about that particularity and to make it a part of his elaborate setting?"

Irma had just finished her second reading of that part where manager Joe Black, thanks to the office, had met Manuel in Mike's small back closet where there wasn't much place to sit or stand. Now that she had been alerted to it, it would have been difficult for her to miss the part that described the very same calendar showing a Coke-drinking damsel in a very chaste bikini. That is, if one were to compare the outfit to what actual taste and tolerance had made everyone used to.

"He could have been informed of it in some way or another, she repeated."

"You are making this up, Pralina snapped at her daughter. "You don't believe what you are saying. If you're going to take Mike's view on this, just tell me plainly. But don't do this. Don't tell me I'm wrong."

"Why, Irma added in despair, Artritis might have visited the barbershop in Enzo's time, let see, from May 1967 up to the time of his death. Why, he could have his hair cut at Enzo when a kid or a young man. They say in his bio that he was born in 1960."

Hearing this, Lyn gaped respectfully at the girl:

"I must admit that I had not anticipated that, she said with some awe in her voice." Here was suddenly demonstrated, as it had happened many times before and always in the same oblique way that an education had not been lost on her daughter.

"What you are saying, then, is that I might be on to something, but I still have some digging left to do."

"And I am saying to you, drop it right there!"

That was Mike breaking in as he seized upon Irma's last hypothesis like a beggar would on a twenty-dollar bill.

"Listen to Irma, he urged. She has just demonstrated that the issue is a dead end."

"Did you?" Pralina asked her daughter.

"What about ghostwriting? Artritis could have his book written by someone else." There was despair in Irma's voice.

"It wouldn't change anything, would it? Whoever wrote the material would have needed to know us. Can you imagine a neighbor of us creating such a piece and giving it to someone else to enjoy all the honor, prestige and triumph?"

"Maybe the ghostwriter was Zielgard?"

"And wait 10 years for publication. No, this doesn't pan out."

"Well, concurred Irma, this is quite alluring. Imagine the explosive quality of the information if your hoax supposition was proven genuine."

"As you say, Lyn approved."

She had at that moment Irma's full attention. All three of them stayed quiet for a minute. Next, Mike stood up, and if his body could have spoken, it would have told the girl, "Don't encourage her in this, for God's sake!"

"Actually, the more I think of it, Irma said, I think it is unlikely that Artritis wrote the novel. After all, this doesn't add up. Why would an author put real existing folks into his narration? The only motive for that would be he wanted to please these same people. So, he would have had to like us. And to like us, he would have had to know us. This qualifies Zielgard. As for Artritis, I can't picture him taking the trouble to do something of the sort. It doesn't make sense. What I say, then, is if he did write that story, he will have a lot of explaining to do."

"What do you suggest, then?" Lyn asked Irma.

"You could ask him."

"As if he would answer me."

"He would if the asking was on TV."

From the kitchen, over Mike very irritated "DAMN" shout of protest, they heard a terrible racket that sounded like a swarm of granules hitting the floor.

"Don't mind me, his voice came from behind the counter, reassuring them somehow. I have everything under control. Which obviously was a lie. He had dropped coffee beans all over the place. Some they could even observe as they had found their way into the dining room, all suspiciously black and, from where they sat, looking like dead flies. In normal circumstances, Pralina would have run to Mike's help and taken, over his uncertain objections, the job of cleaning up his mess. For all his usual proclamations of fixing such a matter, he was prone to talk rather than do anything useful to fix it. This minute, though, Pralina couldn't care less about her mate's exacting predicament. Instead, she grumbled at Irma:

"What is it you are saying, dear?"

"Let's get you invited to the David Letterman Show."

"You mean…next Thursday?"

"It would be fun, don't you think? And I bet after hearing your side, the director will beg you to appear on the show."

"I couldn't do that, Pralina protested, in a bit of panic. I won't go on TV.

Coming from the kitchen, they heard Mike's happy pronouncement of:

"That's a relief!"

"Would you?" Pralina asked her daughter.

"It sure could be fun to do that."

"But the show is in New York, her mother objected."

"I will get there, don't you worry! As you already suggested, when told about my inquisition, they most probably will be very happy to pay for my trip and lodging in the Big Apple."

"We should do a little digging, though. There were traces of excitement in Pralina's voice. If the doctor wrote that story, it had to be in his house at the time of his death, I mean the manuscript. We must establish how it came to fall into Artritis' hands. Who sold that place? We must find the agent who did it and start from there."

"I can't believe I'm hearing this, Mike complained, not doing much else in the way of fixing his mess in the kitchen."

XVIII

Governor Pat Allanson had had more than enough of the polemic that engulfed his administration over that mad sorcerer. The woman had defied for almost a decade all the state's efforts to put her to death and to satisfy, in so doing, a manifold of courts' decisions from the lower jurisdictions up to the highest in the land, the Supreme Court of the USA, that august tribunal whose attention the case had solicited too many times and from so many sides of the issue. In the end, just reading the thousands of pages of legalese, these mostly whimsical and erratic, would have sufficed to send the unfortunate lady into an everlasting zero land.

The governor, for his part, didn't care for the useless polemics that were part of the judiciary distractions, and which made lawyers and judges indispensable arbiters, presiding over the silly controversies people's sensibilities imposed in cases such as Rosa Maman Tour de l'Isle's. Allanson had served in the Army most of his active life. Hence, he had no lost sympathies for the due process of law, tortuous reasoning, and endless dispute. The armed forces worked things out in a different way. A better one, at that. You either did something or you didn't. You didn't try anything when you knew from the start you couldn't and would not get to the end of it. He had attained the rank of Colonel. He had been lucky that his fellow Mississippians attributed to him the US Department of Defense's decision in 2008, which was to concentrate, in their sovereign state, all infantry activities in the country's southwest. Also, the measure had come with hundreds of administrative jobs and thousands of troops moving inside their state's borders. This had paved the Colonel's way to governorship two short years later, and speeded his retiring from the forces after more than three decades of loyal service.

He sure had enjoyed his new quarters in the state's capital. He wasn't that happy at this moment, though. From where he stood, looking out of one of his luxurious office windows, he could spy out a mob-like crowd of turbulent and disruptive invaders. The unsavory rabble occupied the street with placards and signboards that displayed idiotic injunctive scrawling that they shouted mantra-like in his direction. What a sorry sight those ragged misfits offered the world. From his point of observation, he couldn't hear the horde's indignant clamor. He didn't need to, though, since he figured they were parroting the lines written on their signs. The crowd most probably expected to win influence over his future politics with its most unwelcome cumulative wisdom. Their troubling incantations stated:

KILLING ISN'T JUSTICE.
USE YOUR POWER TO COMMUTE.
DEATH ISN'T THE RIGHT PATH.

Damn them, these romantic assholes, he mumbled between his teeth. He could see he was in a bind. Those people out there with their slogans directed at him made it impossible for him to forget the matter that had troubled his peace of mind for much too long, now. He had always fancied that he would be looked upon, in his public life, as a man of decision. Somebody who didn't mind accepting responsibilities. A commander who knew that to lead was to show the way. A politician who wouldn't shunt duty. A chief that would honor the saying, "The buck stops here." That would be his reputation. In such a way, he had managed his career in the Army. As a politician, he had gained a reputation for decisiveness. Whatever his bad calls, and there must have been some, as he reluctantly admitted to very close friends over too many drinks - he would have publicly fought anybody with such a notion, though - quick determination and fast action were the name of the game he had learned to play. Always had been. Always would be.

"Whatever you miss for moving promptly," he would trumpet to his obliging audience, "you gain tenfold by having a situation settled, which could have festered otherwise." He had been successful in both his previous and current career for having put forward such posture and attitude. Fortunately for him, he hadn't faced any great challenges up to now, but that had changed with the foolish witch incident, which explained the idiotic lot downstairs strutting in the sun under the Biloxi constabulary's benevolent and amused indifference. What a grotesque jurisprudence that ludicrous case had yielded, growing out of control like a malevolent cell left loose, which speedily became a monstrous alien that threatened the structure of whatever body it had attached to. He couldn't believe this was happening. Why in hell had they prosecuted the lady in the first place?

That decision hadn't been for him to make. He hadn't even been there at the time. He had been stationed somewhere in the Far East when the shady Zielgard character had died of a stroke. Would he have permitted it? He doubted it. And then, he had no say in such matter. He was not a lawyer. Would he have forced his attorney general to interfere with the case and call back his dog, that is district attorney Ollie Devott? Perhaps he would and maybe he wouldn't. At least, he had enough objectivity to admit as much, a concession he needed to make if he were to refuse what those people out there were demanding him to do. The doctor's untimely demise wouldn't have made it into the news if not for one wacky, voodoo, senile diabolist forty years in the country out of Port-au-Prince, and claiming ownership for the crime. What about it? He was a man of the world. In any normal jurisdiction he could think of, the woman would have gotten herself a few laughs or been ignored altogether. At worst, she would've been caught and buried in one nuthouse or another with lunatics of her kind.

It certainly had not been that way here back in 2005. The voluminous file that jammed his desk was full of clippings that showed media's vociferations, so loud, persistent, and wicked, that it had engaged all the citizens into a vortex of sanctimonious considerations. Which was fueled by the churches of all denominations as they felt that some article of their faith had to be involved, and God himself was the probable victim of an issue cowardly evaded or wrongly resolved. The hullabaloo this had provoked could be compared to a tornado hitting the ground. You didn't see it coming, and you couldn't resist the calamity.

It hadn't eluded the shrewd temperament and cunning disposition of assistant District Attorney, Ollie Devott, recently recruited, young, unscrupulous, and very ambitious. He was a highly intelligent African American, and an able lawyer. He had talent. He knew his way with a jury, and had used this ability to help his senior partners win a few million verdicts in cases ascribed to him by older and less gifted partners in the big firm that had first employed him.

It was said that he would have members of a jury trade their wedding rings for one frozen Popsicle in the middle of January if he just asked. He had that kind of power. Why not use it to make a pile of cash and become wealthy? An interesting question. Devott didn't prize money that much. Criminal law was his thing. On the prosecution side.

Trying million-dollar injury cases had just been a side thing.

That was Ollie Devott's reputation. It explained why the slick prosecutor was feared. Maybe it could explain why nobody had opposed him much when he had started that crusade against Rosa Maman Tour de l'Isle, and why he had been encouraged by some and left free by others to push the matter that far. Why? The fellow had seen something in the old woman's tragedy and her unlikely victim right from the start. You had to give the guy credit, he could identify a good thing when he saw one. This was a first-class gift, this ability to discern trends before they became an infatuation and eventually mutated into an obsession. And he knew how to use that skill to his best interest. It was an art, no doubt about it. The sly advocate had had an insight that there was more in that file, after it had come his way, though he had been the newest addition in the bureau of the District Attorney in Biloxi. The simple ruling that he was expected to issue was already spelled in red letters on the file, left there by a stamping cachet: NOPRO for "do not prosecute." All he had to do was write a reason.

He would have done that, and he would have most probably remained an obscure bureaucrat ensconced in moronic red tape all his life, trying cases in a dull and repetitive way, as if he were working in a GM plant. Yet, Devott Senior, a Baptist minister, would have told you that this son of his had never been known for choosing the easy course. Here, the kid must have flared for a moment in Rosa Maman stupid pretensions a case that showed great career-enhancing potential, and he had acted upon it with a vengeance. That was what the older man had taught him. If you must strike, do it hard and give it everything you've got.

If it was the only thing he had taught his son, it would have been more than enough, as few parents could show that much with their progeny. Ollie Devott was church going. In his community, prayers upheld everybody's daily existence. The need for asking God and the Holy Spirit to help one into the rightful path wasn't something to be taken lightly on those shores. Beware the east coast liberals who laughed with eccentric fervor, the more so since democratic President Obama occupied the White House in Washington. All those freethinkers believed themselves emancipated of God's ultimate standard. Fortunately, here in the South, people still had their hearts in the right place. They had religion. They were believers. They knew that God ruled over mankind. Not only did they accept that fact, but Ollie Devott trusted that living outside that certitude would be merely existing, that is, in his opinion, a life not worth having.

So, after the file had dropped on his desk, he had thought the issue over and decided to prosecute the sorcerer after all. She had admitted the crime. She told herself that she had conspired with the devil. And then, the malefic demon she had summoned had manifested to accomplish the work she had asked him to perform. To have the case thrown away in such circumstances would have been to show a heretical disposition, like affirming oneself as a nonbeliever. An atheist, he was not. He knew for a fact that God existed. As well as angels. If saints could accomplish miracles, the devil was capable of scheming away his services in assistance to that part of humanity that was wicked and depraved. That was it, then. He would go after the woman. Put the matter in front of the grand jury and see what happened. It was worth a try. This, at least, would get him some attention. And what was there to lose? At worst, his bosses would attribute his failed attempt to zeal and inexperience. On the other hand, if he was to ride that bull properly and manage to hold on to the saddle long enough, who knew where that could lead him? Quite far!

So, concluded Pat Allanson, after he had read again about Ollie Devott in the newspapers of the time, here was the man who was at the origin of the existing turbulence outside. This explained the lawyer's meteoric rise into notoriety, so much so that it was said he had his eyes set on the very office the governor actually stood in, gazing at the annoying vista a hundred yards away. Over the last two hours, more of them had come. Where were they coming from? He saw a yellow school bus turning left on Congress Street, driving away from the scene. It was systematic, planned, and well organized, he thought. Whoever managed the performance was bringing in its audience of fervent militants by the hundreds. He sighed and prepared for a long siege. As he dropped on a couch that occupied half of his western wall, he closed his eyes. Soon enough, his mind surrendered to reminiscences of his newfound adversary's handling of what was now known all over the world as the witch event.

He had been elected governor in 2011, after coming back to the country in 2007. For the first few years, he and his wife had lived in Washington where he had landed, moving little flags on world maps and concocting elaborate briefs over where to attach some others. Coming back home to Mississippi hadn't really been an option at the time. And then opportunity had struck. There had been discussions about needing a place to concentrate all the armed forces' operations in the southeast. He had been involved in those dealings. This had put him in contact with the Mississippi authorities at the highest level. He had renewed acquaintances and made new ones, those mostly of a political nature. In the end, he had helped the state he had been born in to win the disputed prize. Or let them think as much. They had beaten Georgia to the finish line. It had gained him a reputation in the right circles.

That very same year, his wife Louise's parents' old family house on Elm Street in Biloxi had come on the market and they had bought it. They had moved in the autumn of 2009, after putting the old Victorian into shipshape condition. Soon after, a committee of four had visited him at his home. The previous governor had gotten sick, he was told, and somehow, they wanted him to replace the retiring fellow. He knew then that the governorship was there for him to grab. Allan Cormier had all but forfeited in his favor, and let him benefit from his supremely motivated political machine. That would ensure his candidature's final success. His victory had never been in doubt, since he was a good old boy. Both he and his wife had been born at the New Biloxi Hospital in the fifties out of families who had been there for many generations. With the folks around, that counted at election night. Also, he came with the aura of having helped the state to land the newfound Army's largesse.

He couldn't remember when he had heard for the first time of the Zielgard eccentricity. It had to have been before he was elected as the premier magistrate of the land. All he could recollect was he hadn't made much of the bizarre proceedings at the time. He'd kind of disregarded the anomaly as something that came with the territory. As the matter was all settled by the time it appeared on his radar, he didn't put much into it. There was nothing of consequence he could have done anyway. Furthermore, Cormier, who had discreetly presided over the committee created to get him elected, had urged him to leave the issue alone. What he really meant was Ollie Devott. "You do not want to mess with this guy," Cormier, who knew his inclinations, had wisely suggested. The woman had been indicted and legally prosecuted. A jury of her peers had found her guilty, and that verdict had already survived three appeals, two of those to the Supreme Court, who had chosen not to interfere on constitutional grounds.

In 2014, a new bunch of lawyers had taken over the case and started the process all over again, their newfound focus, to jurisprudential everlasting fame, being the alleged shortcomings of the legal representation provided their client by her previous attorneys. Over the years, there had been seven in that group, all local advocates, except for two out of Florida and Alabama. Such tactics were the sorry refuge of men turning against their predecessors in desperate efforts to save a life. Whoever had worked those cases knew that in the end, it would come to that, them being the object of some latecomer's scrutiny.

As it was all for the greater good, those unselfish lawyers didn't mind too much the assault on their skills and competence. It was part of the game they played, the cheap pretext introducing an old debate when eastern, white, agnostic, leftist establishment defenders landed in the South with their unprincipled wisdom, their ungodly notions, and concepts, let alone their inbred claims to higher erudition and learning. Yet, these latest luminary champions hadn't fared so well, either. Their multiple objections and protestations not being received as well as they should have in the lower courts, with the judges made out to look, by those know-it-all brats' arguments, like they were presiding over kangaroo courts. The process had left the responsibility of defending the honor and prestige of the native judiciary on Ollie Devott's shoulders. The happy prosecutor had acted like he had been born for just such a task, and had performed accordingly with artful brilliance. No wonder that riding so successfully on the witch case had won him the District Attorney's office, as he was now in charge of all prosecutions in the state.

What Pat Allanson thought in disgust as he looked out of his office window at the growing crowd outside, was being left in the impossible position of having to decide the fate of the delusional virago while offering Ollie Devott, that cunning little bugger, the opportunity to come after him if he were to do the right thing. If there had ever been a case that deserved a governor to exercise his privilege for mercy, Rosa Maman Tour de l'Isle was the one. As the case progressed over time, he had put his faith in the judiciary to neutralize the silly disturbance and call circus jester Devott to order. Yet, no judges, courts, or tribunal, could put that tricky mackerel out of the water, however sophisticated the fishing devices they used, and they had them all. Devott sure had learned a bit about harpoons, spears, nets, and lines. Henceforth he had choked his pursuers into arguing over principles to their most absurd conclusions. Poor Rosa Maman's dispute had, under his skilled advocacy, metastasized into a jurisprudential rigmarole.

The woman that had been found guilty by a jury of ten churchgoing citizens, would stay guilty. The real victim of this improbable inquisition would die if he were to do nothing. But could he? Because if he were to grace the lady with her life, no doubt the state District Attorney would make mincemeat out of him at election time. Or else, he would be made to look in the right circles like he approved of the ridiculous process and cruel denouement. Either way, he was the loser, and his antagonist the victor. "Oh," he lamented, still keeping watch on the outdoor turmoil, "this is a tough call." He turned toward his desk and walked the distance that separated him from the massive piece of furniture. He sat on the orthopedic chair that his wife had insisted he use. There was a knock at his door, which had been left half-opened, and he could see it was his chief of staff, who would want to discuss the order of the day.

"Hello, there, he cried lamely. Come on in." And shrugging in the direction of the demonstrators on the street, he added, "Some still have to work, didn't he?"

"Do they bother you? Charles Langlois asked."

"Not a bit, he lied."

"Have you reached a decision?"

"I hate to admit it, but I haven't."

"So, do nothing. Take your cue from the highest court and conceal yourself behind state sovereignty and the people's limitless licence to vote for laws of their choosing."

"Provided they are constitutional."

Charles, who was a friend from the era when he was a teenager, laughed at the concept.

"I am telling you, Pat, you stay out of the law as much as you can. Leave the silly legalese to judges and their cohorts. The sorry truth of the matter is this disgraceful escapade into demagogic quackery has seen a revival in church attendance at levels never seen before in modern times. The pious and the scrupulous have become the fanatical apostles of a new creed which has engulfed our politics as well. No doubt it will go away. In the meantime, the debate opposes the secular forces with those of the religious right. They have reduced the issue to its most simplistic terms. If you temper the verdict and its outcome, they'll assume you might be an atheist first, a leftist liberal second and a Trump hater third. Believe me, you do not want to be caught near the water when there is a wave like this.

"Still, the governor countered, what about those out there? All they ask me to do is to show some clemency to this convicted woman, and to alleviate, for human reasons, the harshness of her unjust punishment. The woman is an octogenarian, dammit! How can I avoid making a decision when the whole country, well, the whole damn world, is watching me?"

"Let them, Charles snapped as he shrugged off his friend's unsound wavering. Or else, do as you suggest, and you might as well say goodbye to your chance of winning the next ballot. Better yet, resign this office right now, as going soft on Rosa Maman Tour de l'Isle will get you there anyway."

The governor's eyes locked onto Charle's as he whispered softly,

"Why? Perhaps I will do that. Or perhaps, I won't."

Peter Artritis was famous. In the end, he would be remembered as someone easy to forget, the kind of individual who would not take hold in other people's minds and would remain in the collective memory no more than a name with no substantive existence. He was the talk of the town. They were asking about him all over the country. Where an audience could have access to him, though, he wasn't making much of an impression. Besides, as long as it had no negative impact on sales, he was permitted to show himself if he wanted to, but his handlers had abandoned all hope of getting anything useful out of him. His book was selling. He was receiving money out of the venture, so much of it that it didn't make sense to his rather cautious outlook on all things pecuniary. This was just the beginning, as he was told by those who imagined him a new literati genius. They were already pestering him to tell them what he was currently working on, or to show a chapter or two of the pieces. Publishing houses were now bidding for the right to publish his next book, offering mind-boggling sums for the privilege. A paperback version of Faith was now offered onto stands in variety stores, pharmacies, and food supermarkets. Talks of translations in other languages were on the way.

If that wasn't enough, the great man who was the King of all late-night shows wanted to have him as a guest. Peter felt like not going. But he knew that he must. Why wasn't he enjoying his newfound fame and success? The unwelcome answer to that question was so obvious that he didn't care to formulate it. What had he been thinking when he had started it all? It was like walking the streets of downtown Tampa all dressed up in a three-star general's uniform. Was he a kid? What was the fun of doing this? How come he hadn't realized such right from the start? Now, ten years later, he fully understood how vain, futile and useless his missdeed had been, how hopeless and unfulfilling it would prove to be? What about his actual performance? He should have known he wouldn't be able to play the part of a successful author. What was wrong with him? What was missing in his build-up material that had made each of his living days a struggle? What small and insignificant piece of his DNA had his maker omitted and given to everybody else? He craved for that bit of sanity that had eluded him so far. He had foolishly thought that he could appropriate another writer's work and benefit from the deed. Well, he had been wrong.

He had stuck himself in a dead end. Everywhere he turned to look at that point, he saw a wall. At work, he could read it in their eyes; those who knew him well showed him the kind of indulgence they would pay a skating cripple scoring a goal in one college hockey game. As if he were just a freak or something, an idiot who could multiply. Could it be that what he had presented as his story was so out of character that it took them an act of faith to believe he was the creator of all those tens of thousands of words? More and more, belying what should have been the happiest time of his life, he was now inclined to avoid contact with others, finding solace in being left alone. Colleagues who had never cared much for his tastes and output anyway had said nothing in the beginning. After all, he was a celebrated author and the house would make a bundle of money out of the publication of FAITH. Furthermore, they could all dispense with Artritis being part of discussions over one manuscript or another, since his presence added hours of fruitless arguments over cryptic and irrelevant issues. Hence, they attributed his aloofness and withdrawal to his usual distinctiveness and particulars. Here was a guy who couldn't handle success. They had seen it before. Well, they had been in the publishing business a long time. They had seen it all.

Peter Artritis had enough common sense left in him to know that he had had a good life, and to give himself some credit for a few things he had managed to do quite well. He had married the woman he wanted, and she was still with him. This was no small accomplishment in an era which had forgotten that the real blessed ones were those couples who still loved each other after fifty years of living together, as he knew, he would get there. What was notoriety compared to that? True. Getting notice for one's work was fine. But nothing compared to a happy family life to generate a man's day to day required felicity.

He enjoyed all those things. Who cared, then, if he was a lousy writer? That he couldn't adjust well in society? Or charm his way into instant approval at parties? What really counted was he had a life a hundred times better than anybody he could think of, some of them being serious authors he admired. A few might even envy him his reality.

Still, he acted like if he was on a mission to attack and destroy who he was and what he had built that worked. What had come over him? Once again, his distracted mind lingered over the thought that had pushed him into this painful brooding: being ignored might have been a nuisance. However, unearned praise was a tragedy.

Arthur Morin's office was at the corner of Central Avenue and Fourth Street North in downtown St. Petersburg. The place was a pink stucco bungalow that had been built in the thirties, where a large family must have lived in the beginning, since the structure was quite big. As the town grew larger and Central Avenue developed into Main Street, huge skyscrapers popped out of the ground and soon enough, nobody wanted to live in the area anymore. For whoever still owned the few houses that had escaped demolition far into the seventies, there was just one thing left to be done: take advantage of the bylaw that authorized commercial occupation of such premises and use those buildings for business, as they were proven ideal for all kinds of concerns of a professional nature.

Arthur had bought the corner lot from a chiropractor who was being sued by a suffering fool out of his otherwise happy clientele, because he wrongly attributed his chronic back pain to the man's manipulations. In visiting the practitioner's clinic, a part of his routine when possible for cases he considered handling, he had discovered that the place appeared rundown, as it was announced "For Sale" by the owner. He had also learned that poor Dr. Blain was fifth in a list of other physicians who had tried to help the gentleman out of his misery, and whose unwelcome rubbing had provoked the sickly court-prone litigant into action. This was good, and would have encouraged him to take the case. Yet, he had seen the locale and this had made him think.

Arthur was still in his first years of practice at the time. He was renting some office space in a six-story edifice out on Gulf Boulevard that had a bit of an ocean view, if you happened to be on its roof terrace. Impulsively, he'd decided to check it out and referred the new client to a friend. This would leave him free to buy the property, if he wanted. Dr. Blain's place might not have a water view, but it was still perfect, near the center of everything, just where all the action was. With the rent he was already paying, he might be able to buy the place and build himself a little capital over a twenty-year period. This, plus his RRSP, his tiny portfolio with Merrill Lynch, and the house at Pass-a-Grille where he had just moved that very same year. He would need all that and more when the time came to stop lawyering and start enjoying life.

Happier times were no longer that far away, as he was now sixty-four and didn't take as much pleasure out of working cases. That was, the patience to do so had evaporated over time. Clients nowadays had views of their own, and they wished their lawyers to abide by them. Before stepping foot into Arthur's office, these modern plaintiffs had already created a just disposition of their case, and they came with their own strategies to get their desired results. If that wasn't enough, they were averse to all advice that flew contrary to their partiality and fancy forecast.

As he waited at the light on Central for his left turn on Fourth Street, from the corner of his eye, out of his vintage Mercedes, he saw a girl with short blonde hair who stood alone near the steps leading to his front door, next to the massive bronze plaque that read, "MORIN, FANSWORTH, & HOCHIK, Attorneys at Law." He had salvaged the German magnificence from the Bankruptcy Court by proving he had gotten it for a just consideration, the car being his fee for having represented the Turkish consul successfully in Tampa from the disgrace attached to the file bearing his name and described in the news as the Hurlugolu imposture. That went back three decades at the least. He had had the car when he had moved his office downtown The Mercy was six years old at the time. It still looks splendid though. Arthur Morin glanced quickly at his watch. Eight thirty in the morning. Who could the girl be? He hadn't scheduled a rendezvous with anyone at so early an hour.

The light in front of the Mercedes turned green and the solicitor made it into Fourth Street, moving the car slowly and gently, not really a compromise to his vehicle's handicap of seniority. More like a bow to the imperative of his own quiet and reserved personality. He parked the four-door sedan in the newly cemented parking lot besides the building, which could accommodate up to eight vehicles. He shared it with his two accountant tenants, who were using rooms at the back of the house with a separate access. He credited his unknown visitor with good sense, since she had parked her Hyundai Elantra in a spot that they reserved for guests, and hadn't, as others, invaded into his more convenient space near the main entry door, all oak, majestic, and erudite-looking.

He got out of the car with a frown on his brow, which wouldn't have been there when he started his practice, as all new clients had then appeared to him like a gift-wrapped box with a surprise hidden inside. It was no longer his attitude toward people anymore, though. The money, which had been the real incentive to get him to meddle with others' business, didn't matter so much anymore. And then, if not for that, what was left? The love of justice? That was the judge's concern. His was to win his clients' cases. The love of the law? What was there to love? Laws were the products of society. They were manmade and often corresponded to partisan politicians' capricious impulses. As such, they changed all the time to satisfy the taste of the day. Law was a process, an ever-changing one with rules that adapted to the politics of the numerous. Laws were always approximate in their results as they were interpreted this way and that way and sometimes ignored. The law that was seen as defective fifty percent of the time, both sides of all issues clamoring nevertheless for its indifferent assistance, and in the end, the place for just one victor on the podium. Why, with the odds so low, did petitioners still address the courts? He couldn't figure it out.

So, practicing law, had he liked it or not? An honest answer to that question would have been, "Not much!" Any kind of exact science might have been more to his taste, which was something he learned later in life. He liked it when he looked over a problem and intelligent reasoning got him an answer without the "but," "maybe," "it depends," and other legalistic gibberish of that sort. Uncertainty wasn't fun anymore. Now, he needed certitude, and for one with such a state of mind, law was a very bad servant.

The girl must have observed his unhappy façade because she fidgeted with her purse, like she had a sudden urge to look inside in search of a something. She was well-dressed and very beautiful. He felt pity for the poor thing and forced a smile on his lips. She responded at once to his overture and advanced toward him, offering her hand. She said in a voice pleasant and self-assured,

"Are you Attorney Morin?"

He took the offered hand and shook it.

"Yes, I am, he said. How can I help you this early in the morning?"

"I have been directed to you by the agent Phil Leclerc."

"What about him?" He asked with no idea who Phil Leclerc might be.

She must have sensed it, for she explained what he needed to know, and when she did, it came all back to his mind.

"He is a real estate agent in the Biloxi/Gulfport area. He sold the Zielgard property, as you must know, since you were the lawyer who handled the late doctor's estate and such…"

He remembered Phil Leclerc as the man who had sent the deceased's manuscript that Peter Artritis had declared a worthless piece of shit. So much for Artritis' perspicacity. That call of his, he had challenged without his knowing, to unexpected results. Those things happened. Like winning a case that all living authorities have described as lost before the unexpected triumph in the end. The real miracle in this particular instance wasn't his initiative's happy result, but his having responded to the silly impulse that had made him ask for a second opinion. The proof of his intuition's validity was that the Zielgard novel had found a niche in the bookcase that occupied one wall of the room, and was full of collections of court decisions. It had been there for the last five years. It sat undisturbed in homage of his client's ultimate victory from the grave. It was the materiel Artritis had sent back in 2008.

In 2009, he had met a publisher who had been a witness in one of his cases. The guy was from California. They had become good friends. He had shown him the manuscript. The man had slept at his place for the three days he had been in town. With his help, they had won the case. And he had loved the Zielgard story. He said to the girl:

"Phil Leclerc. That's a long time ago."

"You know him, then?"

"What if I do?"

"You see, the girl answered with an edge in her voice, you are my first lawyer. And you could do a lot better if you cared for me to remember this first encounter with a member of your profession in a positive way.

"So, what is it you want, then? What do you need a lawyer for? He asked as she followed him up the steps and he fumbled with the numbers on the door-locking device. At last, he turned his head toward her and lashed out:

'Would you mind looking the other way? Damn, I hate those silly gadgets.'

'I am sorry if I stared, she commented. Why don't you use a key?'

'You discuss this issue with Hochik, he laughed back. The bugger is about your age and wouldn't be satisfied if this office wasn't equipped with the latest novelty; the more complicated the gear, the better. The man won't be happy unless this office is equipped like an intergalactic vessel.'

This sortie made her chuckle and he looked at her in a more cordial fashion. He appreciated people that responded favorably to his humor. As she just had.

'How old is Hochik?'

'Why are you asking? He might be forty or so. I don't know.'

She offered him her hand a second time. He took it as she stated,

'I am Irma Sanchez, and I'm twenty-four.'

'A young pup, as I said, he mumbled between his teeth.' And then he pushed the door open. They both went in. Inside, they walked through a long corridor past a reception area, still unoccupied as it wasn't yet nine in the morning. There were a lot of doors. Arthur stopped at one that had been left half-open and could have been a bedroom in another life. Instead, what she saw in entering the place was more like a suite made of an antechamber that could accommodate two legal clerks, typists, assistants, or whatever secretaries were called today.

Arthur had his importunate caller enter the larger room where he worked. His desk was as neat as you would expect one in a captain's quarters in a submarine. One wall was covered with bookshelves and the other three compromised between art and fenestration. Irma approached a window that looked over one big multi-story condo complex on the other side of Fourth Street.

'The water isn't far, is it?' She asked.

'You could walk to it. I do it sometimes at lunch time.'

There was a silence and he watched her gazing at the luminous outdoors, hearing the sound of the growing traffic.

'Did you drive that Hyundai of yours all the way up here?' He asked. He had noticed the Mississippi license plate, so there wasn't much risk with the assumption. She acknowledged she had. He was impressed.

'It must have been a pretty long drive, he said, searching for a way to get her to tell him her business and be done with it.'

'Six hundred miles. Nine hours or so.' Irma explained."I stay with an aunt who lives in Tampa. Her name is Paola. She moved here four years ago out of Tallahassee, she added, feeling it necessary for her story to conform to the Faith novel." She believed the lawyer she had made this long trip to consult would know at once all the details that might or might not match in the demonstration she prepared to impose on him. She next searched his eyes for some form of recognition, but saw nothing except aloofness and perhaps a touch of concern. He was probably wondering, "How can I get rid of this nuisance?"

"You must have had a good reason for crashing at your Aunt Paula's place." Arthur expostulates while he sat behind his impressive desk and feigned being busy, which was a tough act to perform since the immaculate and well-polished wood surface was free of all encumbrances that one would have expected in such a sanctuary. He opened the drawer in front of him and faked looking for something.

Paula was what he had called her aunt.

'I am Irma, she repeated. And my aunt is Paola.'

He looked at her as if he had expected she would state the reason for her visit, and now, he was disappointed somehow.

'I am Pralina's daughter, she insisted. My mother has this friend, you know, Mike, the barber who works out of the same mall where Al's Diner is.'

She could see by Arthur's incomprehensible stare that she was getting nowhere.

'Well, he said at last, am I missing something? What is all this ancestry business for, if I may ask? Do we know each other?'

Irma decided at that moment that it would not be wise to unveil all of her newfound discoveries to this man, who obviously was not familiar with the story, as she had assumed he would be. Why should he be? Zielgard's death was twelve years past. If he had read the dead doctor's novel, he must have forgotten its details, as his ignorant responses tended to demonstrate. He might also have had no part in whatever scheming had resulted in putting Artritis' name on the cover. Furthermore, there was nothing to gain by direct confrontation with the lawyer over what she had discovered. She didn't need to convince him of anything. What she needed was intelligence. Better it be given without Arthur Morin knowing he might be betraying his friend or client by doing so. All she required from him was some confirmation of a few basic facts that would come in handy in her efforts at getting herself invited to the Letterman Show, which was scheduled for next Friday. Three nights away.

'You are right,' she half-smiled at him, still standing. 'My family has nothing to do with this.'

'Please, take a seat,' he finally offered.'

She did.

'As I have already mentioned, we all knew Dr. Zielgard, and the agent, Phil Leclerc, told me you were the lawyer who handled his estate.'

'True enough. Thought I can't remember anything worthy in all of Zielgard's possessions at the time.' While issuing this misleading piece of news, he couldn't but look at the patch of brilliant glitter that flashed out of his bookcase, full of book spines of a dull brown color. Irma saw the gesture, but didn't make anything of it as Arthur finished explaining, 'The guy was a drunk, as you must know if you have looked a bit at all that have been written on him and his ill-fated demise. He left nothing much except the place he lived in, plus some junk. I don't remember having seen your name as part of his relatives.'

'We weren't related,' Irma admitted easily.'

'Then, your being around might be related to that woman they'll execute next Saturday. Is that why you are here? You think I will dispense with juicy tidbits because I knew the man that got her into the sorry situation she found herself in? What, you must be a journalist, is that it? This makes sense… I should have seen this co…'

'The point is, Irma interrupted, would you know if there is a connection between Dr. Zielgard and this book? She pulled out of her handbag the Artritis bestseller.' That got her an immediate and very spontaneous reaction.

'Great book, that one. I am privileged to know its author.'

Irma stayed quiet. This bit, she already knew. She contented herself with staring at the lawyer and waiting for more. It wasn't long in coming as Arthur added, as if it were an afterthought,

'Nope, they didn't know each other. But after the doctor died, I showed Peter some of the man's writing. It looked like that doctor of yours had a hobby. Writing stories, I mean.' He said the last as he would have someone affected with an eccentric side. 'Whatever, he or some other at his Oracle Publishing house returned the stuff back with the usual Dear John letter.'

Hearing this made Irma jump out of her seat. Could it be that things could be that easy? She decided to push her luck with the candid solicitor.

'You still have that rejection?'

'I doubt it. Possible though. We don't keep files that long. We are talking ten, twelve years, for this one. But then, Zielgard was special and we might have made an exception. Why are you asking?'

That's where she came up with a story of her own. Just like that. The silly tale popped out into her head in time for her to say:

"I am a teacher in an elementary school in Biloxi. I am working on a project that has to do with Dr. Zielgard and the soon-to-be-dead lady you just mentioned. So, I wrote a short bio of both characters and I now collect pictures and documents as I find them. Hence, this piece you told me about would look good in my presentation. I doubt it would be considered a confidential document, don't you agree?"

Arthur thought to himself, why not? Maybe he should have told her first of finding an obscure publisher for the Zielgard work on the West Coast, and showed her the published book. But now that she knew the book had been refused by Artritis, he felt he owed it to his friend not to make him look like the fool he was. That Zielgard had finally found a publisher, she would discover soon enough if she was doing her research. After all, she was a teacher. True, the book had not appeared on any charts, but somehow, he had been told the novel had gained itself an audience in one of the lunatic fringe groups they had out there. Up to now, Eternity had sold eight thousand seven hundred and sixty-six copies. He had kept count. Not so bad, after all. California was a big state. Perhaps there were still a few bonkers left to buy some more.

Arthur stood up in his turn. He moved toward a door in his office, opened it, and there were filing cabinets on all three walls of the closet-like chamber. She saw him look for the name Zielgard through an index card case with multiple drawers in it. He found the card he wanted somewhere at the end of the last of such compartments.—No problem, he mumbled joyously, as if he were thinking, if this is all it takes to get her out of my way, so be it.

Arthur got up. He went to look into a metal cabinet. There were eight drawers. He pulled one open. In it, there were white cards. After a few seconds of searching, he extracted one with the name of "Zielgard" on it. And then he had a number. And that number was the solution to where the file he wanted might be hidden. As it was, all right! He invited her to follow him in the basement. There were shelves covering all surfaces with just enough space between them to walk on the side while facing the thousands of files cramped along each other. With the help of the card he held, Arthur found the file he needed. He got it out and wasn't long at extracting the rejection letter from it. He then used a copier to make a copy of the document and passed the newly created piece of paper to his visitor without issuing another word. Irma followed him back upstairs after he had returned the file in his place. She saw her time to say goodbye had come.

"Thank you so much for your help, she said before leaving."

But he had already forgotten about her. She followed him out of his office. She could see his back, his neatly cut hair that didn't touch his collar, and his left arm that he moved as if to say, don't bother. The staff was coming in. He stopped to discuss something with an overweight girl with a yellow hat still on her head. As she was already installed behind her computer, looking busy, Irma wondered if she would keep it there. Arthur interrupted what he was doing to open the door for her.

"Have a good trip back, he said."

It was the last she heard of him.

I rma got in touch with the David Letterman Show's producer, who worked out of some CBS studio in Midtown Manhattan. She made the connection while using the phone in her aunt Paola's small bedroom. The woman had caught her doing it, and from the look on her face and her way of frantically pacing the room, it was clear enough that the restive older lady didn't approve one bit of her niece's initiative and the use of her phone to achieve whatever her goal consisted of. She couldn't know it, but Zielgard had hit bullseye when portraying her in his Faith narration, the woman getting all agitated and acting weird after Manuel told her where she had found her lost wallet and the lottery ticket that was in it.

It was the afternoon the same day after her meeting with Arthur. Earlier, she had called the number on the Zielgard rejection letter and asked to be put in communication with the editor who had signed the document and as it was suggested, had read the material. The name was all consonants and not enough vowels. An Eastern European pronunciation nightmare. She did her best, though. She was prepared to spell the word from the letter she was holding, and was surprised when the woman at the other end of the line could easily enough connect the name with the right person. In this way, she had learned that the man was no longer working for Oracle. She couldn't leave it at that. Without thinking, instinct made her ask to speak to Peter Artritis, and when she did, she regretted the silly impulse, for it would force her to disconnect as soon as the publisher came on the line. She felt foolish and she hated feeling that way. They would know where the communication had come from. Her aunt Paola might have had a point after all.

"Mr. Artritis is not in, Miss… Can I have your name, please, so I can leave him a message?"

"It won't be necessary. There will be no message, she answered. I guess he is in New York preparing for the David Letterman Show, right?"

"He will be on a tomorrow morning flight and shall arrive in New York before noon. Is there anybody else you might want to speak to at Oracle Publishing?"

"Well, Irma persisted, do you know where this editor who no longer works with you can be reached?"

"Mr. Zewkzriurdarhzie works for Little Brown in New York City, now."

"Thank you so much. I will try him there, then."

At Little Brown, she got her man on the first try.

"Zewkz here. How can I help?"

She had prepared, and she let him have her little charade. "I am Irma Sanchez from Biloxi. I freelance for the Jackson Sun newspaper. I am working on an article on the witch case. That is the woman…"

"I know about the witch case, he interrupted. A pity what they intend to do to that poor woman."

"As a matter of fact, she explained, this is also my take on the tragedy. My calling has more to do with the alleged victim, though. Dr. Zielgard, I mean…"

Her interlocutor had no love lost for Zielgard, as his next comment made quite clear.

"A drunk who operated on the woman's daughter while in a state of inebriation, and she died. Perhaps she would have died no matter who had been there, but that voodoo-practicing Haitian lady got it into her head that Zielgard was responsible for the calamity, and she took revenge by casting a spell on the man. Good for her, is what I say."

The editor stopped talking and Irma heard him take a long breathing. Then he added:

"Getting serious though, I still can't believe after all those years how in this country, she was accused and later convicted of having killed Zielgard and should suffer the ultimate penalty for no more than having wished the doctor dead. A full decade of debate in courts of law to arrive to such a ludicrous result."

He stopped talking, needing to catch his breath. She realized that the gentleman was old. Irma waited patiently for him to conclude.

"So, he resumed, half-laughing, as if nothing important could come from a part of the country that couldn't distinguish between plain silly and serious matters, where do I appear in this story of yours?"

"It looks like the doctor aspired to be a writer."

The man with the funny name sighed.

"So many of them out there."

"I am told, Irma said, that you have read something he wrote."

"That would be a surprise, came the answer."

"Why is that?"

"Here at Little Brown, we don't read unsolicited material. You see…"

She cut him off. "I am talking about when you were working at Oracle Publishing."

'That is a long time ago. Doesn't change a thing, though. I am sorry to say it, but if at Diland, I hear they have changed their name for Oracle, whatever, if we were to have received the typed manuscript of *Pride and Prejudice* in a brown envelope and no introduction by an agent we know, we would have missed the masterpiece.'

That got Irma's full attention. "You mean nobody would have read the work?"

"Well, that is exactly what I mean, he admitted without a bit of shame."

"Whatever, Irma insisted, I know for a fact that you have read the Zielgard piece.

"When would that be?"

"A long time ago. Many years."

"I wouldn't remember one way or the other, then. His voice was nice, like he didn't mind the interruption and the small talk. "What did he write about?" He asked Irma. "Doctor's stuff? Case stories? The usual bio? Those baby boomers, they are all into it."

This took the young girl by surprise. As she sat in the middle of her still unmade bed in her aunt Paola's second room, she got the rejection letter out of her bag and looked at it. There was Zielgard's name beside his novel title: *The Man Who had Two Heads and Lost One on the Moon.* She had completely forgotten to ask Arthur to let her have a look at the manuscript. And what if she had seen it? Would that have changed anything? It couldn't be the same text that made out the book Artritis had gotten published under his own name. And then, she realized it wouldn't have made a difference. Because Artritis, for having stolen Faith, as there was no doubt he had, must have returned another copy and made it look the same just enough to escape the friendly lawyer's inquisitive eyes. He might have returned some unworthy drivel, for all she knew.

"I am sorry to say, she conceded, that I do not know what the story is about. And the rejection letter doesn't mention much. Just the piece's title and the Zielgard's name."

"Well, if there is a letter, the editor from Little Brown deducted, it must be that Dr. Zielgard was introduced to us, after all. As for remembering my reading of his prose, as I said before, it was a decade ago. You say there was a rejection letter. It means that the novel didn't impress us much. No wonder I have no recollection of it. Why would I? In our line of business, one remembers hitting gold. The digging part of the job, you would hate it."

"The piece is described as obscure, nebulous and esoteric nonsense."

This last bit of information brought a prolonged silence at the other end of the line.

"You don't say!" Her New York interlocutor finally said.

"Why? Irma asked, and then she stayed quiet since she didn't know what to make of the situation.

"Actually, her correspondent carried on, that rings a bell. Those words you just mentioned, they would have described my take on somebody else's work. How strange that you connect them now with this Zielgard fellow. I doubt very much that I would have used those very same words to express an opinion of anybody's struggle at literature except one man's. Amazing! Then, he repeated the words: "Obscure, nebulous and esoteric nonsense." And he started to laugh aloud.

"Sorry, the girl muttered. You sure have lost me there."

The other ignored the remark.

"You tell me some more about the letter, will you?"

Irma obliged.

"It says that you looked over the Zielgard novel and found it lacking. That it was unworthy of publication."

"Unworthy of publication, he repeated. Yes, that would be it. Still, we wouldn't use those words to address a living author. Do tell me, dear, who signed so rude a missive?

"You did, sir. You and Peter Atriritis did."

And then, she heard:

"Oh!"

Which was more like the sound produced by someone being hit in the stomach. A moment later, he said:

"I'll be damned!"

After the time it took the editor at Little Brown to recover, he asked:

"Tell me again. What is the date on that letter of yours?"

"May 16, 2008."

"I couldn't have signed that letter. I left Diland in 2006. For three years, I travelled the world. No specific address. Only a few could reach me and even then, it could take weeks. Sorry, lady but what you have in your hand isn't worth shit."

—◦◦◦❈◦◦◦—

Her aunt Paola was in the room, listening to her private conversation with the representative of the David Letterman Show, and she showed no intention to leave her alone. Her baffled features made it very clear that she disapproved of what her niece was doing. Her mother's sister could be so critical when provoked, while at the same time would help you any way she could with no regard to inconveniences to herself. All you needed in order to profit from her assistance was getting used to her sporadic whining. When Irma was born, she had come live with them in Gulfport so that Pralina could return to work. Every morning, she would go to mass at seven and be back in time to drive her sister to work with the baby sleeping in a basket attached somehow to the backseat of the car. At Al's, the two women would bring her in. Paola would then be served breakfast, just an order of toast with marmalade and a coffee. The routine hadn't varied for a full six months.

Then, Pralina had gotten herself a raise, money that she used to pay for a babysitter, a neighbor who was the mother of a four-year-old boy named Christopher. She took care of baby Irma for the pleasure of her company, and the little money it might bring. Paola would still make the trip back from Tallahassee every Christmas, though, staying with them for ten days. In this way, she came to be acquainted with Dr. Zielgard, if from a distance. He was a regular at Al's, and consumed Budweiser early in the morning out of a mug that he sipped from like it was full of regular coffee. It was one of the man's many peculiarities that weren't to Paola's taste. Perhaps it was due to the abuse of alcohol, but then, it must be said that Paola wasn't so graceless that she was above making an impression on so dispirited a soul as was Dr. Zielgard at the time.

Legend had it that one morning he had gotten out of his booth and brought himself to address her. What words he used, and what might Paola have done to merit such a distinction? The episode left no witness except the two involved. Only Pralina had noticed when, coming out of the kitchen with two plates of bacon and eggs for the sheriff and his deputy, the pair had talked to each other. Her sister was in a state. As for the doctor, she saw his face just before he turned around and shuffled back to his table with the beer he was nursing in his left hand. Pralina was used to her sister's antics. She asked her:

"What is it?"

Paola was as white as a ghost. She seized her sister's arm as if to steady herself and muttered in a voice quite inaudible,

"He…he…he offered me a drink."

"That's it?"

"Put his mug in my face. I can tell it isn't beer he's got there. Some more powerful stuff that smells like hell. The horrible man!"

Paola's hand was like a grip on the other woman's arm. Pralina hissed at her, "Let go of me, will you? People are looking at us."

As far as Pralina was concerned, Zielgard wouldn't have been so bad a catch. The man was the solitary type. He was well-behaved. As for his drinking, it wasn't like he couldn't handle it. He walked straight. He was well dressed. Whatever his numerous imperfections and strange habits, he was still a doctor. He was someone who had gone to a university and obtained a degree. The man had had an education. He belonged to another world, even if he didn't mind living in theirs. On the other hand, Paola would have been a poor choice as a female friend for the silly physician. For the man to have shown such poor judgment by making so ludicrous an overture confirmed Pralina's first impression of him as a doctor never to be consulted except in cases of extreme necessity, when there was nobody else to give advice. Shoving his cup right under Paola's nose. What could have come into the poor man's head? Pralina wondered.

"The deranged old bugger, she lashed out." And then, to her sister, she added, "Be glad that he didn't offer a free consultation. You look like you need one right now."

"But he did ask me out, Paola complained. The nerve of that individual. Can you believe that he suggested we go tonight to see *The Hours* at the Cineplex at Tyrone Mall?"

"Holy mother of God. What did you say?"

"How could I? The man is a Jew."

Pralina threw a hard look at her sister. What kind of reason was that to refuse a date? But then, she knew Paola and her bigotry. Such a reaction should be expected of her.

"How would you know that?" Pralina inquired.

"His name."

"You're being ridiculous, Pralina snapped at her sister."

"He has an accent. I know a Jew when I see one, Paola insisted."

"How did you get out of it? She asked her still-shocked sibling."

"I told him I was married."

"Nice."

"He looked at my hand, though. He asked me why there was no ring."

"The man is a perceptive scoundrel, isn't he?" Pralina observed with a smirk on her lips.

"It is no laughing matter."

"What else?"

"I told him I was married to Christ, Paola piously finished. And then…"

"And then? Pralina repeated."

"He said he didn't mind."

This was in 2002. Irma had witnessed so many retellings of that event over the years that it had evolved from one narrator's performance to another. Her mother always teased Mike with the story with a burst of laughter and confessing in the end, as this was her clue, "Too bad the doctor didn't ask me, since I would have liked to see that Julianne Moore picture."

So that was the tale that she had learned through the grapevine about her aunt's connection with the writing practitioner and his caustic sense of humor. As of now, the heroine of the affair towered over Irma. She was agitated and restless. Irma sat on the bed and talked over the phone with a faraway deputy executive producer in Manhattan. She couldn't explain her case while her troubled relative hissed questions at her like she was a cat trying to get out of a tub full of water. Over a lot of dismayed, "What are you doing?" "Is it a long-distance call?" "Who are you talking to?" and the like, the niece nevertheless managed to plow through the futile blockade.

"…as I know for a fact that Peter Artritis didn't write the novel."

Silence on Irma's end.

"As I already said, someone else did."

More silence.

"Can I prove it to you? You bet I can. Yes, she said again, believe me, I can. Now, please, wait a minute so I can write this up…"

While using a piece of paper, she wrote and repeated at the same time:

"I present myself at the airport. Continental has a direct New York flight tonight at 10 p.m. I go to their counter no later than 8:30 and ask to talk to Mark. He will know what to do. Upon arriving, call taxi Queen and tell them I am one of your charges. It will drive me to the Hilton Garden Inn on 35th Street. They will have a room ready for me."

When she was finished writing, she added, "Sure, no problem. I will be there tomorrow at ten."

More silence. She wrote the address of the CBS building on 52nd Street.

"I will see you tomorrow, then, Irma concluded. Don't worry; I will get on the plane tonight. Meanwhile, you can reach me at this number."

She gave Paola's Tampa number, and then she put the phone down under her host's petrified eyes.

"What have you done?" Shouted the older woman.

"I am getting myself invited to the David Letterman Show Friday night."

"Why would they have you in there?"

Irma showed her aunt the Artritis's novel.

"I'm going to have the alleged author of that book recant his claim of having written it."

"But, Paola protested in panic, this is crazy… This is insane, demented."

She took a few paces toward the door and stopped at the wall. Next, she turned around and let her incredulous gaze fall on her indomitable sister's child.

"What business is it of yours, anyway?" She erupted. "Well, do you know anyone else that might support such pretension of yours? This Peter Artritis, why, he will not appreciate one bit that you're confronting him with your silly theory on prime-time television."

"He stole Faith from Dr. Zielgard, Irma responded."

Paola shouted back the name, and her cry shook Irma so much that she lost her balance and fell on the floor. Her aunt was so rattled that she forgot to ask if she had hurt herself, which was not like her.

"What are you talking about? She growled angrily. That man was nothing but a white trash, no-good rotter who drank himself to death. He couldn't have done what you suppose he did."

"He stole it, though, Irma countered flatly. And I can prove it."

"I can't let you ruin your life, Paola persisted. This is insane. What about Pralina? She can't agree with such a crazy scheme. I will call her."

"If you must. Mom and Mike know I am doing this. They are like you. They don't like it much, but they nevertheless gave me some money to help pay for the plane fare from Tampa to New York. My contribution is paying what it will cost me to stay there while I am doing this. Now, having talked with Paul Craig, it looks like the studio is paying for all those expenses."

"Sure. Don't you see? You tell them you will attack on prime TV the number one celebrity in the country. They sure will have you. Why would they care if you make a fool of yourself? You helped them with their rating, that's why."

"I know what I am doing, Irma insisted."

"You really mean to do this? Her astonished hostess spat. Going publicly on that show and saying to the man's face that he is a fraud? Why? This guy will sue you to your last penny. And your mother, also. And Mike. And myself, if he happens to learn that I have given assistance to this scheme of yours.

"You didn't help, Aunt Paola!"

"I didn't? When you plotted this operation out of my home? Using my phone number? You even gave my number to that coconspirator you were talking to a few minutes ago."

"That means nothing, Irma affirmed with as much conviction as she could muster."

"Don't say I am uninvolved, Paola shouted back at her. I am plenty involved. And honestly, it's not nice for you and your mother to abuse my hospitality this way. Who knows whom you have called from this room, without telling me anything of what you are planning? This is wrong, Irma. I'm telling you. It's wrong."

"Aunt Paola!" Irma protested. Meanwhile, her kinswoman sobbed silently.

"You have me crying now."

"I am sorry, Aunt Paola. I didn't realize this would upset you so much."

"But it does, the other sniffled tearfully. You get into this and what good will it do? You mark my words. I can see nothing but misery coming out of your initiative."

With those last words, she left the room.

Biloxi 2018

Ollie Devott liked being a lawyer. All his life, he had wanted to become one. When very young he learned that he could talk his way out of any situation. Whatever nonsense came out of his mouth was crafted with an aura of authenticity that made his words convincing enough to whoever put form over substance. And this, Ollie realized before he was ten, included almost everyone near where he lived.

People who knew him in college or in law school would remember him under the nickname Wily Ollie. He had been a good student. He could have been described as brilliant, but in relation to him, friends and foes favored words like clever, smart, sharp, or devious. Nobody ever doubted that he would be a success. He would grab enough of the law to be able, at will, to deconstruct it to ultimate lunacy and meaningless outcome. That is, any meaning that didn't support his reading of it. This was a great quality in a lawyer, one that distinguished the ordinary ones from those with real talent.

Local judges of the elected variety were easy to confuse; he would win verdicts out of juries under their benevolent assistance. If his triumph was questionable enough, he would settle the case before its dubious outcome could be reversed by appeal courts. It was nothing but a game. And he could play that game better than anybody. The money was great. Juries liked him. Juries followed his lead. Juries were voters. So, he had gotten into politics. Less money. More power. He had gotten himself elected District Attorney in the county where he lived. And then, District Attorney for the whole state of Mississippi. This was all well and good. But not nearly enough, since he had ambition for a larger goal. He had his eyes on the governorship. And then, who knew?

For those accomplishments, he could thank the witch. It had been a good instinct, the one that had caused him to take that case thirteen years back. At first, they had laughed at him, those smartasses in his legal community who cared for the east coast's legal sensibilities to the point of ignoring what the folks down here in Mississippi were comfortable with. His fellow neighbors were mostly churchgoers, and all were firm believers in one God who had created the world they knew in six days, like it was written in the Holy Book. They were his brothers. He knew them well. He had learned over the years where they concealed all their secret buttons, and could get the most beautiful tunes out of pushing those the right way.

Hence, he had gotten his sights on the voodoo woman, and right then, he had seen it all clearly in his mind, all that was to follow. And it had. He had made it happen. It had all worked out like he had anticipated in that instant of intense lucidity, when he was turning pages in her file and deciding to use his skills as an advocate to take her down. It hadn't been easy. There had been resistance. It had divided the legal community all around the country. It had made him a public figure. Nowadays, he was looked upon as the celebrity he was. His black American face had appeared in newspapers and magazines all over the world. Editorials either relished his efforts or desecrated him for his crass ways and practices with judges and juries. That was easy to write, from a distance, when you hadn't been exposed to the man's compelling rhetoric and intelligent discourse laid out in opened court. Come in there and confront his conclusions where it counted, he wanted to tell them all.

Instead they were rewriting the debate after the fact out of the safety of their office cubicles while servicing a readership that wouldn't care for their guidance in the first place if they were to sing another song. Challenge in the proper way, he had experienced. As the dispute had taken off the ground, it had fast become an issue opposing those who believed in God and those who didn't. All the secular organizations regrouped and tried to creep into the witch trial, sending lawyers, writers, clerics and professors from all over the country that tried to be recognized as an interested party in the debate. Some of those showing the best of credentials, pillars of the law, professor emeritus in top notch universities, writers of books and treatises, all with theories of their own over the case and who had tried to save the silly woman's life.

All those efforts had been to no avail except to maintain their notoriety, and that of the organizations they supported. Thanks to Wily Ollie's clever and skillful direction and help from his side—God's side—the Churches and the religious right had sent their own sets of lawyers as illustrious as those from the opposite faction, with tenure in as good and distinguished houses of higher learning and as many volumes written on the same subjects, but with different conclusions. Those squabbles had evened themselves out. They had also made Ollie Devott one of the best-known lawyers in the whole of the United States. He had won a conviction. The case had made its way to the Supreme Court three times over the last decade, and it had survived the ordeal, the verdict left intact. As well as the punishment, which in the end, was all what it was about. The never-ending debate in the country between those who wanted to apply the measure and the others who couldn't stand it.

What a flair he had shown when choosing to put his career behind that prosecution. That had it all, if you cared for controversial, intense, and spectacular polemics. Now, he was forty-six years old. He was on top of his game. It was 2018. He had his eyes on the governorship of the state, and was quite sure to get it as he had the backing of the most influential republicans in the South, plus the fact that the time for old Pat Allanson to leave the office had come. But the silly bugger wouldn't go the easy way. He would fight him. As he had over the woman. Why? The man had put himself in his way so many times that he had become a man to be reckoned with in the nation's liberal establishments. Some even said that he had his eyes on the presidency. How come such a pussy had been elected in the magnolia state?

What a fool he was, that Pat Allanson. Playing the monkey and mimicking on TV show the attitudes of the blabbering idiots on the left. And thinking the moronic affectation would render someone with his background palatable in sophisticated circles. Rosa Maman Tour de l'Isle's fixed date of execution was three days away, and in the actual governor was all the hope she had for a stay. Ollie had decided not to worry about that. If Pat should choose to grace her, it would mean he intended to desist from the race for the governorship. So much the better for Ollie's chances to replace him, and if it took the witch surviving her crime, then so be it. However, it wouldn't happen, even if Allanson had been provoked to admit the week before on some show on the Fox network that he was still considering the pros and cons of such a determination. Let him! Such wavering was good munitions in Ollie Devott arsenal.

Ollie had been invited to the next David Letterman Show. This evening, he would fly to New York in the network's private jet. Here was an opportunity to fire a volley of bullets at his oscillating opponent. He knew the drill. He anticipated the Letterman researchers planting questions in order for his host to get under his skin. But he knew all the answers. These TV people, they had no more than a few days to prepare. They consulted lawyers to suggest the right questions, but how could the host be able to handle the follow-up? These guys couldn't embarrass him. They were the ones who risked the most, David always insisting on having the last word, and he, in this case, left to decide if he would let him have it. Ollie had argued the case ten times in appeal and three times in front of the full nine judges of the Supreme Court. There was nothing even the most confrontational show host could do except give him an opportunity to shine.

Which he knew he would that night. It was so easy to do so. He could see their obvious questions coming like they were tanks on a football field with cannons firing crowd-pleasing dilemmas at him. Tonight, he would respond to their banality and platitude by shocking them, all those viewers who couldn't take life in stride, who needed protection from the truth, who had invented a new sanitised language and set of attitudes to deal with existence's unpleasantness, who had changed the world he lived in by repainting it in a new color, as drab and dull as political correctness could make it. Tonight would be the last of such performances. And then, he would turn the page on this whole episode and concentrate on getting elected governor of his state in two years. That was his rightful place at that time in his career. Let him do that job for a few years and see where it led him.

His bungalow overlooked a marina. Some boats down there were as big as his building. It was one of the very first houses to be built on his street of smaller homes. Then, two generations later, the real affluent people had taken over the place and erected palaces that dwarfed his residence into insignificance, making it look like a guest cabin at the back of their mansion. He didn't mind. He enjoyed his small piece of property. It belonged to him. He knew he could have made plenty of money, but he had chosen another road. He lived alone. He didn't need much. What he liked to do most cost nothing. His parents had bought the place and had lived there all their lives. It looked directly on the intercostal waterway, which was half a mile wide in front of his dining room bay window. A nice piece of water it was, and the two bedrooms he had inherited were one too many.

He had kept his childhood one and used his parents' for an office den. As a matter of fact, he still slept in the same bed he had had all his life. What about that for solidity and permanence? He had been an only son. His mother and father had loved him so much. They had died twelve years before in a car accident. That was when he had decided for their sake to move back in. The house was still like they had left it at the time of their leaving for that dinner party. They hadn't made it there, though. They had been crushed by a bus on its way to the airport. It was said that the driver has lost the use of the brakes while going down a hill.

He hadn't married yet, and he had no plan to do so in the near future. No woman. No children in his world. It wasn't like he had decided the lack of companionship from the start as a deliberate and premeditated act. The right occasion had just not presented itself. Out of the numerous times the magic could have happened, it never had. Whose fault was it? He was not of the kind to get concerned much over such a dead-end kind of interrogation. He believed in marriage, and could talk about the subject as well as if he were a preacher in a church. He liked to think that his present celibacy wasn't the result of a conscious attitude against the institution. Family was his thing, after all. He just didn't know how to start one for himself. Perhaps it was because he had seen his parents interacting, and to reproduce their happiness and felicity was an act too difficult to be tried. But then, he was still young. There was plenty of time left.

They had told him that a limousine would take him to the airport at eight tonight, as he would fly to New York City in a private jet. Some big shot friend of someone important that happens to visit New York for business and didn't mind giving a lift to the Mississippi district attorney. TOD was fixed at eight forty-five p.m. That left Ollie ample time for an afternoon round of golf. He went inside and picked up his clubs, which he dropped in his trunk. In the mirror out in the foyer beside the living room, he saw his reflection and was reminded that he wasn't dressed properly to play the sport. As he never was. There once had been a dress code at the Royal Oak Country Club. This was long before his time, when the place was exclusive, expensive, and provided for the whims of the well-to-do. All that had changed as the eighteen-hole golf course became public and people of his sort took over. Furthermore, he loved the game and played it with moderate grace. Managed to maintain a score under a hundred most of the time, with no need of funny accounting practices. He might find a friend to play with. On a weekday, there weren't many chances for that to happen. He didn't mind playing alone, though. He liked to walk the course's few miles in solitude, enjoying the breeze, the sights, and the singing of the birds. Chances were that he would have the place all to himself. This would be perfect for thinking of his meeting with David L.

The Royal Oak might have lost its most select clientele of antebellum elite, but had nevertheless preserved the vestige of its ancient elegance and old-world luxury. The clubhouse wouldn't have looked wrong as a pavilion in Louis XIV's garden in Versaille. You had to get inside the building to get an idea of how dilapidated the edifice really was. Not that it was in danger of collapsing. Just that it needed some revamping after forty years of neglect, since the city had bought the location. Yet, the course itself was green enough, and if hitting a ball a few hundred yards at a time was your priority, then the Royal Oak was your kind of place. And you could do it in shorts and a t-shirt with running shoes, or in your bare feet.

He parked his five-year-old Ford Mustang under the shade of the tree that still showed on its trunk's mutilated bark the 'O' of his name, beside the 'N' for the girl he had been in love with when he was eighteen. The silly inscription was still visible to him because he knew it was there. Mercifully, as a caddy who carried others' bag of fancy clubs, he had refrained from going public with the romance, and it had petered out rather ignominiously before the summer's ending. Ness had had a ten handicaps, though, and from her, he had acquired a better comprehension of the many ways to interact with a golf ball. In addition to improving his game, there had been the kisses and some unmemorable séances of clumsy petting in the grass when he was fighting insects to get to her skin.

He walked with his cart toward the rear of the palace-like clubhouse and the pro-shop. He hoped Harry would be there and hopefully give him a time of departure within the next half hour. He had talked with the man that same morning. Harry had told him, "It will be a slow day. Come early in the afternoon. I will find you a spot. No problem." So he was there. When he approached Harry, he saw that there were a few people around waiting to get started. Four women who sat twenty yards away were observing an older player as he took a swing at the white dot resting on a mauve tee, which he propelled somewhat lamely on the left side of the fairway, where it would be lost in woodland. The foursome were all dressed up in proper golfing outfits, and when the lady with red hair under a Royal Oak issued cap saw him, she bumped shoulders with the competitor next to her and murmured something in her shorter friend's ear. Then, all members of the small group looked at him. He was a celebrity. Not everyone liked his politics, though. He saluted them from afar, unobtrusively. An infinitesimal gesture that could have been anything. A blonde woman caught his signal nevertheless and beamed back at him.

After the inept golfer had left the teeing ground, his partner put herself in position and with one elegant swing hit the ball fair and square. It disappeared into the sky, disturbing a few crows that protested the intrusion with angry clamors. Harry yelled at the waiting foursome:

"Your turn in five, ladies." Then he addressed Ollie. "Great to see you, counselors. What's up?"

"Not much. I see you're busy. You think you might get me through the swarm, Harry? You do that and I will be in your debt."

"You already are, Ollie. As you should know."

"I sure do. Let's see. When you commit a crime, Harry, I will make sure to peel away a few years out of your fair sentence. What do you say?"

'Do you mean if I steal the money in the cash register, you will get me off with a reprimand?'

Before Ollie could comment, a voice resonated behind him:

"Is this an invitation to engage in wrongful activities from a pillar of the law?"

Ollie turned in the direction the interruption had come from. Behind him, he recognized the smiling face of Robbie McDermott, the New Jersey chief legal counsel in Rosa Maman Tour de l'Isle's unsuccessful defense. The guy he had screwed over so many times in all those years. He was the perfect archetype of a do-gooder out of a white, upper-class, newly selected aristocracy. The champion of lost causes whose organization used his skills to promote its political agenda. Ollie had come to like this long-time adversary, paying him the respect a fighter might earn for himself in the ring after falling a few times to his opponent's assaults, and yet coming back for more. You couldn't beat these guys. They were on a mission. They could never be wrong. Everybody else was. Ollie didn't care much for that attitude. Being a Negro in white North America had taught him that much. To engage in such naïve and ingenuous behavior and make it a profession, you needed to be born into it, and this excluded someone like him. Turning toward the golf pro, he said with a smirk:

'Don't say a word without the presence of your lawyer.'

Harry shouted to the women, "You girls are free to go. You have a good time, now!" Then, he adressed the prosecutor who carried his driver on his left shoulder. "You fix all your cases this way, Ollie?" he asked.

The prosecutor ignored the question. To Mc Dermott, he said:

"I didn't know you had family around."

"I don't."

"Then what are you doing a thousand miles or so away from home?"

"I felt like enjoying a little round of golf."

"Don't tell me they don't have golf courts in New England?"

"They do. But there is no way I could play them with you, is there?"

"I guess not, Ollie concurred. So, he added, you have made this entire trip just to see me?"

At that, Robbie chose to stay quiet.

"And would I assume wrongly if I say good old Harry here played a role in your being here to ambush me? Am I right?"

Harry butted in, saying rather defensively: "This gentleman called every morning for the last four days. Wanted to know is if you were going to play. This morning, after you called, I told him when you would be here."

"As you should, Ollie reassured the discomfited golf pro. My dear friend here has certainly put himself to a lot of trouble for a chance of meeting with me. He must have holed up in some flophouse situated on the wrong side of the tracks as he waited for the right opportunity."

Ollie turned away from McDermott and looked in the direction of the four women, who were walking out of his field of vision on fairway number one.

"So, he asked Harry in a tone of voice as sweet as he could make it, can you give my distinguished colleague and me a starting time? It would be a shame if an eminent North Eastern barrister couldn't play the Royal Oak after putting in so much of an effort."

"You can go now, Harry responded, his face all contrite."

Ollie then inspected the other lawyer's attire, and as expected, he found it faultless. Robbie had dressed in such a way as to reproduce the image of the ultimate golfer. He was the image of perfection, so much so as to get on someone's nerves. In his usual sarcastic manner, Ollie mocked him.

"I hope you make good use of that outfit of yours. Why, you look like Peter Seller playing the sport in an episode of the Pink Panther."

Robbie followed the District Attorney as he walked toward the teeing ground for hole number one. Ollie carefully placed his ball on a yellow tee and practiced a few swings out of the range of the small projectile. Then he hit his target with enough vigor to send the tiny white globe flying fast out of sight. He liked the noise his wood had made when coming into contact with its target. He couldn't say where his ball had landed, though. His newfound partner in the game bowed in appreciation.

"Straight ahead and beyond the two-hundred-and-twenty-yard flag, he announced."

McDermott, who carried his bag of clubs on his shoulder, let the load fall in the dirt. Ollie smiled at him.

"I can't believe you're going to carry this weight all the way to the end of this round, he uttered in feigned surprise. Why, he continued, ask Harry. He will loan you a cart."

The other man was already getting ready to drive. Addressing Ollie, he mumbled something like, "Don't you worry about that," and then in one quick motion, he propelled his own missile half a football field ahead of his companion's.

"Now, the latter conceded, that was unexpected. Don't tell me you made this entire trip just to see me humiliated."

McDermott picked his bag up off the grass and hung it off his left shoulder. He stared a long time at Ollie without saying a word. Then he turned on his heels and moved out toward the fairway and their game. At hole number 5, it looked for the first time that Ollie would get his chance to beat his adversary from the east coast. It was a par three. McDermott's ball had landed in a sand trap. Luckily enough, his was on the green, ten feet away from the pole. Walking the distance that separated one stroke from the next, Ollie had learned that his colleague had been visiting his parents' vacation condo in Mobile and rode the forty miles from there to this place. The bag of clubs was his father's, as well as the older Lincoln he had driven and that was now waiting under the shade of a tree in the parking lot. So, there had been no cheap motel for him to sleep in, after all.

"The flea house would have made for a better story, though, Ollie had laughed."

His second shot had missed the flag by a foot. It stopped on the other side of the hole in the middle of a slope so trivial that he hadn't cared to bother with it, and now, he had gained no footage over his previous position while his opponent had waltzed his way out of the pit. He restrained himself from throwing his putter where the instrument would rut in eternity. The odds for him to steal the hole were quite nonexistent now, as he readied to save his normal. He missed, and this put him in a foul mood. Losing affected his character. His response to the stress of being second place was always poor. Growing older, he had learned to conceal the worst of it. He forced a smile on his face and got his lips to mouth the usual complimentary platitudes after McDermott hit his third shot right into the hole.

Robbie had once been a semi-professional, and might have made it as a career if there hadn't been Harvard and his family's history with the law. At hole number 10, which he no longer expected to win, the best golfer of the two turned to the other and said,

"You must have figured it out why I am here, haven't you?"

Ollie avoided the piercing stare of Rosa Maman Tour de l'Isle's lawyer and the obvious answer he was not yet ready to pronounce. Instead, he joked:

"You wanted to beat the shit out of me."

He could well discern that there was no jollity in the other man's façade. From that point, McDermott was all business. His eyes were filled with anxiety, wariness, and unconcealed despair. Ollie wondered how the fellow, in such a state, could play a round of golf so well. He knew he was this guy's last hope to make the world a better place. Those silly lawyers had to take everything so damned personal, fighting their cases as if they were crusades against an evil that they alone had the power to define and erase. They felt their self-proclaimed, benevolent agendas were a god-given right to inflict onto democratic society. That liberal bunch respected no codes, rules, or statutes if they got in the way of their philanthropy, morality, or ethics.

"You can do better than that, McDermott corrected with a disheartened sigh." Ollie thought, perhaps, it was because he had just seized his father's heavy-looking golf bag with its full gear of fourteen wooden and iron clubs.

"Then, Ollie pronounced, resigned at last to play into his colleague's game, you came all the way here from New York just so we could discuss Rosa Maman's future?"

"Does she have one?" The other asked matter-of-factly.

They played some more. The silence between them became more uncomfortable as they approached hole number 15. It was forty minutes pass five. He was half an hour from home. He would need time to prepare for his trip up the east coast. Maybe he would make the limousine driver wait. Could he? Have a private jet to miss his schedule for no better reason than his playing a round of golf?

He must terminate this competition, then. The darn case was ruining his game. His second shot disappeared into the woods. Again, he had to suppress the almost irresistible impulse to catapult his wooden number three in the direction of where his stupid ball had hit the ground. But McDermott stood less than a hundred feet from where he was. He would not fall apart in front of this man.

He started walking toward his ball. What club was he to use? Better not to know. That way any that caught his eye would do. Behind him, he heard the vexatious 'clack' made by the connection between two hard objects. Somehow, he knew that his Tiger Wood-like adversary must have hit the green. This contrasted nicely with him, as he would soon be forced to concede a stroke for having lost his Titleist or whatever brand of ballistic he had been using. Damn if he would walk back to the spot where he had last struck. This was not fun anymore. He strode across the ground, all bushes and whatnot in the spot where he remembered having lost sight of his ball. He couldn't have played with a Titleist, though. Those were what McDermott had been using. The fellow had made a show of telling him about the box of twelve he had bought at the pro shop that same afternoon. That had been his way of putting the DA in his place. Now that Ollie thought about it, it had been no different in their dealings together over the witch case. McDermott had always acted as if he were so sure of himself, and he, the District Attorney, was an irrelevant obstacle with arguments not worthy of serious consideration. The guy had looked so comfortable losing to Ollie's antics. You had to be born into this, Ollie resented. There was no way one with his background could learn how to reproduce the attitude. He would never make it into McDermott's crowd.

Later, when it was no longer possible not to discuss the real reason for their encounter, the New York barrister had confided to him,

"I have a meeting scheduled with the governor tomorrow at ten."

So that was why he had come all this way. Ollie was just a side show. What was there to say? Nothing came to mind, so he kept his mouth shut.

"I would like to be able to tell him that I talked to you…"

"Allanson will not like that conversation, I can tell you that much."

"He has the authority to be merciful and save that woman's life."

"Yes, indeed."

"If I could tell him that you do not object to my appeal for clemency."

"Me, who asked for the death penalty right from the start? Why would I do that?"

"The deranged woman should be left alone to die of old age. At least you should know that."

"That's not for me to decide. The jury did it. Remember?"

"Whatever. The woman is a lunatic. She doesn't deserve to be put to death."

"Who does, according to your standards?"

"Well…"

"Your client, she would have cut three babies to pieces and made them into a ragout. You would tell me the same shit, arguing she didn't deserve to die."

"And rightly so, as the woman you just described would have been out of her mind."

"Yet, you get my point, don't you? Rosa the witch is no more than your pretext to be here. It is the death penalty you are after. I can't believe you bother me at this late stage with those same litanies of yours."

"It is a horrible thing to inflict upon another human being, and ten times more dreadful in this specific case."

"You seem to know more about the case than me. As far as I am concerned, Ollie added dismissively, that woman has been convicted of a crime for which the law of the state punishes with death. My job was to argue the case, not to decide upon it. It was your job to prove me wrong. Ten years of legal wrangling, thanks to you people, and look where it has left you, waiting in one governor's anteroom begging for a murderess's life. I wouldn't want to be in your shoes."

"So, will you do it?"

"You must have been told that I harbor the ambition to fight Allanson for that governor's office in two years."

"I wish you luck, McDermott lied."

Ollie looked at the other lawyer. They were now walking hole number 18 in direction of the club house. He had to leave fast if he wanted to make it in time to his home. Why did he feel as lousy as he did? Like he had crashed a party and they were all speaking a language he didn't know.

"The point is, this is all politics. You convince the governor and tomorrow he goes your way, then you help me in my campaign."

He saw real pain pass in his interlocutor's eyes, who started to say something but got cut off by Ollie's continuing conclusion. "This is what his take on the matter might be, mind you. Politics and nothing but. You tell him I approve of your initiative; he will see that as a play from my part. And who would blame him? Voters have the last word, haven't they? It is not as if you would care about that, though. You wish to have things your way? Go into politic. Get elected!"

There was not much golf left in his vis-à-vis, and no argument that he could come up with that had a fair chance of making an impression. Ollie recognized McDermott's posture at the end of a court-debated issue when he realized his words were not being heard. Yet, when in a jam, he was worth listening to, as he seemed capable of recouping under duress, able to rally all the rockets he had left in one splendid conclusion. Now, the same lawyer looked beat up, though. He glanced at his watch and said:

"It's getting late. Maybe we should skip the rest of this game."

Ollie had told him about his Letterman appearance and the limousine at eight that would bring him to a private runway and a super jet with an arrival time in N.Y. City of 10:30.

"A shame, he quipped, always the court jester, just when I was making a comeback."

As they walked past the green and were in view of the clubhouse, Ollie said to his gloomy companion:

"I feel sorry for you."

"Try Rosa, he heard McDermott mumble."

"I am sorry for her, too. As if it would change anything."

"You could let me tell Governor Allanson tomorrow of your new disposition?"

"I wouldn't trust you to cite me correctly, Ollie smiled back."

"Write it down, then. Surely, you can do that much."

From some distance, they heard the word "Fore" and an instant later, the plop of a ball that dropped fifteen feet ahead of them and continued to roll toward the green. Two teenagers far behind with no shirts on their backs were sending signals that could have meant anything from, 'We are sorry,' too, 'Will you fossils move out of the way?' The DA accelerated his pace. He now hoped to reach the end of this quite disturbing tête-à-tête. He forced a laugh out of unsmiling lips, showing his teeth nevertheless, all white and straight, thanks to his dentist's expertise.

"I won't write down such a thing, he disclosed. Sorry means feeling regret. And regret means distress over an action performed. I will not have you babbling to my future opponent that I wish I hadn't accused Rosa Maman Tour de l'Isle of any crime, or hit her with the harshest measure the law permitted in her case."

"So, you used her?"

"I didn't… he started to say."

"That is all this poor woman represents to you. Some kind of vehicle to bring you up on the political stage, is that it?"

"This can go both ways, you know."

"I didn't start this circus. You did."

"Sorry to disagree, Ollie protested. Your client did."

"Right."

They continued walking. They finally made it to the clubhouse's terrace, where people drank beer out of mammoth pitchers. Ollie was dying for one of those. He would have to wait, though, because there was no way he would deliberately prolong the encounter and the irritation he felt. When McDermott was in his car and ready to go, the prosecutor informed his New York counterpart, as if it were a departing gift he was offering him:

"I tell you what. Tomorrow, you tell Pat Allanson that he is free to do as he pleases."

XXII

Peter Artritis was at the studio with other guests. He would not be asked to sit beside the great man before late in the show. So he had been told. The stage he was on was like a beach under the sun on a summer day at noon time. It was hot. The light was brutal, with an artificial incandescent brilliance. He felt the rays hit him like they were physical particles. Out there, protected from the discomfort of his position by what looked to him like a black hole, was the audience. They were mostly cheerers, and they certainly were good at it since no joke, sally, or quip went unnoticed, or was left without the right combination of applause, laughter, chortles, or giggles. He wanted to close his eyes, but he fought the impulse. The first thing an assistant on the set had told them was not to do that, since they were on television. People were watching the show by the millions, and who wanted to get caught that way in his life's minute of fame? Not that he was part of that crowd of easy listeners, though. The telly, he didn't watch. Not the regular programs. Not the news. Not the presidential debates. Not even the devastation of hurricane Katrina and other calamities when they happened.

What about social media, then? Just looking at the people near him, he could well see them all occupied at fixing their phone using frenetic fingers to write down four or five words pointless messages. Another activity the same assistant had banned while on the stage. Still Peter could see his neighbors anticipate the instant they would be free to use their gadget and post insipid brew to be look at on similar machines all around the planet. Not him. He had resisted the infatuation. When in need of a phone, a quarter was all what he needed. Angela had a Facebook account and visited the place regularly. He had one too but never contributed anything.

Then, he must be missing a lot, he was often reminded, and he had the good sense to agree. Still, those mediums left him cold and indifferent.

He forced himself to look around. At his sides were chairs occupied by other guests. In front of them sat David Letterman, separated from his invitees by a desk-like table. On the left side of this setting, he observed a mobile platform with people sitting on theater-like armchairs, three rows and five seats each. These places were filled by a dozen individuals. He had been told that they were part of the program. A selected cast made out of people in the know, mostly journalists, invited because it was felt they were in a postion to chat with the invitees du jour as there was a time in the show where they would be offered an opportunity to discuss and question the visitors. In the lot, a girl attracted his attention. She had striking features and blonde hair. She held a book in her hand. From a distance, he could discern it was Faith. The lass was in her twenties. What was she doing there? He had been told questions could be thrown at him coming from the audience. He hadn't paid attention when inform of such. Would she try to embarrass him? If not, what was the point of her presence? The girl looked at him. He forced himself to smile at her. She didn't respond. That sent a chill down his spine. He hoped he was mistaken and that she hadn't been looking at him after all.

Now, the host had both his elbows on the hard surface between him and the black man he was conversing with. There was a file open in front of him. His hands picked out pieces of paper and his eyes cast a quick glance at their content while his invitee talked. What was it about? He should have listened. Letterman must have found a juicy morsel because he shouted a question that sounded more like a dilemma. The applauding crew approved with a lot of cheering. "Who is this guy?" he asked the smaller lady sitting beside him. She had black hair and a face like a bird. When she answered him with a smile, he was surprised she didn't squawk him back her answer.

"Ollie Devott, the celebrated prosecutor who won the Rosa Maman Tour de l'Ile conviction, chirped the woman."

As Peter was looking through her without seeing, she added:

'The witch.'

Peter wanted to retort, "What witch? What conviction? What the hell are you talking about?" But he couldn't. There was no gain in letting his goose-looking neighbor know about his ignorance. This fellow Devott looked like he knew his business. Some of his snappy retorts got him a few rounds of applause of his own, and Peter could see that that worried his inquisitor. This Devott was obviously sharp. He sure could handle all the teasing his host directed at him. Letterman's biting irony made him look like not much more than a "faire valoir" to his guest's panache.

Peter Artritis had enough sagacity to recognize éclat when it was put in front of him. He couldn't but ask himself if he would, when his time came, perform as well as this member of the bar, though. The man should've had a tough time in the suffering chair he sat upon. The man, he learned when making sense of his answers, had prosecuted an old Negro woman for having bewitched her prey dead. If that wasn't a silly enough piece of litigation, what about the fact that the wretched creature was now waiting to be put to death by lethal injection the day after tomorrow at six in the morning? The story was vile, and yet, those two were acting as Bob Hope and Walter Matthau might have in a funny movie where everybody knew that, in the end, all would finish well, that the condemned victim would be delivered out of her dungeon, and the barbaric sultan would accidentally fall in a pool full of piranhas, though the fish wouldn't show an appetite for his flesh. But this wasn't a scene in a movie. This was real life. There were more repartees from the Afro-American District Attorney, which elicited sympathetic approval out of the studio's anonymous darkness.

Peter couldn't but ask himself how the spectators of that sorry performance could react in such an inept and asinine manner, all of them gullible and partial to the juggling lawyer's demagogic proficiency with words, beliefs, and ideas, as well as his irresistible sophisms to express it all. Artritis could detect the fault line in the barrister's reasoning. Still, he couldn't come up with a better assault on the chap's elaborate show than what David Letterman was actually doing, which wasn't much. He then recalled that a jury made up of similar people had acquitted O. J. Simpson of any wrongdoing in the killing of Nicole Brown. That explained it all.

The blonde girl's hair flowed freely down her shoulders. A knockout, she is, he thought. She had her gaze fixed on Ollie Devott, and he could see that she sided with Letterman. He laughed at himself for the silly thought. As if Letterman were free to have an opinion. All he did was play the devil's advocate to his invitees' idiotic conclusions, because there was no other tune he could sing at the moment. Yet, the comedian would argue the exact opposite if there was a need. It all depended of whom he ended up interviewing. Those damn broadcasting mercenaries. All the same, Peter could sense that the girl was clever. It showed in her pose and bearing. Whatever intervention she was there to make, he hoped against all good sense that it would be directed at Devott or some other guest. The hardcover she was holding, though. That worried him. It must mean something.

For now, Letterman looked like he had run short of gags and embarrassing gibes. As a result, the Mississippi District Attorney was like a 400 HP Ford Mustang let loose on the highway, unrestrained and able to ramble without interruption as he made one distasteful argument after another, and the host let him. Clearly, Ollie Devott had taken over the whole circus. The trainer in the ring was no longer in charge of his animal.

What in hell was the bugger talking about now?

It was a tale about growing old.

There was no doubt that the chap had talent. He certainly could tell a story. Artritis, as a would-be author, could recognize that much. He heard the crafty shyster's narration. How when he was at work a few years back, his assistant interrupted whatever he was working on to tell him that some witness he had wanted to take a deposition from was there to see him. It had been John Wilbur, a fireman. When he was in his office, Ollie had been surprised by how big the man was. His hair was cut short. His jaw was square. You could see he had shaved, and yet his cheeks looked rough. The DA still remembered the strange feeling that had gotten when looking at the fellow. The guy had been a full-grown adult. That was the way he remembered his father from the point of view of a ten-year-old kid.

He had invited his visitor to sit on one of the government-issued chairs that were part of the room's furniture. He then searched for the proper form that he needed for the kind of statement he had in mind. There were specific spaces for the name, address, date of birth, and such. He asked the obvious questions. The answers came out in a baritone. Safe and firm. The information was reliable, as one would expect from a grown-up. Just what was required. No embellishment, small talk, or idiotic digressions. Not a word said in vain. One couldn't but admire such a specimen of humanity. A real adult.

Ollie confided next to his smitten audience, in preparation of his little anecdote's denouement, how he had wondered if he would ever be like that man.

He had written down the information he needed on some conflagration or other, and then, he'd taken notice of the box where, a few minutes before, he had penned the four numbers of the fireman's year of birth.

1960

He compared the experience to being hit on the head by a baseball bat. Why hadn't he caught the meaning of that number when he had first put it there? He'd been born the same year as the man. The year they had elected Kennedy as president.

The damn fireman was his age. He was John Wilbur. Could others see him as he saw the fireman? No doubt they did. And yet, when he had looked at his image in the mirror that very morning, all he had seen was the nineteen-year-old teenager he still believed he was.

At last, Letterman's chin revealed some tension. From his position, Peter author could see some discomfort in the otherwise jovial disposition of the host. Would he be able to shut down this loquacious, ebullient joker? The lawyer was an accomplished crowd pleaser, though, winning more and more approval, as shown by the vigorous clapping coming out of the subjugated audience.

Ollie Devott, who must have realized that his time was up, concluded his monologue with, "Never saw myself in the same way after that."

That was the host's cue to take over. But he missed it. He looked over his guest's head to someone making signs at him. Ollie caught the great man's attention back when he added, "Well, I guess I am finished here. What do you say?"

That was it!

In this way, he got the last word, as he always did, those who knew him the best liked to observe. It was later noted in a celebrity magazine that had apportioned one paragraph out of a longer piece to comment on his very unusual interview's termination. The piece's juicier subject was the immense scandal and public discomfiture of the newly discovered and celebrated author, Peter Artritis, son of mogul Spiros Artritis, over the writing of the world bestseller Faith, which had just been made into a mega budget movie.

According to reporter Canarie Tottletale, what happened was:

Ollie Devott left his chair while Letterman tried to recover by telling a joke so he could share in his audience's exuberant display of appreciation. Then, a boy tapped on Peter's shoulder. "You come up next," he was informed. They had already explained to him how it worked. Letterman was no longer in his central place. He could see him talking with a guy who had a lot of equipment attached to him or around his person. He had a cup of coffee in his hand and was sipping at it while listening to the technician's instructions. The interruption would last four minutes, after which David L. would go back to his seat and his next guest would be called. A young man looking buzzy was just behind him ready to tap his shoulder expecting Peter, upon that signal, to walk toward the great man, who would stand to shake his hand and invite him to sit.

While Peter waited, he felt nervous. He felt nauseated. He couldn't believe that he would manage to find in himself enough force of character and discipline to make it to the seat assigned to him, let alone express himself in a coherent way in front of millions. What was he doing there? On the wall's electronic countdown device, the number changed from three to two.

Two minutes left.

There was still time to bolt. Run away. The heat was punishing. He would say to them that he wasn't feeling so good. That was the truth. Or he could decamp without saying anything. Why not? He didn't owe these people anything. What could they do to him? Nothing. His book was already published. His was a big success. The movie was being seen in hundreds of theaters. Renowned Hollywood stars were already acting the scenes. They wouldn't stop on the grounds of too timid an author.

One minute to go.

And he was still there. He caught the eyes of the young blonde woman. He could see that he was the object of her silent scrutiny. He smiled at her. Not much of a smile, at that. She didn't return it. She looked away from him. Why? Perhaps he hadn't smiled enough. Maybe he was just imagining the damsel's unlikely prying on him. And what if she was? Was he not somebody worthy to be curious about? What was wrong with him? Why couldn't he enjoy his newfound fame the way he had dreamed he would when the time came? It wasn't supposed to be like this. He was afraid. What was there to be frightened about? Nothing. But still he was.

A thunder of clapping interrupted his musing. It was too late for him to get out of the game.

Apart from dropping dead, that was.

David Letterman was comfortably installed in his seat. The audience calmed down. The author of Faith could hear his heartbeat accelerate. They told him to stay still and wait to be called. Why wasn't he? His mind was in total chaos. The pounding inside his arteries reverberated crazily under his skull, each pulsation like a detonation. One thing became clear. He might not survive the ordeal.

Letterman was telling one stupid joke after another. What was he supposed to do? He could sense the boy's presence besides him. The waiting was killing him. He wasn't made for this kind of life. He shouldn't be in this studio. This was a mistake. He had no right of his own to be there.

And then, the host emitted his last quip. Peter heard his name being shouted and then, he responded to the delicate pressure on his left elbow. The sound system discharged a quick introduction that described him as the distinguished author of the book everybody in town was talking about these days. He surprised himself for being able to get on his feet. Mercifully, his heart was no longer a problem. He realized he could walk toward the great man. He was calm. This was a miracle.

And the girl in the audience? What about her? Why worry?

She was just a fan.

Peter left the studio in a state of enormous confusion. He remembered vaguely having walked out of the set, bumping into a technician and making him drop an instrument he had been holding. He was running away. He must have been. Because he was no longer around to hear the sound of the device crashing to the hard floor, or the tumult that followed his hasty departure.

He hadn't bothered to wait for the lift. With water running down his cheeks, his vision impaired, he had barged into the stairway, and it could have been said that he flew his way down four steps at a time. Outside, he had skipped the limo that he had been told had been left at his disposition, and would normally have brought him home.

All he wanted at the moment was to vanish into the night, namelessness and invisible. He felt like a character in *Back to the Future.* Would he find his way back to his previous life? That is, if it would have him.

It was not yet eleven o'clock. There were still a surprising number of people ambulating on the sidewalks, like they had nothing else in mind, nowhere to go, and were walking around downtown without direction. Happy and without a care in the world.

As for him, like in the Leoncavallo's opera, *Pagliacci,* he had been given his line.

"La commedia è finita!"

The temperature was mild. A light breeze and his swift pace sent his disheveled hair into his eyes. He couldn't see that well anyway. He realized he was crying. All those tears gushed out all over his face. He couldn't recollect when he had let himself go to such a state in public.

How could ordinary life continue for everyone else when the air he breathed oppressed him and was no longer life-sustaining?

One couple from the other side of the street stared at him. The woman wore a red dress, and was alone with a cute outfit among a throng of female passersby who had jeans or shorts on. The red dress lady was addressing her escort, and from the look of them, he could discern it was him they were talking about.

He changed direction and ran as fast as he could away from their curiosity, wiping clumsily with the back of his hand the ill-timed deluge from his face, not thinking, oblivious to his surroundings, searching for a lair to hide in, and well aware that for him, there no longer existed such a place. Raw luminosity on his left told him he was approaching a store. What could be still open at that hour? Flashing green neon lights projected the PHARMACO's name onto the darkened avenue. When he passed in front of the establishment's automatic doors, they opened. That made him stop in his tracks. In his quite confused state, he saw this as a message of some kind.

Maybe the solution to his trouble was inside. He went in. There was nobody there except him. No employee or other customer in sight. But the place was huge, and there were so many lanes of shelves peddling everything, chain store like. Someone could clothe himself with the stuff on display there. He could also survive on the dry and frozen food that was offered. Or get the basic junk his car needed to run properly. Even remodel his house out of a well-apportioned tool section that sat beside an outside furniture area. It was filled with the usual folding tables and chairs, all colourful and comfortable looking. He felt the appliances had been left there, waiting for him to choose one to sit on and tell his story. He let himself fall into a robust, light blue, plastic easy chair that sat beside a big 200 BTU colossus of a barbecue-like device. He closed his eyes to protect them from the harsh glare of the fluorescents, which dispatched maximum wattage white light mercilessly and uselessly.

Some remembrance of his predicament made it back to his troubled mind, and anyone could have seen on his features how hard he was fighting the recollection. It was so difficult to relive the scene.

That girl!

He had known from the start that she was there for him. Whatever he had led himself to believe had been delusional and nothing else. Misleading himself. Something he was good at, wasn't it? The girl had been waiting for him in one cruel ambush. She had left him with nothing he could have used for protection against such an attack. He could well see now that he had been finished before it even started. All his answers to her accomplice, Letterman, was just more rope for him to hang himself with. The wretchedness of it all. To think the great man had known it all from the start. Playing him and his deception, like a cat would have with a mouse. Those two must have foreseen the scene-crowning finale, anticipated his ultimate implosion and the grotesque escape that followed.

How would he survive the discomfiture and humiliation? All the people he knew, all their friends and numerous relations would have put themselves in front of their TV set on his behalf.

What about his wife?

He couldn't think of Angela at that moment

The incongruity of his surroundings took his spouse out of his distraught mind, and that, at least, was a relief. The sound system was playing a song. It was Tony Bennett's "I Left My Heart in San Francisco." The light was unbearable and again, he shut his eyelids. As darkness took over, so did the dejected ruminations. And that persisting question he couldn't push away: how would he get through his disgrace? It was an impossible proposition.

The ballad stopped, to be replaced by a very poor improvisation on the theme of the hit song, "If I Were a Rich Man" from *Fiddler on the Roof.* He couldn't care less for the carnage of the cheerful melody. He then relived his painful encounter with fame and how nice it had all felt in the first instants when the attending public had given him a standing ovation. One well-orchestrated piece of business, getting the obliging crowd to show its appreciation of a newly discovered author. Well, he very much understood now that it had all been part of the malevolent performance, getting him as high as they could so his fall would look the more spectacular.

He couldn't but see himself as he must have appeared to the millions of spectators watching the show and smiling benignly to their enthusiastic welcome. After a time, David L. or some member of his staff must have been sent a hidden directive, because, in a matter of seconds, they had all stopped their silly exhibition of infatuation, as one would calm a dog by throwing a bone in its direction. Their master gratified the lot with a brief movement with his head, while his lips mouthed a few words of thanks. Or perhaps it was something else. Peter Artritis, who had then found his seat, thought he had heard his host articulate, "Fricking idiot" instead.

Enough of that.

That was more like it. Was it at that moment that he had developed an instinctive dislike for his smiling companion? Or was it when he comprehended that he was to share the spotlight with some foreign baryton player who had landed in town to perform the role of Papageno in the Metropolitan Opera's adapted version of *The Magic Flute*, which they had made to fit the New York urban décor of 2000? The already seated writer had tried not to show his annoyance for being branded second-tier entertainment, a wrong the hangman lawyer Ollie Devott hadn't been made to suffer. Peter Artritis couldn't have known, and if he had, he would have been grateful for the short respite. Some music out of the Mozart masterpiece was being played on the studio sound system.

It had the beneficial effect of calming him.

XXIII

ngela and Peter had married in 1985. They were so young at the time. He was the only man she had ever known intimately. She'd been nineteen when she'd met him. He'd been twenty-two. The rest had been the most beautiful adventure of her life. And it still was. He had fallen for her as Warren Beatty had for Natalie Wood in Frank Capra's *Splendor in the Grass*. Theirs had never been a teenager romance, though. Both had known from the start that neither of them could live and be happy without the other.

And it had worked out marvelously. What a perfect life they had had together. Was she naïve in entertaining such a belief? After all, what experience had she of what a perfect union between a man and a woman should be? She couldn't compare her husband with any other man, could she? How did she know, then? How could she be satisfied and secure in the notion that the older you grew, the more you appreciated the virtues of a singular fusion, with no meddling in the process? Spiros used to say that love was like an investment. You respected your capital. You treated it properly and it would grow bigger and bigger.

As for herself, she might have expressed the same in another way. When she looked at a movie or read a book about a great love story, she would marvel at the fact that no lovers in those tales had had it better than she had. Few could say that much nowadays.

She was alone in their St. Petersburg domicile. Peter was in New York. The day before, she had driven him to the Tampa Airport. And now, late at night, she was watching on channel 4 a cocky African American lawyer whose fame relied on his ability to ruin innocent people's lives. He did so by gathering together members of his community who were gullible

291

enough to do his bidding - if he could reunite them in a jury and share a courtroom with them.

It was a pity, the free ride the annoying individual had been given, his inquisitor poorly informed and appearing ready to let the merciless debater have "le dernier mot" on all issues. At last the importunate jurist had exited the set. But not before having left them with a little story of his own, a nice one which showed that the soapbox orator had a bit of style after all. Besides, what he had said was so true. When one looked at himself in the mirror, what he sees has nothing to do with reality.

Then they called her husband's name. And there he was, sitting with David Letterman and looking his usual self, worried and uncomfortable, the poor dear. He had never been at ease when he was the center of attention.

The image on the screen changed. The crowd's applause dimmed. An enchanting music took over. She had no trouble identifying the Mozart piece. Once, when they were still quite young, she had bought, on an impulse, tickets for *The Magic Flute*. They'd been in Atlanta. Their children, Patrick and Tammy, had been with their grandparents for the weekend. She and Peter had been invited to her cousin's wedding on a Saturday. The trip back required them to be at the airport at six p.m. on Sunday. As for *The Magic Flute*, it was a matinee with a one o'clock starting time. It would be finished in time for them to make it to the Hartsfield-Jackson Atlanta International.

Sophie's wedding had been nothing if not an extravaganza of bad taste, which was a perfect example of the countless ways one could throw money away. That high a degree of silliness couldn't have been achieved by her aunt alone. She must have been helped, for her exuberance to manifest itself in such a frenzy of absurd spending. Well, money was like alcohol. One better be able to handle it. Angela was soon to learn the culprit's name. While they had waited to get inside a thirty-five feet long limo, her ecstatic relative had pointed at an overweight lady as she was helped into another strange-looking vehicle. She was Florice Merriment, and she owned a business that went under the name THE FIRST TIME.

Do it once

Do it well.

Do it big.

Do it expensive.

The first time is always worth remembering.

While caracoling on the dance floor of the four-star hotel that hosted the celebration, with Peter working hard not to make a fool of himself, she told him about her Amadeus initiative. He had had a few drinks, and she might have found him more receptive of the idea for that very reason. He hadn't said much, too busy counting steps and bumping into their fellow dancers. Then, they'd gone back to their table. A less graciously predisposed mind than hers, for all Peter's clumsiness as a waltzing partner, would have seen in the trampling of her feet some deliberate disposition on his part. He sat on his chair and she could perceive relief in his eyes. At last, he addressed her.

"We're going to an opera, aren't we?"

"Yes, she had said."

"Those things are endless. What about our trip back home?"

"The show starts early in the afternoon. We will be out of there before four at the latest."

"And you got us tickets?" As if he wouldn't have believed her capable of such a deed.

"It will be a good way to spend the day, and this will give us the opportunity to visit the Atlantic Center for the Arts."

He had stared at her, a sort of half-smile forming on his lips. It hadn't stayed there long, though, and she couldn't figure out what passed through his brain. Luckily, he hadn't asked how much it had cost her to get into Atlanta newly built opera house. Instead, he had pronounced with a wink,

Don't ask me to dance anymore, will you?

They had made it to the Center. Angela had been very excited about the prospect of listening, for the next few hours, to mostly older, bulky performers hollering love duets with stentor voices, then dying, killed either by rivals or by their own hands. Such had been her husband's take on the genre, anyway. He had been twenty-nine-years old at the time. He hadn't known much. Angela, for her part, had sure been ready to learn, as she babbled nonstop about how this trip could be seen as a good starting point for their, up to that moment, quite lacking cultural life, if one was to discount picture shows like the *Roots* miniseries. Now, she had argued, was the time for them to look upon the Tampa art scene. Go to concerts when they were offered in that city, or in St. Petersburg, by both their philharmonic orchestras. And assist the Grand Opera at home as such performances were proposed in town, even in Sarasota and Orlando, for the devoted amateurs who didn't mind traveling a bit.

Peter had sat beside Angela, reading something that wasn't the program. He heard his wife's pitch. He knew music. He had listened to a lot of the stuff at home as his old man used to read himself to sleep while tuning the PBS 89.1 classical radio station. However, he was not yet there. One day he might be. But it sure hadn't looked like it would happen that afternoon in that auditorium.

Finally, the lights went out, the maestro was called to the pit, and the orchestra delivered the overture's first notes. This had the advantage of slowing down Angela a bit in her scheming to become a pillar of the arts in their community. He had sat through the *Flute*'s first part, looking at his watch, and might have slept before it was finished, but a big ruckus in the end, with all of the singers yodeling their parts in a kind of very excited and disorderly confusion, brought him out of his torpor. This might be the finale, he'd assumed. But he'd been wrong, and was made to endure another half hour of the silly nonsense. That had left him ample time to reminisce about the emperor Joseph II's character in the movie *Amadeus*, telling Mozart over one masterpiece or other,

- My dear young man, don't take it too hard. Your work is ingenious. It's quality work. There are simply too many notes, that's all. Just cut a few and it will be perfect.

Now he knew what the fellow had meant. That had brought a smirk to his face. Or perhaps it was in appreciation of the curtain falling down, at last.

As their seats were on the second balcony in the middle of an alley, there was no way to get through the multitude of beaming opera lovers and gain a fast exit from the place. Angela was sure making a good show of clapping, overdoing it a bit, as a matter of fact. The noise coming from her display of blissful gratitude… Well, an older lady in front turned to look at them with an air of silent reprove. Then he'd realized that it wasn't Angela the woman was staring at, but him. Or not him, really, but his hands, which weren't producing any sound, since they were still, and he was quiet. That had somehow started him up with his own display of appreciative fervor.

It took them an eternity to clear their section. Nobody was in a hurry. There were not enough stairs to go down. Those people in the audience were no longer in their prime, to say the least. They moved slowly, and didn't seem to care if it were to take them a lifetime to make it to street level.

He wasn't that way. Not yet. So, he fumed noiselessly. He fretted behind his wife with heroic restraint. She ignored all the overtures in the crowd and missed opportunities to shove her way forward, as he would have gladly done given half the chance. Finally, snail-like, they had reached the huge reception lobby. He could see the exit gates two or three hundred feet away, and a patch of reasonable open space if one were to go through the left and follow the wall of the edifice.

As he started in that direction, he sensed Angela resisting his impulse. Worse, he saw her moving toward the center of the great hall where the throng of strollers gathered like a cluster of avid bargain hunters around a stand that trumpeted the sale of a recording of the afternoon production highlights.

This was too much. Still, his vain protestations were nothing to his wife's enthusiastic errand. Obviously, it was not enough to have at great cost suffered through three hours of *The Magic Flute* live, but now, it looked like the "chef d'oeuvre" was to be brought home.

At a price. They had some nerves, these artsy folks, peddling their wares like gypsies in a bazaar. Such a prank. And him the mark that fell for it. Under his incredulous gaze, he saw his wife approach one salesperson and happily complete the transaction. Next, they navigated through the press of gawkers, he sensing in his back their smirks and silent criticisms for the sucker he felt he was. Yet Angela was elated, and wisely he managed to keep his displeasure well concealed.

The day after, around six p.m., he was in his study on the second floor of their home in St. Pete. He was reading. Angela was preparing supper. Both Patrick and Tammy were playing with the kids next door outside. He could smell the fragrance of the roast cooking downstairs, thanks to his spouse's judicious assiduity.

And then, there was something else. What was it that had made him lose his place on the page he was blindly staring at? He was hearing something. It was coming from their living room. Music. It was vaguely familiar. As he was concentrating on listening, he took more of the piece and kind of enjoyed it, as when one might fancy a lake's cold water after having suffered the first two minutes of immersion. He liked so much the overpowering rhythm in the cadenzas that a couple of singers were purring in each other's direction that he couldn't help getting out of his seat and barging down the stairs toward the kitchen.

"What is that?" He asked Angela.

She had half her head in the oven. He could see the meat and its perfect color, like the music that was now coming at him loud and clear. That tune was irresistible. Something inside his guts wanted to grab Angela and dance it through its stunning finale. From the stove, she told him:

"This is the duo between Papagena and Papageno."

"What are you talking about?" He countered with a shrug.

She looked up at him, showing no surprise at his inadequate response.

"It's from *The Magic Flute*. I'm playing the record we bought, remember?"

The record we bought, he repeated in his head. Now he would get credit for a gesture that he would have denounced not half an hour before as a daft extravagance. He must have made an odd picture as she added:

"What is it, honey? Is everything okay?"

"You mean… he mumbled. And then he added through his teeth: "How did I miss this yesterday afternoon?"

The next few weeks, he must have played those highlights ten times or more. Then, he bought the whole opera and listened to it some more. It wasn't long after that that he discovered Mozart's big three: *The Marriage of Figaro, Don Giovanni,* and *Così fan tutte.* By that time, he was already into Verdi, and when the CD came to life, he had already built himself a sixty-two title vinyl collection. He had gotten through the lot and loved them all.

What he had learned from his first unwelcome encounter with the world of lyrical music was that, like many other things in life, one must keep an open mind. Give oneself a chance. As for the musical, it might translate this way: if you liked anything at first hearing, you might not like it for long. On his first introduction to a musical piece, one hardly heard anything. The mind did, though. Appreciation came with familiarity. You listened to some work while doing something else. You did that a few times. There was no need to pay attention. In this way, the music got into you, penetrating and growing inside you in a kind of insidious manner up to a moment when the magic operated. This was when you stopped dead in your tracks, transfixed because suddenly, you recognized a passage and you realized how much you liked it.

The Romanian baritone had just put an end to some comment on the Russian ex-Premier Mikhail Gorbachev's heritage, which Letterman used to issue a crack of his own. That got Angela out of her reverie. She couldn't make heads or tails of the joke, and blamed herself for not keeping ahead of world affairs. And then, the great man with a discriminating grin turned his undivided attention to her unsuspecting husband.

t was past eleven at night. It was Friday. Arthur Morin had had a long day in court, and he hadn't achieved much as nothing had worked as it should. A witness hadn't shown after he had talked to her two weeks before, and the woman had been more than cooperative at the time. While looking at the summons, he had caught the blunder about the room number. 212 on one side and 512 on the other. His eyewitness must have gone to the wrong place and been told to get lost one time too many. He knew the staff on the fifth floor, and one would have needed to work hard to get help from those fellows.

He'd had to ask for a recess. He wouldn't win the case by the weekend, as he had promised his now very unhappy client. It would have to wait a few months at the least since his opponent hadn't missed the opportunity to play his, "Oh, I am so busy" act, not finding a hole in his schedule before early the next year. He'd fumed, but couldn't say a word without risking being rebuke by the presiding judge in front of a very pissed plaintiff. All this was his recently hired secretary's fault. How would he survive the calamity of losing Lisa, his previous assistant, who had worked for him for thirty-one years? She'd quit and was moving to Australia with her new husband.

He wasn't that young anymore. A lawyer's job was difficult enough without one's efforts being impeded by blundering clerks. Now, thanks to that silly woman, the big verdict he had committed to deliver for his client's pain and suffering was pushed back to a later date, and there was no way he could explain it away to the very dejected lady that had walked out of the courthouse besides him. It was his fault. So, he told her so and offered to cut his fees from thirty to twenty-five percent. She had been most generous, for she had refused. A grand gesture on her part.

He was now at home glued to his big-screen TV. He had found out by chance Peter Artritis participation in the Letterman t.v. program. How come this bloke who was his client and a friend hadn't let him known in advance of his presence in the show? He would have been invited to sit in front of a camera anywhere and he sure would have called upon everybody he knew well and less well to let them know about his performance to come. He lowered the sound to a minimum, since he didn't care for what the Eastern European baritone had to say. He was perusing his Merrill Lynch monthly report. Well, he thought, there was more than enough for him to stop working. He could sell this place and retire to his late aunt's condo in Pt. Brittany. Why wasn't he doing just that, he asked himself for the hundredth time.

Upon returning to his office after the dual-date subpoena episode, the work he had expected to be done wasn't. The machine the substitute lady used to transcribe his words on paper from his dictating tape had broken down. Worse, he had found her in deep conversation with some family member and she had been crying. He made out somehow that an uncle of hers was very sick. So, he couldn't say anything. Work was piling up. He would have to get used to it. He couldn't live like that. Not at his age. He realized how lucky he had been for having been blessed with Lisa for all those years.

Suddenly, he saw her as the camera moved around the set, taking in the people that were there, first the audience and then, the contingent of the public's representatives, who were seated closer. They were part of the show, and there would be a time reserved for them to fire their questions at one invitee or another.

There she was. He recognized her easily. She was the same blonde girl who had barged into his office unannounced and asked him about Dr. Zielgard. What was it that she had asked him? He tried now to remember as he worked his remote to get the sound up. He must have been quite distressed with the sorry situation at his office to have forgotten the damsel. What was her name again?

Irma!

He had that politician's gift of never failing to remember a name. She had asked him if there had existed a connection between that long-time dead fellow, Zielgard, and Peter Artritis. What a strange question, since she must have known there was one. The rejection letter that he had given her. The story about her being a teacher who was interested in the witch's case. This was no more than a tale that he had gobbled up like a very junior rookie. And now, there she was, a thousand miles away from home, sharing the stage with his friend, and he couldn't but anticipate mayhem with the up and coming confrontation.

Finally, the camera focused again on both Letterman and his bestseller writer guest. It had been many years since he had asked Peter to check the Zielgard's story, and since then, they hadn't seen much of each other. His friend looked older, as he obviously must. How fast time passed, he mused. And soon, we will both be in our graves. Thinking again of the trouble in his office, he thought, "Do I really need this?" I have been a lawyer for thirty-eight years. Sure, it was fun, as long as I had the proper backup. Yet, going to court and having to double check everything and being insecure all the time, he wasn't too good at that, or at looking over all the smaller details of a case, something he had forgotten how to do since he was used to having it done for him by his previous perfect assistant.

Artritis did look older. Like that black lawyer had said, so was he, even if he couldn't draw the correct conclusions when looking at himself in a mirror. With his friend, it was another matter. For one immensely successful author, he didn't appear much pleased to be sitting where he was. Why did that guy always appear to be out of focus with his surroundings? Like he was on a faraway frequency that was difficult to catch? Arthur had known Peter a long time and never really connected with the man. It might have had something to do with the fact that he favored friends that showed a bit of sport, jest, and jollity in their rapport with others. He liked his buddies to have funny nicknames, and addressed them that way in pool parlors, on the golf course, or at their Friday night poker games.

Peter Artritis was not that way. He was the serious type. Grave. Solemn. Grim. Once, in the late eighties, he had tried to build a relationship with him, inviting him and his wife to some Italian restaurant in downtown Tampa, and was later invited to the couple's luxurious residence that looked on Tampa Bay. Things had not worked out. They couldn't find a subject to talk about. The publisher was unreceptive to his small talk about court cases or political comments, issuing now and then odd obiters that were like stray bullets in a field, impossible to figure them out, leaving one wondering where the hell the shooting was coming from. He had like Angela, though. She acted in a way so protective of her husband. The man must have had something going for him, though, having been able to secure such a companion and getting her to adore him so much. As it went both ways. Just being with them five minutes, one could see that clearly.

He turned off the light. On the screen facing him, his client's placid façade reverberated in the sudden blackness that now surrounded Arthur. You could sense the man's nervousness as he prepared to submit to his interrogator's intrusive prying. He knew witnesses well, and this much, he could judge from afar.

There was nothing to worry about, though, and there could be no doubt that Peter would do well. Like if he was in a court of law and answered Arthur's probing with carefully edited responses. He had forgotten all about the girl and the unease created by her curious presence.

At last, Peter had told it all, who he was, where he lived, whom he was married to, his children and family, what he was doing for a living, Oracle, what he liked, whether he was a fan of football, as he obviously was one of baseball. In this way, they talked of the novel he had written. When was it written? He told the viewers that the Rays' success in season 2008 and its ultimate demise at the hands of the Phillies in the World Series had inspired the story. And what a great story it was, Letterman had then offered as he brandished the book over his head for all his audience to see. This provoked a spontaneous round of applause from the gathering of fans. What about his other stories, Peter had been asked. When had he started writing? Had he published anything else? Or tried to? Perhaps under another name?

That was when Arthur had discerned something, a shifting of the eyes, a quite imperceptible signal, very difficult to detect to an unsuspecting bystander. The solicitor had seen enough of the same in his law practice to recognize when a witness was no longer telling the truth. Peter was still there doing his Peter act. And then, something somehow was out of sync. Arthur concentrated on what he was looking at. There was a kind of laser-like precision in the questions being asked. It reminded him of a deposition when he threw a hostile defender a set of well-concocted queries.

Yes, there could be no doubt about it, something was definitely wrong with Peter's performance. He could also detect in Letterman's attitude that he, too, had sensed a bit of discomfort in some of his guest's less than candid clarifications.

Letterman was now working Artritis like he was an opponent lawyer building his case. Each question cried for an objection that he was not there to issue. He didn't know why, but Arthur had an idea of how this would finish.

Bad!

In his experience, it always did. Peter was plowing his way through it all the best he could. For each of his responses, he fell a little bit more into the hole he was digging for himself, and would soon be pushed into it and buried. Arthur could see it coming. It was happening right before his eyes.

And then he knew Irma's presence on the set had to do with his premonition of a disaster yet to occur.

"Have you ever been in Biloxi, sir?"

This was the girl. The young woman had a nice voice. Her diction was precise. She wore casual clothes, but they all did since it was summer. She alone in the panel had shown an interest in Artritis. Two other participants had addressed the Magyar baritone and gotten bitten by his assertive, derisive riposte that left them wondering if they had asked the right question, and certainly cut out their impulse for an encore.

Peter looked at the blonde female who had spied on him since he had sat down beside Letterman. He didn't know the lady. Perhaps she was just a fan of his. Still, for reasons unknown, he resented her attention. What kind of question was that? Why would she care what places he had visited? Biloxi! Who in his right mind would want to go there? A place on the Gulf. A gambling place, at that. How long would this thing last, anyway? He had been told that questions might come from a panel of people chosen out of that day's audience.

There was not much for him to do except indulge the girl's curiosity. "Why do you ask?" He said. Are you a travel agent?

That got him some cheers and a short round of applause. Still, Irma was undeterred.

"What if I am?" She smiled back. "I gather you didn't, then?"

"You might."

"What about your characters, sir? How do you get them?"

"Well, he answered back, with a bit of annoyance showing in the lines on his brow, I create them where there is a need. Really, there is nothing to it."

'So, it's that easy, isn't it? How come then, Sir, most authors complain of finding that part difficult?'

Arthur didn't like this 'sir' business. The cold formality of it. It was highly disturbing.

"I don't know about my fellow writers friends. As for myself, things just pop out in my head and I use what I find in there."

"The reason I ask, sir, is I was told some authors will look around and pick people they know and use them as characters in their stories."

Arthur was transfixed in front of his TV. So, he thought, this is what it's all about. That was where this confrontation was going, wasn't it? Peter might have worked Joe Black out of one of her folks, and now the daughter or the niece or whoever she was wanted a piece of the action, some sharing of the wealth, a percentage of the movie rights and whatnot. The solicitor sigh in relief. What silly nonsense. If that was what had induced the girl and she fancied she could get herself a piece of the action with such a notion, she had another thing coming. He Arthur sure would see to that.

He hoped it was that simple. Why was he apprehensive? Why the butterflies in his stomach? Why was his heart beating so fast? He must take hold of himself. Could it be there was something wrong with his acumen?

"So, you question those I used in my book?" Peter retorted rather flippantly. The word 'question' he had used discharged like it meant 'harass' and he was the victim.

Back in his living room, Arthur pondered, why is he on the defensive? Somebody in Peter's position should smile twice as much as considered necessary in normal society. He should look cool. He should answer all questions as if he appreciated them being asked. He should… He should… Peter had the look of a suffering party on the dentist's chair. Now the audience was all rigid in their seats and he could well see they were picking up the same vibes he was. The smirk on Letterman's lips was devilish. The crafty fellow must have known something was up.

"What about the location, then?" The girl persisted.

"As you must know if you have read my book, Peter said, all the scenes happen where I live, in St. Petersburg, Florida. As for the setting, it is the same as the characters. I made them all up."

"So they are not real, is what you are saying."

That angle again.

Arthur would have shut his client up right there. He would have asked for a recess. He would have found a place to talk in isolation with him. He would have done it even if it would have meant feigning having a heart attack, like the one he felt he was on the verge of being hit with right now if he was made to endure this little scene much longer.

But Arthur wasn't there, was he? That was why he couldn't do anything.

"If you mean, is the story real? No, it isn't."

"Have you ever been introduced to Pralina Sanchez?" Irma asked next.

'She is a character in my fiction.'

'Still, have you known her personnaly?'

"I'm not good with names. I might have and I don't remember. But if I did and give her a speaking part in my story, I would know. What is it with that lady?" He responded.

"Or her daughter, Irma? Perhaps you have met her sister, also? Or maybe her boyfriend?"

He was confused. He didn't think straight. He should have remember who she was talking about. It was a long time he had not read Faith. He couldn't come up with the obvious answer that is remembering the scene where Irma and her family are introduced in the tale let alone those people's surname.

'Well, he felt like explaining, they are just people I created in order to write my story.'

'People you created in order to write your story, is that it, Irma repeated in a voice made venominous by her sarcasm?'

Peter had on his face an air of such innocence that it was pitiful. Arthur had read the other man's story a long time ago. Still, he remembered there was in the story a girl who had organized a kind of secret meeting between Manuel and his manager. In some shop or another. He grabbed the book that was on a shelf in a bookcase near where he stood. He was used to browsing through written documents, mostly depositions, and finding his way fast to their juiciest parts. It was no different with this one. He heard Peter articulate after a time:

"Now, you are mocking me."

"You do not know what I'm talking about, don't you?"

The lawyer saw there was nothing Peter could think as a retort to that. On the other hand, Arthur had found the right page. He had figured it all out. Why hadn't Peter, yet? Pralina. Irma. Paola. Mike the barber. Was it possible that Artritis had forgotten those names? Highly unlikely since he had written Faith the year before. And then, why would he care if they were names he had made out of nothing? That girl though, she must have a point. Her name was Irma. Could it be that her mother was named Pralina? What about an aunt called Paola or her mother's beau going under the name Mike? If these four characters were somehow the source of Peter's inspiration, he couldn't but know about it and it should have been very easy for him to debunk his intrusive stalker with the right anecdote. Why then did Peter looked so vulnerable? He remembered the girl asking him for the rejection letter. Could it be… He had send Peter the Zielgard manuscript a decade ago and the letter now in Irma's possession was what had closed the matter. Coud it be… Could it be there had been something fishy in that conclusion? Could it be this third degree, her presence and untimely insistence be explained by her non believing Peter Artritis hadn't authored the book? A shiver full of worry passed through him. If he had not written the book, then who had? Well, it must have been Zielgard. He brushed the thought away. This was insane. Out there, the silence was becoming uncomfortable.

"It figures, the inconvenient vixen persisted. When was it that you read this book of yours the last time?"

The very question Arthur would have asked. The lass had talent. She didn't wait for an answer. As if there had been one coming.

"No, let me guess, she continued, her tone cold and uncongenial, a decade ago?"

What was that? What is it the girl suggested? That Peter wrote the Faith story a decade ago and sat on it? Letterman should have objected to Irma's inquisition and put a term to the ridiculous performance. But he didn't. This was entrapment. Could Letterman do that? He would sue the bastard if given half the chance. What was Artritis waiting for to stand up and leave? He must have realized he was in hostile territory and couldn't cope much longer. Arthur saw that Artritis was at a loss. At last, the poor man mumbled rather pitifully: "I don't understand."

The charge didn't make any sense to Arthur. All the same, his friend had taken a hit, he could tell. Peter was bleeding, though there wasn't yet an open wound with blood gushing out. Still, the haggard face of his friend revealed it all. What was happening here? That damn Letterman scrutinized his guest with a debonair smile on his otherwise cryptic features.

—∘∘⦅◉⦆∘∘—

Artritis, for his part, had his eyes transfixed on his tormentor, his imploring and dejected individuality reduced to no more than a plea for mercy in one silent and useless prayer. Somehow, she knew. The maddening thought engulfed his mind. How could she? He couldn't say. True, he wasn't thinking straight.

He wanted out. He could still get up and leave. It looked easy enough. Yet, he was paralyzed in his seat. He was unable to move, not much more at that instant than a fly imprisoned in a spider's web. In his throbbing head, there was a question that collided against both sides of his brain in one crazy gallopade. What had he been thinking?

The girl was right. He should have read the silly potboiler before coming in New York to be shot at like a rhinoceros in the wild plains of Africa. He remembered having done so upon receiving the Zielgard's manuscript, without counting his getting through the tale to make the necessary adaptations, like changing the baseball clubs' names, as well as the location where the action took place from Biloxi to St. Pete. Those didn't really count though, since they hadn't required a full reading of the piece. As for his getting through the book last, he had been reluctant to perform the task in the first place. And a task it would have been since executed without pleasure nor gratification. He'd felt no inclination to read those words again.

As they were not his.

Except for some additions, that is.

Did the girl expected him to tell her that? Had he read the book? He had written the goddam novel for chrissake. At least, that was what they were all supposed to believe. Which she didn't obviously. This was her point, isn't it?

As for reading the Zielgard story, he had done it a long time ago only to realize it was a good one. Why in God's name had he put himself in this sorry situation? What pleasure had he imagined he would take from falsely attributing to himself the merit of producing a work that was the antithesis to all his previous efforts at writing original prose? What an abject failure he was. And what a callous critic of his own achievements he had proved himself to be. He was worthless. His life had been worthless. He had sold himself short. And for that, he had been paid a few pieces of gold. And tonight, it was payback time. He could feel the hideous hand of the devil brushing his shoulder. Soon he would be shown the bill. These names she was throwing at him. What if they were those of minor characters in the Zielgard story? They must be.

These were his thoughts while sitting under the studio lights with cameras point at him multiplying his image on millions of TV screens all over North America. No wonder he wasn't at his best.

Pralina. Irma.

He couldn't tell. He should have taken care. His perusing through the book wasn't that long ago. How come he was that helpless and inadequate? Pralina. Irma. They were part of Faith. He remembered now. Secondary actors that had found their way into the story to make Manuel look good. Now that he thought about it, they sounded vaguely familiar. Pralina. Like the French name for some kind of candy. Was it a Christian name? What a loser he was.

"Tell us, sir."

The silly girl was going at it again.

"Have you ever met with or talked to real estate agent Phil Leclerc?"

"I don't remember."

"What about lawyer Arthur Morin?"

On hearing his name shouted at him over the screen, Arthur jumped out of his sofa as if he had been hit by a defibrillator with five hundred joules of electricity in an *ER* episode. Now what? What was going on here? Why was this bitch mentioning his name, and that of Phil Leclerc? Did she intend to hurt him? On an impulse, he seized his cell, as if this would be the first step in initiating a direct connection with the network and putting an end to the idiotic exhibition.

He had given Irma a document that had been in the Zielgard file. It was Peter's letter rejecting the dead man's manuscript. What had this to do with the man who was now being grilled to death in front of a swarm of millions? Again the disquieting thought. Could it be that the Zielgard manuscript he had shown Peter...?

Again, he discard the notion. How could that be? He had gotten it back, hadn't he? It had been returned to him, hadn't it? The piece wasn't good. So he had been told. No big surprise there. Rejection was the lot of most Sunday scribblers. Zielgard had been one of the lucky few though, benefiting from the fact Arthur had later been in touch with those Californian gypsies in the publishing business, because he wouldn't have bothered to question Peter's opinion by showing the Zielgard piece around.

The rejection letter, then. The one he had made a copy of and gave to Irma. He can contemplate the girl's resolute and fierce bearing as there is now a "gros plan" that makes her visage fill the screen. She waits for a reply to a very easy question. What is wrong with Peter that he can't answer with a simple, 'Yes I know Arthur Morin. He is my lawyer.'? Arthur is no mafia-type lawyer that an honest client will chose not to admit having been seen near him.

"He is my firm's solicitor, Peter concedes in a voice frail and hesitant. Why do you ask?"

The firm's solicitor, a bemused Arthur repeated in his mind. Why not, 'He is my lawyer friend?' Why did it look like Artritis wanted to put some distance between them? The lawyer went back to his meeting with Irma. She had asked him if he had read Zielgard's novel before sending it out for review. He hadn't made much of the question at the time. He remembered the joke it had generated. All those judgments from the high courts of the country that he had yet to look at. Now that he was thinking about it, he could see that his insouciance had been unprofessional. He kind of anticipated where all this was going. To his eyes, he looked more and more like those clients he'd dismissed as pinheads because they rarely provided the right answer to his inquests. Well, he could have made himself a copy of the material before sending it away, couldn't he? Then he would have been sure that what he had gotten back was… He desists from that line of thought. This was crazy. Peter wouldn't… He recalls the manuscript that had been returned to him, and it was the same he had sent. He would have caught it if there had been a difference. Wouldn't he? Or Lisa would've. When had she missed anything, that one?

"Do you know Pralina's boyfriend? His name is Mike."

Arthur had read *Faith* after publication. It was not so long ago that he couldn't recognize the names he was now hearing. They were characters in Peter's novel. Why does Peter show himself in such an apathetic manner? Why is the man acting so dull? It looks like he doesn't know what the blonde chick is talking about. Lyn. Irma. Paola. Mike. The barbershop. The mall. Al's Diner. He could have barked back at the girl that they were all creations of his fertile imagination and be done with it. Would he? After all, the Oracle's CEO had affirmed just that right from the beginning. Now, he shows no other response than sipping at a glass of water and using the stratagem perhaps to justify his silence.

"Have you ever visited Al's Diner? Irma perseveres."

How long will this be tolerated to carry on? Arthur suddenly has a vision of what might come next. Still, the ominous concept isn't making any sense. The manuscript sent back to him with the rejection letter had been good stuff, nonetheless. Worth printing material, as a matter of fact. It had been published in California. 'Eternity.' One softcover edition. Eight thousand copies or so being sold over the last seven years. Zielgard had been shown to be a writer of some talent in the end. Who would have used such good writing as a substitute?

"No, I didn't."

"Have you ever visited Mike's barbershop?"

What was it the girl had asked a few minutes ago, when he could make neither heads nor tails of her words? "When was it that you read this book of yours the last time?" A decade ago, she had suggested. That's when he had sent Zielgard's manuscript to Peter. Well, right at this moment, it sure looked like his friend's perusing through it was a long time ago, Arthur mumbles to himself. It was the only way to explain Peter's inferior performance. It was obvious that he hadn't read Zielgard's manuscript for that many years, or if he did, something was wrong with his head because it appeared to him Peter must have forgotten the narrations' particulars, let alone the characters' names. He realized he had just referred to Faith as Zielgard's manuscript. So, what was it Oracle had sent him back? He was not much of a judge as far as belles-lettres were concerned, but the stuff must have been good, its prime quality proven by his finding these bohemian peaceniks on the west coast that had like the work enough to want to make a book out of it.

Again, he relived the scenes when he had been referred by an artsy client to an Oregon writer who had ended up winning a Pulitzer. Steve Wilbur was the award-winning author's agent. After Arthur had helped both to settle a dispute over some option the laureate had granted Harper Collins to publish his novel, on his way back to the airport, he had bestowed agent Wilbur the Zielgard manuscript. As he had expected nothing, it had been a real surprise to hear from the fellow a few weeks later and to listen to his announcement of having found a community of hippies and marihuana smokers that might want to give the piece a try if Zielgard didn't care to get royalties. Arthur had agreed and renounce all profit out of the venture up to the first five thousand copies sold. Last year, he had received a check for $732.76 with a letter explaining why so low a return. He hadn't cared to investigate. The money had found its way into the succession account.

Who then, Arthur reflected, would steal some junk and send back valuable shit in return? Then he returns his full attention to the forty-inch screen of his Sharp TV set. Had he missed anyhing in the last few minutes of his jumbling around in his head silly concepts and awfull conclusion? Peter appeared pale and defeated. He was sweating profusely, and thanks to one merciful cameraman, there were no more full-screen pictures of him. The poor man had already endured a few rounds too many in the ring, and there was no arbiter to stop the fight.

Peter was getting beaten mercilessly and couldn't do anything to defend himself. Peter didn't have in him what one needed to fight his way out of trouble. His friend and client had, one way or another, done something unthinkable…like abusing Arthur's confidence, and stealing for himself the *Faith* story. Peter must have replaced it with a piece of his own, a piece that he hadn't cared to show around. A piece that he must have liked, but despaired over his inability to protect it against his entourage's indifference.

And he, being of a resigned and submissive nature, had let the matter sleep. He had written good stuff and done nothing. He had not believed in himself. He had had no faith. No wonder he had thrown himself on the Faith manuscript. He must have seen it as a sign. Like Joe Black, who decided to use Manuel at bat after he talked to his lawyer and got confirmation of the youngster having been right in the crazy bullet's case. He must have seen it as an omen that his time had come. That he was now offered his great opportunity to shine.

Well, he had been sorely mistaken. Because right now, the man looked like a fish snapped out of the water and discarded on the beach to die in agony. There was no sound coming out of him, and it wasn't for lack of opportunity to elucidate.

"I assume your answer is a 'No,' then. You never visited Mike's barbershop, didn't you? Irma insisted."

They all see Peter when he shakes his head from left to right and then again. Arthur thought he could discern a kind a cruelty in the girl's tone and attitude. She was in total control. She was obviously enjoying what she was doing. Could it be that he had been that way when destroying a witness with abrasive questions that had no reasonable answer? When he acted as the executioner who was doing the killing, he didn't show much commiseration for the victims of his implacable logic, since he asserted they had put themselves in their seats and were ready to lie to get their way.

"I am showing you now Pralina Sanchez's driving permit. This is my mom, by the way."

On one screen everyone present realizes suddenly existed appears the aforementioned document with the photo of a woman in her late forties.

Well, Arthur concludes. No need to speculate no more. This has been well prepared in advance. Still, the advocate no longer considers fighting over the issue.

Peter stays awfully quiet.

Irma persists by unveiling her own driving permit, then Paola Sanchez and Mike Gordelli's. Irma and Pralina share the same address. Follows a picture of the Al Diner restaurant with Pralina, Irma, Mike, Paola and a man dressed like a cook who must be Al, all five smiling in front of one front glass where one can read breakfast, menu du jour, quick meal, hamburger steak, we serve liquor. The next slide is one of an old man drinking a beer with Pralina sitting besides him. Another shows Enzo's barbershop with Mike at the door. That last picture that lets observers apprehend that both places of business are on both sides of the same dilapidated plaza.

"Can you explain Sir, how come you describe all those places and characters in your novel with perfect details and exactitude?"

Artritis acts like he is out of it. He looks around with eyes half-closed, seeing nothing and acts like he has difficulty to breathe.

"You can't, isn't it? Because you have never contemplated the possibility that some of the characters in the story you stole were real people and couldn't have found their place in that book of yours if it was you who had authored it. What do you say Sir?"

No answer.

"Have you known Dr. Otto Zielgard?"

When he hears Zielgard's name, Peter collapses in his seat, looking like an abandoned puppet. Whatever was left of the author's composure disintegrated at once. Could it be that he is surprised at this late stage with that last query? He must have seen it coming. But then, perhaps not. Arthur had seen so many of those inarticulate lying felons who had stumbled into their fraudulent scheme thinking it was easy. As it might be, most of the time. As long as you didn't find one wicked Irma-type in your way.

'He is the one older gentleman seated near my mother in Al's restaurant.'

'Your mother, Peter repeated as if it were his last words.'

There was one issue left, though. What was it that had alerted vindictive Irma to his harried friend's deception? And then, he knows. As Peter does, sitting alone and defenseless to his badgering tormentor's cross-examination. It comes to Arthur in one flashing revelation. The girl must have known Zielgard, the physician who fancied to put real people in his novel.

Irma. Paola, the aunt from Tallahassee. Her mother, who must have been a waitress at Al's Diner. A genuine truck-stop kind of place, without a doubt. All this in a mall not too far away from one Interstate or another. In that mall, you might also find a barber shop with Mike as its operator, and Pralina's paramour in addition. On reading the book, they would have recognized themselves and known somehow whom the real author of Faith was.

"Sir, let me ask again. Have you ever been in personal contact with Dr. Zielgard?"

He hadn't. Peter Artritis says so.

"Then, have you ever been in contact with him through an intermediary?"

Now is the time, Arthur tells himself, as he is riveted in front of the tube and his heart stops beating. He addresses the small figure of the woman that appeared on his screen, mumbling through his teeth, "Go for the kill, you merciless bully. Put an end to this poor man's misery."

Why had the network allowed that brutal and unfair exhibition? They should have put a stop to the disgusting circus a long time ago. And then, why would they do such a thing, as it was evident that they had been behind the whole execution-like business right from the start?

Irma had procured the rejection letter from Arthur's very own hands. How stupid could one be? What was the bitch waiting for? She had yet to throw it in his face. You finish him up, you damn harpy. Don't you like it, the squeezing, the wringing, the squashing, and the crushing sensation? There is nothing like it, is there? As he knew, for having imposed himself on others in that same way.

Irma was brandishing, at that instant, a piece of paper in front of her quarry. Artritis keeps his eyes closed and appears no longer concerned. Why was the dolt acting this way, Arthur censured mentally? Why is he staying there, taking it all, acting like he was already lost? Just shut the fuck up and walk the hell out, he wanted to shout at the hollow figure that was being deconstructed in the semi-darkness of his living room. Artritis sure didn't look like he was going to obey his faraway counselor's silent injunction.

"This, sir, Irma intoned, is a letter from Oracle Publishing, dated June 10, 2008. Its subject is a manuscript by one Otto Zielgard. Faith is the title of the work referred to. Are you aware of this letter, sir?"

As there was no word or sign coming out of the diminishing shape that sat on the seat beside an aloof and grinning Letterman, the girl continued:

"This letter is addressed to lawyer Arthur Morin. Its apparent purpose is to inform this gentleman that your publishing house has judged the outcome of Zielgard's efforts unfit for publication. Can I suggest to you, sir, that this letter has been authored by one, Peter Artritis, CEO of Oracle Publishing? Is that you, sir?"

This elicited no reaction. There were talks, protests, and murmurs coming out of the audience. More of this and she risked losing them. It was time for Irma to close her act and make some point.

- Might I suggest, sir, that this is the way you got your hands on Zielgard's manuscript. She didn't wait for a proper authorization as she pursued with her implacable conclusions. "I suggest that you were asked by the Zielgard estate's lawyer, Arthur Morin, to evaluate the piece. I suggest that you have appropriated the work for yourself by changing a few things, like the locations where the action takes place, as well as the names of the baseball clubs involved. What I suggest, sir is that you have not authored Faith, this book that you have been invited here to discuss. What about it, sir?" Irma challenged her subjugated target. "Can you say, here, that I am wrong?"

This was when Peter Artritis opened his eyes and stood up. He looked around and found the girl. Their eyes locked onto each other. And then, recovering as much self-composure as he could, he pronounced distinctly, his voice poised and aristocratic:

"You are right. I don't know what came over me. I'm sorry."

With those words, he walked away. Yet when he had reached the tip of the stage where his image could still be caught by the cameras, he turned and addressed them all, making sure that he wouldn't be forgotten by pronouncing:

- It is not finished till it is finished.

At that, he departed. And then real pandemonium hit the studio.

BOOK THREE

ANGELA

n their home, Angela had not remained idle in front of the TV while watching her unfortunate husband getting pilloried to death. Five minutes into Irma's denunciation, she rushed to her house phone and dialed the CBS number Peter had given her in case there was some kind of emergency. Before she heard a second ring, someone, far away up north, screamed at her:

"Are you out of your friggin' mind? I told you not to call back!"

"Who is it I'm talking to?"

Back in New York City, the man with the loud voice and the crude words tried to recoup.

"Sorry, he said, I thought I was addressing somebody else who has been hounding me non-stop. I am Charlie, by the way. I'm kind of in charge around here, for whatever that means. And who are you, if I may ask?"

"I am Angela Artritis. Peter Artritis's wife back in Florida. And to tell you the truth, Charlie, I don't much care for the way my husband is being handled right now. I demand that you put a stop to the trashy spectacle at once."

The voice took on a regretful tone.

"I'm sorry, lady, but this is live TV. I couldn't do what you ask even if I wanted to."

"Why? You are the producer of this disgraceful scene. You put my husband into it, and he was unaware that he would have to face a third degree grilling from hostile harridans with crazy agendas. Charlie, I am telling you. You stop this insanity now, or I will have our lawyer sue the hell out of you all."

Thanks to his experience of many years, the producer didn't laugh in Angela's face. Instead, he said, using his most reasonable and neutral tone,

"Your husband was told he might face questions from the audience. And he signed a discharge."

"Then you knew beforehand, she replied without really fully knowing what she meant."

"What is it that we should have known about? You know something I don't, you tell me."

She realized the impasse she was in. The man was making sense. What was there to know? Irma would soon be running out of gas. And Peter being Peter, he would always look bad in all situations, if given half the chance. That might have been reason enough for her to wish to put an end to the stupid circus. Charlie wouldn't see it that way, though. Peter was like that. She had gotten used to it. His fans would, too.

As she saw she couldn't do anything from her end to terminate the sorry exhibition, she asked him:

"I must be with him. He'll need me after all this is finished."

One thing one must give credit to those big New York studios, they were not in the habit of counting pennies. What they could do easily was given if they could, and without making a fuss.

"Let see, the man hesitated."

Followed silence at the other end. Angela figured he was going through charts and schedules. Then she heard the man's voice coming back on the line. "That might be arranged. We have a company plane in the air right now flying out of Miami. I will have it land in Tampa in order to pick you up. Can you make it to the St. Petersburg airport in half an hour?"

"I'll leave now. Where to?"

"Gate 12. You ask for Bill. He will be there waiting for you with the network jet. This way, you will be at the St. Regis before two in the morning."

She called a taxi as she dressed hurriedly, and watched in total incomprehension while Irma drew to her incriminating conclusions. The taxi was already waiting for her when she left by the front door. Twenty-five minutes to go. She told her destination to the driver, afraid he wouldn't be able to make it in time and listening a bit reassured when he mumbled back that they had ample time to make it at this late hour.

Then, in a state of disarray, she called Arthur. Somehow, Arthur would know what to do.

He always did.

Arthur couldn't trust what he had just witnessed: Peter and his swift exit, followed by images of pure chaos and disarray, all those folks milling around David Letterman, who no longer appeared in charge of anything. The picture on the lighted frame changed to be replaced by some soap publicity. As he was now standing in front of his set, he pushed the OFF button. His friend's sudden disappearance had put him in a kind of frenzy-like turmoil. What about the implications and consequences of what had taken place in the last twenty minutes?

There were so many, and he felt like his mind was like a four-way Interstate suddenly reduced to one narrow lane with one mile of traffic behind waiting to get through. Could it be that it had been a dream? After all, it was late. That aborted trial had left him exhausted and depleted. He looked at the couch he had slumbered on while waiting for the David Lettermann show to start. Maybe he had slept through the performance. Could it be that he had imagined the entire drama? Perhaps it was just his mind playing tricks, and the foolish visions were nothing more than too much wine at supper. The abuse that could have generated the sorry ramblings were likely fished out of a pool of shameful recriminations against Peter Artritis's inadequacy for his rejection of Dr. Zielgard's otherwise good work.

Was that making any sense? Absolutely not. He couldn't think straight anymore. He was sorely in need of a stiff drink. What was it Artritis had said last? "It is not finished till it is finished." It wasn't like the Oracle editor to talk that way. Was it a quotation? Yogi Berra had issued a lot of those cliché-like utterances. More probably, the Yankee manager might have said, "It ain't finished till…" though. A catchy, cute, little attention-grabbing phrase. Definitely not in Peter's usual range. What, then, had come over him? His friend was most probably the last individual in the country who would know who Yogi Berra was, let alone pick from the man's repertoire of smart repartees and bons mots.

What had he meant?

There was something ominous in the communication. Like Peter knew those words were to be his last on this earth.

Now! He was doing it again. Where was that bottle of scotch? He needed a glass. He had to calm himself. He would drink himself to sleep. Yes! That was a plan. Where was Angela? Why hadn't she been there in New York with Peter?

Perhaps she was.

He tried to imagine the state of shock she most probably was in. She too, he thought, must have found it odd, Faith coming out of her husband later in life. So much out of character. Yet those egghead types, they had a knack to do the unexpected and jolt everyone out of their assumptions. Hadn't he been taken in really well himself? And he was the lawyer.

WORSE!

He was the agent who had shown Peter the Zielgard's story in the first place. That same not-so-gifted friend scribbler that had not published anything of his own out of the useless material he had written over four decades. And then, the same individual, under the pretext of the last World Series, had been stirred into producing the perfect novel, a bestseller, a sure bet moviemaking book? A clod who wouldn't know the first thing about the game of baseball if his life depended on it?

No! This last inning grand slam by an improbable .150 hitter was too good to be true. It was like finding some serious musical masterpiece in the affairs of a present-day, dead, junkie, lowlife rapper. What a dupe he had shown himself to be.

He was in the kitchen of his condo in Pt. Brittany. From his living room, he could see water everywhere, and a mile away, the Morocco-like structure of the Don CeSar that sat on the beach at Pass-a-Grille.

He had a half-empty bottle of Johnny Walker in his hand. All that was missing was a glass. He moved toward the cabinet where he used to stack his disparate collection of fancy containers and such. He hesitated between a silly-looking flute and an ordinary orange juice glass ending up choosing the last. As he was pouring himself a generous serving of the amber-colored liquid, the phone rang.

He looked around. It wasn't that long since he had moved into this place. Where was the damn apparatus? It was black, attached to a wall, and was old, familiar, and friendly. Better! It was constant and reliable. He liked things that didn't change positions all the time. And it worked all the time. He took the communication and recognized Angela's voice instantly.

"I knew it was you as soon as you spoke, he said."

At the other end, the woman seemed disturbed. "It's Peter."

He couldn't keep himself from sharing his thought with her, feeling an overwhelming urge to express to Peter's wife his exact emotion at that instant. So he interrupted, doing his best to sound affable and unworried.

"I was thinking about you, Angela. As you were obviously thinking of me. It must have to do with some psychic phenomenon, don't you think?"

"Arthur, came the voice, are you with me now?"

So much for extra sensorial perception and mental telepathy. He started to answer,

"Well…"

Only silence came from the other end. And then, he could hear that Angela was crying. The woman was distressed. She had good reason to be.

"I saw him, he admitted. I don't know what to say."

"He will need me, she sobbed. Will you come with me?"

His first instinct was resistance.

"Angela, he reasoned, you can't go to New York at this hour of the night."

"I am in a taxi right now heading toward the airport, Angela said, regaining some control over herself. "I shall be there in twenty minutes. If you can make it, I will have them wait for you at gate 12. A private jet will be expecting us and we might be in New York around two thirty a.m. Then at Peter's hotel fifteen minutes later, perhaps."

Where he lived, Arthur was a quarter of an hour away from the airport.

"I am on my way, he articulated. But before he had time to add anything else, the line went dead."

He didn't bother to put clothes in a suitcase. Since he was still dressed, he picked up his jacket and left. Outside the temperature was stifling hot and humid. He walked toward his vintage Mercedes.

The car was parked in the lot that served building one, where his unit was. The place was assigned to him, while visitors had at their disposal their own area. Then, some cloudy concept hit him, and he stopped dead in his tracks. He hesitated, his hands moving as if in a spasm. After what looked like a bit of erratic equivocation, he returned to his front door.

His apartment stood on the first floor of a V-shaped building, of which there were three. His one-bedroom unit stood on the waterway on the ocean side of the Pinellas Bayway. He had had a big house, once. The passing of his wife followed a few years later by his aunt dying and leaving him this place had made him consider alternatives to his otherwise very well organized and secured existence.

Such as moving into a smaller place. No need for five bedrooms and three bathrooms if you lived all by yourself. He was well into his sixties. Eight hundred square feet was more space than he needed as he rebuilt his aunt's unit from scratch, installing bookcases on one free wall in the front section that overlooked the water, and making a study of his bedroom, the bed in there looking like a decorator's ornamental afterthought.

This was two years before. He was a mile away from his old house in Pass-a-Grille. He didn't miss it. There was a time to live big. That time had passed. No big deal.

Back in his unit, he grabbed his briefcase and put in it the Faith book plus the Zielgard's file. Giving way to an impulse, he had brought it home after Irma's recent visit to his office. The work had had a cryptic title. Arthur laughed at seeing it again on the copy he had kept after giving the original to those West Coast freethinker entrepreneurs.

The Man Who had Two Heads and Lost One on the Moon.

He must give it to them. The first thing they had done was change the silly masterpiece appellation.

Eternity, the work's new title.

Better. Even Arthur could see that. He must still have somewhere a copy of the book published under that title. He was almost out of the condo when he decided to bring it in New York with him. He found it and left.

He opened the door of his car. It was massive and heavy. It clicked in its frame in a reassuring way, the noise it emitted like some well-thought conclusion at the end of one of his own oratory performances. He still could smell the leather's subtle and discreet aroma, he alone being capable of that feat, and resenting his occasional passenger who wouldn't partake in his amazement over the matter, some even having the nerve to dispute his pronouncement and dismissing his car like an eccentricity that would pass.

The space behind the wheel could have accommodated a much bigger driver than he was. There was no chair around that rivaled the comfort of the one he sat in right now. He could sleep there if he wished. These seats were that good. With a beaming smile, he started the engine. It caught instantly, emitting the exquisite humming of a purring cat.

While speeding over the limit on highway 275, he couldn't but think: Who in his right mind would brand a novel with a name like that? What kind of silly story could derive from such a poor name? Why would an author care to put such useless nonsense on paper? Two heads! The moon! Was there someone on this planet who might want to read anything bestowed with such a poor title? How had the work found an audience? He couldn't say.

Now, it was a sure thing that Peter Artritis must be the author of the "Two Heads" lunacy, and Zielgard, of the *Faith* bestseller. This was more like it.

Not much of an accomplishment. Yet, Artritis might be glad to learn somehow that his words, against all expectations, and thanks to his solicitor's efforts, had found an audience of lost souls who considered him their prophet, and would follow him on an interstellar trip if he asked them.

Perhaps it would help Peter to get over his ordeal, this success of his, fished out of the water in extremis, yes, but still a realization of some sort, quite modest if compared with the prize he had been made to forsake in a rather brutal fashion. Well, who knew what made those writers happy? He didn't, but it was in his nature to try to find out anyway he could and not to be the judge for the sins of others.

He enjoyed driving the Mercedes. Maintaining the car in perfect working condition cost him as much as driving a brand-new Malibu and changing vehicle every few years. Yet, the feeling of driving his old lady, as he used to call the ancient machine, couldn't be described in words, as he was no poet.

He parked the car where there was the least chance he would be bumped by some deadbeat motorist, who wouldn't mind this sort of contact as he would be driving an undistinguished and outdated relic.

He met Angela on his way to gate twelve. She was marching along an endless hallway. The moving carpet he was on passed her by. He jumped over the railing and had some trouble regaining his balance after touching the ground, as he had misjudged his previous velocity. She looked like she had aged ten years since he had seen her last, and that was not yet three years ago. He had been invited to their thirtieth wedding anniversary at the end of 2015. The Rays had won their division's championship. Peter had told him at the time that he was working on a new project. He hadn't paid much attention. The running joke around Peter was the balderdash kind of literature he persisted to write. Being in touch with Oracle's management, he was well placed to know what Peter's colleagues thought of his so-called "projects." They even had a name for those. They had nicknamed them MMP as in "Money-Making Proof."

He had never gotten personal with the publisher, or discussed the man's literary ambitions and achievements, as he was too afraid of being asked to look over the pointless narratives and expected to emit some sort of opinion. Neither had he ever discussed Zielgard with Peter. Clamoring the doctor's success in faddish California would have been bad taste, like boasting over someone else's mistake.

He saw at once that Angela had been crying. She held a wet Kleenex in her right hand and her eyes were a mess. She hadn't dressed properly. She didn't carry any luggage except her purse. When she noticed him, she sighed and cried out:

"Oh, Arthur! I am so glad you were able to make it."

"You will get through this, he promised, as if he knew."

She didn't challenge his banal guarantee as she squeezed his hand in hers, and, in this way, expressed the gratitude she felt for him being there. The light was crude. They were alone except for a solitary misfit playing guitar a quarter of a mile away.

"You know where you're going? He asked.

There were lines of different colors on the wall on their left. She pointed at them and answered:

"I was told to follow the red one."

They reached a crossing that exploded into a circle-like structure with six identical passageways. There were so many lines of all colors and shapes that for a few seconds, they lost their guide, and when they found it again, they trailed after it, feeling like Hansel and Gretel looking for breadcrumbs in the forest. They reached gate twelve two minutes later. An officer in full uniform stood from the chair he had occupied while waiting for them. He addressed Angela with an air of professional efficacy.

"You must be Mr. Artritis's wife."

Angela offered him her hand. He took it in a firm handshake.

"I am Maurice, he said. I will assist Captain Clark on this trip."

"I am Angela, she said. And this gentleman here is Arthur Morin. A friend and Arthur's lawyer."

At that, Arthur winced. Could it be that a little show of force was the reason for his presence on this offhand, snappy escapade? He shrugged off that notion, not believing Angela capable of that much cunning. He would have been an architect, or a history professor, and she would have introduced him the same way. Still, the people back in New York might take notice.

"Charlie hadn't mentioned two passengers, though."

Arthur was fast with a quip of his own:

"Two small a plane?"

"I couldn't do the trip alone, Angela explained. I do hope that your captain can accommodate the both of us."

The smile she had forced on her face was of the kind that couldn't be resisted. Water poured out of her eyes and before Maurice could issue his next words, she was sobbing again. They followed him toward an exit door. Arthur had known the couple for a long time. Of the two, he liked Angela best. And now, he could see the woman had been hurt. Her world, completely secured before now, was on the verge of collapsing. He put his arm on her shoulder and pressed her against his chest.

"It won't be a problem, Maurice, showing a bit of uneasiness, countered."

He opened the door and then they found themselves outside on a metallic platform ten feet off the tarmac. They got down a set of stairs where a golf-cart-like vehicle had just appeared out of nowhere. Maurice took the seat beside the female driver. Angela and Arthur sat at the back. Next, they were on their way, moving thirty miles an hour or so along service roads buzzing with the noise of airplanes around them, expecting to get hit anytime soon and hoping for the best.

Five minutes later, they had made it to their destination. It was an immense hangar with planes of all forms and sizes nearby. One of those, which must have been the smallest of them all, was up and running, a glittering jewel in the night that threw light away from all crevices and interstices. Their craft was marked with a discreet reproduction of the CBS network logo on its tail. Its door was open at the top of the steps, which would be rolled up back into position as soon as they got in.

Another man, obviously the captain of the plane, occupied one of those steps. As if he had assumed his subordinate had already done the welcoming aboard bit, he nodded hello to them and left. There wasn't much amicability shown in his posture. The man looked as if he had had a long day, and Arthur could well imagine the phone call out of the Big Apple that had gotten Clark out of his way for that special assignment. As their captain made it back to the cockpit, they followed Maurice to their seats. There were four around a table made out of a very rich material. By the time they had sat, the jet had started moving.

"This is the boss's specially assigned jet plane, Maurice informed them. Quite a nice little trinket of a toy, don't you think?"

Arthur tried to look impressed, but couldn't come up with anything worth uttering.

"Better strap yourselves in, because we will be off the ground soon. I must go back there myself, now. If you need me while we are airborne, use this phone and I will be here in a sec. If you need a drink, there is a bar with some stuff in it. Also a fridge with sodas. You look for yourself and take whatever you want. I might make coffee later if you care for some."

"Thank you so much, Angela interrupted, but don't you worry about us. All we crave for is to get in New York as soon as this plane can make it. When will that be, if I may ask you?

Maurice looked at his watch. He shouted his answer before vanishing behind a partition that isolated the front cabin from the passenger's area.

"This trip's ETA is two thirty-five in the morning."

Angela turned an uncomprehending gaze at Arthur. He decoded the acronym's significance for her.

"Estimated time of arrival, he translated."

"Boys will be boys, she smiled back at him. This, at least, will likely never change, will it?"

They suddenly felt crushed against their seats; the stress on Arthur's back was stronger than anything he had ever experienced in all of his previous flights.

"I wonder, he said to his companion, the speed of that bird. After all, New York is more than a thousand miles away, and if we are to land in… He took a quick glance at his watch …one hundred and seventeen minutes… Well, you do the arithmetic."

Angela had her eyes closed, looking unconcerned by their carrier's performance. Finally, they were off the runway and climbing at such a ridiculous angle that it challenged at first their otherwise well-entrenched view of physics. The table in front of Arthur was no longer a table, but appeared to him more like the chalkboard hanging from a wall in his office. How long would this aircraft be able to maintain an ascent as perpendicular as that one? His head was upside down, looking at his feet and finding his shoes in want of a polishing.

At last, Captain Clark must have found the plane's correct altitude, because it slumped fast into a more conventional horizontal position, which did a great deal to improve their level of comfort. Arthur, who had freed himself from his seatbelt, couldn't hold back the silly notion of both he and the woman beside him starting to drift around in their weightless environment. That thought started a low rumble in his throat that stopped just short of becoming a laugh when Angela asked him,

"Are you okay, Arthur?"

He looked at his companion. It was the second time in less than half an hour that she had cut him off, seemingly worried with him being there, once, and now asking if he was okay. Both times, he had felt like, in a kind of a poetic disposition, wishing at first to digress into the field of extrasensory communications, and then, into the one that dealt with the orbital trajectory of flying objects. Angela hadn't perceived his mood and countered his preposterous wanderings both times with an inadequate response. True, she had a lot on her mind, and still, she was the Angela he remembered. Not much of a dreamer, a fantasizer, or a star gazer, that writer's wife. As she must have been a poor tambour for her eccentric husband's odd fancies. Angela would see a tree for what it was. Building material. Paper. What must she have thought of her spouse's implausible production?

Arthur pondered the question.

There could be no question that the woman loved her sophisticated mate. She wouldn't do anything that might hurt him. Of course, she would be supportive of her man the best she could. But one couldn't walk a rope if he hasn't been raised into it. Angela couldn't be receptive to Peter's esoteric nature any more than she could transform herself into a trapeze artist. She wouldn't understand her husband's written words, and neither could she recognize the moods which fed them.

As for making sense of his stories, nobody did. Still, how unfortunate all that was. He felt for Peter, left alone, ignored, and unappreciated. And the woman he so adored powerless to cheer him up. She would read his works without having in herself what it took to produce proper feedback, the right comment, the expected praise. Or she would, in a cliché like manner, end up doing more harm than good.

She might have like Faith, though. He bet she had. He could well imagine the defeated woman sitting beside him wanting to make up for all her previous inadequacies by extolling the baseball narrative. A nice and easy story that one, Arthur concluded. A tale that Angela must have understood and praised, as millions of others had done. What a hard lesson it must have been for Peter to endure, seeing his beloved wife falling for Zielgard's book.

Who said that life was easy? No free ride existed. There was always a price to pay in the end. That was what Arthur believed. It had served him well, up to that day. Permitted him to avoid most of what the world had to offer of silly enticements and nonsense of all variety. Just like Angela, he deduced that he would've lacked the proper attributes to commentate on Peter's talent. The man that could be described as an exotic piece of potted greenery in need of water, which was never to be provided.

How had he ever been able to cope in such a habitat, let alone add more and more words to his collection of solitary output? Writing solo, without any readership. And not enough spring in his backbone to fight for his work over his Oracle colleagues' resistance. The guy was the ultimate loser. And the woman who loved him the most couldn't help. This was so sad, Arthur thought as he was half-sleeping in his seat. But all was not lost. Peter was a success after all. And Arthur had with him the published proof of it. The Eternity story. A smile illuminated his face as he fancied himself telling this to his hopeless client and seeing him come back to life somehow. This could be his own part in this drama, more of a tragedy, a scene not yet written, but he might give it a try. To make sure the play at least had not so bad an ending.

He was a lawyer. He was an optimist. Things would come out okay. That's what he did. He was a fixer. He would fix this.

"Angela, he said, are you sleeping?"

"No, she answered promptly. What about you? Are you all right?"

Again! Was this some kind of an obsession? Or maybe she wasn't all right and projected the same for all. If so, she had good reason for it.

"Why are you asking?"

"I'm so afraid, she sobbed."

"Come on, he objected. He will get over it. I'm telling you."

"How can you say that?" She countered. He has been destroyed publicly."

"We will find something for him to say. I will have a statement ready to give to the members of the press tomorrow."

She turned to him, her skeptical gaze piercing into the solicitor's devoted blue eyes.

"I do not need pious reassurances like that, she snapped. What is there to say, anyway? You can't lawyer your way out of this one, Arthur."

"Oh, but I might, he insisted."

"What about all that money that came his way and should have been paid to Zielgard?"

Arthur recalled the German cousin. Here was a lucky bastard.

"Peter won't mind giving it back, I am sure."

But she must not have heard him as she lamented:

"I should have been with him."

"As a matter of fact, he responded, I wonder why you weren't."

"I let Peter convince me not to go. He told me this was a hit and run kind of trip, you know, all to be bagged in less than twenty-four hours, no luggage, him leaving late yesterday morning and promising to be back home before six tonight. Besides, Tammy wanted us to visit a house she and her husband want to buy, and it was scheduled for this afternoon. Peter would have missed it, obviously, but as he is not much into houses at any rate, it might not have been her father's advice our daughter was actually seeking, if you know what I mean."

They had been in flight one hour when their captain decided to make an appearance. He showed himself over a protective curtain that separated the crowded pilot's cockpit from their more comfortable quarters. He must have felt or been told that his prior attitude of showing his displeasure to his passengers wasn't good policy, and now, by his mere presence, he wanted to make up for it. Arthur, who has sensed all that, chose to make a joke out of the situation. He asked:

"Are we crashing or something?"

Angela, who might not have heard her companion puerile query, welcomed their host with a question of her own.

"We can't be near our destination yet, are we Captain Clark?"

"At your service, madam, the first officer retorted with a bow and an amused grin on his face. As for your litigator friend, I am sorry to say that he will have to find his next big case somewhere else, as I will make sure this flight gets you both to Manhattan."

"Charlie told me about you, Angela carried on."

"As he must, came back the fast reply."

But Angela wasn't finished yet with her small talk.

"Whose plane is this?"

"Nobody's in particular. It belongs to the network. Whoever needs it uses it. This one though is the smallest of the fleet. So, the network's president likes to think it's his."

"Then there are more than one of those?" She replied in real astonishment.

Clark laughed.

"One in every city that counts. About half a dozen or so in this country alone."

"And Tampa qualifies? That's a surprise."

"Los Angeles, Phoenix, Houston, Chicago, New York, Miami. We picked a guest in that last city and I was bringing her home when I was informed of you two."

"A woman guest, Angela blurted out. Where is she?"

Clark showed them a door behind them. "There is a bathroom you can use the other side of that door. Facing that bathroom, another door that opens on a small cubicle with a bed in it. That where our third passenger lies, sleeping most probably."

However, Angela had turned her face toward the window and the moon. She didn't care for the TV conglomerate jet set up. Seeing this, Clark resumed into his function and closed his exculpatory act by adding:

"We will land at 2:40 a.m. Maurice must have told you folks where the booze was, if you should want some. I have been told that the Verizon CEO who was on this plane a month ago left a very rare bottle of Lagavulin scotch. Sixteen years old. The best value of all whiskeys. I figure there is still a good ten ounces of the stuff left. So, help yourself, if you wish."

Seeing their unenthusiastic response, he concluded:

"Would you care to have coffee? My partner has just started a pot."

They said they might. They were fine. There was no need to worry about them. Clark was satisfied, somehow, that he had done all that could have been expected of him if his guests were sensible enough. He gave the couple a last irresistible smile and left.

"Nice fellow, Arthur said. He sure won't sleep in his bed tonight."

"Neither will we, his companion responded."

Arthur couldn't help but throw a probing gaze at Peter's wife. What kind of answer was that? Why should that man suffer because she was in misery? He wanted to ask her. The Angela he remembered was not that way. He decided she must be very upset, to issue such a useless comment. What was the point of being angry at others because they didn't share in your misfortune? Or wishing them to partake in it, as if adversity was contagious? Angela that couldn't find in herself one bit of compassion for the chaos she was inflicting on another person's routine. Worry did that to people. Arthur had seen it in his own clientele of suffering litigants. Those who lost and couldn't handle it. Turning sour and wanting the world to do likewise. Although she had suggested nothing of the sort, what if Angela suspected her desperate husband might be pushed into one extreme gesture or other. He decided not to get there. Now were the worst moments of this sorry episode. The sooner they see Peter the better. And at least, he had with him a bit of news that was sure to bring some comfort to the couple soon to be reunited.

"Peter must have been in quite a desperate and disheartened state to do a thing like this, he said to fill the silence."

"I thought he had done it, she murmured, and he had to work hard to hear her whispered words over the buzz of their airplane's reactors." "I had always asked him to write something easy. A nice story that I would like. Well, he did it, didn't he? I thought he had so performed to please me. And I knew from its very first pages that Faith was going to be a success. I told him so. I was so proud of him, she sobbed."

"Still, Arthur suggested, it wasn't like him to produce such a tale. Why I didn't connect the dots...?"

"What do you mean? You think it's not in him to write that well? She snarled.

"Well, he defended himself, I mean that I could have been more discerning... I was the Zielgard lawyer and I am the one on brought him the piece."

"Arthur, she interrupted, he is brilliant. He always has been. If he were to put his mind to something, he could do anything. He once told me that he liked writing poems in ancient Greek because doing the same in French or English was far too easy."

Which, as far as the lawyer was concerned, was Peter's first problem. Specializing in useless skills for a worldwide audience of a dozen or so half-dead venerable academicians.

"Actually, he insisted, what I want to say is that I am responsible for this mess. I started it all in 2008."

"Those were bad years. He became sick, or something. I recall doctors despairing over the right diagnosis. It might have been a bit of depression, I think. But he didn't want to see a psychiatrist. He fought this thing alone, though. It took him years to get over it."

"Well, I am sorry to have missed it," he offered. "Can't say we were seeing each other much at the time." And then, he added as if speaking to himself, "Sure, you couldn't know, because Peter would never have spilled such a secret, not event to you."

"What is it, Arthur?" She snapped at him, her voice suddenly hard and metallic.

He realized suddenly she didn't know what part he had played in this mess. He told her about Dr. Zielgard and the witch. Regarding the manuscript he had sent her husband and receiving it back with his rejection letter. He told her about Irma and giving the girl a copy of the cunning missive. She knew the rest. How was poor Peter to have foreseen that the author of Faith, whose merits he had been asked to evaluate, had put real people in his book, secondary characters that would ultimately recognize each other? His project had been nothing more than a disaster waiting to happen. The real definition of a snare. It was a tricky device that had caught her spouse really well.

"And he waited ten years to play his hand, can you believe it? I find this amazing, Angela cried out."

Arthur was a good conversationalist. He had a quick mind for capturing the real meaning in other people's half-expressed statements and sentiments.

"He built the trap that got him in the end, which is usually the sorry result of all such poor souls' efforts toward one unlikely triumph or another. I saw all sorts of similar defendants in my office as I helped them to fight their way out of prison."

Angela looked at him with unmitigated horror deforming her face.

"Has Peter committed a crime?" She gasped.

Arthur put both his hands on her arm. He pronounced with a voice decisive and firm,

"I'm sorry, Angela. I should have thought before I started babbling all this nonsense."

He let go of her and stood up to pick up his briefcase, which had been discarded in the luggage compartment just over their heads. After he had regained his sitting position, he got out Zielgard's book. Then his eyes fixed on Angela as he tried to comfort her.

"You don't have to worry about anything. I am the one who could complain about a crime having been committed if ever and be assured I won't. But you do not yet know the whole story. There is more to come."

Next, he proceeded to explain how he had met that agent in California and had decided on an impulse to show him Zielgard's material. Getting a second opinion. Not that he didn't trust Peter's judgment, but who knew? Furthermore, that West Coast guy owed him. So, it would be a free consultation. Why not ask, then, and see what happened? Anyway, that agent of mine, he found this wave-catching, coke-sniffing, sun-loving beatnik couple. They loved the piece. They asked for more. He had been told that the man with the long hair had been very dispirited when learning of the author's death. And when being told of the doctor succumbing to some villain witch's magic, the silly joint-user had declared kind of knowingly, "That figures!"

Arthur couldn't but laugh in a disgusted manner as he recalled the idiotic observation. Could someone prove himself more of a blathering fool in not so many words? And this was the guy who had seen some potential in Zielgard's manuscript.

Well. The Californian dope head must not have been that crummy and inadequate after all. He had guessed it all right, somehow, because he and his wife put the work into print, and believe it or not, the work had achieved a modest success in some nook or niche of the artistic West Coast's bohemian crowd, because it had sold eight thousand copies.

Arthur showed Angela the soft edition of the book that had a Dali-like picture on its jacket, in a surrealist style. As she didn't move nor saying anything, he carried on.

"I didn't say anything to Peter at the time. After all, he had rejected the Zielgard material, and it would have been rude on my part to boast of my newfound triumph, against his advice. It is unfortunate that I let such scruples have the better of me. Don't you see?" He insisted to his quiet audience of one. "Peter dismissed his own writing as unworthy of being published. Isn't it fate's ultimate about-face? If I had told him, he would have divulged his subterfuge and renounced his not yet completed machinations. Imagine how happy it would have made the poor wretched man, finding himself appreciated somehow, even if those who loved his work belonged to the lunatic fringe. But nothing is lost, is it?"

He must have found Angela's response missing in ardor, for when he started talking again, his voice was not as persuasive as he would have liked.

"Look, Angela, I am here, and I will meet your husband in the next two hours. As desperate as he might be, I am bringing him the most marvelous news that you can think of. Don't you see? I am bringing him the very air he needs to breathe in order for him to live through this calamity."

"You think so? Angela finally pronounced, her voice faint and flat."

How come she couldn't see this by herself, he wondered. Something must be eating her by the inside. Still, he persisted, finding nothing else worth doing:

"I know so, Arthur insisted. Think about it. He now has a readership, people who have built him into some kind of cult-like character and will crave for the kind of stuff Peter is able to produce at will. He most probably has drawers full of previously written stories that have never seen the light of day. He will be the next great shaman of a new literary artsy craze that will have word clusters looking like a Picasso drawing. No, Angela, you take my word for this. Peter is on the verge of something great. Oh, I know he will do well. And, well, he could even make a bit of money out of his writing."

"Peter, she broke in, doesn't care for money."

"Whatever, Arthur said. I can tell you, though. What he cares is being read. You believe me now. He will like success that is genuinely attributable to him.

"What then?" She asked. "If Peter took Faith away from the doctor who actually wrote it, he could make a complaint, and Peter could end up being charged with some felony or other."

"Zielgard is dead, don't you remember? I told you that."

"So, she countered, his estate, then... What about that?"

"I am the one who represented the so-called estate, Arthur revealed to her, quite happy with his little exhibition and at being in the center of all things. At first, he clarified, there was no such thing worth to be called an estate. Whatever money Phil Leclerc got for the house went to pay Zielgard's debts. And the furniture wasn't even good enough for the Salvation Army. I got lucky with his twenty-year-old Cadillac, which was sold to one of his neighbors for two thousand dollars, because the fellow knew the car to be in good working order. The doctor had no family in Biloxi, and nowhere else in North America, for that matter. Not that I lost much time with research, though. From his doctor's association dossier and the University where he got his degree, I learned that he was the only son of a Hungarian couple who left their country before the Great War, when it was part of the Austro-Hungarian Empire. He was born in 1929 in New Orleans. Their only son. It looked like his parents were of the Jewish faith, but I couldn't find anything in his place to show that he cared for one religion or another. I found him a cousin in Germany. That's where I sent the money that was left after having disposed of all the man's assets. Not even two thousand dollars. A physician! Hard to believe, isn't it?"

Arthur suspended his long monologue to look at Angela. Not sure of what he saw, he asked her:

"Are you listening to me?"

She nodded her head yes.

"Stay with me, he insisted, there is a lot more to come."

"Please, tell me, she implored him, will he be indicted? Will he have trouble with the law?"

Arthur couldn't help but to sigh with displeasure. Angela was no longer looking at him, her eyes wandering listlessly around as if she were trying to spot an annoying fly. He had been there before. It was the look of someone at the other end of one of his lectures, and he was seeing in their shifting gaze and restlessness that they couldn't wait for him to make his point. He hated the judges who were in the habit of doing that, cutting him off with factual questions while talking him out of the proper foundations that were essential to fully appreciate the subtle music of all those facts click-clacking nicely into their rightful places in his well-prepared arguments.

"No, Angela. Don't you see? I am the one in charge. And I will make sure that this matter settles nicely. The cousin in Germany will be too happy to discover himself a multi-millionaire to complain about how his new found fortune happened. Let me finish and you might understand what I mean. I have a plan. I will have a press release ready for tomorrow's paper."

"You will?"

"You, Peter and I will call a press conference this morning and explain it all."

"What is there to explain?"

"I am working on it. I will find something. But please, do listen to me. It helps to put my thoughts in order."

"I am sorry for the interruption, she yielded."

He studied her. He could well see that she was afraid, and it might have been for the same reason that he was. He couldn't bring himself to visit the subject that tormented him. The poor woman. She would have him talk about anything but what lurked in both their minds.

"Where was I? He asked."

"His assets were two thousand dollars or so…"

"Then, he was a drunk, wasn't he? It cost him his life in the end."

She fixed on him a perceptive gawk.

"Now, she said, you surprise me, Arthur. Are you siding with the prosecution on that poor negro woman's case?"

"I am not, he protested."

"You just attributed to her Zielgard's ill-fated demise."

"Why, he admitted, you are right. Silly parrot that I am! I am just repeating what everybody says on the street. That's all. Doesn't mean anything."

"Still, the woman is actually waiting to be executed. When will that be, I wonder? The last time I read about it, I remember thinking it was coming fast. What a pity!"

"I know. Nothing much we can do for that unfortunate lady. Better we think about something else."

"I have a strange feeling that she has a connection with Peter."

That sent a jolt through him. Why would Angela say something like that? And still, it touched a nerve. In some ungraspable way, it brought back his anxiety about his friend's fate. He decided to play down the association. He showed her the book Eternity.

"This novel here is all there is between those two. No! We better think of something amusing. Like my meeting with this agent in California. The fellow who took an interest in your husband's writing. What a marvelous denouement this is. I am so glad for Peter. I am telling you, Angela. This is the miracle cure to all his past vexations and discomfiture. The guy got his book published. And then, amazingly, it caught some wind. From my perspective, it was like a lonely prospector who, after a lifetime of futile digging, falls at last on some lode of minerals one thousand feet underground. Well, Arthur persisted, it activated the agency to move a bit toward finding some relation to the now many-year-dead Zielgard. They put some kind of notice in Biloxi's newspapers, and then, one of the doctor's cousins manifested himself out of Leipzig in Germany. A lady, who had bought Zielgard's previous house, saw the ad and managed to get in touch with Siegfried or someone back there. She had once received a letter addressed to Zielgard and couldn't locate him. Only God knows why she would have kept the missive for all those years. The thing is, there was a return address on the back of the envelope. So this cousin on his mother's side was all the family the good doctor had. And he was the one who had received the proceeds of Zielgard's book. You can see now why this Siegfried will not make a fuss. This guy comes from behind the iron curtain. He was born into communism. He has studied Marxism. He might even have believed once that his side had it right. Anyway, this fellow's idea of being rich is being able to buy a car. So now, if this guy don't believe in God, I am telling you, he will soon. And you know who that God might be, don't you? You have him sitting beside you."

Arthur was enjoying himself. Angela could see that. Enough to forget that it was approaching two o'clock in the morning and they should both in more ordinary circumstances have been fast asleep in their own beds. She asked him:

"What about the other people involved? Anybody around who might feel like he could initiate something?"

"This is why I must come up with a little communiqué for the press that will wrap things up. I am not sure yet what I will tell that lot, but it will take care of that somehow. No intermediaries or middlemen will suffer from this readjustment. What I intend to do is very basic. I will swap the book rights from one legal entity to another. I will have an accountant to establish how much money came out from both east and west coast initiatives and determine who shall be indebted to the other. I am afraid to say that Peter might find himself on the wrong side of this equation. Yet, I very much doubt that this will change his mood. I am sure this book will change his professional life beyond his wildest dreams, and in a way that he has always been too afraid to anticipate."

Angela took Arthur's hand and he looked at her. He couldn't hear what she said, but he could read her lips as she mouthed,

"Thank you, Arthur. You're the best."

He put his right hand where she had rested hers, and they kept that position of close proximity and understanding as long as their mutual feeling of friendship subsisted. Then, he disengaged and showed her the book he had been talking about. That was the first time Angela had a look at it. Like Faith, it wasn't an inch thick. It must have been three hundred pages at the most. The jacket was colorful. The title of the piece was in bold letters, each word in a different color.

"Eternity, she read."

"They change the title. Peter's was: *The Man Who Had Two Heads and Lost One On the Moon.*"

Angela looked at Arthur.

"This sounds familiar, she said."

"Looks like Peter's stuff, you mean?"

She was now perusing through the pages. After a while, she affirmed:

"I might have read this. It's been a while, though. Twenty, thirty years back, I guess. You know, he always showed me all of his writing."

Arthur couldn't help but ask her his next question.

"What did you think of his stories?"

She turned her face away from him and stayed silent. Arthur would have liked to take back the question. He said, "I understand."

Linden airport, New Jersey, October 18, 2018

I t had been quite a let-down for Ollie Devott, since he wasn't used to playing second fiddle to anybody. Still, he felt that way after his appearance on the David Letterman Show. That silly blonde bitch had ruined his act with her career-wrecking pursuit of a schmuck she had labeled a thief for having stolen the Faith book. The book was on all the bestseller lists, and Hollywood had made a movie out of it. He hadn't seen it yet. Now, he knew he would. And read the book too.

He sure hadn't seen it coming. He had been waiting that moment and when it happened, he knew he had shined. Still the appearance immediately after him of that no good son of a bitch followed by the so-called author eradication out of the hands of one young white-blond vixen, that's what he hadn't anticipated. Who would remember him after an earthquake of that scale, big enough to have shaken all listeners out of their comfortable settee? At first the celebrate scribbler hadn't look like serious competition. He remembered having asked himself how such a loser-like character had been dealt a winning hand as momentous as the one he was proclaiming to have received.

The man hadn't felt real. He was as dull and boring as a fish in a bowl. His answers to all questions were beside the point, and were used as no more than the excuse for starting him up in one useless divagation or another.

And then, it had happened. That Irma girl had stood up and washed away the nonentity into utter oblivion. As much as he had resented the girl's performance for meddling with his own, he couldn't help but to be mesmerized with the way she had achieved her task of striking out the false idol, the same as a chemical would have in disintegrating a batch of expendable molecules.

He mused over the bad luck it had been for him to precede such a breathtaking extravaganza. The worst of it was, everybody around, even his friends and family that were present in the assistance, were now talking in his face about only one thing and that was his fallen alternate ominous last words: "It is not finished till it is finished." What could the charlatan have meant by that?

What a waste it had been, having been invited on national TV and not once given the opportunity to advance his case toward the governorship of the great state of Mississippi. When he had put the matter of his ambition in play and expected Letterman to give him a shot at developing his ideas and projects, the great man had stopped him dead in his tracks and insisted he talk about The Rosa Maman Tour de l'Isle next execution. He had done well to explain himself but still, judging by the reactions in the audience, he knew that subject in ultra-liberal New England would bring him nowhere.

The silly woman would die in less than seven hours, and he couldn't make one bit of her situation work for him. To think that he had left his house in that posh part of Biloxi that overlooked the Gulf of Mexico and suffer a night of half-sleeping in an anonymous hotel room for such a miserable outcome. Now, he had to get back home to make it to the state prison, where Rosa Maman's execution was to take place the next day at six in the morning.

Ollie glanced at his watch. It was eleven o'clock at night. He sat in a small room somewhere in New Jersey. The local airport was so trivial that the edifice in which he was made to wait looked like the visitor area in the emergency section of some back-country minor hospital. They had told him to be there at nine. He had reached the desolate premises at eight.

And then, nothing.

True, there had been an employee who had moved around a bit. He couldn't say if he was management or the janitor. After a while, the man had seemed to notice his presence and told him not to worry, somebody somehow would come and take care of him. They usually did.

He fumed. He was still waiting. He had no book to read. The one he'd brought had been left on his seat on his previous flight. He had been told he would find it, since he would be traveling on the same airplane that had brought him in. The usual bookstalls with the potboilers "du jour" were nowhere in sight. There was a rack in one corner of the room, with a few magazines showing their worn-out pages to his unconcerned myopic glance. Later, with nothing to do, he had approached the sorry-looking device with its appendage of trashy prose. What kind of people were hanging out in this place, he had wondered as he fished out two five-year-old *Reader's Digest*s in German. All the remaining material was aimed at those with a disposition toward the mechanical. He had observed all those ludicrous publications that had words like dynamic, automatic, robotic and what else in their headings. If he would have been in a better frame of mind, he might have appreciated the place's readership's obvious preference for the high-tech, and would have hoped the material to help somehow in keeping his next plane from crashing.

XXVII

The taxi driver was so tall that his shaved head touched the car's ceiling at every rough spot on their way. They were driving on Park Avenue, with Central Park on their left. Then, they turned on some street. Even at this late hour - it was 3:35 in the morning - there was quite a lot of traffic. People must have gotten out of nightclubs, bars, and cabarets all at the same time, because the sidewalks looked like downtown St. Pete in the middle of a weekday. Chico was their chauffeur's name. He was a black man from the West Indies. And he sure liked to talk, as he had done nonstop since their departure from the LaGuardia Airport, where he had picked them up. He had been there in the passenger arrival area carrying a placard with Angela's name on it. Arthur had been the first to notice it.

"I think I'll like these TV folks, he said. They certainly know what it takes to make someone feel important."

"Like you needed help to achieve such result, she said with a smile."

Things were looking better at that moment. Peter's proximity might have helped somehow to alleviate her sense of dread. He acknowledged the charge, not wanting to risk breaking the mood with some lame protestations of innocence.

"I'm so glad they didn't have us drive in a cigar-shaped limo, she added. I hate those silly-looking contraptions."

"As long as it gets us to our destination, Arthur replied."

"I am so afraid, Angela whispered."

"Maybe we could call him."

"I put my cell into his luggage but he won't use it. As for calling him at his hotel, we were in the plane from midnight to three. Calling now and

343

be directed to his room, he is either already there and sleeping, hopefully, or he isn't and this, I will learn soon enough."

He didn't ask her to elaborate, as he well knew what she was scared about. He, too, entertained sketchy vibrations that something somehow was amiss, out of focus, or unconnected. They had followed Chico to his glittering presidential older-looking black Lincoln. The interior of the car was all smooth leather, and its accommodations were designed for ultimate comfort. They sat in the back, settling in the luxurious decor that might help them forget their other troubles. Or so Arthur hoped.

"No luggage, the chauffeur had commented as he discarded his signboard in the trunk of the limousine."

"We don't expect to stay long, Angela explained."

"I am sorry to hear this, Chico answered back. There are a few good shows on Broadway that you might have cared to see. And Charlie told me to get you folk's tickets for a few of those, if you like."

"This is all very considerate. Be sure to thank him for his generous attention, as well as for you being here for us right now. I am here to pick up my husband, as you might already have been told. I am quite sure he will want to leave as soon as possible. So, we will have to decline Charlie's invitation."

"There was some restraint in Angela's voice that felt to Arthur like a silent rebuke. Chico might not have sensed it, though. As soon as he had the car moving, he had started in on his life's history, and in this way, they learned everything that it was possible to know about him. The interesting part was his basketball career. He had almost made it. Could have made it, mind you, if it hadn't been for a stupid injury at the age of twenty. The worst of it was it had happened after he had been spotted by a talent scout, who had gotten him a meeting with a coach, and a try out in the NBA. He had made the cut, he told them without the expected bitterness or discomfiture. An organization had offered him a contract. He had proved to be an apt center in Charlotte, where he had played one season. And he would have had a very a good chance to graduate with the big club in Cleveland, if it hadn't been for his breaking a leg in a stupid motorbike accident. He had stayed at his friend's house and had decided to try his host's 1000 cc Honda without asking for permission, and had thought - rather stupidly, as he could well see after the fact - that he could operate the machine with just the scrap of data he had caught by observing his pal running it. Well, it was a bit embarrassing, Chico disclosed from behind the wheel with the right accent of chagrin, as he hadn't been able to move the damn thing much. The silly gizmo had been the same as an untamed mustang, and had had the better of him in seconds, falling on its side and over his leg as soon he succeeded at making it roar his way forward. What a fool he had been. Not yet three weeks pass his twentieth birthday. He had been lucky, though. The bone had made a full recovery. But the ligament in his knee hadn't done as well. Thus had ended his career of leaping and springing behind a bouncing basketball. That had happened ten years ago, they learned. Plus many other details in their most unfortunate driver's biography.

Angela was no longer listening to the man's narrative of his two botched marriages. He was small talking his audience to death. Basketball. Another of those childish recreations that they made so much about in this country. Like baseball. Look what the silly diversion had done to her beloved Peter. No doubt he had been lost in that world of concrete truth, where nature, reality, and actual facts imposed their heavy loads on the characters' behaviors in a story. It might have been too much for him. He was used to living in his own protected environment, with complete control over all possible contingencies left into her own hands, since she alone could protect and shield him against perils coming from outside.

This, she had done all her life. And she had been good at it. She was the armor to Peter's delicate makeup. Her husband was still a child in so many ways. He had never developed into a full man, like his father, who'd been a man's man. An Anthony Queen image of a man. Who could ever compete with such a person, when nothing of what he possessed would have been his if not for the old man? Spiros Artritis was the personification of the words, 'success,' 'power,' and 'money.' He had created it all out of nothing. Spiros, when in a room, would force his ascendancy on everything and everyone without even trying. For him, just being there was enough. Quiet or laughing, his mere presence imposed its benevolent dominion on all living things. Angela didn't resent her father-in-law for his overwhelming personality. What was one to do against forces of nature? Was the wind to be blamed for the damages it inflicted on a weak structure? Perhaps

Spiros had crushed Peter somehow, but she knew he was a good man, and he wouldn't have done it on purpose.

It might not have been easy to live around him, though, having such a role model, and knowing full well it was a silly notion to imagine yourself following in his steps. Peter must have been aware from the very start of his life that to make it just half as well as his father would need continuous effort and dedication, with no certainty of triumph in the end.

Who would care to try with such poor odds? Still, Peter had, without really knowing how. He had striven to do it in his own way, by writing. Writing himself into another dimension, a field he must have been sure his father wouldn't care to visit or compete in.

He had done it with nothing much to show for after a life's dedication to the task. And she couldn't help him there. She had no idea how to assist him. Her husband lived in his own private domain. When he was in it, writing his stories, she knew he was happy. As she also was, and always had been.

He had been a good husband. Still was. She had been a good wife, too. And still was. They loved each other. Always had since the very first day they had met. Theirs had been a blessed marriage—if one could settle on a definition of such an institution in the early days of the twenty-first century. She had made it to fifty-five without ever looking back or longing, in sleepless nights, for a fancy prince right out of a fairy tale. But then, she only alluded to her own experience. She knew in her heart that she had been the only woman Peter had ever touched. They had been so young. They had learned it all with one another. And looking back, one certainty she now entertained in life was that their way was the way. That whoever was lucky enough to find the right partner from the start and love him till the end must be blessed somehow.

Someone coming out of a younger and more promiscuous generation might have questioned the wisdom of such a stance. He most likely would have labeled it as raw and lacking practice. For him and those likes him, it would mean a shortage in one of existence's ultimate pleasures.

So, in this way, it could be said that their life had been a success. If success was defined as being happy, their life together would have been the foundation of this most vital of all emotions. Could she have been mistaken about Peter, though? He was so timid and shy. The unassertive sort. Somehow sheepishly so. There were times when she'd had to take over. The man could reveal himself a real nuisance sometimes, artfully inept at most of his fellow man's activities. Except for the fact that she didn't care about those deficits, as anybody on the street could cover them for him. What he could do, he alone was able to perform. She knew he was good at his work at Oracle.

As for those stories he persisted writing, she couldn't make heads nor tails of them. She couldn't say if they were good or not. They might have been, though. He wouldn't show them around much. And she didn't push him, either. Perhaps she should have. Still, it looked like Peter had achieved some kind of equilibrium over the years, content to produce his fiction and not worrying too much about his stories being read or not. What if she jostled him into showing his work to publishers, who would retaliate with heartless rejection slips?

She had once told him to use his upper hand as Oracle's CEO to force the way for some of his better material to make it into book form, but he wouldn't hear of it. This would have been as good as self-publishing and wouldn't count. What was the problem with self-publishing? She had asked him once. You write. You produce a book. Who cares who paid for the damn thing?

"I do!"

That had been his answer. Not a word more. She had let the matter drop. And now, this!

The pull of their taxi lowering its speed stirred Angela back to downtown New York nightlife. Mercifully, Chico had finished talking. They were waiting for a light to change. Suddenly, there was a knock on Arthur's window. She saw a black man's face with yellowish-white eyes and a ten-day-old beard. His mouth moved and yet, they couldn't hear a thing. Just by glancing ahead, she discerned two other such pathetic beggars who were assaulting the vehicles in front. Before Chico could object, she opened her purse and caught a five-dollar bill that she then passed through the hole Arthur created, for he had obeyed her silent intimation. She thought she heard the words, "God bless you." But she couldn't be sure as the window closed with an angry whine, cutting her off from the wretched individual's blissful marks of appreciation.

"Those bloodsucker hobos, Chico complained. They now work in crews and you might find them at every street corner. A pest they are, that lot. They won't leave you in peace anymore."

"Shame on us, Angela murmured, not caring to be heard."

"Now that you slipped them some cash, persisted the man behind the wheel, you watch what happens next!"

As she could already see, all the sorry-looking pariahs agglutinated around the Lincoln with their proffering, imploring hands. It wasn't a sight to make anybody comfortable. Arthur echoed Chico's previous comment with his own, "Pretty disturbing, indeed."

There was a crowd of the messy supplicants all over their limousine, now. Where had they come from? Angela pondered. There were too many of them to be explained by the few she had seen on the street before she'd handed out the five-dollar bill. Some were blocking the Lincoln's way forward, each pressing upon the others to get better access to the car's hermetically shut overtures.

"A plague they are!" Chico erupted as the light turned green and the vehicles ahead had started to move. He didn't have to use his horn for the unsavory cohorts dispersed by themselves as if on cue.

"Look at that, Arthur marveled. They know it would be bad business to block traffic."

"See where they are now, their driver emitted with undisguised contempt."

A cluster had already formed on the other corner, where a few cars had immobilized. As they passed them by, Angela could discern some worriedness in an assaulted driver's posture, who was showing off in a Corvette with no top.

"You don't have those where you come from?" Chico asked them, and Arthur discerned in the man's voice something like a brag. He at least lived in a big town, even if it came at times with a bit of a drawback.

None of his passengers cared to answer, Arthur lost in his thoughts and Angela recalling what she had learned about Zielgard's book. The Faith manuscript precipitating a chain of events that now appeared to her both unbelievable and ineluctable at the same time. What a beautiful story it was, and how splendid an ending for Peter rather lamentable trial at success. He had been wrong for acting the way he had, there could be no doubt about that. What was it that had pushed him into the sorry deed, though? He must not have been thinking straight. An uncertain smile formed on her lips. After all, the notion of her husband entertaining thoughts that would stand to reason was a bit unrealistic. Money couldn't be a motive. Then what? Approbation? Consideration? Respect? That might have been what had driven him to such drastic and uncommon behavior.

Being read. Being admired as a writer of some distinction. Proving himself in front of his peers. Getting to see his name on a book's jacket. So, he had put his hands on Zielgard's manuscript and he had done the unthinkable. He had stolen the man's words, paragraphs and chapters for himself. He had duped the man who now sat beside her. How could he have done such a thing and still envisioned it would make him happy? Had he even been?

Angela was suddenly afraid, as if she had found herself in a difficult spot on a mountain-climbing expedition with nothing to secure herself to anywhere in sight. What if Peter hadn't been happy, as she'd always thought he must have been? This idea was so alien that she started to cry. Arthur extracted an immaculate handkerchief from his vest pocket and offered it to her.

"I'll be okay, she promised."

"We are almost there, Chico stated, as a way of comfort."

Peter and Angela. Angela and Peter. They had been together. What could be more important than that? In all that could be achieved in one's life, they had prevailed with its most essential requirement for attaining real happiness. They had loved each other. In doing so, just for that fact if nothing else, they had had the perfect life.

And yet, it hadn't been enough for Peter. He had committed the unforgivable, perpetrate the unthinkable. In secret, without telling her. Worst, he had shown her the piece as if it had been his own. How she must have hurt him for all the idiotic praise she had dispensed toward the work, since she had never before shown similar appreciation for anything else he had written. Right there, Peter should have realized whatever he expected from his action would produce more pain than relief.

How sad. Peter craved to be read. And his clever sleight of hand hadn't done much to improve that outcome. A sleight of hand it might have been. Whether it was a clever one was another matter. Peter was highly intelligent, but adept, smart, and clever were not words to apply to his sort of brilliance. He had now been smashed into pieces right in front of all those fans he had so desperately been seeking. What good could he have expected from this hopeless business? He must have known that whatever readership it brought him, they couldn't care less for his real self and his own literate accomplishments.

What a waste! Her husband had been given everything except the ability to believe in himself. And she hadn't done much better for thinking that writing stories was like collecting stamps, a business that one did in solitude. She would have died before letting a complete stranger read her poem - if she had ever cared to write any. In her world, words needed to have a purpose as immediate as possible, otherwise they might as well be the useless ramblings of lost souls.

Then, is this what she thought of her companion's best efforts? That notion frightened her. She had no simple answer to that daunting question. She didn't know. She was confused. She couldn't face the subject. This squabbling over her past attitude toward her spouse's creative initiative couldn't do her justice. As she was inclined to blame herself, it would be easy to overdo it in her current frame of mind. This wouldn't be fair. She was not at fault for the way she was.

True! She didn't read creative fiction or novels. If she was to leaf through anything, her personal taste would get her into stuff like biographies and memoirs of the historical or political variety. If she must suffer criticism for not having been appreciative enough of her husband's writing, then so be it. He could have been a chef and she would have loved him still, even if she never ate his cuisine. Well, she might have been a vegetarian, perhaps. She wasn't, mind you. All those silly people that were in search of a creed.

Now. She was doing it again. There was this side of her that could be so judgmental, dismissive of others' belief and partial for her own. There couldn't be any doubt that she must have been influential on her partner. A squeeze on his otherwise easygoing personality might have left a poor impact if one's estimation took into account past events.

Her chest constricted. She felt a pain as she sensed there was no air left in the car, and she would suffocate if this trip was prolonged. Fortunately, the Lincoln stopped under a canopy. She heard, but couldn't distinguish who had said what.

"Here we are."

Arthur touched Chico's shoulder with some money in his hand. The man move his neck in one illustration of a NO sign.

"It's all being taken care of, you don't worry about anything."

Arthur addressed Angela who was preparing to get out of the car.

"Are you all right? You look awful"

Already, attendants all dressed up in their Hotel Pierre attire had opened all four doors of the car, all three looking for luggage and finding them missing. The light outside was excruciating and made it hard for them to hide a bit of chagrin at having to welcome such poorly equipped travelers. The outside air put some strength in Angela's bones, and she was helped out of the car with the assistance of an eighteen-year-old boy's arm. The youngster had stared at her purse like it was too much of a burden for her and that he must carry it. Seeing she wouldn't let him, he had smiled at her and pronounced,

"Bienvenue to the Hotel Pierre, madam."

She smiled back at him. She could read his name on the front of his colorful garb. FRANÇOIS. She started to open her purse, but Chico showed her some bills in his hand.

"Let me take care of that, he said."

A drop of water hitted the car windshield. Looking at the sky, he added:

'You see all those clouds? Better be inside. Rain is coming.'

She walked around the Lincoln toward Arthur. The place was grandiose, with Central Park nearby. After their chauffeur had disposed of their porters, she saw him give the Lincolns keys to a valet, whom he must have known because of some familiarity in their small talk and gestures. Then, he turned in their direction and said, "Shall we?"

They followed their guide inside. Somehow, the crushing sensation was gone, and Angela rejoiced in anticipation to be soon reunited with her husband. Whatever state of helplessness she might find him in wasn't a great concern because of her conviction that she was all that Peter needed. Thanks to Arthur's most improbable initiative, they were at that moment in the enviable position of bringing him the most wonderful news ever. From her, from them, he would learn that he had been a success after all, that he had had a book of his own writing published, and that he had found a niche for himself in the restricted universe that he had so much craved to get into. And that was not all. Had he not grown a following that begged for more of his work? People that looked at him as a role model, his prose seen like the work of a mentor? Those marvelous fans out there in California had found in his words what was needed to appreciate her mate's originality and inventive qualities. She was suddenly filled with immense affection for all of Peter's unknown devotees and supporters, whom she knew he needed on his way to healing and complete recovery. Of such a rosy outcome, there could be no doubt.

Arthur had calmed her fears of the law getting involved in the matter. Had she not been told that he represented the estate? This ensured somehow that it wouldn't initiate legal action against Peter. If there was no complaint, there could be no involvement by one politically ambitious District Attorney or another. As if that sort wouldn't want to get into Peter's case if only given half the chance. The prize of such a hunt likely to be tremendous with all the publicity that was sure to be attached to it.

As for civil prosecution, Arthur would make them useless by initiating an accounting of the earnings generated by both Zielgard's and Peter's novels, and see that the latter reimbursed whatever amount it might be proved he had received in excess. In this way, there would be neither victim nor reason to sustain a complaint. That was what she contemplated as she crossed the Hotel Pierre's majestic lobby toward the reception desk.

She had seen her share of grand hotels around the world. Still, she was impressed with the splendor of the place. Working behind the counter, she could discern an employee busying himself with some computer work. The man was slim, with not much to show on his bones. His arms and legs looked like poorly fixed devices on a piece of machinery. He had not yet noticed their coming in. There was nobody else around as far as she could see. No wonder! It was the middle of the night. Who in his right mind would care to check into a hotel at such a time? With an effort, she put a smile on her face. Soon, now, she would be reunited with Peter. Soon, she would make everything right.

Soon!

She looked at Arthur, who was following Chico's steps. The lawyer had been there for her. She felt immensely grateful to the man. Yet, she was getting ready to take away from him the pleasure of announcing to

Peter his almost miraculous stunt. Well, he must have thought he had won the right to tell the tale. She would let him. It would be nice enough to be there and see the happy solicitor bring joy into Peter's eyes.

And then, they were there. The desk attendant, whose name was Stéphane, addressed them with a slight French accent.

"Welcome to the Hotel Pierre. How can I help you?"

"Charlie must have left you with some instructions about those folks, Chico said as he took charge."

The instant he heard the name 'Charlie,' the man's features clouded. Angela saw the alteration and was filled instantly with a sense of dread that she couldn't explain, while she knew instinctively that what was coming wasn't good. Arthur must have deduced the same, because he put his arm around her shoulder and pressed her against him. She let him, as her legs might not support her for long.

"You must be Mrs. Artritis?" Stéphane asked in a low voice.

She heard the desk clerk speak, but she couldn't answer on account of some constriction in her throat. With her eyes fixed on Arthur, she implored him silently to make things right. The clumsily-built Frenchman then added, after glancing briefly at his screen:

"Peter Artritis's wife, and you must be Monsieur Arthur Morin?" Stéphane persisted, looking at the lawyer like he was trying to guess the number of gratuities he could expect from the man just by the way he dressed.

"Our plane touched ground half an hour ago, Arthur disclosed, feeling silly at the same time."

"I hope you guys had a good flight. I have an aunt who lives in Tampa. She showed me around as I intend to reunify with her someday."

By the sickly look of him, Angela doubted he would live long enough to make it to retirement on Florida's west coast. Worse, she had the intimate conviction that the small talk was all for show, just a silly way for the receptionist to gain some time in telling them what he must.

"I believe, Chico suggested, that there is a room reservation for Mr. Morin, and that Mrs. Artritis should be escorted to her husband's suite. She is quite anxious to be reunited with him."

"Well, answered the employee with some uneasiness, I have a bit of disquieting news. We received a call from Bellevue Hospital. It looks like your husband, madam, was brought there. I know how this news might sound to you. Yet it's most probably nothing to be worried about."

Angela's knees gave way and Arthur had to assist her to a chair nearby. Over his shoulder, he shouted,

"Did he call by himself? Has somebody talk to him?"

Stéphane had a very small head perched over a chicken-like neck and under stress, it moved left to right in a distractingly annoying periodic rhythm. He looked at Arthur, and at the woman who had changed color. Why make matters worse? Whatever they would learn, they would learn soon enough.

"Well, I think he did, he lied. He would have reached Monsieur Charles."

"How do you know for sure? Implored Angela"

Stéphane was ready for this.

"We were told to expect Monsieur Atritis around 1:00 a.m. and he didn't show up. Then, hospital attendants must have found his room key in his pocket. That's when we were called. Moreover, we have been in touch with Monsieur Charles, who checked with us as soon as he received the news. It must have been Monsieur Artritis who called him."

Charlie had been informed of his guest's inopportune presence at the Bellevue, since his number was also found in the author's affairs.

"As you would have been too, madam, Stéphane added, now addressing a very white and sickly-looking Angela. But you were not home."

"What about my husband's condition, she pronounced as distinctly as she could."

"They will not disclose this information to some stranger on the phone, Stéphane answered. I did ask, mind you. He is alive, though. I am sorry not to be able to tell you more."

"This is a nightmare, Angela mumbled to Arthur, who stood by her and didn't know what to do or say."

Chico, for his part, said the obvious.

"I know where the Bellevue is. You come with me. It is five minutes away. I will drive you there."

XXVIII

The weather in Biloxi, Mississippi, can be quite extreme at times. The temperature has been awfully hot, with such a level of humidity as to make the notion of a Turkish bath sound refreshing. From his living room's patio door, Ollie Devott scans his yard with a disgusted air. His garden is as attractive as the moon's surface, everything looking dead. His patch of grass yellowish no matter what amount of water he manages to sprinkle on its surface, against the county's restrictive regulations in such matters. Everywhere his disenchanted regard looks is bleached out and colorless. His palm tree has no palms. Who had first called the silly scrub of a species a tree in the first place? He has two Spanish oaks that are not, at that moment early in the morning, making much of a reputation of the Spaniard epithet.

The trees are washed out and as wretched as he is. He landed at 1:45 a.m. thanks to the one hour difference between New York and Gulfport. He slept in the plane and might have bit since his arriving home. Sitting in his living room, he sees the implacable sun make its unwelcome appearance in his kitchen window, which looked upon the Gulf of Mexico. Twenty minutes later, clouds takes over, of a very sinister black variety. Soon enough, any blue left in the sky is obliterated. The air conditioning device in the lawyer's bungalow is stretched to its maximum capacity to give relief, the system emitting strange disturbing noises and rattles, the machine on the verge of collapsing into a state of useless indolent inefficacity. To think he could still be asleep and ignore the discomfort for that very reason. He looks at his watch.

It was more than time to go. The state prison where Rosa Maria Tour de l'Isle was scheduled to be put to death is twenty minutes away by car.

He drops his eyes on the open pages of the day's newspaper, which he left open on the kitchen table beside his unfinished toast and coffee. They have announced severe storms with risks of tornados. Then, the first clap of thunder shakes the house, a crack so hard and deafening that he drops his keys on the floor. He stares outside. No rain yet. A flash cracks the horizon. He counts one, two three… still, the ensuing blast takes him by surprise. It shakes the house and the floor moves under his feet. He feels nervous, apprehensive, alarmed even. He should have eaten. He has no appetite. That damn daybreak execution was taking its toll after all.

He picks his keys on a hook near the entrance door. He drives a Saab. He likes cars that look a bit exotic. He walks out. Perhaps the gods who orchestrate their silly display of bad temper will soon show their pique with some rain and loosen up a bit on the heat.

He goes out. A strong blast of wind almost takes his jacket off his back, sending his tie flapping riotously against his left cheek. His car is outside, near his garage. He gets hit by the first drop of rain. Oh boy, we're in for the real thing, he thinks. A big splash of water exploded angrily on the windshield as he opened the door and engulfs in the vehicle. Better get going, then, if he wants to make it to his destination.

He starts the engine and takes off in the direction of the prison. By law, he needs to be there. He is one of the few officials required to sign the condemned prisoner's death certificate. He wouldn't say that he enjoys that part of his job. He sure could have dispensed with the burden. However, since he is the one responsible for putting the woman there in the first place, he might as well be there till the end and see for himself the ultimate result of his labor.

From the small enclave he lives in that looked upon the Back Bay of Biloxi near Hill Park, he turns left on Veteran Avenue toward the National Cemetery, Old Park Road, and Highway 90. The facility is on the Gulfport section of the town, not far from the Gulfport-Biloxi International Airport. When he reaches downtown, he notes that a tree has crashed unto the wires of some traffic lights, which are no longer operating on a street corner. It is no big an inconvenience at dawn, though.

He has been driving for ten minutes when another flash of lightning split the horizon with a snapping querulous strike. He counted one…two… three… He reaches number six when he got hit by the most earsplitting sound he has ever heard. It is like the world has been cracked open. He could have sworn his car has been affected somehow, feels it moving like it had been lifted up in the air and dropped back on the ground like a useless piece of junk. The resounding interruption of rolling thunder that follows has a kind of natural normalcy, though. Ollie becomes at once aware of where he is and why he is there, in his Swedish indulgence at so early an hour. He took a deep breath, realizing he could use some air. Then a strange notion popped into his mind. How long was the half-life of fear?

He glanced at the clock on the instrument panel. 5:50. He might be late.

Well, he is almost there.

- Damn that witch, he mutters.

He finishes his trip with not much time to spare, if any, and worries he will not be able to run the distance from his parking space to the door before the sky opened up with a summer deluge. However, it is raining, and he will get wet. Damn the bitch, who has well chosen her time. She is quite good at making his life miserable.

The prison doesn't look like one. It is not much more than a six-story building in the shape of a box. Nothing sinister. Nobody who wasn't in the know would have imagined what the site was for. Officially, the structure shelters the administrative office of the Mississippi Bureau of Prisons. Plus a few other public organizations, like the Mississippi Department of Public Safety and the Mississippi Highway Safety Patrol. Just another silly bureaucratic bazaar for pencil pushers, then. Which the place obviously was, but that didn't take into account the second basement, to which he will be escorted in a moment. The very secret area is protected by doors nobody would ever see, with their skull and crossbones under the words RESTRICTED AREA.

The entrance he is looking for was on the left side of the building. There was a black Mercedes 550 parked just in front, beside a big dumpster and some old office furniture that waited there to be disposed of one way or another. Ollie wonders who the owner of the luxurious sedan can be, and how the fellow has been indulged to leave it there. After all, he can read No Parking in this area written on a signboard hooked up on the wall just in front of the Mercedes less than five feet away. As he is about to ring a bell on the right side of the small portal, the steel door is opened by a Creole officer who has in his hand an electric light, as the area behind him is like a black hole.

"There's no power, the agent emits with a contrite look, as if he is somehow to blame for the disruption."

Ollie can well discern the lighted screen that must have permitted the man to see him coming, and is casting faint greenish phosphorescence. He goes in. The site is like a tomb inside an Egyptian pyramid. He refrains from asking whose car it is near the admission slammer. Instead he observes:

"The close circuit television works, though. You must have some kind of a backup system, don't you?"

"If we do, it's not working so well. I have been told to bring you to the warden's office as soon as you show up."

"So, let's go, Ollie responds graciously. I'll follow you. It's you who has the beacon, after all."

They walk through endless passageways that seem like tunnels, and once in a while, there is another glimmer of light approaching them from far away. The idea of meeting another train in the subway came to his mind. The District Attorney has been here before but there were lights and the place didn't look that sinister. He shrugs and says:

"This place sure looks like a sorry mess."

"Well, it is the witch screwing us good, his guide retaliates."

"The lady's fault, is that what you're thinking?" Ollie couldn't but laugh at the concept.

"If she wished somebody dead, she might wish this place to disappear."

"Right, approves Ollie. Still, I believe the thunderstorm outside is to blame for our present bit of discomfort."

"As if I knew, come the answer from the guard ahead. You're the lawyer."

"Just a friggin power outage. Nothing worth getting all excited about or needing to be explained with this voodoo bullshit, he adds and not trusting his words as much as he should have."

They walk some more, approaching an area that radiates the kind of luminosity obtained with kerosene lamps. He hears the man conclude:

- On le verra bien.

His name is Dieudonné. Ollie can well see the badge with the strange inscription on the man's chest through the glow that comes from the warden's office.

"Why?" Ollie challenges, and it is difficult to know if he is referring to his cicerone's previsions, the language he has used or the improbable yellowish brightness that now engulfed both of them. He can see the white of the guard's eyes, and that brings to his mind the erratic stamp of those in his church who prays as if they expect a miracle to happen in the next five minutes.

"As a matter of fact, there is a backup system. It ain't working properly, is all, Dieudonné repeats, and not making much sense at that."

"Yeah...and Rosa Maman is to be blamed for that, Ollie sneers dismissively."

"You meet the warden. You ask him."

At that, Dieudonné makes a volte-face and disappears fast into total obscurity. Ollie knocks at the door and hears the invitation to push it open. He gets in. Thanks to candlelight everywhere and the kerosene lamp already mentioned, there is a semblance of luminance in the room that is all glittering and scintillating. He can well make out the people inside. They are difficult to distinguish from their trembling shadows on the wall. After the person in charge of such mayhem has introduced himself, the visiting lawyer can't resist a wisecrack.

"After you kill a man, walk a mile in his shoes. After that who cares? He is a mile away and you got his shoes."

"Are you showing an interest for the prisoner's footwear?"

The individual who has just talked is big. Like, three hundred pounds big. He has a very red face and not much hair on top of it. It is very hot in there, and the warden is pissing water from every pores in his skin. Due to their special circumstances, there isn't an ounce of humor left in the fellow. Changing subject, he snaps:

"I presume you are the DA's representative." In the penumbra, the man sits behind a massive desk that looks like some altar in a place of worship.

"Where are the others?" Ollie inquired. He could see on the wall over his interlocutor's head an electric clock that had stopped its strolling at 5:57.

"Sorry business, this is."

The voice has come from the left. The prosecutor turns slightly in that direction, and yes, he can recognize the form of the medical examiner, who sat on a sofa. There is a glow from the cigar he is smoking. Ollie wonders if Lester Rayle is the owner of the Mercedez he has seen outside. He can, since it is said he is wealthy on his wife's side. He says hello from afar. No use in an excess of affability and risking tripping on anything and breaking a bone.

They are interrupted by the explosive bursting and crashing tonality of some wave-land type of verbal communication. A very antiquated device, by the sound of it. They hear the warden mutter:

"Where is the damn thing?"

When he has put his sticky hand on an appliance that resembles a walkie-talkie, the gadget hisses angrily like a cat that is seconds away from being thrown into cold water. The man in charge, who doesn't look much in charge of anything, addresses them all.

"The phone won't work."

Then he shouted angrily into the machine.

"Crosbie here! What is it you damn want?"

"O'Brien at Central, comes the answer in a blizzard of clattering interference. We went to fetch the old lady. Sir, there is something wrong with her."

"Why? Is she giving you trouble? You get her where she needs to be, you hear me…"

"Sir!" O'Brien cuts him off, and through the interruptions, they all can make out what he is saying.

"It isn't like that, said the voice on the other side of the communication. The woman isn't responding, sir. The dame looked kind of sick, sir."

The warden rolls his eyes, as if this is one complication too many to the accomplishment of this day's duty.

"What is it you mean? He asks, feeling the need to inquire."

"I mean, sir, she was okay one hour ago when I woke her up. Now, she's all dressed up. She's lying in her bed…and…and…you should come down here, sir, and see for yourself."

"Perhaps we should go, Lester Rayle suggested from the couch."

"Stay put. We will be there in a minute! Crosbie roared into his speaker."

Then, he juggles erratically with the machine till they all can hear the liberating click that kills the device's maddening struggle to screech its way back to life.

"I'll be damned, the warden concludes."

He appears extremely disappointed, but tries to look like all is under control and he is o.k. He will get through this, his enormous frame seems to project. It will take more than a witch few tricks to interfere with his duty. The big man opened a drawer in his desk and out came a flashlight. They all followed him into the disquieting darkness. Ollie, the doctor and two other officers. The warden didn't care to do the introductions.

"There will be no lift, I presume."

This was the doctor, who received the retort so inept a remark deserved, "You presumed correctly."

From that point, Ollie decided to credit the warden and discount the physician. Then, what could be expected from someone who drives a Mercedes 550 and considers himself pre-eminent enough that he can leave his car where he pleased? That kind of person annoys him immensely.

They walk in succession, following the big man's lead. Somehow, their small group makes it to a set of stairs. He can detect, outside the beam of glimmering brightness ahead, the shadows of a priest's silhouette. The man is sitting on a chair when the warden and his group approaches.

"Father Arkadiusz. I didn't expect you in here, warden Crosbie erupts."

They all stop in their tracks and Ollie bumps into silly Rayle, the German aficionado who whines in surprise:

"What, what? I thought I was the last in line."

"Then, you thought wrong, sneers Ollie, taking his cue from their host's manner of addressing the medical examiner."

The priest stand up. There wasn't much of him to be seen as he is short, and appears to Ollie as if he has survived a long fast.

"Here is as good a place as any to wait for you guys, Father Arkadiusz replies to the warden. His voice was low-pitched and resonant.

But I would have thought you would have liked to be with her, Crosbie responds."

All could hear that the subject made him uncomfortable.

"She didn't want me there, the priest explains in a basso, quite a surprise for a person his size. "God, he adds rather piously, won't impose on someone who isn't ready."

"How long did you sit there all by yourself?"

"Can't say. A few minutes before the black out. The coffee machine got me here, I guess."

"Then you were with her for a while, after all?"

"So you say. Not that it made much of a difference, though. But, queried the priest, what about you? You don't intend to go through with the procedure right now, do you?"

Crosby shrugs his massive shoulders, a move that nobody could have observed as they are all in the dark, except for the part of them that from time to time get caught in the glare of the lamp. Still, they don't miss the frustrated sigh that accompanies the warden's next utterance.

"I have a job to do, and it will be done if I must do it myself. You better come with us as I have been informed that she might be in need of your ministrations."

Crosbie takes the stairs, grabbing the handrails and wheezing his way down. They follow next, one after the other and counting the steps, as they have been told. There were ten to a landing followed by ten more in the opposite direction. This would put their group on the first floor under street level. One more to go, then. In this way, they all tailed their guide and his beam of light, which would bring them, hopefully, to the witch's sanctuary.

They arrive at an iron gate. As soon as he sees the warden, the guard tries to operate the door in a manual fashion, but the portal resists all his efforts. At last, he admits piteously:

"It won't open."

"Of course, Crosbie grunted. It's all electrically controlled. Use the emergency code and punch the number by hand, will you?"

"I did just that, protested the other. It won't work, though."

"Get somebody from the other side to do it, then, Crosby orders."

"There is no one around on the other side, sir."

"You get their attention somehow, okay? Use the phone or sound the alarm."

"Yes, sir, the guard responded."

Then, he starts to bang on the gate, first with his naked fist, and then with the hard part of his electric torch. After one or two minutes of such racket, they see some light coming their way. From the other side, a set of keys was plunged into a steel box built in the wall and then, the obstacle screeched open, swiveling lazily on its hinges. At last, they can progress toward their destination without further delay.

The cell where Rosa Maman Tour de l'Isle is waiting to be dispatched into a better world is well illuminated, thanks to many flashlights that stood along the partition opposite the built-in cot that protrudes from the concrete wall. On the bed, the woman is lying on her back. Her hands are joined over her ample belly. She appears peaceful and at ease. Her eyes are closed. She could have been sleeping. Still, Ollie who looks at the woman at that instant don't believe this to be true, as no one in his experience sleep this way. The position the woman is in looks more like a person already dead lying in her casket in a funeral home. The district attorney knows the witch is gone just by looking at her corpse.

"This lady is as dead as can be, he announces."

"Who arranged her this way? Crosbie asks the guard who is nearest to him, and still remains somehow hidden in the surrounding shadows."

"This is how we found her, a voice coming from behind Ollie affirms."

The warden turns toward guard number two and glares through him, as if some disgraceful noise or other had escaped his body. He then turns his suspicious stare on the woman who lay on the bunk. The incongruity of the situation is enough to make him forget common sense and protocol. Such as checking the prisoner's vitals. Rayle pushes him away and says as he leans toward the inanimate, placid lady:

"May I, please?"

All those present must have realized at that instant that something really important was taking place, because complete silence suddenly imposes itself while the medical examiner takes the woman's pulse. Then, he declares matter-of-factly:

"She is quite dead."

"Then, you will all miss your little ceremony."

That is Father Arkadiusz, who approaches the corpse and proceeds with his own ritual ministrations. His sally is obviously directed at the director.

"What a shame! He adds after a few seconds of the latter's vacillating silence, as he appears to be in a state and can't conceive of anything worth throwing at the troublesome cleric. The last three words must have hurt him somehow though. They suffice to get him out of his irresolution.

"This is uncalled for, Crosbie barks angrily at the priest."

What could be expected from that sort? The warden think. He doesn't know that the deceased was a Roman Catholic, as there were not many of those around. Rosa Maman must have originated from Haiti. Well. She sure hadn't cared for this fellow's last rites and silly ceremonies. For this, at least, he could credit his reticent captive. Leaving the priest to his punctilious shenanigans, the warden now turns his scrutiny on the physician.

"What got her? Can you tell? Did she kill herself?"

That got him a concert of vehement protestations from the officers present.

"Not a chance, they shouted in one unhappy chorus. Nothing came in. Nothing got out. We had her under constant supervision."

Crosbie interrupted them all. He addressed the highest-ranking officer in the cell, who was a woman named Percy.

"I couldn't say just by looking at her, she admitted. What you have suggested shall have to be checked out. Yet, she was well enough when she dismissed all spiritual support. And this was at five thirty this morning. We had her under nonstop surveillance, as you must know. I personally saw her lie down on her couch. She was already all dressed up. I didn't think about it. She could rest if she wanted. Then, you received that call in your office that brought you all down here. That was ten minutes ago. It is now ten past six. I presume she was discovered the way she is right now a few minutes before the communication went out. Let's say, then, that she has been dead fifteen minutes, and she survived at least to the time I saw her lying down. I can't say for sure the exact time I observed her, but it must have been five forty, maybe forty-five. This leaves us with a fifteen-minute window of opportunity. I do not know of any substance that acts that quickly without leaving traces of some sort on the victim's features."

The doctor interrupted this lecture to illuminate the witch's serene face with the glare of his flashlight.

"As you can all see for yourselves, this lady's physiognomy is calm and gentle. I would put my money on natural causes."

"You mean to say that she put herself on her cot, got into that comfortable position with her hands on her chest, and then she just died? Is this what you suggest? Crosbie asks Rayle in a tone of extreme skepticism."

'Still, Percy added, there was that thunderclap that made a lot of noise a few minuts ago. So loud powerfull and deafening that for a time, I thought that the building would collapse. This is when the power went out and we were left with complete blackness everywhere. I remember looking the hour on my phone. It was 5:57. If I had to guess, I would say she died just at that moment.'

She then looked at Dr Rayle and asked:

'What about the hour of death? Could it be as I just suggested?'

'Who knows? I won't risk myself into such conjecturing.'

All the others, if they had an opinion, kept quiet about it. Father Arkadiusz, for his part, terminates a prayer with a sign of the cross and pronounces, as if he has been offered the choice of putting an end to the issue:

"God's ways are inscrutable."

Nobody there was ready to argue with his conclusion. Ollie looks at his watch, but he can't make out the hour hand from the minute. Neither does he feel like asking for someone to share a bit of light. He would find his way out of this shithole soon enough. He feels somebody bump against his back. It is the padre. Somehow, the small man has put his hand on a flashlight, and now, he beams the device into the DA's face. He can't see much of the other's visage as it was lost in shadows, the glare of the lamp like a blinding sun to his half-closed eyes.

"So, he hears the deep voice of the little fellow address him, you are the one we shall be thankful to in eternity for having been the initiator of this sorry satire."

Arkadiusz's tone is sarcastic, and Ollie don't like that approach one bit.

"I prosecuted the old lady, if this is what you mean, he answers, doing his best to ignore the sneer that corrodes the cleric's words.

"This, you did, Arkadiusz responded. This, he repeats, you surely did, didn't you?"

Ollie frees himself from the glare of the torch and makes to get away. The priest chases him into the darkened corridor. He could use some light. He walks fast and he senses the little man working hard to follow in his steps.

"You must have been good at it, the annoying individual insists, because once trapped in your web of silly legalese and mindless obfuscation, she was lost, wasn't she? You must have enjoyed the ride, haven't you? It is not every day that people like you have an opportunity to fight evil and live to tell the tale."

The lawyer crashes into something and almost collapses on the ground. When draped in the beam of the blazing lamp, he sees the fallen chair and an open door, which must have been the office it has come from. The guard is nowhere to be seen, though. Showing the flashlight the priest was holding in his left hand, Ollie smiled at his companion.

- Can't you use this properly and cut the homily?

Ollie didn't mind the clergyman's attitude, as he was used to that kind of talk. He had had plenty of the same from the press, mostly from the North Atlantic big cities. The way to deal with those oppressive liberals is to let them palaver. As for him, he has made it his profession to get people to talk over their lawyer's objections. In his playing field, he was used to having the last world. He could well let that useless priest have it right now. He didn't give a damn of the man's opinion of him. Who was bound to profess it, anyway? He, at least, wasn't receiving his orders from some alien, papist, foreign jurisdiction. Nothing this troublesome father might tell him could take away the fact that he was in peace with his conscience. He had done what needed to be done, and the churches where he lived had approved, as had his fellow citizens, who lived by the scripture the same as he did, and whose opinion surveys had shown a quasi-unanimous approval with his style of worship. He saw himself as a warrior ready to fight for their beliefs. He must have said so to his invisible interlocutor, because he heard him repeat the words.

"A warrior, then."

"What about it? Ollie asks without thinking, as he worries about obstacles in his way."

"A combatant with an agenda from Heaven. Why is this sounding familiar? This is really fascinating. You and me, we should…"

Whatever Father Arkadiusz wanted to add, he is interrupted by the sudden appearance of radiant and blinding luminosity. When it happens, they had reached the stairs and were soon reunited with Crosbie and Rayle, who had walked not so far behind them.

"I'll be damned, the warden shouted in surprise."

From there, they all made it to his office. They could all observe the hand from the seconds on an electrical, government-issued wall clock moving slowly from one quadrant to another.

5:57.

Ollie takes his leave and is followed by the priest. While they walk into an endless passageway toward the exit, Arkadiusz engages him again.

"So, you really believe that she killed this Ziegler guy?"

"Zielgard, he corrects."

"Whatever, the other sighs."

"She sure claimed she did."

"Oh, spare me the lunatic discourse, will you?"

"Then, you do not think she could, is that it?"

"Are you making fun of me now? The priest barks. The woman was just showing off. She didn't expect to be taken seriously. Why did you?"

"Murder is serious business, wouldn't you say so?" The DA countered.

"As you should know, sickness is another."

"The lady's sanity was court evaluated. Psychiatrists had her for a whole week, mind you. She was judged legally competent. That is a fact."

"Delusional competent. Is this what you had in mind?"

Ollie made a gesture of discouragement.

"Have it your way, he says. But she still jinxed my victim really good, and a jury found he was dead because of her. End of story."

"He was dead because of her, the cleric repeated. How, may I ask, was she able to accomplish that?"

"I would have thought, Ollie countered, that it was more in your line of work to answer that question. I mean, miracles and stuff."

"So, Arkadiusz hissed at him, this is what religion is about, some sort of supernatural freaky phenomenon bullshit?"

"As you must know, the woman either spelled Zielgard dead by pinning needles into his puppet effigy, or used one or another of her magical voodoo devilish tricks. You tell me. Whatever she did, it worked just fine. And why, she did it again, I mean her exit this morning. Isn't this enough to convince you this lady wasn't just one lunatic mad woman."

The priest caught Ollie's arm and they both stopped walking. The exit was ten feet away. Outside, a hard rain felled viciously. They wouldn't make it to their cars without paying a heavy price. What a horrible day, the lawyer thought as he faced the hideous orange-brown walls of the corridors. Fine drops of perspiration could be seen on his companion's brow, as he must have been forced to walk fast in order to keep up with the prosecutor.

"Let go of me, the DA demanded. I am tired of this silly polemic, and to tell you the truth, what I feel like now is getting some breakfast."

"I am happy to see that you have an appetite."

Ollie had had enough. "Now, sir," he growls, "you pack your bag of laments right this minute and you leave me alone, you hear me?"

"Were you afraid of her? Arkadiusz insisted."

There was, in his eyes, the signs that foretold of erratic manners and unreliable urbanity, his tone of voice harsh and unfriendly.

"The hell if I was, Ollie shouted back as he made for the door."

"You are full of it, Ollie Devott. You know that, don't you?"

They were outside, still protected from the rain by some canopy-like structure. The noise of the water falling over their heads abates and then stops. The lawyer plunges first into the foggy drizzle, not caring about his bothersome escort. They both pass by the plush Mercedes without Ollie hitting the car with his foot, as he would have liked to do since he was pretty upset. The priest was really getting on his nerves after all. He accelerates his pace, forcing his smaller companion to trot beside him.

"You never believed, even for one minute, that she was capable of killing that doctor, did you?"

"I proved she did, the DA erupted."

"You're full of it," the other said again. Ollie could well see that it was an effort on the part of the priest to navigate those never-visited waters of tasteless and scatological bad form."

"Now, you are repeating yourself."

"If you had," Arkadiusz insisted, "you would have been scared to death. Tell me, Devott. Aren't you surprised to have survived the prosecution?"

"Make sense, man!"

"And the judge who presided over this absurd circus? And all those who got involved in one appeal or another? Not to forget Crosbie, who had her under his supervision? And the executioner who was to inject her with a lethal dose of poison, and would have if not for her timely departure? And all those others who must have got on her wrong side since she was arrested and detained? What about them? What about the arresting officers?"

"So, Ollie barked back, you tell me. What about the lot you described?"

"They are not dead, are they?"

His first instinct was to respond, how am I supposed to know that? Yet, even from his perspective, it would have shown too much callousness on his part. Instead, he muttered between his teeth:

"I would have known, I guess."

"As they should have been, if you were half-right and she was the witch you made her out to be."

He answered nothing. He couldn't.

"Don't you see? The other carried on: "You should have been very much afraid of her. What am I saying? You should have been terrified of the woman. You argued successfully that she was responsible for your 'so-called' victim's passing. But what? Since you initiated this sinister business, you slept like a baby."

The priest washed away from his face the tears, the rain that were running freely on his cheeks. He had stopped pursuing the lawyer, who was walking away as fast as he could. In one last effort, Arkadiusz shouted at his foe's diminishing back:

"You were not scared. Tell me why you were not scared."

That was when Ollie made a quick volte-face, watching the little man one last time, and then he said before entering his car:

- She willed herself dead, didn't she?

- You are such an asshole, the black cloth ecclesiastic screamed at the departing Saab.

XXIX

They all hated the night shift, but MTA driver Hanyu Pinyin didn't mind traveling through Kips Bay in his bus between ten p.m. and six in the morning. True, the timetable prevented him from having a life. But then, everybody who knew the man would agree that he didn't have anything that could qualify as a life anyway. Kips Bay was a nice section of the New City borough of Manhattan. Since there were no official boundaries for the New York City neighborhoods, the limits of Kips Bay were vague, but it was considered by most to be the area between East 23rd Street and East Thirty-Fourth Street extending from Lexington Avenue to the East River.

Within Kips Bay, the sector along First Avenue was dominated by the institutional buildings of New York University, which included the NYU Grossman School of Medicine, The Rusk Institute of Rehabilitation Medicine, and Bellevue Hospital Center, most often referred to as Bellevue. It was founded in 1736, and its staff took great pride in it being the oldest public hospital in the United States.

Not that Hanyu Pinyin gave a damn for those historical niceties, though. He'd been born forty-one years before in some shithole in China, and was lucky enough to have a grandfather that had got him shipped to the other side of the world where he had landed, joining his gramps, in an uncle's enlarged family. His uncle was Hanyu's dead mother's brother, who had started him at once in his dry-cleaning business. Not yet five years old, he had been made to learn to stitch shirt buttons. He'd become quite good at it. All this was before he'd gotten to know his letters. Not the silly-looking kind, mind you. He was in America, after all.

Life at his uncle Zhang's in the Bronx hadn't been so bad. As an orphan, he hadn't expected much in the first place. Now that he could look back at those years with a perspective, he allowed that things could have been worse, all things considered. He had made it to the right level of education to get a job at the Metropolitan Transportation Authority. This was no small accomplishment as he was one of a kind out of the thousands of employees that labored there. The MTA was the largest public transportation provider in the western hemisphere. Its agencies served a region of 14.6 million people spread over five thousand square miles, and moved more than eight million customers on a daily basis.

Those silly statistics. What had gotten into him? Couldn't he chew over some other topic? As if there weren't enough of those. Then, wasn't this the point of his dumb musing? Better the data than anything his otherwise unsettled mind could come up with on his own.

He was piloting his enormous diesel-powered vehicle on Route M-9 with two passengers. One was quite drunk and would soon become a nuisance if he didn't stop thinking up new ways of producing annoying noises with his mouth. Better to assume they were from his mouth, anyway. The man had revealed himself to be a real pest. Those white devils could be really disgusting when they put their minds into it. No Asian could debase himself this way even if he were to make it his life's mission. They lacked the imagination to be good at that sort of thing. No one would care to compare the nauseating fellow to any living beast. It wouldn't be fair to the animal. He knew he might be partial in his judgment, but the actual sight of the inebriated, worthless, unwashed, belching individual in his rear-view mirror made him want to throw up.

This wasn't good. He couldn't let some deadbeat lowlife ruin his peace of mind. He forced himself to forget about his repulsive rider. He could view affluent First Avenue as it passed by on both sides of him. Against his best efforts, he recalled his gloomy life. A life! As if he had one worth talking about. Since his wife of fifteen years had left him, he felt like he'd been dropped in a pit, with nobody caring to help him out of it. Worse, he was digging in the wrong direction, making the hole deeper and deeper. Who would give him a hand? He had made the wrong kinds of friends, running around with the gambling crowd. And if you knew gambling, you knew nothing if you hadn't made it into the Chinese high-stakes betting culture.

As he had. And they were sucking him dry.

He heard some more fireworks coming out of the useless drunk in the back, reminding him of an elephant making wind. The brainless bugger had started him up into this melancholic nonsense. The hell with him.

His friend Lyu had told him to stay away from the betting crowd. Hanyu was a good man, in his own way. He didn't fool around. He didn't drink. As a husband, he'd been mostly okay. Hadn't beat the wife or abused her with foul language. She'd had little to complain about, and had admitted as much. There was this one thing, though. His card playing had gotten out of control lately, and she hadn't been able to take it anymore. It would kill her before those few he was in debt with killed him. Lyu knew what he was talking about. Lyu had been there. He was well placed to give advice. He had told Hanyu to quit the game before it was too late. Then his buddy had disappeared. No one could say if he was dead or back in China.

When looking at his nephew's situation, his uncle Zhang would adopt the posture of the family sage and pronounce:

"Heaven has a road, but no one travels on it. Hell has gates, but fools will dig under them to get there."

It was all the advice he would get from him in all situations, be it his gambling or misfortunes in matrimony.

It had been no use to beg his wife to stay with him. As for demanding it, he was enough of an American to have adopted the relaxed and tolerant ways of the natives. He fully realized that a show of authority would get him nowhere. His uncle Zhang might have repeated a few times his saying about heaven and hell, but hadn't cared to help much beyond pronouncing those words. Yet, he had given his kinsman another bit of guidance. If Hanyu was to lose face, he had cautioned, better to have the smallest possible number of people to know about the ignominy. Avoid the fight you can't win, and there was no way he could have won that one. The deck had been packed against him.

Not only that. He could perceive the same thing by looking in his children's eyes, who hadn't said a word. No need! What had they done? They had stared him out of the small apartment they shared with uncle Zhang and his wife's mother. He was still expected to pay his share of the rent, though. As if he could. This would require him to win some of his money back. That was it! Everything could be put right again. Those damn dice. Since he had started to cast the tiny things, he had had a streak of bad luck that made all the previous ones appear like kid stuff.

After his present shift, he was to meet the guy who might buy his car. If the price was right, that was. That would get him ten thousand dollars, at least. Maybe he could bluff his way to twelve. He still owed a few bucks on the Camry, but the fellow didn't seem to mind. No way would he go below five figures. He needed this money really bad. He would keep two thousand for tonight's action and distribute the rest between the most aggressive of his creditors. Yes, ten thousand would do the trick. He wasn't yet ready to go back to the old country.

As if this wasn't enough, there was some pressure at work. A black man he had fleeced in a poker game had been in debt with him for twelve hundred dollars. He still carried his fellow worker's watch: an Omega. He didn't know watches and hadn't believed it when Baldwin swore the silly object was worth forty-five hundred friggin' dollars. Then he had shown him a similar item on the Internet. Speedmaster. Automatic. Chronometer ultimate. The device looked like it could fly for all its showy display of useless intelligence. Still the bauble had a thirty-six hundred English pounds list price. Quite impressive.

Now, the problem was the guy's wife, whose father had offered the gadget to his son-in-law. Somehow, the daughter had learned about Hanyu and his little pawnbroker act. The vexatious wife had made it into an official grievance at the front desk. That wasn't good. He had received a letter from some big shot at MTA and had been urged to relinquish his prize jewel. As if he gave a shit about the toy. Would these rich white devils in suits care to pay him his twelve hundred dollars? He laughed at the notion.

The drunk in the back of his bus was quiet now. That was a relief. His sorry debtor had proffered the expected protestation of innocence and had offered a shitload of meaningless assurances of future cooperation in settling the matter, as well as some harebrained story made out to explain his powerlessness in getting his hands on some cash right this instant.

Well, he believed Baldwin had had nothing to do with his wife's interference. What was he to do? As if he were left with a choice. He would end up handing the Omega back and hope for the best. Couldn't risk fighting the MTA over such an issue. It would be nice if things would work out this way at home. He could use a break. If his wife would accept to take him back, things would get better, of that he was sure.

What about his own creditors? Perhaps they could act with him as he was made to with his own deadbeat defaulter. That was a good one. As if he could exert influence over both Big Joe and Little Felix. They were both cook in one big Chinese restaurant. What if he was to call their boss and complain he was being scalped by those two?

It was two o'clock in the morning. He was approaching the A&E building on his left. There was a bus stop at the corner of second avenue and forty-Second Street. He had waited at a red light at Fortieth Street. When it had changed to green, a very red Mazda Miata convertible had passed him by at fifty miles an hour and he'd gasped in disgusted astonishment. It distracted him from seeing the man who walked the sidewalk alone. He must have come from the McDonald's nearby, because he still carried a super big cup of some beverage or other with the hamburger giant's colors on it. When Hanyu was still a hundred yards away, the man stopped walking and looked him in the eye. Even from that distance, the bus driver could discern that something wasn't quite right with the guy. There was something off in the way that he stood there motionless, looking transfixed at the moving vehicle. Hanyu started to decelerate. Suddenly, he felt afraid. He would be a hundred feet away from the bus stop when passing the pitiful individual, his speed still over twenty miles an hour when doing so. The drunk had walked shakily toward the bus's front door. And then, from the corner of his eye, he saw the gent with the goblet in his hand throw himself in front of his moving cab. He heard a pop-like sound, like when a baseball was hit real good and the happy batter knew he would never see the little shit again.

Pure instinct made Hanyu apply his foot on the break in panic. He pushed so hard that he was surprised when the metallic partition ultimately resisted his shoe's agonizing pressure. The bus kind of jolted out wildly, flattening up in front as if it wanted to enter the ground. The drunk flew through the open space to land rather brutally against the windshield, and then, detached from its glass surface. His surprised mug as he collapsed on the floor showed an expression of intense outrage and dissatisfaction.

He finished his journey toward the floor looking not much better than a bundle of unclean laundry. The idiot boozer should have stayed put in his seat, as it was written everywhere that he must. In his field of vision, for a fraction of a second, he saw the shapeless blur of a body drifting above street level in apparent weightlessness. The steering wheel pressed against his bladder and he crumpled on its circumference, his chest activating the horn that started its noise-producing cacophony and wouldn't stop even after he had regained a semblance of control over his much shaken constitution. By that time the bus had come to a full stop without further mayhem. The bus stop was still fifty feet away or so. There was nobody there waiting to get in, though. Thanks for small favors.

Hanyu's heartbeat had gone manic. He couldn't remember a moment in his life when he'd been as much afraid as he was at that moment. What the hell had happened? He didn't know. Had he hit somebody? It couldn't be. But then, it had felt like he had. On the other hand, he could swear there had been nobody on the street he was driving on. Not one soul around except that McDonald's guy who had been walking on the sidewalk just as he was driving by. The man hadn't showed that he had any intention to cross First Avenue. He had just been there in the last second, no more than a flashing image of an older fellow looking at Hanyu. He had seen his eyes, though. He could still recall the misery he had perceived in that dejected stare. It had sent him a dreary signal, not yet a warning, mind you, those eyes that, now that he thought about it, had already been dead.

Beside him, the irrelevant, inebriated nonentity grunted, which revealed everything about the infamy of his most unfortunate position. The drunk trying to get up brought the driver back into his more immediate reality. Hanyu opened the door. At least they would get some fresh air. The wino was a stinking mess, and looked like he was going to throw up. There was a deafening noise that wouldn't let him think properly. Ambulances didn't emit that kind of sound. Where was that racking clattering coming from, then? He realized somehow it was his own bus's useless protestations for the way it had been handled. His angry fist hit the protuberance that was in the middle of the steering wheel and as a result, all instantly became mercifully quiet. When he looked again for his unsavory passenger, the vagrant was sleeping. That left him some time to look around.

He could now observe some activity outside. People were coming out of McDonald's. A white BMW 535 stopped erratically just in front of the MTA carrier and Hanyu saw a lady getting out and running toward the motionless body of the man he had smashed. Not without throwing a scolding glance at him.

The dazed bus driver knew he had important things to do. There was a protocol that he must implement. How could he be expected to act in any sensible way while his mind was in such turmoil? Still, this wouldn't do. He had to react. How long before he called the front desk and reported the incident? If he didn't, he'd better be incapacitated and on his way to some intensive care unit. Some air coming from outside helped somehow and he found his cell. The number was written with the usual basic instructions on a piece of paper scotch-taped on the left window. He couldn't make it, though, his hands shaking so much, his fingers so big that they hit the push buttons two or three at a time. That was when he started to cry. He didn't recall ever having wept this way since he'd arrived in this country. He knew he was making a lot of noise, sobbing like a baby, and still, he couldn't help it. It was more than his present predicament. He howled for his lost wife and family, the sorry mess he had created for himself, for being the man he was and not being able to do better.

The emotional, childish display diminished. He was surprised when he saw the last of his passengers walk by himself to the front exit. The distinguished-looking black man with an attaché case couldn't but detect the pitiful state Hanyu was in, and said to him in the guise of consolation,

"Don't you worry, man. That poor dude had it coming."

And then he stepped over the drunk, making sure his clothes did not come into contact with the individual. Hanyu couldn't say if the departing man had meant the inebriated wreck on the floor or the one lying on the street outside. The fresh air might have benefited the snoring derelict, because he suddenly righted himself into a sitting position and used the steps as his bench.

"Are you okay?" Hanyu forced himself to ask.

"You sure drive funny, the drunk answered." And then, his balance still precarious, he stood up and left.

He saw him disappear away down the sidewalk, stumbling across the street and looking like a circus animal walking on its hind legs. Well, he was the captain of the ship, and he had disembarked all his passengers to safety. He might survive this episode after all. He next called the emergency number and put the phone to his ear. It worked.

From then on, everything went quite fast. The lady in the BMW, who had been a doctor at Bellevue, arranged for an ambulance to be dispatched at once on the site. In this way, he had been told that the unfortunate stroller wasn't dead. Yet! He couldn't figure out how anyone could survive an impact with a moving vehicle such as the one he had been driving. All the same, who could tell? Those ER people were quite good on TV, fixing moribund people and bringing them back to life.

Patrolmen materialized soon after the paramedics. He could see them talking to witnesses and taking notes. When they were ready for him, one officer moved toward his bus's open entrance and looked inside. He was accompanied by one of the witnesses. The bystander was dressed in a suit. Who would be on the street at this late hour in such attire? Then, he was no witness at all. He was a lawyer. Half an hour into the calamity and here he was. That was fast, he marveled. Those guys at the Metropolitan Transportation Authority didn't lose time, did they? They took care of business, as this mouthpiece would do as of now. That was what he had been told. Do as he says, and all will be fine. This was what he wanted. Somebody, not him, to be in charge and make this displeasing sequence of events, as well as their consequences, simply wash away. This counsel looked the part very much. In his middle forties with a nice appearance, the chap could have impersonated George Clooney, if not for his receding hairline. His name was Latmi Deluidis, and he was a third-generation Greek. Better, he was a fixer. He was the help MTA had sent.

The police officer stood on the sidewalk waiting for the driver to leave his seat in the coach. When he wouldn't move, the lawyer jumped in and said,

"I will need to confer with my client. You give us a minute or two, will you?"

Before the officer could object, Deluidis was already issuing instructions to his new protégé, hissing between his teeth as he was getting up.

"Stick with the version you already gave over the phone and you will be out of the woods."

Then, he pushed Hanyu outside the bus. The officer started by asking the driver for his name and Deluidis answered, managing to get it right on the first try.

"So, officer Trillit carried on, you must be the driver...?"

"He was, Deluidis answered in his place. Who else would care to sit where you found him?"

Then he turned towards Hanyu and introduced himself properly.

"I am Latmi Deluidis. I am the lawyer MTA got out of bed to deal with your situation. And this here is Officer Trillit, who will ask you a few questions. He already knows the answers for having talked to a witness. So, you don't worry. Tell us all about that jumping suicidal man, will you?"

"You are leading a bit, counselor, don't you think?" The cop objected.

'Sorry pal. I won't do it again, a laughing Deluidis promised, not contrite in the least.'

Trillit had his notebook open, with his hand holding a pen on a white page he was anxious to fill in, at the ready to immortalize Hanyu's next few words. Hanyu looked at the sollicitor with imploring eyes and received silent encouragement to proceed. He stuck with the version he had already given to his handler on the phone forty minutes ago.

"There was this fellow, he articulated as well as he could. I took notice of him as I was preparing to halt at the corner of Twenty-Sixth Street. He had some drinking goblet in his hand. I remembered thinking he was standing in the wrong place if he planned to get on the bus." Hanyu interrupted himself, out of breath. He glanced at the beaming barrister. As he knew he was doing well, he persevered. "I couldn't do much. The bus was there, doing his thing. Well, I was coming up his way. Not fast. Reducing speed as a matter of fact in order to come to a halt at the next bus stop. He saw me. All the bloke had to do was stay where he was."

At that point, there was a break in the narrative and Hanyu wiped his face with his left hand, his gesture a bit clumsy, as he didn't know what one was supposed to do when dripping water all over his cheeks. This made his interrogator uncomfortable and he withdrew the pen from the sheet of paper. Deluidis put a comforting hand on the troubled driver's shoulder.

"What happened then?" He whispered. Tell us."

But before he could, Trillit interfered:

"Was there anybody waiting to get in at the bus stop?"

"No."

"Then, there was no need to reduce speed, wasn't it?"

"Still, I did. It's in the book. You reduce speed at a bus stop at all time, no matter what."

"O.K. You continue. What happened next?"

"He jumped at me, Hanyu whimpered. There was no time for me to see much, though. Just a sudden move out of the corner of my eye followed by the popping sound it made when I sent him flying."

"We could tell you hit the brakes fast enough, Trillit offered as comfort."

"What about him?" The driver asked. Is he dead? Will he make it? Can I see him?"

"Well, the other replied, as far as I know, they got him to Bellevue. So you will have to ask them. Some doctor took care of him, though. He must have been alive somehow. As for seeing him, it is not my call."

He then finished scribbling Hanyu's last sentence in his notebook and added as he was folding it:

"I guess we're done here."

After they had seen him turn back in the direction of his patrol car, both the lawyer and his client got on the bus. Deluidis turned towards his disheartened charge.

"You did well, he approved."

He offered him a clean handkerchief. "Now, he pursued, you wash yourself clean and then, as you have suggested, we are going to investigate what became of that poor basket case."

"I can't leave the bus, a disconsolate Hanyu objected. It's against regulations."

The lawyer shrugged dismissively.

"Forget the damn routine. You will bring that bus back soon enough. Anyway, our technical people at MTA will want to take pictures and measures. This bus needs to stay where it is for the time being. You close that door now and I will have our new friend Trillit make sure nobody comes near it."

Thus reassured, Hanyu did as he was told. They both made it to Adult Emergency Services of Bellevue Hospital. The Bellevue AES was a level one Trauma Center, and a major paramedic receiving establishment. It was said that the combined annual volume of its AES and urgent care area topped eighty-five thousand visits. It also served as the standby hospital, linked by special line to White House Security whenever the President, Vice President, or leading public figures traveled to New York City, as it offered all major specialties and subspecialties. All year long, twenty-four hours a day, without interruption.

When they went in, the place seemed quiet, if such a lieu could ever seem that way. The only hospital urgency Hanyu had ever come near was the one in the *ER* television series. He followed Deluidis, and soon enough the fixer had managed to talk to a doctor, then another, who stopped a nurse and told both of them to follow her. They reached a room where they were told to sit and wait. The doctor who was in charge would come and talk to them. Hanyu recalled what he had thought on receiving that piece of news. He must not be dead. If there was a doctor, there must be someone under his care. He sat and looked at the clock on the wall. It showed 3:30 in the morning.

XXX

Traffic was light and the Lincoln flew through the city's streets at fifty miles an hour. Those sitting inside couldn't feel it, so big and comfortable was their luxury car. On its back seats' cream-colored leather, neither Arthur nor Angela were saying anything, both lost in their thoughts.

Chico stopped the car at the ER entrance just as a group of paramedics ran about in a kind of crazy ballet, fussing over one very sick-looking patient. As much as he longed to exit the limo, Arthur knew better than to open the door by himself. He waited for their chauffeur to come to Angela's side and help them out. The man looked concerned and Arthur, who noticed details of that sort, liked him the better for it. He followed his unhappy escort toward the unknown fellow lying on a stretcher, saw her looking at the man's flustered face as if she had hoped somehow to recognize her poor suffering husband. Finding out it wasn't him didn't alleviate her burden, though. This man was very much alive, and she could tell that he would make it through his ordeal. What about her poor Peter? What if he had done something foolish? She trod on Arthur's heels. Thanks to Charlie, they were expected. Someone greeted them as soon as they passed the emergency center's entrance door. They were brought into a room and asked to wait there. Angela couldn't resist asking:

"How is my husband?"

The nurse couldn't or wouldn't say. Whatever tidbits she cared to impart with were about a Doctor Ryan who would be there soon. And then the woman disappeared as if they were lepers and one more minute near them would get her infected.

381

The waiting room was filled with empty orange plastic chairs, save for one that was occupied by an Asian gentleman with plenty of very black hair. He was wearing a uniform and staring blandly at the wall with a well dressed man standing beside him. The companion was speaking, but whatever he tried to convey, Arthur could tell his words weren't getting through to his audience of one. They sat without looking at the couple that had preceded them in. Not long later a harassed-looking male nurse pushed the door wide open. It crashed on the opposite wall with a bang. The newcomer ignored them all, standing there, quiet and motionless. At last, the medical attendant approached a table with a coffee machine on it. He seized the still half-full pitcher and turned toward the frightened woman who was now peering through him.

"You care for one cup?" He asked her?

As Angela wasn't responding and Arthur was looking elsewhere, he filled his own with the substance and left in the direction of the Asian man and his companion.

As soon as he took notice of the nurse's presence, Latmi Deluidis interrupted his monologue and addressed him in his usual garrulous way:

"Finally! I will say this: to be ignored in a place like this has its advantages. At least you're not dying."

But the nurse passed by them and didn't stop. Arthur, though, greeted the "bon mot" with a smile. Then he made for the coffee table. That was when he heard the same voice calling to him:

"I wouldn't try that if I were you."

"I'm not that fancy, Arthur answered back."

"As you wish."

He served himself a cup of the insipid beverage. At best, it was hot. Arthur walked toward the talkative fellow. He should have stayed with Angela, but she was lost in her thoughts and wouldn't miss him anyway. Besides, the man had a friendly attitude and Arthur could use the diversion. He approached the good looking individual and saluted him with his drink. He noticed the stranger's half-empty mug and concluded:

"You already discovered the best the place has to offer. You guys must have arrived before us."

"As if they care. You are the first human being I've talked to since me and my friend here entered this waste of a place."

"You were right about the coffee, Arthur offered."

"You know how many lawyers it takes to screw in a light bulb?" Asked his new acquaintance.

"Another of those silly jokes. Arthur, who had heard that one before, laughed ahead of time."

"How many can you afford?"

The punch line must have come as a surprise to the small Asian man, because suddenly his body started to move and in no time, he was laughing hysterically in a high-pitched and clumsy manner, the sound he was making evoking the hihihihihi of strange alien characters in the cartoon he had read as a child. That was when Arthur noticed the man's outfit. His companion put his arms in a protective way on both his shoulders, concluding:

"You liked that one, didn't you?"

Then the merry jester turned his attention toward the newcomer and enquired:

"What are you doing here?"

Arthur dodged the prying and said instead,

"You must be part of that unfortunate lot yourself. You do look like one, and I've got an eye."

"Well, Deluidis admitted, I hope you meant that as a compliment."

"It was a very cold winter this year. I must have seen you, for a change, with your hands in your own pockets."

This started the bus driver on another seizure-like spell of crazy giggles, a display that eventually put a skeptical smirk on the other man's lips. And then, Arthur offered his hand and presented himself as a colleague.

"And your name is?" He then asked, both their hand still shaking.

Deluidis identified himself. The Tampa lawyer gulped the last of his coffee, glancing at Angela, who was still sitting where he had left her. Her eyes were closed like she was sleeping.

"This your wife?" Deluidis asked. "Who are you here for? Your mother-in-law? A child?"

"Her husband, he responded rather distractedly. We were told he was here. We know nothing. We hope for the best."

"He hit someone, Deluidis explained in return. With his chin, he pointed at the Chinese bus driver. A poor downcast who must have been thrown out of the house one time too many and saw fit to put an end to his misery by throwing himself in front of a bus."

This put Arthur instantly on edge, and he was enveloped by a feeling of apprehension and dread. What were these people doing in here? He wondered. This was obviously a special place. Made for waiting, yes, but not of the kind they put you in if you drop into the ER as an outpatient. This must be another department, one of Bellevue's numerous categories like cardiac, neurological, obstetrics, toxicological, and such. He and Angela had been made to linger there because some specialist was supposed to tell them about Peter's prospects. And then, here was this fellow bus driver and his jocular mouthpiece sharing the same space. That must meant something, Arthur speculated.

"Then, he forced himself to ask, do you know what happened to the guy?"

"As If I knew. We've been made to wait here for the last hour."

"Why would you, anyway? Arthur wondered out loud. After all, he is no family of yours."

"Well, my client over there would sleep easier if this jumper wouldn't die on him, Deluidis rightfully suggested."

There was some noise in the corridor nearby and Chico made his appearance with a scratch of paper in his hand. As he was about to pass it to Arthur, it fell on the floor. "Charlie asks you to call him at that number," he said. Deluidis bent to grab the note that had landed at his feet. He looked at it and the writing on it inspired him into another of his jokes.

"Doctors at a Brooklyn hospital have gone on strike and put their demands in writing. Hospital officials say they will find out what the doctors want as soon as they can get a pharmacist over there."

Arthur took the written message back to Chico and smiled at him.

"The man has a point, don't you think?" He said. "You believe you can make some sense out of this scribbling?"

"I am sorry, the newcomer admitted easily. Charlie has asked you to wait till 4:30 before calling him."

Chico then proceeds to pronounce each of the ten numbers distinctively while Arthur write them down. He terminated by repeating:

"That's where he will be at 4:30"

"Is this all? Arthur insisted. Looks to me like there are a lot more words in there than those you've prononced."

"That, sir, Chico explained with a smile, is my grocery list, sir. That's all I had to write upon when I got hit with this call from my boss."

"Fine, Arthur concluded. Perhaps we will know more by then, and hopefully I will be able to give him a full situation report by that time."

"You mean, their puzzled driver retorted, they told you nothing yet?"

"We have not been here long. I am pretty sure someone will come shortly now."

Arthur was saying these words when a short lady dressed in a white doctor's frock made her appearance. As soon as she did, Angela was out of her seat and standing before her.

"Please, tell me, she implored. I am his wife. How is Peter? Can I see him? He will need me. You must bring me to him. At once, she insisted."

"You will see him, the physician answered."

There was no smile on her lips. Her voice was quiet and her tone decisive. Then, she added:

"I am Doctor Helen Ryan, the chief of neurology here. Your husband, I am sorry to say, is in a coma. He has had a CAT scan, which shows a hemorrhage to the brain. It is under control right now. We've also done an EEG that shows some hope for a possible recovery, but it is too soon yet to know for sure. He may come out of it in hours, or days, or maybe weeks. There's no way to predict."

"How come he is in a coma? What happened to him? Bring me to him, please, pleaded Angela.

"Sure. Another thing, though. I have asked Dr. Vikram Daruwala at the Presbyterian Hospital to give a second opinion. Dr. Daruwala, as you might know, is the leading neurosurgeon in the country. He is the one who has written the Bible on the traumatic injuries of the brain. He also was my professor at Harvard."

"Thank you, Angela, now sobbing, whispered."

White as a ghost, she added:

"Please, let me see him now."

"What happened to him? Arthur asked to the departing doctor as both she and Angela were leaving."

"He has been involved in an accident, she replied over her shoulder. I have been told he got hit by a city bus not far from here. Now, will you follow me please? I will bring you to your husband."

Both women left the room and disappeared around a corner. It took five minutes for the remaining occupants of the room to do the same. But not before Arthur had the time to learn from Hanyu Pinyin what had happened to Peter Atritis. Before exiting the premises, Arthur gave his coordinates to the girl in charge of the front desk. In this way, Angela would know he would be waiting for her in his room at the Hotel Pierre.

Bellevue Hospital, Saturday, 4:00 in the morning

He was sleeping a lot. He dreamed, seeing mostly the playback of his life. This made him happy, because he'd had a good one. There were times when he might not be dreaming, because he could think inside the dreams. In addition, he could hear them somehow. They said it was an accident.

Well, he knew it wasn't.

Why had he done it? It wasn't like him to do anything drastic. All his life, he had managed to avoid unpleasant or challenging issues. He had had many of those. Still, he had made it through them all. It had to be an accident. There was some comfort in this notion. To think otherwise was inconceivable. It would destroy Angela. Knowing that he had deliberately chosen to put an end to his existence was a concept that she wouldn't be prepared to deal with. He might not survive his coma, God forbid. Would she his death? Somehow, he knew that she would get through the ordeal of his dying. But the other thing, if it was proven true, would get to her. No way could she grow old if her husband of so many years had seen fit to put en end to his life and leave her alone without an au revoir. But the word was out that it had been an accident. Better that way.Then, if his death had been casual and fortuitous, it would have been out of his hands.

She would have realized he was upset. It would have been so like her eccentric spouse to act in odd and unusual ways. It would be easy for her to envision him as he walked through streets and boulevards without regard to anything except his thoughts. Getting hit by traffic. It happens all the time. The more so if one is distracted and inattentive. She would buy such a story.

An accident, then. Was he dreaming? He had made it into his late fifties, and he could well remember never having deliberately broken anything since his early childhood. His toys, objects, furniture, cars, and whatnot, he had always cared for, using those things with a protective scrutiny.

And now this.

He knew he had been blessed with good fortune. He had enjoyed everything that counted in life and more. And then, there had been this other side of him. The loser side. The side that messed up all the winning hands that he had been dealt. Why? He could be served with a full house and would play his predominant hand in such a way as to lose some chips over it, or make trifles where another would have robbed the bank.

Hours passed. Or were they minutes? And then, he knew she was there. He felt her take his hand. He felt her hair brushing his cheek and the wetness of her tears on his skin.

Angela smiled. This was her Peter. He never cared much for silly competition, all those games people indulged in to position themselves against others in life's so-called struggle. She was near him now. She had walked the Intensive Care Unit's long corridors beside Dr. Ryan who had explained to her the reasons of Peter being there. They were passing open doors left and right. Behind each of those was a sorry exhibit of some personal drama, of worlds collapsing and new frightening beginnings. Peter's room was at the end of one those endless passageways. His left shoulder was in a cast. Otherwise, he looked whole enough. He had a bandage around his head, but apart from that, his face was intact. His eyes were closed. He could have been sleeping normally if it hadn't been for the tubes coming out of his body, connected to a clattering life support device that emitted an ominous rhythmical beeping.

What a horrible place this was. Intensive Care Units could reveal quite an intimidating environment, the more so if the person lying there was a loved one. Strange sights, smells, and sounds had a way to put her in a state of constant alertness, which was good since she didn't want to miss the moment when Peter woke. Which obviously he would. There could be no doubt about that. There existed no conceivable alternative scenario.

Through the door, she saw nurses walking by. She had been asked to wash her hands and to wear a green hospital gown over her clothes. She had been asked to turn off her mobile phone, for it could interfere with the functioning of the sophisticated medical equipment in Peter's room, or elsewhere. From far away, she heard an annoying shrilling sound of a monitor gone awry, as if it was protesting the subject under its care for being a quitter. The way of the machine to protest an ailing patient that no longer played his part of fighting in a game where one's existence is at stake, life's prolongation the ultimate prize. The racket must have been some sort of alarm, for it sure caught the right people's attention. Soon enough, she listened to the banging of doors and attendants running in panicky haste. Better someone else. Perhaps she was just imagining things. The terror was in her.

She looked at all the pieces of equipment surrounding Peter. She wished them to stay quiet. There was a sort of TV that showed on its screen all sorts of wave line patterns as it kept track of his heartbeat, blood pressure, body temperature, breathing rate, oxygen saturation, and such corporal functions. What if it was the monitor Peter was attached to that went berserk? What would become of her then? Would she be able to take it? Would Peter survive such a trial?

She was still holding Peter's inert hand in hers. He was wearing no ring. He never had. His wedding ring had been lost. She recalled him buying the cheap trinket, since he knew he would use it just one time at church. Then, it was an imposition that couldn't be evaded; he had smiled at her and showed the wedding band he had procured. It was metallic and gold in color. From far away, it looked like the real thing. It would do. His skin was warm. Would he respond to her caress, as he did when they were in the bed they shared back home? She concentrated on her sense of touch and tried to detect some kind of reciprocity that wasn't there.

Yet, he was breathing. He was alive. That was what counted. He wouldn't die on her. This couldn't be. She had to give him time. God wouldn't permit them to be reunited just to take him away. She looked at her sleeping husband. She had some irresistible intuition that he must have known she was there. That was when she started talking to him. She told him that she had always loved him, and would till the end of time, that she needed him and that he must come back to her. Tears came to her eyes and she fought the impulse to break down. Was there a smile on his lips? She must hold herself together. In a fluttering voice, she recalled the night they had first met, using the exact same words he'd used when telling the episode, as he liked to do when they were in company. It made for so wonderful a story. That had been their story. What a great tale he had made of it. Hearing her own words out loud had a soothing effect on her nerves. They had assisted at a Harry Belafonte concert. When half into the story, a brief knocking at the door distracted her. She turned her head toward the light and saw a young woman who said:

"Hello, I'm Lyn. I'm a social worker."

Angela stared at Lyn with uncomprehending eyes. The other got her feet into the room and asked:

"Would you care to see a priest? Father O'Brien will be making his rounds at seven o'clock. I might ask him to stop here."

"What for?" Angela asked in panic, knowing instantly that this was an inadequate response. Lyn must have had some experience of dealing with spouses in pain, because she didn't argue her case. She just stepped back and disappeared. So, that was it, Angela thought. Peter who would soon be meeting his Maker, and he needed a proper introduction. What a nightmare all this was. Those professionals, they sensed the end was near, and they'd sent her signals that she must prepare, somehow, for the inevitable. What were the chances of surviving a coma? In movies, they always did, didn't they? Peter was there. He was hooked up to all sorts of life-dispensing apparatuses. And he wanted to live. It was an accident. One couldn't die for such a stupid reason. He had been disturbed. That horrible girl. They had let her have the better of her beloved Peter. The poor man wouldn't have known the first rule of engagement for such an encounter, let alone escape unscathed from a deliberate and aggressive provocation. Those people in show business, they had left him no way out. Whatever he had done, he deserved a chance, and it had not been offered to him.

And then, he was here, lying unconscious. She was at his bedside. What if it hadn't been an accident? She must not go there. She must put her mind to some other things. This idea of Peter taking his own life was so shocking that she couldn't deal with formulating it. This had been a random event. A fortuitous calamity. Some bad luck, like everybody experiences in one way or another. He would find his way back to her, and then, he would explain it all. Never again, she promised herself, would she leave him alone. She would be there for him. He needed her as much as she needed him. Always. He would make it. She knew it. He had so much to come back to. She started telling him about his publishing success in California. Arthur wouldn't mind. Time passed. She stopped talking. Peter wasn't listening. There were a clock on the wall. She looked at the seconds hand for a full five minutes.

At 6:35, she jumped out of her reverie. Had she not sensed some pressure on her finger? She stopped breathing, all her senses alert for one improbable vital spark. Could it be that he was coming out of his coma? She concentrated on his eyelids, expecting Peter to look at her and smile like he used to at home when their eyes met.

But not this time. The rhythmic beeper that came out of the device flustered her to the point of madness. What, then, if he had been sick? Could it be that he had been depressed? Was it possible that he had and she had overlooked his condition? So much for all this love. It was a silly pretense if such was the case. They were growing old. Look at Spiros, who had been as fit as an olive tree until the day he had died in despair.

She recalled that family picture of all of them taken a few years back in Kalamata. That was the place they all came from, thanks to the great-great-grandfather who was said to have died in good health at ninety-six, the result of a boat accident owing to some raging Mediterranean Sea's capricious impulse. They had all been there near the antique stone house overlooking the blue water. Those timeless elders with their faces as callous as sandpaper, by reason of three days' worth of stubble, and not one of them under the age of eighty-five. The women hadn't done so well, though. There was only one in the picture, Spiros other sister's death being the excuse for the old man's trip home and the taking of that photo. It was the last visit Spiros was to make to the country of his forefathers. Or so he had said. They had gone with him. Peter to see his uncles and cousins. And her accompanying him for the fun of the trip. Spiros had sure looked healthy enough. He'd been in the center with all his teeth showing and both his arms up, a Zorba-like posture, as if he was getting ready to dance the Syrtaki. That was why, seeing them, she had always assumed that she would be the first to go. She couldn't say why, but that conclusion had been a reassuring thought. She couldn't see herself doing all those tasks one was supposed to perform at times like this. She couldn't conceive living alone. Better to leave Peter that burden.

And now, he was there in a hospital bed, and perhaps he would never make it out of that coma. How could that be? What had happened? What was he doing there in the first place? What had gotten into him to account for the fact he had traveled from the CBS Studio to that McDonald's near the place he had been hit by a bus? He should have been driven back to the Pierre. Then she remembered his exiting the set in haste, and his ominous last words, taken out of Yogi Berra's grave: "It is not finished till it is finished." What the great man had said was more like, "It ain't over till it's over." But Peter wouldn't have known that, would he?

What had he meant by using the silly quote? The words sure didn't sound like Peter. His normal self would more likely remember some Plato citation like, "Great is the art of beginning, but greater is the art of ending." She knew a bit of Plato. Peter had introduced her into the philosophical world from morning to night with the proper quote for all life's occurrences. He must have been pretty agitated for such a sentence to come out of his mouth. What had come into him, then? He didn't knew sports, and still, he liked the Zielgard story about baseball enough to discover its value and excellence, loved it enough for him to do the unthinkable. He had been right, the novel had been good and gained him instant acceptance among all writers left and right. She had always marveled at her spouse's ability to catch up fast on any subject he chose. If he were to put his mind to it, he could learn anything, and be better at it than the average Joe in no time.

That McDonald's, then. The distance between that place and the CBS Studio wasn't so great that they couldn't be walked. Peter might have wandered, going nowhere, just wanting to be left alone. Somehow, he must have seen the big yellow M of the fast-food chain giant and decided to get in. He had visited the burger diner for the cup he had been carrying when he'd been hit by the bus. What was it, then? He had seen the bus and ran to catch it? And he had tripped on something or other. This would explain his dropping in front of the vehicle, as he must have.

She looked at her husband resting on the metallic bed. The last time she had seen him, he had been preparing to depart for that horrible place. He had been excited. He had made her promise to listen to the show, and she had. Peter had been a celebrity. Not that it had changed him in any way that she could have noticed. Her Peter would always remain the same. Her Peter. The one who didn't care for anything except their life together and finding enough time to read and write his stories. Would he ever be able to do that again?

He had to get better. Fate couldn't be so cruel that it would spring him out of the play before his act was finished. Peter had yet to experience real success, the one he would soon enjoy, thanks to Arthur. The lawyer that would put an end to all dispute by attributing earnings of the Faith book to its rightful originator. Somehow, a switch would be done, and an explanation furnished that would clarify the entire situation. Perhaps the sorry mess could be blamed on some confusion in the publishers mishandling of both pieces. And if such an ending was too much to ask for, as she could well realize her idiotic deceptions were not making any sense, then so be it. Peter would readily admit whatever wrong he had done. Who would complain? Arthur had disclosed to her that the only family Zielgard had had was one cousin in East Germany, and that kin would be so overcome by his newly acquired fortune that he wouldn't even think of lamenting, let alone making a fuss about the whole mess.

No! This, they could manage together. With Arthur's help, they would find a way. And Peter would get better. And he would be a celebrity in his own right. This would make him happy. He would be liked. What an odd idea, the notion that her husband would have cared for such trivialities as receiving homage from his fellow men. Spiros would have shrugged over such a concept. He had liked to quote Charles de Montesquieu. "The fewer men think, the more they talk."

From her angle, seeing her sleeping husband's profile, Angela could see a resemblance between father and son. Peter might end up with some of his father's facial characteristics. The aquiline nose, the compressed, narrow lips, and a two-day beard on his cheeks could do miracles to bring back home the ancestors. She would have liked to be able to call her father-in-law. Whatever the problem, Spiros had provided solutions. While alive, the man had shown enough vitality for both himself and his son. He would have been able to bring Peter back to life. Well, at that instant, it sure looked like she couldn't. She had been in that room for almost two hours now, expecting Peter to wake up, but that wasn't happening, and there was no way to know if he would survive, let alone emerge from his coma and be with her for the time it takes to say goodbye.

The clock in the room showed 6:44. It was difficult to know if it was night or day. She must have dozed. No wonder. She had had no sleep for the last 20 hours. She couldn't use her cell. To accomplish the task, she would need to leave the room. What if he awoke and she wasn't there? She brushed away the useless objection. She'd slept, hadn't she? And he could have died on her then. What about that? Well, the life-sustaining device would have taken over then, and she would have known about the calamity. She would have to leave somehow. How long would he be sleeping this way?

That's when it happened. It took her by complete surprise. A clash of thunder so loud and deafening that she felt like being swallowed into the detonation. Peter's bed trembled, walls oscillated around her. For a brief instant, she worried about the building collapsing. And then, a semblance of calm. She kind of sensed a bit of pressure on her hand where Peter's thumb touched it. She looks at him intensely. Nothing.

She considered calling someone. Tammy. Patrick. What would she tell them? Their father was lying in a coma in a room in some Hospital Intensive Care facility and he might never come out of it alive? What good would that do? Either they would insist on coming, or they wouldn't. One way or the other, it wouldn't change Peter's prospects, or the time he would need to get out of his present state of unconsciousness.

She was crying now. So much for taking charge of things. The reality of it was that she craved to talk to someone, because she really needed some support. Spiros would have known what to do. He always did. She caught a tissue out of a Kleenex box on a table near the bed and dried her tears. No, she decided, better wait. She looked at the cot that had been placed against the far wall. Perhaps she should try to sleep a bit more. The monitor was still casting its cheery beeping through the small space, each of its throbbing pulsations and hopping graphics on the screen some indication of Peter still-working engine.

Five minutes passed. This slight interval had seemed to her like half an eternity. She heard another rumble, far away at first that reverberate through her before maturing into an explosion that took her breath away, so strident and ear splitting that she almost fell on the floor. Hopefully, the deafening roar decreased to a distant clamor and the machine that kept her husband alive continue purring as if nothing had happened.

When a semblance of calm returned, she stared at her husband and she thought she saw one shivering shifting of his left eyelid. Was she hallucinating? Her heartbeat accelerated and she felt weak from anxiety and lack of rest. Also, she didn't remember when she had eaten last. She pressed Peter's hand between her trembling fingers and whispered soft words in his ears. She sensed the semblance of pressure on her palm, the touch so light that it must have been the product of her restive imagination. And then, there could be no doubt. In one fraction of a second, Peter's eyes opened and fixed instantly on hers. She could see recognition in his haggard features. He was looking at her and through her. She stopped breathing. Her heart constricted in her chest. She should have been relieved, and somehow, she wasn't. Peter's subdued stare made her so afraid because it came from a place she couldn't or didn't know how to reach.

He was there and yet, he wasn't. His eyes were wide open. There was enough light for her to see every minute detail of his afflicted gaze. She saw his lips moving. The beeping coming from the machine beside her was pounding crazily against her temple with an explosive regularity. She bent and put her ear near his mouth. She sensed on her cheek the sting from his stubble. She could see he was trying to tell her something. She begged him between her sobs to lay still, not to exhaust himself. That he should rest. That there was all the time in the world for him to tell her what he wanted. There would be time to talk later. All would be fine. They both could see that now. He had no need to say anything at that instant. She was there. She would stay where she was. She would never leave him. She loved him so much. And she was so happy. He would be well soon. She couldn't ask for more.

The sound of Peter's voice, weak and yet vivid and understandable, silenced her. She blamed herself for her insipid prattle. What if she had missed some of what he was painstakingly trying to tell her? She gulped down her tears and listened. What he was saying to her made no sense.

"Joe and Barbara, they... That part was mine..."

"It's okay, she mumbled, ignoring what he meant and not wanting to ask."

Tears were rolling down her cheeks and she could see them raining down all over Peter.

"They were my words, for you, Angela, Peter said."

"You should say no more, she implored him." She saw the strain to get the words out was too much of an effort for him. "Please, dear, you rest. I'm so happy that you are here."

And then, as his eyes locked onto hers, he said:

"I love you so much, Angela."

Those were his very last words to her. His sad eyes stopped seeing and somehow, she knew. Once more, the heaven opened up to blast the city with another call for judgment, this one more vociferous et resounding than the last, thundering over her and Peter for so long, multiplying the clashes that burst one after the other in a cacophonous collection of roaring blasts. The room lost its light. She was engulfed in total blackness. The emergency system might have taken over because all became bright again. Still, the lines on the monitor started jumping, the device issuing angry protests, a shrill noise that filled her with instant terror. That was when she started to scream, but before she could hear the sound of her despair, someone from the emergency team of operators came in and took over.

The clock on the wall showed 6:57.

EPILOGUE

Summer 2019

It had been a difficult time for Angela.

Arthur read the line and stopped writing in his journal. Those words couldn't express the desolation that had followed Peter's passing. Devastation seemed a better term to express the utter despair, misery, dejection, and wretchedness that had befallen Angela in the hours, days, and months after her spouse's demise. He had worked some kind of settlement with the transit authority, Angela renouncing all claims for the unfortunate death in exchange for a declaration by the driver of the bus affirming that it had been an accident. He had been made to meet Hanyu Pinyin, who had told him in detail all that he reminded of that horrible night. Arthur could well see in the fellow's unsettled eyes the face of his writer friend in the half second it took him to elect to put an end to his existence. It had not needed a lot of persuasion for Hanyu to change his story and adapt his discourse in a way that was best for all parties involved, himself included. Arthur had left New York with the driver's signature at the bottom of a declaration that said Peter had stumbled over something or another and dropped in front of the vehicle, with no time for the driver to do anything. In this way, Angela would not have to deal with the worst consequences of her companion's final gesture in life.

Early in the morning, he had received a call from some nurse or doctor in the hospital. They required his help to handle Angela, who refused to disengage from the recently deceased Peter Artritis, and they needed to do something since protocol would not and could not tolerate such anarchistic displays of passion and devotion.

When he appeared in room 1209, he saw that Angela, overcome by despair, had entangled herself with Peter, and would not respond to ultimatums to let go of him. The male nurse who had brought Arthur to the room approached the bed and, for an instant, Arthur was under the impression that the man was about to grab the desperate widow by whatever morsel of her anatomy he could catch, and disengage her from the prize she was protecting from invasion, seizure, and usurpation. The nurse, Maurice, would do whatever was necessary, and just needed him there as a witness in case the heartbroken woman claimed she had been attacked and molested.

He did not approach Angela, though. What he did was turn his face toward Arthur. There was no need for the attendant to say anything as it was clear what was expected of him. The man left, closing the door after him. The lawyer stayed where he was, watching Angela. Peter's left foot was imprisoned between her two legs. She had one hand closed over his right wrist, while the other looked strongly attached to his hair, which he had in abundance at the back of his neck. Her eyes were fully open and stared into nothingness. She seemed as dead as Peter. Arthur moved near the bed, not sure what he should do or how to do it. He had been told Peter's had died at 6:57 that morning. He had been called at 7:35. His watch now showed 8:20. Could it be that Angela had been in that catatonic state for the last hour and a half? He remembered how she'd been the last few days and could not believe it was the same person he was contemplating at this time. He must do something to get her out of her torment. He'd been standing there for the last five minutes without having done or decided anything, and he felt tired suddenly, not sure anymore if his legs would support his weight one minute longer. He looked around and moved to the nearest chair and sat in it. Well, falling into it would be nearer to the truth. So that is what he wrote in his diary.

While he was contemplating the past events, it was difficult for him to put them down on the paper, even though it was eight months later and, thanks to his workload, old habits, and the beaten path, things had settled into their usual and reassuring routine. As for Angela, she had finally consented to put an end to her self-imposed coma, but he doubted she would ever be capable enough to enjoy life the way he knew she had when both she and Peter were together. He had been sitting in the chair for a long time. Perhaps he had slept, because when Angela pronounced his name, he was dreaming of someone calling to him, and in his remembrance, it had been a judge from a very high court, and he had been afraid, somehow, because he knew he would not be able to answer any question the man might ask him. He had been relieved to realize it was just Angela whispering 'Arthur' in a voice that appeared to be coming from outer space. And then, reality hit him hard. The picture of Angela all entangled in her dead husband legs and arms was nightmarish, spooky, and macabre enough. It took the jurist in him a few seconds to regain his wits. When he did, Angela was sitting on the bed and he took comfort in the fact that the most difficult part of his mission was accomplished without any unwelcome intrusion from his part. Still, no words came to his mind as he furiously tried to issue a few words that wouldn't sound so insipid and conventional that he would regret having spoken them for the rest of his life. He had accumulated a few of those cliché-like utterances over the years, and they were into the habit of coming back to pester him when sleep wouldn't come easily. It was Angela who broke the uncomfortable silence with a question of her own.

"Did you keep a copy of the Zielgard's text that you sent to Peter in 2008?"

It was a matter he would have preferred to be left untouched. He had no choice but to answer in the negative. Because he sensed some criticism in the scowl he imagined seeing in the woman eyes, he felt compelled to add:

"Well, I had no reason to suspect any wrongdoing by Peter."

"If you could put your hand on the original you sent Peter, I would like to compare the text he wrote to the novel he published as his own."

He reflected on what was asking of him. And then, he saw the absurdity of it all. He wasn't thinking straight. Angela had excuses. Did he?

"I gave him the Faith manuscript. What he returned to me was his own work, what has been later published in California under the title Eternity."

"True. Excuse my confusion. I will look home and see if I can find it."

"Why would you want to do that? He asked."

"Peter told me the romantic part in the novel, I mean Joe being still in love with his wife and telling her so, all that had nothing to do with Zielgard. For that part, we have to give him credit since he wrote it."

"Peter told you, Arthur repeated in a daze. Are you telling me that he came out of his coma and spoke to you?"

"Yes, he did, she admitted sadly."

"What else did he tell you? Arthur asked."

"Just that he had written that part all by himself. That was when all light went out and the stupid machine interrupted with its absurd racket."

Arthur could well recall the segments Angela was referring to. He had reread the work the day before in the plane, en route for New York, and then finish the short novel in his room in the hotel Pierre, while waiting to get some news of the progress he hoped Peter was making under the supervision of the medical staff at Bellevue. There had been longing, sentimentality, yearning, homesickness, regret, and nostalgia in the tale, obviously the longings of one spouse who was still suffering for the loss of a loved one. And what about the scene when Joe showed Barbara the lost earring that was attached to a chain around his neck? Could Zielgard have written those words? How could he decide? But Peter coming out of the grave just to tell Angela he was Joe and she was the woman of his life no matter what, that sure made far better drama. Arthur liked good stories, and being the lawyer he was, he chose to go with the one Angela had delivered.

He was alone in the room that served him as an office in his domicile. There were books everywhere around his desk. Not just around his desk, but on all the other walls also, even around the window that looked outside. He stopped writing to have a glimpse at the water. He saw white foam over waves that pitched left and right, and a small vessel sailing through them. The owner was acting in panick as he tried to diminish the sail area, and didn't look like he knew what he was doing. His obvious difficulties weren't enough for Arthur to start worrying about the ineffective sailor's predicament. He was thinking at that moment about how the issues of Peter's creative impact on the Zielgard piece had been settled. Angela had been proven right in the end.

It had all happened this way.

Angela stood. She was pale and looked like she was going to throw up. He prepared for the worst. What were they to do? Go back to the hotel? Maybe use the place and try to sleep. He wouldn't even if he tried. They should go home, the sooner the better. Find a funeral house that would put

Peter in a casket and ship it St-Pete. If Angela were to insist on staying with Peter remains and fly with him, he would separate from her. Her decision.

Then, she said:

- Better go now.

She turned toward Peter, whom to Arthur's eyes didn't appear sick at all. He could have been sleeping and on the verge of waking up. He saw Angela lean over her husband and put her lips one last time on his brow. She was almost at the door when Arthur said:

"You might want to take his clothes with you."

"They will need what he was wearing to dress him up before they let his corpse leave this place."

Arthur hit his head with his fist.

"What was I thinking? You're right, of course."

Since he was already rummaging through Peter's effects, he managed to extract from his pockets some coins, a set of keys, and a wallet. He heard Angela asking him:

"Are you coming?"

He had opened the wallet and was going through its contents. Nothing worth making Angela wait for him one minute longer. As he was preparing to catch up with her, he sensed something angular, hard, and pronged in the section of the wallet that was supposed to contain change. He pushed open the small compartment. What he discovered hidden there was a little piece of jewelry. It did not take him long to recognize what it was. Barbara's blue earrings, the pair she must have lost, and the half of that duo that had hung on Joe's chest for forty years. There was no need to ask Angela about her losing the small trinket when she was eighteen or nineteen. Arthur already knew the answer to that question.

Angela would too. But not now. Later.

It was proof enough that Peter's claim of having written the chivalrous part of Zielgard's bestseller was true. He put the small object back where he had found it. It would be returned to Angela in time. Better she was alone when discovering what he had.

If it were him, he would not have liked to break down in front of others.

What about Ollie Devott?

Of course the fellow merits some attention from this writer, and the reader shall not be disappointed with what follows. There was in the New York Times of marsh 23, 2019, this little item hidden between one recipe of Mexican guacamole and the sorry tale of a Brooklyn transgender person uncomfortable with the surgery that had cut some important part of his body. No longer happy with the procedure, he was, twenty years later suing the government for having improperly denied his parent's petition to the court. The parents had been begging the tribunal to compel their son to get psychiatric help and for him to be committed to a public facility where he could have been evaluated before making such a radical decision.

The part concerning former district attorney Ollie Devott read like this:

"We learned yesterday that the Mississippi Attorney General, Ollie Devott, has been chosen to replace former DA Bill Gallagher in the Trump cabinet. The latter desisted the position one month ago by reason of health. Attorney Devott will occupy the same position in Washington as the one he had in the Biloxi's legislature.

The former Attorney General of Mississippi is the well-known District Attorney who gained immense notoriety when he decided to hunt down Maman Rosa Tour de l'Isle for having cast a spell on her victim, a crime normally associated with legends and fairy tales. This did not prevent that famed barrister to persevere and sway a jury of twelve Mississippians in voting her guilty of the crime not counting the requiring of the death penalty and being rewarded for his efforts by the right ruling.

Just recently, he enjoyed the result of his unlikely crusade and Herculean efforts. Those helped him fight his way to victory, notwithstanding numerous (frivolous, to be sure) appeals. They include the last, but not the least, one year ago, when seven judges of the Supreme Court of this country decided not to interfere with the way one state chose to govern itself. A decision that reinforces the principle of state absolute domination over matters that fall under its jurisdiction, be it criminal justice or the kind of punishment people living in that state should or should not receive.

No less than four months ago, illustrious lawyer Ollie Devott achieved the fulfillment of his mission. Last October, Rosa Maman Tour de l'Isle succumbed, as dictated in her sentence, but the lady had the good sense to achieve such a result by her own means. We doubt the newly appointed Attorney General of the United States lost any sleep over the matter, as long as justice was done. No doubt such a zealous righter of wrongs will prove a valuable addition to the Trump presidency.

THE END